I WILL DANCE AGAIN

A Novel by

Antje Keller Simunac

Published by Oak Branch Publishing

ISBN

979-8-218-21622-1

Acknowledgements

Many thanks to my mother, Annemarie Hermann, who patiently sat with me through endless interviews about that time.

I owe gratitude also to my friend, Edith Ellis, for sharing her family's courage to survive World War II.

Also, to my sister, Ingrid Bojanowski, whose help enriched these stories, Julia Tolentino, as well as to my niece, Dr. Christine Bojanowski, without whose skills I could not have finished this book.

I am also thankful for my publisher, Gregory J. Ferris, of Oak Branch Publishing.

And most of all, I am indebted to my editor," Mary" Ernie O'Dell, President of Green River Writers, for her countless hours reading and editing this manuscript. And, most of all for her friendship and belief in me.

In loving memory to my mother, whom everyone called "Schecko".

PROLOGUE
Burghof Village, May 1945

The howl of a dive-bomber moves closer.

And der Fuhrer asks you to sacrifice for the final victory is ours, the radio blares. "Idiot," Annemarie Peterman speaks out loud and quickly looks around. But she is alone in the makeshift apartment, two rooms upstairs next to the hayloft of the old farmhouse. "It's 1945 and you've got nothing left to shoot with, except your mouth," she mutters. "I want my children to play with toys, have fun, go to school and - Scheiss." She hits the off button so hard that the radio tumbles to the floor. Anna, six, and Inge, four, were playing outside in the farmyard. Damn war. Sirens, planes droning, bombings and fires, and no coffee. Oh, a real cup of coffee. But this is normal now.

She gets up and stands in front of the mirror. "God, I'm so skinny, I look like a twelve-year old boy." But she smiles at her face and brushes back her short cropped brown hair. "After the war, I'm going to let my hair grow and…" Everything starts with "after the war" and ends there. Her eyes are big and blue in the mirror. "Ha, Lily Marlene." She wraps her arm around an imaginary lantern post and starts humming.

She glances out of the single dingy window at the sky, so blue. Not a cloud. "Oh, sun, spring, beautiful May," she sings.

She thinks of Alfred, how he had hugged her before he left for the western front in France, or somewhere. "I'll be back soon, Liebling," he crooned. "Don't worry, the war is almost over." She has not received a letter from him in eleven months and thirteen days. Letters from the front are unpredictable. *Blue skies, sunshine.* A letter could arrive today. At least he is not at the eastern front, where the Russians are killing and burning everything. But is he already dead, somewhere in a ditch? The pain settles in her chest like a cancer.

Then the howl and screech of a dive-bomber comes close and Annemarie bolts away from the window. A deafening boom splinters the glass, and her scream is drowned in the fiery roar. She falls and scrambles to the stairs, where she is hit in the legs by shrapnel.

CHAPTER 1
Burghof Village

Anna Peterman heard the car coming closer, turned and pointed at the gray military sedan chugging down the deserted country road. "Look, Karl, he's waving at us." She jumped up and down, waving back at the soldier behind the wheel.

"I know, it's the Major." The boy saluted and yelled, "Heil Hitler."

"He gave me candy once," Anna said.

"The Major is coming to see my father, the mayor." Karl was nine, four years older than Anna, and had lived in the village all his life. His father owned the biggest farm in the village. "City girls don't know anything! Poof, poof." He pointed his gun finger at Anna.

It was late afternoon, and Karl was looking for the flock of geese to herd them back into the barn. Anna and her sister, Inge, were helping him.

"Farmer Munster said your father is a big fat Nazi pig, I heard him say it," Anna shouted,

running a few steps out of range so he couldn't hit her.

"My father could arrest Farmer Munster. I'm going to tell him what you said." Karl glared at her.

Four-year-old Inge joined the quarrel. "My mama's friend has a gun. He can shoot you! He's a soldier," she shouted, clutching her sister's hand.

1

"You're a baby. You don't understand." Karl brushed her off.

"We were evacuated," Anna proclaimed. But when Karl asked what that meant, she didn't know. "We've been in the war," she shouted. "When we lived in the city the house across the street got bombed and I saw people on the roof jump down four floors! You don't know anything, Karl."

The children often played war, the boys pretending to be the Russians, coming to attack, the girls hiding behind trees, bushes and in ditches. Anna remembered in the city the howling of the sirens in the middle of the night when they had to rush down three flights of stairs to hide in the bunker. But her Mama had said they were safe living here in the village in Farmer Munster's hayloft.

"Look, the Major is almost at our farm now. Let's go, we don't want to miss him." Karl pointed to the gray military car speeding by. He pushed Anna out of the way.

Suddenly, Anna's sister started to cry.

Anna kneeled in front of her. "What's wrong?"

Inge pointed to the sky.

Anna put her arm around her. "Don't worry, they can't find us here." She looked up at the planes, which sounded like angry bees, their hum growing as they came closer. Her mother had told them that if planes came, they should jump into a ditch and cover their faces.

Their roar was so deafening that Anna had to cover her ears. "What about the geese?" she hollered, but Karl must not have heard. As they started running towards the village, one of the planes appeared to dive right at them. Anna grabbed her sister's arm and started to run but Inge kept falling down. Frantically, she dragged her into the ditch and threw herself over her sister, who shook and cried.

"Mama, I want Mama," Inge screamed. The plane dove over them with an ear-piercing roar. Dirt flew into

2

Anna's face, sticks and brush hitting her cheek. She wrapped her arm around Inge, pushed her head down and grasped at clumps of grass with her other hand. A cloud of dust and exhaust engulfed them. Anna pressed her face into Inge's hair.

As the sounds of the engines faded, Anna sat up and crawled up the embankment. "I think they are gone." She took a deep breath, grabbed Inge's hand and pulled her out of the ditch.

"Don't cry, she said," wiping the dirt off her sister's face. "Oh, you are bleeding! A rock must have hit you." She used her sleeve to dab the trickle of blood away. "Let's go find Mama."

Just before they reached the Munster farm, where they lived upstairs in the makeshift loft next to the hayloft, they heard several loud booms. The earth vibrated.

"Back in the ditch, quick," Anna yelled, pulling Inge off the road. They flattened their bodies against the damp earth and covered their heads. Then it was quiet. Anna waited until the roar of the planes turned into a distant hum. She got on her knees and peered over the edge of the embankment. She pulled Inge up. "Look." They stared at a plume of grey smoke rising from the Munster farmhouse. The air smelled burned.

"Come quick, we've got to get to the house and find Mama," she shouted, and pulled Inge with her.

"Mama!" Inge cried.

"Mama!" They both shouted. They ran past Karl's farm, past the white villa where the retired sea captain lived and around the bend towards the Munster farm.

The farmyard swarmed with people, some of them German soldiers who were stationed in the village. Anna tried to scream but could not make a sound. The front of the farmhouse was ablaze. Flames leaped into the air like dragons, devouring everything. Under the big oak tree, she saw the Major's gray military car resting against the hedge.

"Mama." Anna yelled, pulling Inge behind her like a rag doll. Confusion and chaos swallowed them, people scurrying around, shouting and carrying furniture outside. "Mama!" She ran through the barn door, into the big hall past several pieces of farm equipment, trying to get to the wooden stairs to their loft. Anna heard the blare of the village fire engine as it turned into the farmyard.

Flames were leaping down one side of the stairs.

"Mama, Mama!" she screamed. Somebody grabbed her from behind and pulled her back. She fought but could not escape the iron grip. The extreme heat was strangling her. Sparks flew all around.

"You can't go up there," a man's hoarse voice shouted.

"But my mama is up there." She twisted and tried to forge ahead.

"The bomb hit up there and nobody could be…" The voice stopped and so did Anna's heart.

"Where is my sister?" she whispered, but the man just dragged her back towards the door.

"We've got to get out of here now," he hollered, "the stairs are going to collapse."

And then, her mama emerged at the top of the stairs and started to hobble down. A hush fell over the crowd. All was quiet except for a few muffled blasts and the crackle of the burning wood. Annemarie Peterman did not scream or say anything, just hobbled from step to step, unsteady, keeping away from the burning rail. Her dress was torn, and blood streamed from her legs.

"Mama!" Anna screamed and tried again to lunge out of the man's arms.

Her mother saw her and reached out, lost her balance and fell down the last few steps. Amidst screams and gasps two soldiers jumped forward, lifted the small woman by the arms and carried her outside.

The man carried Anna and ran out behind them. A loud crash. "The stairs have collapsed!" he hollered.

Dusk soon engulfed the scene and people moved about like ghosts in the thick smoke, the yellow and red flames reflected across their faces, illuminating them briefly as they emerged from the smoke. Anna coughed and looked around for Inge. A ladder had been raised from the fire engine and Anna stared at the fireman spraying the house like she had seen them do in the city many times.

"Mama… Inge," she whimpered. "Let me go, please let me go."

"You can't, Maedchen," the man said in a soft voice, hugging her to him. "She'll be all right. The Army doctors will take care of her."

But Inge – where was Inge? She swiped at her runny nose.

"There." He pointed at a vehicle with a big red cross painted on the top. "They're taking Mama away to the field hospital now. And your sister? There is a sister?"

She stared at the soldier who was holding her. His face looked old and wrinkled, covered with soot.

"I don't know." He turned scanning the crowd. "But we'll find her."

"Those Russians, they hurt my Mama." Anna started to cry.

"No, not the Russians, girl, the British. They were British bombers trying to hit the Major's car."

Anna buried her face in the soldier's chest.

CHAPTER 2

Anna woke up and peeked from under the down comforter. Where was she? Where were Mama and Inge? The room smelled of smoke. A ray of daylight beamed at her face through a slit in the curtains. The bedding smelled musty, and she sneezed. She peered around at little painted roses covering the walls like the wallpaper in her grandmother's bedroom. A tall chest stood against one wall with a framed photograph of a soldier next to a vase of dried flowers.

She pushed away the comforter, slid off the bed and stepped on to the cold wood floor. She noticed a mirror mounted on the wall next to a stand that looked like a tree, only it didn't have leaves. A hat perched on one of the branches and a jacket hung next to it. Anna stared in the mirror and tried unsuccessfully to wipe the dried dirt off her skirt. She picked up the photograph. The stern face of the soldier looked back at her. On the bottom, a name. Jacob, 1941. Jacob was the Munsters' youngest son, the one they had not heard from in over two years. Mr. Munster often said that Jacob was probably dead at the Russian front and that's when Mrs. Munster cried and wiped her face with her apron.

So, she was still at the Munster farmhouse. She slipped into her sandals and ran to find Gertl, the Munsters' farm maid, to find out about Inge and Mama. It was cold and Anna shivered. She tiptoed down the long hallway, passing the door to Farmer Munster's office, which the children were not allowed to enter. People said that he had

6

been mayor of the village before the war. The door next to the kitchen led into the parlor, which was never used except maybe at Christmas. Curious, she opened the door and saw beautiful china displayed in a tall cabinet, a dancing ballerina on a music box, and ornately carved chairs surrounding a long-polished table. A large picture of a woman in a flowing white wedding dress and a somber-looking man in a black overcoat and hat hung above a long sideboard. One picture showed a baby posed naked on a white fur rug that looked like a bear. She had often wondered if it had been a real bear but was afraid to ask, since she was not allowed in the parlor.

Then a loud noise from the kitchen, and Gertl's voice shouting, "Verdamt." Anna put her hand over her mouth. Her heart pounding, she closed the parlor door and stepped into the kitchen, a large, square room smelling of fried potatoes and bacon.

Gertl was on her knees, picking up pieces of a plate. "Don't move. There could be glass on the floor."

Ignoring the warning, Anna ran to her. "Gertl, where's Inge?"

"We'll ask Mrs. Munster." Gertl finished cleaning up, rose and wiped her hands. She stroked Anna's hair. "You need something to eat, Maedchen. Here, drink this." She turned and handed Anna a glass of milk. "How would you like a slice of bread with molasses?" She did not wait for an answer but cut a thick slice from the loaf, buttered it and heaped the sweet molasses on so thick that it was dripping off the sides. Dancing up and down, Anna watched her work. Molasses was her favorite. She wiped away tears and took a breath. She sat down and ate every last bite.

Gertl looked at the empty plate. "Why don't I fix you a couple of eggs?"

"No. Not now. I want to go find my mama and Inge. But where are they?"

Gertl stopped and gathered Anna into her arms. "I'm not sure, Maedchen, but after you eat, we'll find out." Gertl turned to the stove and cooked the scrambled eggs, which Anna devoured quickly, despite her worry, leaving not a morsel on her plate.

"Let's go now," Anna said.

"After we peel potatoes. Come over here and help me." Gertl sat down on a bench next to the sink and poured potatoes into a bucket. She motioned Anna to sit next to her. "You hand me one and I will peel it. That way we will get done faster." She smiled and pulled Anna over to the bench. Unhappily Anna sat.

Farmer Munster flung open the kitchen door, came in and sat down at the table. His wife, Ida, and Jake, the farm hand followed him. "Damn, if Major Rudi hadn't stopped right under our tree, they wouldn't have hit our house. That fool never did have any sense." He shook his head and popped his suspenders.

"He is a Major," Jake mumbled, fiddling with a piece of straw. Anna knew Jake was friends with the Major because she had seen them going to Braun's tavern together.

Mrs. Munster wiped her eyes. "We can be glad that they just strafed the house. Had they used a bomb, we'd all be dead now."

"We can fix the roof on the front, so it doesn't rain in. But all the hay is burned up," Jake lamented. "What're we going to do now?"

Mrs. Munster rose and picked up the pot. "Coffee, anyone? Maybe Gus Schultz can help us. He's got more hay than anybody."

"Ha, that big asshole Nazi isn't going to help anybody, especially not us." Farmer Munster pounded the table. Anna dropped a potato and slid closer to Gertl. "Oh, he'll give to his Nazi buddies, those big shots who joined

8

the party and kiss his ass." His fist slammed the table again and a spoon fell.

Anna covered her ears. "He said that word," she whispered to Gertl.

"Not so loud." Mrs. Munster looked around, her lips twitching. "You never know who is listening."

"I'll be damned if I can't talk as I please in my own house," her husband yelled.

Anna reached for Gertl's hand, shivering. Farmer Munster, a big man with a mustache, was always nice to her, like her grandpa. She had never seen him angry like this.

Yanka, the watch dog who was chained at the front door, barked ferociously. Anna knew that a stranger was coming. Gertl put down the knife and looked towards the door. "Hello, Gus." Mrs. Munster placed a calming hand on her husband's arm. "Join us. Something to eat or coffee?"

Anna held her breath. Karl's father, Gus Schultz, the man Farmer Munster hated, had arrived with Ben, his farmhand, in tow. Gus was a short man, rotund, with a round face and red apple cheeks. He always wore a ball cap. "It's because he's bald," Karl had told her once. Schulz walked with a limp, stopped at the end of the table, and stood there stiffly, Ben shuffling his feet, looked at the floor.

"What the devil do you want here?" Farmer Munster shouted, leaning forward, his arms on the table.

"I have some important news." Gus puffed up his chest, beads of sweat appearing on his cheeks.

"Oh, yeah, you've come to help me fix my burned house, right?" Munster pounded the table so that the cups rattled and slid around. Anna cringed.

Gus took off his cap and twisted it in his hands. "I can send you my farm hand to help clean up the mess. Looks like you got lucky. Only the front of the house burned."

9

"The hayloft burned, and all our hay is gone." Jake did not look up.

"The hayloft? Isn't that where the city lady, Annemarie, stayed?"

"Farmer Munster nodded, stroking his mustache. "Yeah, and she was damn lucky. Got out alive."

Anna stopped breathing, her heart thumping like a drum.

"We've got one of her children with us, the young one." Gus smiled at Anna. "But we can only keep her for a short time. I'll need the room for my daughter when she comes home."

Karl had told Anna that his older sister, Erika and her baby, where coming home soon.

"Well, if that was your news, get out of my house. I don't want no Nazis here." Munster got up and took a step towards Gus. Anna leaned back; afraid he would slap Karl's father.

Mrs. Munster pulled him back. "Sit down, Otto. Gus is just doing his job."

Gus took a step back. He swung his cap in the air and cleared his throat. "The war is over."

Stunned, they stared at him. Anna could hear the water bubbling on the stove. He took a handkerchief from his vest pocket and wiped the sweat off his face. "As of yesterday, it is over. I heard it from a soldier. All of them left the village during the night."

Ben yelled, "Heil Hitler," and raised his arm and saluted. Gus turned and elbowed him, and he stopped, put his hands in his pockets and looked at his shoes. Gertl dropped a potato and it rolled under the table. Anna jumped up to retrieve it, but Gertl pulled her back.

Everybody began talking at once. Mrs. Munster stood up, her arms flailing. "Oh my God, that means Arnold and Jacob will be coming home. " She covered her face with her apron and sobbed, her body shaking.

Anna looked at Gertl. "Is she crying?" she whispered. Gertl shushed her.

"Nobody knows what's going on," Gus Schultz continued. "There's no order out there now. Nobody knows who's in charge."

"You mean *you're* no longer in charge?" Farmer Munster roared, shoving his chair back. A cup fell off the table and shattered on the tile floor, but nobody seemed to notice. Anna hid her face behind Gertl and squeezed her hand.

Farmer Gus ignored him, but his face had turned red. "No, I'm no longer mayor. It really was too much. My farm needs work and my health is bad. I can hardly walk, with this gout."

"What you are saying, Gus, is that all the old Nazis are bailing out, right?"

"If I were still mayor, I could have you arrested, Munster. You always were a damn socialist." Gus's voice sounded shrill, and he took a step towards Otto Munster.

Anna sat very still. She didn't know what they were talking about but hoped they would say more about her mother. At least she knew that her sister was with Karl at the Schulz farm.

"Get out of my house before I get my pitchfork." Farmer Munster shook his fist. "I have two boys serving on the front, and you know that. They could be dead. And where is your son, huh, where has he been all these years?" He shouted so loud that Anna covered her ears.

Mrs. Munster having recovered, shook her fist.

"Archie has diabetes," Schulz growled," he's not been in good health, and you know that and ---"

"Shut up, both of you menfolk."

Anna had never heard Mrs. Munster raise her voice before.

"I need to find out where my sons are. They declared Jacob missing two years ago but they made a mistake. He'll be coming home soon. And so will Arnold." Her tears started up again. She dabbed her eyes with a handkerchief, her voice trembling.

"If I can help you find out anything, I will do that." Gus said, his voice turning soft.

Then Farmer Munster jumped out of his chair, knocking it over, turned and stormed out of the kitchen slamming the door behind him.

Anna clung to Gertl and started to cry.

Mrs. Munster picked up the chair. "Can you also find out where they took Annemarie? We need to get the girls to her." Her voice was normal again.

"Sure, I will," Schulz said. "We've got our own to take care of. But everything is in chaos. There is nobody in charge now and the military has disintegrated. Everybody is afraid of what will happen next." Gus raised his arms, accidentally striking Ben. He shook his head and slapped his cap back on.

Mrs. Munster wrung her hands. "But you will try to help us, Gus? And don't mind him. He's just upset about the house burning and our boys gone. It's been hard on us." She stepped towards him and reached for his hands.

Gus nodded. He pulled a gold watch from his vest pocket and motioned for Ben to follow him out the back door. Karl had told Anna that the watch and the golden chain were a gift from the Fuehrer.

Anna jumped up. "I want to find my mama."

Gertl put her arm around her. She opened the lid of the metal box on the table and handed her a cookie. Mrs. Munster turned to Anna and stroked her cheek. Anna saw her lips quivering.

"I want to see Mama, please," she begged, trying hard not to cry.

"Don't worry, we will find her." Mrs. Munster took Anna into her arms, rocking her back and forth. "Go visit with Yanka, she's asked for you."

Anna shook her head. "Dogs can't talk." She pulled away and stomped out of the room.

Yanka, the gray shaggy dog, lay chained by the door. People said she was mean and would bite anyone who came close, but Anna knew that was not true. She sat down on the steps. The dog rolled on her back and licked Anna's hand. Anna stroked her scruffy fur. Yanka closed her eyes.

"You're not mean," Anna said. "You're just lonely. You have no mother and no sisters." Anna felt her throat close, and her eyes welled up. "Nobody loves you." She kept stroking the dog's belly. "But I do. I love you, Yanka. I wish they wouldn't chain you like this. I know you want to run in the meadows with us and play."

Yanka's brown eyes narrowed to sleepy slits.

"Do you miss your mama?" Anna caressed her ears. Yanka rolled on her side and put her big wolf head into Anna's lap. Anna sniffled and wiped her nose on her sleeve. "They don't know where my mother is either." She buried her face in the dog's shaggy neck.

CHAPTER 3
1945 Army Field Hospital

Another attack, Annemarie thought, with a heavy sigh. The drone of a squadron of bomber planes, coming closer. A radio blared propaganda. "Shut up," she said aloud. She lay in a hospital bed staring at the white ceiling, the large room was cramped with beds, and a strong odor of disinfectants hung in the air. The gray curtain that separated the six women patients from the wounded soldiers was stained and torn on one side. Radio propaganda pierced through the mumblings and moans in the ward.

"Somebody stop this," Annemarie muttered, looking at nobody in particular. "It's 1945 and they say we've got nothing left to shoot with. Stop the fighting, I want... She stopped as a nurse pulled back the curtain.

"Don't worry, I agree," nurse Lisbeth said with a big smile. Annemarie guessed her to be in her early thirties, shapely-plump and big busted. Frizzy hair protruded from her white nurses' cap. Her full mouth, painted bright red, stood out like a signal demanding attention. Annemarie had never seen a woman with painted red lips.

Lisbeth opened a window. "It stinks in here. We've got to air you out. It's May, and a beautiful spring day. Now, breathe. Breathe, I said." She looked around, and everyone who was conscious followed her orders. "Doc Hartmann will be here soon. He's in the annex on his rounds. So, make yourselves pretty, ladies. I'll be right back."

14

"Ha, ha. Make yourself look pretty," Annemarie mimicked, grinning sourly at the two women patients next to her. The other three were too injured to respond. When Annemarie earlier asked Lisbeth about them, she'd just answered, "In a coma or dead," shrugged, and went on with her business.

Annemarie had frowned. "That sounds so harsh and uncaring, Lisbeth."

"Look, Miss, we get thousands of wounded coming through here, most of them half-dead, or let me say for your benefit, half-alive. I can count the number of doctors and nurses on one hand. We all work double shifts, and we sleep right here in the barracks. Only a few hours, then the day starts all over again. We try to fix them up, ship them back out, or we cart them away, because another one is waiting for the bed." She stopped to catch her breath. "We're short on medication, short on bandages and well, young lady, ask me what I can do for you today, and I'll jump to take care of it.'" She stood, her hands on her hips, her face flushed.

Male patients clapped and yelled, "Bravo," Heil Hitler," and "Come over here, Freulein, I'll make you feel better."

Lisbeth dropped into a deep curtsy, prompting her ample breasts to almost pop out of her snugly fitting uniform. Soldiers whistled and clapped.

But Annemarie sank into her pillow and cried softly, wiping the tears with her sheet. She did not know how long she had been in this wretched military hospital and what had happened to her children. They had gone to the Schultz farm to play. Surely, one of the farmers had taken them in, but she sobbed. Little Inge, always worried, so scared of the Russians. Annemarie wanted to hug her and tell her everything was going to be all right. But Anna had been with Inge and that should help comfort her. Brave Anna, who had survived tuberculosis, who always wanted

15

to be her little helper. She cried harder, sinking into deep despair. The days were stretching endlessly. It seemed as though she was on another planet, except for the drone of the bombers passing over day and night. Sometimes, lately she didn't even hear them. But at least they drowned out the incessant speeches the Fuehrer inflicted on them day after day. Rumors circulated that the war was over. A wounded soldier reported that the German Reich had capitulated, but no one was sure. No announcements had been made by hospital officials.

"Shut off that damn propaganda, I can't hear what I'm cutting," Dr. Hartmann had been heard shouting in the OR. That could have proven dangerous for anyone else, to insult the Fuehrer, but the head surgeon and a genius in fixing damaged bodies was said to have a big brass Nazi friend. Some said it was the Commander himself, who was in charge of the hospital and had connections to the elite in Berlin. There were also rumors that it was the commander's wife, but nobody was sure.

Annemarie groaned in pain. At her bedside, Doc Hartmann had explained her injuries in his simple, straightforward way. "You were shot through both thighs by shrapnel." He'd examined the wounds, touching and squeezing. "How'd that happen?"

"All I remember is, I was sitting at the table darning a sock in the room Farmer Munster had given to us next to the hayloft. We had been evacuated from the city. I was lucky we ended up at the Munsters, since they liked children. A lot of farmers do not like city folks but were forced to take them in. So that created a lot of friction."

"So darning socks is what got you in trouble." He grinned.

She sighed. "I don't remember what happened, just that I heard a loud boom and got hit. I touched my leg and felt blood. Then I saw the flames. I knew then I had to get out of there and look for my children."

Doc Hartmann took her hand. "Oh, Maedchen. You only got hit in the legs. If shrapnel had hit you in the body or head, you would not have met me. See? You are lucky." He patted her on the cheek and walked away.

Lisbeth came in with a serving tray and set it on Annemarie's nightstand. She closed the curtains around the women's ward.

Annemarie told Lisbeth what Doc had said, and she shrugged. "That's Doc. What can I say?"

"My legs hurt." Annemarie bit her lips.

"That's a good sign. If you feel pain, you know that you still have legs."

Annemarie tried to sit up, and Lisbeth helped her, propping two pillows behind her back.

"My God, is that what I think it is I smell?" Annemarie raised her head, closing her eyes and taking in the delicious aroma.

"Just for you, ladies." Lisbeth grinned and filled four white mugs with steaming hot coffee. "Sugar and cream?" she asked as though they were at a cafe in Berlin.

The women picked up their cups and slowly savored the delicious brew.

"Oh my God, I'd fuck the commander for this," one of them whispered. Everyone laughed. "Just an old fashioned kaffee klatch," Lisbeth remarked, "but don't ask me where I got this. Questions are strictly *verboten*."

From that day on, Annemarie and nurse Lisbeth became friends. She knew that the patients loved Lisbeth, even if all she could do for some was hold their hands as they died. Annemarie also liked Doc Hartmann, whose unorthodox bedside manners were legendary. Lisbeth said that every female patient in the ward and all the nurses had a crush on him. "No gloom and doom in my hospital," she heard him declare. "Everyone in here is happy and leaves happy."

He was a young man, not much older than thirty, Annemarie guessed, well built, and charming. Some of the other doctors frowned on his behavior.

"I want you to come up with three jokes a day so we can pass them around," he said to Annemarie the first day he examined her, "and there'll be no censoring."

She had been sedated and didn't remember how she got to the hospital, but his words stuck. Everybody followed his request, eager to come up with jokes, play the game, and lighten up this place of suffering and death.

"Sourpusses and complainers get priority and will be fixed up and get a first-class ticket back to the front," he declared with a smile, looking like a college student with his slicked back blond hair.

He smiled at Annemarie when he examined her. "What a gorgeous young thing you are, yum, yum." She had pulled the gown over her body, but soon learned to appreciate his humor and enjoyed bantering with him. "I can't wait to go dancing with you," he'd said as he checked her bandaged legs. "Do you like to dance?" He looked up at her out of the corner of his eye.

"I love to dance, but now..."

"OK, it's a date. We'll go dancing as soon as this damn war is over, and I'm not falling asleep standing up."

She'd laughed. "You actually take time out to sleep? I think we'll have to report you to the authorities."

"Good idea. Have them look me up. I'll be the one leaning against the wall in the nurses' lounge."

It was crazy, but his attention always made her feel better--and desirable-- if only for the moment. "I think he actually smiles with his eyes," Annemarie told Lisbeth. "Sometimes they are deep blue and then they turn to steel gray with speckles."

"We are falling for the charming Doc, are we?" Lisbeth chuckled. "Don't pretend you aren't. I notice these things, trust me, I do."

Annemarie shook her finger. "Don't be silly, Lisbeth. I'm not a schoolgirl. I am married with two children."

"So?" Lisbeth raised her eyebrows. "I think Doc likes you."

"Sure, he's in love with me and every woman he meets, past and present. He's a real Casanova, that charming doctor." Annemarie smiled. "I know what's going on. I admit, he's hard to resist but we all look forward to his sweet lies."

After Nurse Lisbeth left, Annemarie lay with closed eyes, numb from the medication and everything that had happened. *God, I'm a twenty-six-year-old with two small children, and now no useful legs. What am I going to do when the war ends?* Her thoughts drifted to Alfred and she touched the ring he had given her before shipping out to Normandy. He had hugged her and promised to come back alive. His words rang through her as though he had spoken them yesterday. "I'll be back soon, Liebling, don't worry. The war can't last forever, and we will be together then, I promise you." They had kissed for the last time and held each other. Though she had not received a letter in many months, she knew letters from the front were unpredictable, plus they might not find her right away since she was at the hospital now. Maybe the Americans liberated his unit, and he was a prisoner of war, safe until all this was over. Her mother had always said she was a lucky girl. A letter could arrive today. She pressed her face into her pillow and drifted into restless sleep.

CHAPTER 4
Army Field Hospital

Another beautiful spring day had ended. The sounds of spring surrounded the hospital barracks. Birds chirped, searching for mates, and the scent of flowers drifted into the open windows of the ward.

"Don't forget our dance date," Dr. Hartmann reminded her and winked, sitting on the edge of Annemarie's bed.

She remembered Lisbeth's words and thought that he liked her. "Will I be able to walk again?" she asked, feeling herself choke up.

"Well, I'm not a magician, so you'll have to be patient and let your body do the healing."

She covered her face with her hands.

He reached for them and gently rubbed them. "You're a young woman, Annemarie, you'll get through it. I'll help you; I promise!" He squeezed her hands, stood and turned to the next patient.

As much as she wanted to believe him, it seemed as if he had given her evasive answers.

Wounded soldiers arrived every day and told of the collapse of the eastern front, of masses of refugees bulging some of the cities to capacity and of German military units retreating to the West with the Russian army in pursuit. Villages burned, roads were clogged with refugees, starving, dying, their bodies littering the sides of the road, while the mass of the able-bodied pushed on. Was Alfred's mother on that road? Annemarie shuddered. Strangely, the daily radio broadcasts kept on. *We must sacrifice for the fatherland. Every man, woman and child must stand strong in unity against the enemy.*

"Somebody forgot to push the off button," Annemarie said to Lisbeth. "Where exactly is the Fuehrer?"

"Somewhere in a bunker, I guess." Lisbeth rolled her eyes. "He's not going to let them shoot up his grand old ass."

"Ssh." Annemarie covered her mouth. "One of these days they're going to come and get you."

On this balmy late afternoon, Lisbeth had appeared with a wheelchair. "We're going out," she proclaimed. "About time you got yourself moving."

"But Doc Hartmann said"

"Oh, pfui, he's not here." Lisbeth helped Annemarie out of her bed and into the wheelchair.

"I feel like a sack of potatoes," Annemarie grumbled, grabbing the handrails and shifting her weight to the left side of her body.

"Yeah, all one hundred pounds." Lisbeth wheeled her through the ward, down a hallway and out a back door.

Annemarie looked around, exuberant. She stretched out her arms. "I forgot how wonderful it is to be outside." She took a deep breath. This was the first fresh air since she had been wounded. She closed her eyes and turned towards the sun, letting its rays caress her face. The scent of the flowers reminded her of Lisbeth's Eau de Cologne. "I will be dancing soon," Annemarie sang out as Lisbeth turned and went back inside.

She returned in a moment with a tray holding liver pâté, cheese, a loaf of rye bread and two bottles of beer. "For now, we'll just sit out here and have ourselves a little picnic."

"Where on earth did you get liver pate?"

Lisbeth smiled, pulled a bottle opener from her pocket, opened the beer and handed her one.

21

"Bavaria St. Pauli Beer. Wow! I haven't seen that in a long while." Annemarie held up her bottle and they toasted: "To the end of the war."

"Tell me that we won't be sent away if they find us out here," Annemarie joked, but with a tinge of fear in her voice. She wondered what man was showering Lisbeth with gifts and privileges. Not Doc Hartmann. Someone higher up. The Commandant? When she'd asked earlier, Lisbeth had smiled and said, "A birthday present. Don't worry. I've got friends in high places."

Annemarie reached toward the tasty spread. "Are you, I mean are you sleeping with …?" She blushed, embarrassed. "I don't mean it that way, and it really isn't any of my business."

"It's all right, I don't mind." Lisbeth sipped her beer. "I could be here alive and have food on the table or stayed and be dead. It was easy, believe me. Those who took the high road are now rotting somewhere, after the Russians got through with them. I made my choice and I'm glad I did. I'd rather be soulless and alive than pious and dead."

Annemarie stared at her. "I don't understand."

Lisbeth took a big gulp of beer. "We heard from the few who escaped when the Russian army passed through. They pillaged, they burned every house, and they killed all the men, old people and even children. And we heard stories how they brutalized the women before they killed them, too. They're barbarians." Lisbeth's voice showed no emotion. "Those who didn't believe what the refugees were telling them were fools." Lisbeth's face looked hard.

Annemarie's mouth dropped open. What she had always dismissed as Nazi propaganda was true. She shuddered.

Lisbeth raised her bottle. "Prost! To life and the good things to come." They finished their beers.

22

"What about you?" Lisbeth asked. "Are you married?"

"Yes. Well, I was. You know I have two children. Inge is four and Anna will be six in July."

"So, what happened? Where's your husband now, on the front? Just a moment, let me get us another beer." Lisbeth got up.

Annemarie looked at the sky. A beautiful spring. How nature was able to succeed and renew despite the human race trying to bomb the earth into oblivion. She closed her eyes, breathing deeply. Doc Hartmann had said he would help her. She could still feel his warm hands on hers.

The sudden howl of the air raid sirens brought her back. Air raids during the day? They mostly struck at night. She searched the sky. Where was Lisbeth? Frantically she grabbed the arms of her chair, put her left leg on the ground and tried to scoot herself closer against the building. She covered her head with her arms. The drones moved closer, then a tremendous boom, and pieces of wood, dirt and metal flew all around. She cowered in her wheelchair, shrieked and leaned to the side, knocking over the empty bottle. As quickly as they had come, the planes were gone. Annemarie raised her head and looked around. Everything looked the same. She turned and saw Lisbeth step through the door. "Oh, my God, Lisbeth, I thought I would die." She put her hand over her mouth.

"Nope. They missed. A clump of woods got hit back over the hill. They're trying to put the fire out now." She swung the beer bottles around. "Lucky for us. Are you all right?" She pulled Annemarie up in her wheelchair and peered at her.

Annemarie brushed some dirt from her lap. "Do you think we should go inside?" Her heart felt like it would jump out of her chest.

Lisbeth handed her a bottle. "They're gone – let's enjoy the sundown. I'm hungry."

"I could have been hit with that flying metal."

"Hm, but you weren't." Lisbeth waved her arm as if to brush away Annemarie's fears.

Annemarie reached up and put her arm around her. "You are an angel, Lisbeth." Her voice quivered.

"Ha! Me an angel? I'm just a woman playing her cards right, girl. I know what I've got, and I use it. And maybe I was also lucky," she said. "I'm a survivor. And so are you." She smiled at Annemarie. "Remember, I have friends in high places." She pointed to the sky – "so relax."

Annemarie shook her head and laughed. She drained half of the bottle. "I'm relaxing."

They sat quietly for a while, enjoying the food. Finally, Lisbeth spoke. "You don't have to tell me, about you, I mean, if you don't want to. It's all right with me either way."

"Oh, I don't mind," Annemarie replied, licking pate off her fingers. "I can't believe how naïve and stupid I was." She leaned back and shook her head. "We were all so young, and it was so crazy, so exciting, you know. We poor city girls got to travel and get out and have fun. My father had lost his job. He was never interested in politics and didn't care to join the party. He was blacklisted and couldn't find work and that made him grumpy all the time. And Mother thought it would look better and he might get a job if I joined the Hitler Youth. People noticed if you weren't participating. I had a big argument with my father because I wanted to join. You know, all my friends … had." Annemarie looked away, thinking of those turbulent days.

Lisbeth nodded vigorously. She understood. "You look like a sixteen-year-old girl, so young, pale, and so fragile. I wish we could put some weight on you."

24

"No, I am not fragile. I was always small. Short, with a boyish figure." She giggled and pointed at Lisbeth's bosom. "I'd give a lot to have some of that."

Lisbeth laughed.

"So here goes the next part of my tale," Annemarie continued. "Being seventeen, I wanted to live, enjoy life. In the Hitler Youth group, we had so much fun. We went camping, took the train to the Baltic Sea, visited other cities and met young people from those groups. Sure, we had the meetings. Brainwashing is what my father called it, but we didn't look at it that way and we didn't care."

Lisbeth nodded and chewed on her cuticle.

"It caused a lot of stress in our family," Annemarie went on. " As I said, my father was totally against it. And most of my relatives felt the same way and were afraid that I, who had become a Hitler Youth leader, would turn them in. So, they stayed away and we were no longer welcome at family gatherings."

Lisbeth nodded. "That happened to a lot of families."

The sound of more planes flying so low made the windows rattle. Annemarie shivered and dropped her bottle. It felt like the attack on the farmhouse all over again. A piece of concrete from the window vibrated loose and fell, narrowly missing her wheelchair. She slid back in her chair and shrieked, then glanced at Lisbeth and continued. "I did get burned out after a while. It was after they sent us to the farms. It really was slave labor, cheap help for the farmers, who treated us like dirt. A girlfriend and I ended up on a farm where they made us work twelve hours and never paid us a penny. I lasted six months and quit, disillusioned about *pride in work and helping the fatherland.*" Annemarie laughed. "One funny thing that happened there. I got my period, and I had no idea what it was. I thought I 'd caught some disease. God, I was so naïve." She frowned and shook her head.

25

Lisbeth looked sympathetic.

"My mother just never talked about such things, you know, like sex, oh no." Annemarie briefly covered her mouth. "I had to write home to ask her to mail me sanitary napkins because I had no money."

Lisbeth laughed: "We were all naïve. My sex education came by way of our biology teacher, old man Maurer. And all he ever talked about was peas and beans and how they propagated. How that was supposed to relate to us still beats me." They both chuckled. "But I had a brother eight years older than I, and he taught me a thing or two. In fact, he got a girl pregnant and had to marry her. Guess that's why he volunteered for the army."

"Where is he now?" Annemarie asked.

"Dead. Killed in Poland early in the war. He was just a kid, really. But he loved the Fuehrer, and he died for him. Rest his soul."

"Sounds sort of like me," Annemarie said after a pause. "I met Willie, my husband, at one of the Hitler Youth outings. God, he was handsome, tall, well built." She smiled. "Every girl was after him. Blond, blue eyes-- steel blue-- he could charm you into doing anything he wanted. "Yah, tall, strong." She shook her head. "I wonder what he ever saw in me?"

"I can see why he picked you." Lisbeth paused. "Who knows? When he comes back, he may be a changed man. The war has changed all of us."

Annemarie shook her head. "It seems like a long time ago. I think it was 1938, and our group took a trip to the Isle of Fehmarn in the Baltic Sea. It's beautiful there. White beaches, swimming. We were so carefree and happy. And him being twenty-four and I just really a naïve kid, I believed every word he said. I had never been with a man, you know, intimate." Her face felt warm.

"So, you fell for him, right? And got pregnant?" Lisbeth laughed.

"How did you know? But you are right. I certainly didn't think that you could get pregnant after - after only one time. Well, you know lovemaking and how it works and all. We were on the beach, and I was so excited that he chose me over all the other girls. I would have done anything for him." Annemarie shrugged and threw up her arms. "It all happened so fast. And it hurt. I didn't have any fun and I did not want to do it again. I cried, and he laughed when he found out I'd still been a virgin. But I still loved him, and everybody thought that I was so lucky." She took a swallow of her beer.

"And then it hit me. I, the leader of the Hitler Youth group, was pregnant! And I had just started as a salesclerk at one of our big department stores." Annemarie shook her head and gazed at the swaying trees. She stopped and looked at Lisbeth, who was listening with a slight smile on her face. "Should I stop? I'm just rambling. We can continue another day."

Lisbeth waved her off. "Keep talking. I can't wait to find out what happened next."

"As you can imagine, my father had a fit when I told him I was pregnant and, of course, he blamed it all on the Nazis. When Willie took me home to the Baltic Sea where his parents lived in a small town, I was so excited. What a letdown that was."

"What do you mean?"

"His mother. A thin woman, sort of haggard looking. She had on a black dress, no warmth, no smiles. She immediately disliked me; I could tell. She said I was not good enough for her son because I did not know how to iron, that I had trapped him by getting pregnant, if indeed it was his child! And that I was poor trash from the city."

Lisbeth interrupted. "And his father?"

"Oh, he is just a big smiling teddy bear who does what his wife tells him. But, to make a long story short, Willie had applied for a job with the water department of

27

Fehmarn, but he could only get the job if he was married because they provided a house for the family to live in on the island. So, we got married, and Anna was born three months later. Ha, ha, ha!"

"So, you lived happily ever after." Lisbeth's words had a sharp edge as she gathered the empty bottles. Dusk engulfed them and it was getting chilly. "I'd love to find out what happened next," she said." Sounds like a love story, sort of."

"I will tell you more when we have another chance, my friend. There are many twists and turns before I become the grieving widow of the blond Germanic man every girl pined for."

Lisbeth wheeled Annemarie back into the ward. The air felt sticky, and a peculiar odor hung in the room.

"I know what you think. After being outside, it smells rotten in here." Lisbeth commented dryly.

"Lisbeth, really," Annemarie protested.

"Guess I've turned into a heartless witch. That was supposed to be a joke."

Annemarie grimaced. She was in pain now, and exhausted from the long journey into her past and her first venture outdoors. "I think I'm slightly soused. I haven't had so many beers ever."

"Two. You only had two beers, girl. But I'll give you something for your pain. I do have a heart, really, I do. And I'm not even on duty tonight." Lisbeth helped guide her back into the bed, dug into her pocket and produced a pill. "Here, take this." She handed Annemarie a glass of water.

"Thank you, Lisbeth," Annemarie murmured.

"For what?" Lisbeth raised her eyebrows.

"For being such a good friend." She sank into her pillow. "They've really crowded us here, rolled four more beds into this small area last night when the nurses from the

28

bus attack were brought in," Annemarie said, listening to the moaning all around her.

"Damn the Tommie's!" Lisbeth cussed under her breath. "Why did they have to shoot at these poor girls? They just wanted to go home after work. All young nurses that we need so desperately." She sighed. "And the war is almost over, so why shoot at the bus and then kill these innocent girls running for the ditch?"

"Oh my God, is that what happened?" Annemarie rose from her pillow, white-faced. "Why, in God's name, tell me. Why?"

"How should I know? The bus was traveling down the country road, and the bombers dove down and shot at it. Guess they had nothing else to do, since everything else has been bombed to smithereens. I hope the Tommie's rot in hell, if there is such a place. But these few girls did survive, barely." She went to check on the patients in the adjacent beds.

"Who is on duty tonight?" Annemarie murmured, fading off into sleep as the pill took effect. She thought she heard Lisbeth's voice grumbling, "Nobody, I guess. Nobody gives a damn anymore."

CHAPTER 5
Burghof Village

"How will Mama find us here in farmer Schulz's hayloft?" Inge sat on a plank of wood, her arms wrapped around her knees.

"Oh, Inge, she will. You know that Mama knows every secret, she always does."

"So how does she know that?" her sister asked.

"God gave Mama a special heart, like a radio, so she can hear where we are." Anna had made that up, but believed it was true.

Inge looked at her sister with worry in her green eyes. "This hayloft isn't going to burn down too, is it?"

"Of course not, Inge, there is no more war. The planes all went away. And farmer Schulz is an important man. Karl said so. Nobody would mess with his barn. He'd call the Fuehrer."

"What about Ben and his mean wife? Could they come up here when they do the chores?"

Anna shook her head. "Oh, stop it. If they come, we'll hide under the hay. Look at me. I'm not afraid. I'm almost six and I'll protect you."

Inge nodded, looking up at her sister. "I know you will, Anna. Mama said so."

"So, what did you do yesterday when I had to stay at the farm and help Gertl with the garden?" Anna liked helping in the garden, but she also missed her little sister and worried about her.

"I got to ride along with Karl and Ben to the moor. They let me hold the reins of the horses. Their names are Bertha and Bodo. Bertha is my favorite. When she is in her stall, I give her carrots and she eats them right from my hand." Inge jumped up, bubbling with excitement.

"She doesn't bite your fingers. With those big teeth?" Yanka's teeth were little compared to those of a horse.

"No, she doesn't bite. She has big puffy lips and takes the carrots softly," Inge explained.

Anna didn't know what the moor was and wished she could have been along yesterday. "So, what do they do at the moor?"

"They dig out pieces of the bog, that's what Ben called it, and they put them on our wagon and then Bertha and Bodo tow them back to the farm and Ben and Karl throw them on a pile to dry in the sun."

"And what do they do with them after that? Feed them to the pigs?"

"No, silly." Inge put her hands on her hips. "They burn them in the stove in the winter."

"Oh, yeah. Like we use coal at home in the city. I wonder where *that* comes from?"

Anna scratched her arm. The hay made her itch.

"It was fun." Inge went on. "I want to ride a horse sometime. But Ben said Bertha is too big for me. So, maybe she'll have a little baby horse some day and then I will get to ride."

Anna got up and hugged her. "You are the smartest little sister in the world." She tousled her hair.

"You know what else?" Inge cupped her hands over her sister's ear and whispered. "We had a fire."

Anna's mouth dropped open. "What? A fire?"

"Yes, Karl said his father cleaned out papers from his office. It's all empty now."

"They burned up all the papers. All of them? Are you sure? Why?"

"Yes, they did," Inge insisted. "But it's a secret." She put her finger on her lips. "So, you mustn't tell anyone, promise?"

"Hum, why would they do that, burn all the papers?" Secrets were always fun, and she could usually get Inge to tell her.

"Karl said it's got to do with the war. The Fuehrer wanted everything burned up."

Anna shrugged, losing interest in that story. "Want to know what I did yesterday? I was sitting in the garden helping to shell peas for supper. You open a pod and then all those little peas fall out. I always thought peas grew on trees."

Inge nodded. "Me too."

"And guess what? Arnold has a girlfriend. Her name is Rita."

Inge looked puzzled. "Who is Arnold?"

"Gee, don't you remember? He's the Munster's' oldest son, I told you that he had come home, remember?"

"Home from where?"

"Home from the war, dummy. Don't you remember anything I tell you?"

Inge stuck out her lip.

"I really like Rita." Anna smiled, trying to distract her. "She likes me too. She's Arnold's fiancée. Rita said she'd take me swimming in the Burghof Mill Lake. I can't wait."

"Can I go too?"

"Of course, you can. You will like Rita. Mrs. Munster says she's a floozy."

"What's that?" Inge wrinkled her forehead.

"I don't know. I think she doesn't like her much. But farmer Munster likes her. She's pretty. She's got black curly long hair and red lips. She let me paint my lips."

"I want to paint my lips too," Inge whined.

"You will, I'm sure. But I had to wash it off so Mrs. Munster wouldn't find out and get mad. I wish I could have kept it on to show my friends in the village. Oh, and Rita gave me a bathing suit. It's red with flowers on it. It's so pretty."

"I don't have a bathing suit," Inge wailed.

"Well, you're little, you don't need one," Anna said.

But her sister started to cry. "I want to have a bathing suit too. Mama will make me one."

"I will ask Rita. I think she can get one for you, too. You know what?" Anna went on. "When I was in the garden with Gertl and Mrs. Munster and we were shelling peas, Rita came in and she gave me chocolate." Anna pulled a small wrapper from her pocket and handed it to her.

"What's chocolate?" Inge looked at it suspiciously.

"Try a bite," Anna urged. "Just put it in your mouth. I like it a lot."

Inge unwrapped the bar and took a bite. "Ugh." She spit it out. "It's bitter. I don't like it." She handed the chocolate back.

"More for me." Anna popped it into her mouth and let it slowly melt on her tongue.

Inge rose from the hay bale and slipped her hand under her skirt, scratching her bottom.

"After Rita left, Mrs. Munster said to Gertl that Rita's father is a big wheeler dealer and those Pollacks are all alike." Anna said.

Inge shrugged.

"I asked Gertl,'what's a wheeler dealer?' They both looked at me and laughed and said I wouldn't understand."

"Hm," Inge said. She brushed pieces of hay from her blouse. "I'm getting hot."

"All right, let's go outside and see what Karl's up to." Anna took her sister by the hand and, after checking to see that nobody was around, they climbed down the ladder and ran across the farmyard to the Schultz's' house.

Karl was at the kitchen table eating a ham sandwich. "Want some?" he mumbled; his mouth full of bread.

Anna made a face. "Ham? No, thanks." If it were molasses, she would have eaten it, of course. Inge looked longingly at the food and Karl handed her a sandwich.

"Karl, what's a wheeler dealer and a Pollack?" Anna asked. She wanted to find out what they were saying about Rita's father.

Farmer Schulz stepped into the kitchen. "Ha. Is that what old man Munster called me?" He scowled at Anna.

She was afraid but answered, "No, no," then explained that Mrs. Munster said Rita's father was the wheeler dealer and a Pollack because she always gets nice things from him.

"Ha, ha, ha!" Karl's father bellowed. "Pure, holier-than-thou Munster. He always has to have something to gripe about. Rita's last name is Zombrowski, isn't it?"

Anna nodded. She really wanted to go outside and play, but farmer Schulz told them to sit at the table and listen really good. Anna took Inge's hand because she looked scared.

Farmer Schulz stood up and faced them. "Rita's folks are Polish refugees and live in the tenement cottages on the west side of the village behind the church. He has started working for the British because he speaks English and translates for them. That's his job now. He don't have a farm so you can't blame him, he's got to make a living, right?"

The children looked at the floor and said nothing.

"The world is changing, and you've got to go with whoever is on top. The British are rulers here right now.

34

They call the shots and Rita's father is a smart man to join them. Pollacks didn't get treated well here in the village. I know that for a fact, so, he's lucky now, and on top." He coughed and cleared his throat.

The children stared at him.

Then Karl spoke. "Father, why don't you work for the British too? Then you could be mayor again." He looked up at the big man.

Farmer Schulz broke out in a bellow of laughter. "Son, I don't think they'd take me. In fact, I'd rather they never find me. He pulled his gold watch from his pocket. "I have chores to do, Karl. I've got to milk the cows and get the corn planted."

"Yes, father," Karl replied dutifully, "but are you still a very important man?" He looked unsure.

"Yes, of course, Karl." He patted his son on the cheek. "Run along now." He turned and opened the door.

"The British are our enemies, they hurt my mama," Anna blurted.

"Well, things change," he said. "The war is over. Now they are the Allied occupation. And you better do what they tell you." He shook his head.

Anna looked at Karl and shrugged her shoulders.

"Come on, let's go outside," Karl urged. "I think the water in the creek is really high. It always is after the rain, and we can wade in it and catch frogs."

Inge finished the last crumbs of her sandwich and stood up.

Anna was glad to get away and ran outside, her sister in tow. They followed Karl into the meadow behind the house. "What did he mean?" she asked.

"Oh, he's just angry that he's no longer mayor in charge, you know. He thinks the Fuehrer should come back."

"Back from the bunker? Didn't he burn all his papers too?"

"I don't know," Karl yelled over his shoulder and started running towards the creek.

"I hate the British," Anna shouted, running after him. "Hate, hate! They hurt my mama."

"Hate, hate," Inge screeched, "I want my mama!"

CHAPTER 6
Army Field Hospital

"You're healing well." Doc Hartmann nodded approvingly. "Freulein Annemarie, your left leg is ready to go out for a walk. We've got to get you up and moving."

"What about my right one?" She smiled. "It takes two legs to dance, if I remember correctly."

The doctor paused and sat on the edge of her bed. He looked serious and that made her tense.

"Your right leg is giving me a bit of a challenge. One of the wounds, the big one in your thigh, is healing nicely."

"But?" She held her breath.

"Well, it's too soon to say." He smiled, but she sensed it was a forced smile.

"I really need to know, Doc." She raised her voice. "I'm tougher than you think."

"The wound in your foot is giving me a little trouble," Doc Hartmann continued in an even tone. "It is healing very slowly. There might be an infection and possibly some nerve damage affecting the circulation."

She lay there, eyes wide open, facing the horror of what that could mean. Then she tried to speak but could not utter a word.

Doc Hartmann got up resolutely. "Annemarie, you are a very special lady. I promise I'm going to fight for you and do everything I can to save your leg. I've got a few tricks in my bag that I hope will work. And, to celebrate your progress, I've instructed nurse Lisbeth to get you up

37

on crutches. Moving around will help, so you will do what she tells you, Liebling." He flashed an encouraging smile.

Annemarie nodded, her lips quivering.

"You better come up with your three jokes for tomorrow, remember? And our dance date still stands." He squeezed her hand and moved on to the next patient.

She lifted the blanket off her legs and stared at her thighs. The wound in her left thigh looked like a crater, welts and holes of different colors, bluish, yellow, red and purple. Healing well, Doc had said, well enough to remove the bandage. She bent to examine her right leg. The thigh was completely bandaged and appeared swollen. Her foot had swelled to twice its size and a yellowish discharge was oozing from her toe. She sank back and closed her eyes, feeling as though she had received a death sentence. *Fight to save your leg*, he had said. Helplessness and despair gripped her. The constant moans and screams from the wounded soldiers followed her into her dreams. *This is what hell must be like.*

She still had not received a letter from Alfred. He was probably dead, somewhere in faraway France, taking their dreams for the future with him. And her children? She had not heard a word. Desperate for information, she had talked to anyone who would listen, but nobody seemed to know anything. Her parents - they were frail and not in good health. Did their apartment house survive the last fire bombings? Did they have enough to eat? She had to find some way to get a message to them. If her mother thought she was dead, she would not have the will to live.

She wept for herself, for her children and for her mother and father and the two brothers she lost. She had to be strong, had to go to her parents. Perhaps her sister Margarete was checking on them to make sure they had food. Oh yes, Margarete, her well-to-do older sister. No, Margarete would not be there for them. "If you ever need help, don't count on your sister," her mother had said.

"Find a friend or even a stranger to help." Why had her mother told her that? She'd never offered an explanation. As the youngest child, born when her sister was already ten years old, Annemarie had always been close to her mother. Spoiled, her sister insisted. Annemarie and her mother talked about everything, read books together and laughed. Annemarie knew that she was the reason her parents kept on living after the death of their second son, her younger brother, Otto.

Thinking of sweet Otto made her cry again. He'd been only sixteen when he enlisted on a merchant marine ship. The letters he wrote brimmed with enthusiasm about the ship and the many exotic places he had seen. She fondly remembered the pretty red coat he brought for her when he came home after his first trip. Everybody was so proud of him. And then the telegram arrived. They had found him hanging on the ship's chimney and had buried him in New York. Suicide, they claimed. Her brother, Otto, who was so looking forward to his future. Her father said they were covering up something hideous but did not have the means to fight the shipping company. After that, Father kept much to himself, barely talking with anyone. Those were sad days at home. Annemarie cried harder, her whole body shaking. She pulled the sheet over her head.

"Hello, anybody home?" Nurse Lisbeth's cheerful voice brought her back. She lifted the sheet from Annemarie's tearful face. "Feeling sorry for ourselves, aren't we?" She handed her a handkerchief. "Not in my ward, Maedchen. Remember Doc Hartmann's rules. You can be miserable before you come here and after you leave, but here, we support each other and keep a stiff upper lip." She looked around and beamed. "Doc Hartmann tells me that everyone here is doing much better today. I knew my girls could do it." She opened the shades. It was a gloomy day and rain pelted the windows in a monotonous beat. "It's almost June. We need a little rain to keep those pretty flowers blooming," Lisbeth chirped. The blue pinstripes in her crisp uniform accentuated her figure and complimented her perky demeanor.

Annemarie sat up in bed. It was impossible to stay sad for long with nurse Lisbeth around. She sniffed the air. "Is that what I think it is? My sister uses that scent. Expensive."

"A birthday gift." Lisbeth grinned. "From a friend in high places." She flipped her head and pursed her lips in a kiss. Then she said, "I have some news." She looked down at Annemarie. "You have a visitor."

"What? Me, I have a visitor? Who would find me here?"

"It's a gentleman, that's all I know," Lisbeth said. "Why don't we put you into a wheelchair, doll you up a little and then I'll take you into the nurses' lounge, so you have some privacy." She didn't wait for an answer. "Come on, let's go, I've got other patients waiting." Lisbeth helped Annemarie out of the bed and into the wheelchair. She wheeled her into a medium-sized room, sparsely furnished, with a gray linoleum floor, a brown sofa on one wall and a few chairs around a table in the middle of the room. A large sink filled one corner and several mugs lined up on a drying board. A large bulletin board covered with notes and papers took up almost one entire wall.

"Now let's see what we can do to spruce you up a little."

Annemarie waved her arms in protest. "Really, that's not necessary."

But Lisbeth rummaged through a small leather case she had brought, took out a brush, powder and a lipstick. "Don't argue with me, child. You look like somebody who has just risen from the dead. We've got our reputation to think of."

Annemarie laughed. "All right, make me look like Lily Marlene if you must." She flipped her hair, brushing strands of off her face.

"And now put this on." Lisbeth helped Annemarie into a light blue jacket decorated with small white flowers. "Ah, ah, no argument, Lisbeth knows best."

"I look like a baby doll," Annemarie said. She felt light-hearted now and eager to meet the mysterious stranger.

"You look pretty, girl. You should always wear that color lipstick." Lisbeth nodded approvingly.

"I have never owned a lipstick." Annemarie said.

"Then you should. I'll give you one if I can find another in that shade." She left to fetch the visitor.

Annemarie shook her head. Lisbeth amazed her. When others were scrounging for food, she managed to find lipsticks.

Lisbeth returned followed by a young man. "But I don't want you two to be long. The nurses will need the room for their lunch break." She winked at Annemarie and closed the door behind her.

The man stretched out his hand and introduced himself. "Rudi Mueller." He looked unsure of how she would receive him. He wore civilian clothes, a beige windbreaker over a rumpled white shirt. Annemarie guessed him to be twenty-eight or so. He had short-cropped sandy hair and was of medium build.

"I think we've met before," he said, "in the village of Burghof. I was stationed there with the military."

"Burghof. That's where I lived where we got bombed." She took a closer look at him. "Yes, I have met you with Jake at Braun's Pub."

"Yes, we've met at Braun's," he acknowledged. He pulled a handkerchief from his pocket and wiped his damp forehead.

41

She remembered him. He was a major with the unit stationed in the village. She decided not to ask why he was not wearing his uniform.

"I came by to tell you that I am sorry." He looked at his feet. " It was stupid to drive into the village, I know that now. I should have jumped into a ditch." A nervous smile came and went on his face.

She smiled back, confused. "Major, why do you think you were involved in my being injured?"

"You really didn't know? I was the one they were shooting at. I had driven down that road and parked under the big oak tree. And now, look at you. I've ruined your life. It has really bothered me that you were hurt. I am just glad that you made it out alive." His voice cracked. "I want you to know that I am not a bad man." He pressed his handkerchief against his eyes. "Please believe me it was unintentional. I wish there was some way I could make it up to you."

The man was sobbing now. She reached out and touched his hand. After a pause, she said, "Did you know Alfred Schapen? He was also stationed in Burghof. I think he was shipped to Normandy."

"Hmm, yes, some time last year, I recall." He slowly lowered his eyes to hers.

"I have been waiting for a letter," she continued in a halting voice. "He wrote to me often, but I have not heard from him in a long time." Her heart was beating so loud, she wondered if he could hear it.

He looked at his folded hands. "So much has happened. Everything is in turmoil, it's almost impossible to get around now, you know. There are no soldiers left in Burghof. The military has moved out. Everyone left during the night," he went on, "so it's almost impossible to find out anything. I promise if I hear something, I will let you know."

Annemarie took a breath and tried not to cry but she could not hide her disappointment.

A pause stretched between them.

Finally, he said, "I am so sorry, and if I can ever make it up to you, I will. You have to believe me."

She almost smiled at him. "If you can help me with this, I will be forever grateful. Are you still in Burghof?"

"I have not been there recently, but I plan to go back as soon as possible. My wife and three children are there with my sister-in-law, Eva Weller. You might know her."

Her face lit up. "Of course, I know Eva. She works at Braun's Pub. Major Rudi," she pleaded, "my children, Inge and Anna, were left in Burghof after the bombing of the Munster farmhouse, and they took me away. I want you to find out if the girls are safe, where they are now. I have not heard anything at all. I don't even know if they were hurt or." She bit her lips.

"Oh, I can answer that," he interrupted. "The children are fine, not hurt. They were outside and one of my soldiers kept them out of harm's way during the fire."

She grabbed his hands. "Oh my God, thank you!"

"I know they are safe. Now I remember, Eva told me one of the girls was taken in by the Munster family and the other by farmer Schulz."

She took deep breaths until she was able to speak. "You don't know how happy you've made me. Oh, my God, oh my God." She covered her face with her palms.

A nurse stuck her head through the door. Major Rudi rose. "Looks like they need me out of here." He spread his hand at her, turned, and started towards the door. " I'm glad I've been able to bring you good news."

"Oh, and promise me one more thing," Annemarie cried. "Please go back to Burghof and tell my children that I am fine and that I miss them and that I'll be back soon to get them." She shouted, out of breath, "Or could you bring them here to visit me? I want to see my girls. I need to see my children."

He stood there and folded his hands. "Miss Annemarie, I will try. But I can't guarantee anything."

She stared at him her stomach dropping.

"It is not safe to get around, you see. There's still sporadic fighting, especially in the countryside. Some towns are still being defended. God knows why they don't surrender, but they want every able-bodied man to fight till the end. If they catch me out of uniform, they'll shoot me on the spot. They've taken every young boy they can find, even thirteen-year-olds. Poor boys, how can they expect them to fight the British army and their tanks with just a gun? It's terrible. Just terrible, they'll all be mowed down by the tanks, every one of them, believe me." He was talking faster, and faster, almost in a frenzy. He stopped abruptly and took a breath. "I've got to lay low right now, you understand, don't you? I can't risk getting caught. I have a wife and children to consider. It wasn't easy to get here. I almost got caught and the British came close to shooting me. It will be all over soon. But for now, it is very dangerous out there. It would be a shame to die now when it's almost over and most of the country has surrendered." He was still gesticulating, flinging his arms around, defending himself against imaginary soldiers.

A group of nurses entered the room, alarm on their faces.

"But you promise, Rudi." She rose, almost falling out of the wheelchair." You will bring my children here." She grabbed on to its arm with one hand and spread the other to regain her balance. "You will bring them, promise me."

He turned to the door, his shoulders sagging and his face expressionless. "I promise," he said in a barely audible voice. "If I make it through alive."

A moment later, as the nurses settled around the table with their cigarettes and coffee, the sound of low flying planes approached from the west. A tremendous boom rattled the furniture and a mug tumbled from the drying board into the sink. Annemarie shrank into her chair and held on to its arms as it spun against a wall. As quickly as it had started, the roar turned into a hum and melted into the distance. None of the nurses took notice.

Then Lisbeth barged in. "Something got hit." As the nurses scrambled out the door, Lisbeth turned Annemarie's wheelchair into the hallway and ran her down the center of the ward towards her bed.

Annemarie looked back towards Lisbeth. "My children are safe; they are with the farmers."

But Lisbeth shook her head. "Later," she shouted, "I must get to the village. There are injuries." She helped Annemarie into her bed and rushed away.

CHAPTER 7

"Oh, my God, Lisbeth," she said, after Lisbeth returned. He saw my children. He said they are safe. I'm ready to dance." She was laughing as they passed Doc Hartmann in the hallway. He smiled and blew her a kiss.

"I tell you what, I have to check on the patients wounded by the attack on the village," Lisbeth said, "but I'm off later this afternoon. If it is not raining, let's get out and have another picnic to celebrate your good news. Now, get some rest and do a little praying to the weather god."

Resting was out of the question. "My children are safe. They are with the farmers, so I know they'll get plenty to eat," Annemarie blurted to the women in the adjacent beds. "They are so young, only four and six. I miss them so much. Major Rudi promised he would bring them here to see me." She babbled. "Inge is afraid of the Russians. But my Anna, the oldest, she takes care of her little sister." She smiled; her eyes moist with joy. The words were bubbling out of her in a continuous stream. "My God. I can't believe it. My children are coming." She looked around. "But I have nothing to give them." She clapped her hands. "I could knit something, like a hat or a scarf." She stopped, remembering that her yarn and needles were lost in the fire."

"Ask Nurse Lisbeth," her bed neighbor, a thin woman with a missing arm, said.

Annemarie leaned back on her pillow. If Lisbeth could find lipstick, surely, she could find some needles and yarn.

Later when Lisbeth stopped by to pick up the lunch tray, Annemarie asked about knitting needles and supplies. "I want to knit a hat and scarf for Inge and Anna. Maybe red, yes, Anna likes red, and pink for Inge." She smiled at Lisbeth with expectation. "Lisbeth, my children are coming. And they are safe. Major Rudi told me so. Thank God, they had a guardian angel."

"Yes, yes, dear, you already told me five times. But you must get some rest now. You've been up for hours."

"When the girls come, I want to have their presents ready. So don't forget the needles."

"Knitting needles. That's one request we've not had at this field hospital." Lisbeth laughed.

She glanced out the window. "Looks like the weather god is happy for you too. I see a patch of blue sky over there."

After the initial euphoria of Rudi's visit had subsided, Annemarie sank into a deep sleep.

... Alfred was there. He promised her again he would come home and give her a ring, his mother's. "Alfred," she cried, and reached for him as his image faded. She ran down the bombed-out village road, ruins on either side still smoldering in the ghastly sky. "Alfred, Liebling, I'm here, I'm coming," she screamed, scrambling up a hill on her hands and knees, trying to get through debris, craters and burned brush, then huge explosion...

"No," she shouted, reaching for him, but when she opened her eyes, she was looking at Lisbeth's smiling face.

"Are you all right?" Lisbeth placed her hand on Annemarie's forehead.

"I saw Alfred, Lisbeth. He smiled and called out my name."

"Sounds like a pleasant dream. Tell me about it, did you have a good time?"

Annemarie was trembling. "No, I never reached him. A big blast knocked me down. Everything was burned and no one was there."

"These are war times, girl. We all have nightmares. Talk to the soldiers, they'll tell you that your mind mixes it all up."

Annemarie nodded. "I thought maybe he was giving me a message that he --"

"Stop it right now." Lisbeth leaned over her with a stern face. "You will drive yourself crazy if you keep this up." Her voice softened. "Let's have our picnic. Unless you prefer not to go out today?"

"Of course, I want to go. We have to celebrate." She tried to smile.

It was dusk when Lisbeth returned. She helped Annemarie into a wheelchair and pushed her outside to the small patch of grass by the back door. It was warm, with a light breeze fanning the rain-laden leaves, spreading the fresh scent of moist flowering plants.

"It couldn't be more beautiful, so peaceful. You would never guess that there is a war right over the hill." Annemarie said softly.

Lisbeth nodded.

"Major Rudi said that the war is almost over and there is only sporadic fighting." Annemarie looked at the sky. "The same stars everywhere. Even the British and the Russians are looking at them. I wonder if they, too, make a wish when they see a shooting star." She sighed. "I wish for a shooting star right now."

Lisbeth passed her a bottle of beer. "Sorry, no liver pate this time. But we've got cheese. Hmm, Gouda, my favorite, and chicken, bread and vanilla pudding." She handed Annemarie a plate and fork. "But I managed this beer. A new delivery must have come in. Some things still function. Cheers to your shooting star." She stood and lifted her bottle to the sky. "I think your gentleman friend is right. The war is ending. We were told at our staff meeting yesterday there could be an end to the fighting any day. Commander Herberger left two days ago."

"What about all the patients here?" Annemarie stared at Lisbeth, alarmed. "We don't have any place to go."

"Nothing is official yet. I'm sure some type of arrangements will be made. I won't just run off and leave you here."

Annemarie smiled hesitantly. "Prost, Lisbeth!" She raised her bottle and took a big gulp. "I really want you to meet my girls. Hey, how would you like to be an aunt?"

"Aunt Lisbeth, I like how that sounds, yes, I do. Let's toast to that."

Annemarie filled her plate and relished every bite, sensing that it was probably their last feast "I'm on my second beer." She giggled.

"Doesn't sound good, 'nurse gets patient drunk'. We'd better slow down, girl. Listen to Aunt Lisbeth."

Annemarie ate another Kaiser roll and stuffed a big piece of cheese into her mouth. "I can't believe how much I'm eating."

"That means you're getting better, and your wounds are healing. Eat good now. From what I am hearing there's not much food on the outside. People in the cities are dropping dead from hunger. We have enjoyed privileges here at the hospital, Commander Herberger saw to that." She wiped her mouth with a ragged napkin. "But let's not think about that now. Tell me more about that love story of yours with gorgeous Willie."

Annemarie tried to think back to 1939. "Hmm, where to begin?"

"You got married, had a baby girl and moved into a house on an island in the Baltic Sea," Lisbeth prompted.

"Right, that was a happy time. I played house and had no worries, just a young wife starting out." Annemarie smiled. "I didn't like sex, but I did get pregnant again."

Nurse Lisbeth's lips formed an O, faking surprise.

"But then the war had started, and Willie volunteered to join the Navy. Everything changed after that. We had to move out of the house because it was tied to his job, and I refused to move in with his parents."

Lisbeth raised her eyebrows. "They never changed, I mean, now that they had a grandchild?"

"Nope, I guess I was stubborn, too. I have my pride. My family is poor, but we are decent, hard-working people, and nobody calls us city trash. I never forgave his mother for that."

Lisbeth shook her head. "So, what did you do, with one little kid and another one on the way? I've never had children, but I can imagine that it was not easy."

"I went back to the city, poor as a church mouse, and my daughter, Inge, was born there three weeks later. I stayed with my parents, but they lived in a one-bedroom apartment and my father is a heavy smoker, so we were living in a cloud all the time. Anna coughed a lot, so I had to do something."

"What about your sister? Didn't you mention she is well off?"

"Oh, yes, she was and still is. I remember visiting her for her older daughter's birthday party. She has two girls too, about the same age as my girls. Her apartment is huge, three bedrooms and just beautiful. My kids pestered me for months after that visit to go back to play with those beautiful doll houses and toys. But we weren't invited again. My sister is the wife of a Captain Heinrich Bowman. And I am the poor relative from the other side of town. I had a hard time explaining that to my children."

"Did you ever ask your sister why she treats you that way?" Lisbeth said. After all, she's your only sister."

"It goes back to our childhood. She was born before the last war, and she never had any of the things I had. She claims that my mother loves me more than her. To this day, she brings up that I had a rubber ball to play with and she didn't."

Lisbeth shook her head and handed Annemarie another bottle of beer.

"Thanks." Annemarie took a long sip. "When I had to move back to the city, I asked if she could lend me thirty-five Marks, which I needed to pay for a one-room apartment down the street from where my parents lived."

"Did she give you the money?"

Annemarie laughed aloud. "No. She said her husband would not allow her to loan out money because I wouldn't pay it back and then I would need more."

"What a witch. Your own sister. And you with two little children. I would hate that woman."

"I don't hate her. I guess she's just a poor soul, you know, not a happy person. And I think she drinks, probably an alcoholic, or close to it."

Lisbeth frowned and shook her head. "Boy, I'd like to meet this Mrs. Bowman and give her a piece of my mind."

"Maybe you will." Annemarie smiled and took another sip of her beer. "Anyway, somehow, I got a small apartment with my mother's help, and I went back to work and she looked after the babies. When you are young, you just work things out."

"When you are young. You make me laugh. Like you are an old lady now."

"Sometimes I do feel like an old lady, so much has happened so fast."

"When did Willie come home, or is he still on the front?" Lisbeth leaned back in her chair.

"Get out your hanky, Lisbeth. You might need it when you hear what happened next. You know what?"

Annemarie held her empty bottle upside down. "I could really use another beer."

Lisbeth stared at her. "I just gave you one. All right, I'll get you another one if I don't run into Doc Hartmann. He will fire me if he finds out I get his patients drunk."

"Nobody will fire you, Lisbeth. Remember, your friends in high places?" Annemarie grinned.

Lisbeth disappeared and came back with two more bottles.

Annemarie took one and drank. "That tastes so good. Maybe I'm turning into an alcoholic like my sister."

"Nonsense, Annemarie, three beers, once a month? You are such a naïve, innocent girl. So, tell me more, I've got my hanky ready." She waved it in front of Annemarie's face.

"It was a couple of years ago, 1943 I think because Inge was born in January of 1941 and Willie had never been on leave to see her. He was stationed somewhere in Norway, near the arctic. At least in his letters he mentioned ice and snow and dark, foggy days that felt like nights.

My oldest daughter, Anna, had gotten sick, very sick. My mother and I took the streetcar to a clinic, one of the few still open, where an old doctor told me that she had bronchitis. Anna wasn't quite four. She got worse and worse, and we thought she was going to die. She was screaming all the time. The old doctor just said that's what little kids do, scream. *I* was getting hysterical and screaming at *him*."

Lisbeth scratched her head. "He's probably just an old man left to run the clinic because all the able-bodied doctors are at the front. That's why we are so short here at the hospital too. But since this is an army hospital, they let us keep a few like Doc Hartmann to fix up the boys and get them back to the front."

"You are probably right, Lisbeth. But I became desperate and went back to the clinic the next day. We had to drag the poor sick child on the streetcar again since there was no other transportation. The old doctor was not there. Maybe he croaked. Sorry. But an older nurse saw Anna. She took one look, examined her, and asked what the child was treated for. When I told her, she had a fit. She did a few more tests and told us this was an emergency and the child had to be admitted to a hospital immediately. And that's what happened. Hardly any beds were available, but somehow, she got little Anna in."

"What did they say she had?

"Pneumonia and tuberculosis."

"What!" Lisbeth leaned back in her chair and slapped her thighs. And she was treated for bronchitis all that time? Unbelievable, it's a miracle that she survived."

"You are right. They told me at the hospital that my daughter was dying." Annemarie choked up as she thought of that dreadful day. "I was going to lose my little Anna. They asked me to report this to the military authorities so the father of the child could be notified and come home immediately."

"Oh, my God, Annemarie, you poor thing." Lisbeth bent and gently brushed a strain of hair from Annemarie's forehead.

The scent of Lisbeth's Eau de Cologne soothed her, and, for a moment, she felt safe, like everything would be all right.

"They sent a telegram to his outpost and granted him emergency leave. The plane scheduled to bring the next group of soldiers home for leave was filled to capacity, and they bumped another soldier so Willie could take his seat. I remember that day as if it was yesterday. I was beside myself with fear of losing my child and couldn't wait to have my husband by my side." Annemarie had to stop, realizing how much this was still upsetting her.

"But you were lucky, your daughter lived." Lisbeth gently placed her hand on Annemarie's arm.

53

"Yes, little Anna pulled through. It was amazing even to the hospital staff. It was a miracle."

"You are right, Anna is a little miracle. I'm glad you told me to bring a hanky." Lisbeth dabbed her eyes. "I've seen a lot at this field hospital, but this..."

Annemarie watched the branches swaying in the breeze like they were following a symphony. "I did not see Willie again. He never got to meet his little daughter, whom I named Inge. I'm still sad when I think about that."

"But what happened? I don't understand."

"I received a telegram the next day. They regretted to tell me that my husband, Willie Peterman, was killed in a plane crash. I heard later that the plane took off in fog and slammed into a mountain. They have those around the fjords in Norway. There were no survivors."

Lisbeth stood up, bent to hug her, and said in a trembling voice, "I am so sorry."

Annemarie put her hand on Lisbeth's. Nurse Lisbeth was not so tough after all.

"Wow," Lisbeth exclaimed. "Now I'm ready for that next beer. I bet the soldier who was bumped off that flight is happy. That is a miracle for him too. If I were religious, I'd say it was God's will."

They sat quiet for a while, listening to the leaves rustle. A bird chirped.

Annemarie reached for the last chunk of cheese. "I went to apply for his widow's pension. You know, he died for the Fatherland, since he was on active duty. It wasn't much, but it would have helped me a lot." She gazed into the shadows of the trees.

"So, you didn't get it?"

"I went to fill out an application and they asked me if I was Mrs. Peterman. Stupid question, I thought, and told them, of cause I was Mrs. Peterman and showed them our marriage license. They told me that there was another

54

Mrs. Peterman who had two children and that I had to share my pension with her."

Lisbeth laughed. "You are making that up. It's a joke, right?"

"No ma'am, I wish it was a joke. I was shocked and told them that it must be a mistake, argued with them. But it did not do any good. And that's not all. A few weeks later -- it was a Sunday - I was just about to leave to take the train to the sanitarium where Anna was recuperating from tuberculosis. You know they isolate those patients, I mentioned that did I? I was about to leave when there was a knock on the door. My mother had come over, since we always went to the hospital together. Poor little Anna. Five years old and all alone at the big sanatorium, waving to us from behind the window. Her face always looked so pale, and she did not smile. After a few moments, she raised her eyes to Lisbeth's.

"Anyway, my mother said there was a woman with a child to see me and she let them in. She introduced herself as Mrs. Muller and her daughter Helga. And then she dropped the bombshell. She told me she was engaged to Willie and they had planned to get married after the war. And she pointed at Helga and told me that she was Willie's daughter."

Lisbeth's mouth dropped open. She shook her head, gulped her beer, spilling a brown stain on her uniform.

Annemarie rushed on. "At first, I did not believe her. And then I took a closer look at Helga. She looked just like Anna. I had to sit down or else I'd have fallen. Then I asked Helga how old she was, and she told me almost five. I quickly did the math. She was born almost the exact time as Anna. The woman told me Willie stayed in her little town on trips with the Hitler Youth and that's how they met. She said they fell in love instantly and he came back to visit her often. I was crushed. She said we could be friends, but I broke down and cried and told her to

55

leave and that I never wanted to see her again." Annemarie took a deep breath. "So, who knows how many little Annas are out there? I didn't want to believe it, but Willie was a Don Juan. His good looks and charm got him into bed with any woman he chose."

"I know what you think." Lisbeth said. "In a way, he got what he deserved when the plane went down, right?"

"I'm not sure what I was thinking. I had to go on with my life, you know, a toddler, a job and a sick child in a faraway sanatorium. My grieving-widow status changed instantaneously. All I could think was, that bastard! He cheated on me, he betrayed me, he just married me for the convenience of a job and a house. And he took up with other women even while I was pregnant with our first child."

"Did you ever tell his parents?"

"I wish I had. I probably still could. What fun that would be to look at his mother's face and tell her of the many bastards her son has made." Annemarie laughed. "It's not really funny, but in a way -"

"You can still do it. I would," Lisbeth said with conviction.

"I might, I just might. But I'm not sure I can face that woman again. You know I applied for child support since my widow's pension was cut in half. I was told that his parents had to contribute, but I don't know what the legal terms are. They must have sent some papers to them, because I received an envelope with a note that said, 'onetime payment for child support.' You know how much it was? Twelve Marks." Annemarie's voice brimmed with anger. "His parents, his children's grandparents, sent me a check for twelve Marks marked 'One-time payment.'"

Lisbeth slapped her thighs. "I can't believe that."

"I got so angry that I took the check and mailed it right back to them and told them to keep it. That's life for you. Maybe they will get their payback when they go to hell which I hope there is, for their sake." She gazed up at the stars and took deep breaths.

"Everyone has a story. Unbelievable. Lisbeth gave Annemarie a motherly pat on the cheek. "You're holding up pretty well. Though you almost got killed and you can still smile." She looked warmly at Annemarie. "But you know what? From now on it will all be wonderful for you, like Cinderella."

"I hope you are right, I really do," Annemarie murmured. After a long pause, she continued. "Well, here is the grand finale. After the firebombing started in earnest, they ordered all women and children to leave the city, to evacuate. I wanted to stay with my parents, but the rules had to be followed. Anna had returned home by then and we were sent to Burghof, a small farm village northeast of the city. Those farmers didn't want us. But the military gave them no choice." She slowly sipped her beer. "You know, in a way it was a blessing in disguise, because we had enough to eat there. Anna and Inge made friends with the village children, played outside, and got to see cows and chickens. It turned out to be a happy time, especially, of course, after I met Alfred." Her face lit up.

"And then you got wounded and ended up here. Unbelievable." Lisbeth sighed. "But we go on, don't we? You are a survivor, Annemarie. You have dealt with a lot of hardships, and you look like a young girl. You can still laugh. Next time, you have to tell me all about Alfred. Cheers." She held up her bottle.

"To Alfred, the love of my life," Annemarie whispered and looked at the sky, wishing for a shooting star.

CHAPTER 8
Burghof Village

"I am a princess." Anna pranced up and down the kitchen showing Gertl her new dress. "Rita sewed it for me and she made one for Inge too." She twirled around to make sure Gertl was paying attention. "Look, it has a big white bow in the back."

"The wedding is not till two o'clock, Anna. Don't you think you should take the dress off now? It might get dirty."

"What time is it?" Anna asked. "I am not taking this dress off."

"Ten o'clock, Anna. It is morning. We've got a lot to do till then, and I thought you would help me get the vegetables ready."

"But I want to go over to Karl's farm and show them my dress. All my friends will be there." Anna curtsied. "Please prettily."

Gertl shook her head. "You do such a good job shelling peas and stripping beans. I could really use your help today. I'm worried that I'll not get it all done for the banquet."

"All right, I'll help. But only for a while." Anna stomped out of the kitchen and walked to the rose room, the one with the little rosebuds on the wallpaper. It was so pretty. It was her rose room. She stood in front of the mirror and looked at herself. Never before had she owned such a beautiful dress. Oh, if only she could show it to her mama. It was made of blue, shimmering taffeta and went

58

almost to her feet. Rita said it would cover her worn old sandals, the only shoes she owned. She wondered if Rita would let her paint her lips again.

Anna really wanted to go to Karl's farm now and show the dress to everybody, especially to Inge, since Rita had made the same dress for her, just smaller. Inge would look so pretty in it. Reluctantly, Anna took the dress off and carefully laid it on her bed. She put on old slacks and the checkered blouse she hated because Mama had made it from worn old kitchen curtains. Here, in the village, the children probably wouldn't notice. But she still hated it. "Ugly, ugly, ugly," she muttered, walking back to the kitchen. But soon, she'd be back in her pretty dress. "This is the first time ever that I will be a flower girl at a real wedding," she said to Gertl.

Gertl laughed. "Yes, Anna, you've told me at least ten times already."

"So, what are you going to be in the wedding?" Anna asked, picking up a pea pod.

"I'm going to be right here, preparing food for the guests. And then I'll be serving it, hopefully with extra help." She sighed and tightened her head scarf.

"When are you getting married?" Anna asked.

Gertl raised her eyebrows and peered at Anna.

"Rita told me you have a beau. She saw you dancing with him at Brauns." Anna grinned.

Gertl put down the knife she was chopping carrots with and folded her arms. She always did that when she got serious. "Oh, what else did she tell you?"

Anna shifted from one foot to the other. "Just that – that – um, that he is a soldier and that he is your boyfriend."

"She told you that?"

"Not really, but I heard her say it to Jake." Anna squirmed. Gertl suddenly looked ten feet tall.

"I think we have to wash your big ears out with green soap tonight," she said, but she laughed.

Anna was not afraid of her. Gertl was her friend and made her scrambled eggs. Back in the kitchen, she clapped her hands. "The whole village will be there. I'm so excited." They had already decorated the Munster farmyard and moved Yanka to a barn in back. Anna dropped her hands in her lap. "How late is it now, Gertl? Gee, how many more peas do we have to shell today? Nobody can eat that many."

"It is only eleven o'clock now, child. And, yes, we have to shell all of these peas because Rita's family is coming and a lot of other guests."

"Inge and I will be sitting in the wedding carriage up front with Jake on the way to the church. I wish my mama would come. She could suddenly arrive, couldn't she? Maybe she heard about the wedding." Anna put her bowl down.

Gertl tossed a carrot at her. "Here, eat that, it's good for your eyes." She wiped her hands on her apron and sat down at the table next to the child. "Anna, let me tell you a secret. Remember Major Rudi?"

"Yes, I remember him. He always gives us candy."

"He went to visit your mother in the hospital. I heard it from Eva Weller yesterday. He said your mama is feeling much better and her legs are healing. And you know what? Major Rudi said that he will take you girls to visit her."

Anna crowded onto Gertl's lap and threw her arms around her neck. "Can we go today, please?"

"No, Anna, the wedding is today. But soon, I hope. I am sure he will stop by and tell us all about his visit."

Anna jumped up and down. "Can I tell Inge about visiting Mama?"

"No, no, you must not tell your sister. She'll just cry. Promise, you won't tell her yet please?"

60

"Oh, I forgot, I better not tell her." She sighed. "But it will be hard, Gertl, really hard to keep it a secret."

They finally got done with the peas and Gertl let her go. Anna ran down the road to the Schulz farm. Karl, her sister Inge and several other children were sitting on top of a wagon, the one they used for hauling bog, because there were pieces of it all over.

"I am going to be a flower girl in Rita's wedding," Anna announced to them all.

"Me too." Inge jumped down and took her sister's hand.

"Wait till you see our new dresses, Inge. They are so shiny, with big bows on the back." Anna pranced around and curtsied as though she was at the wedding. Inge watched and started to hop around in a circle.

The children looked at them, but no one said a word.

"Everybody is coming to the wedding, right?" Anna glanced around perplexed at their reaction. "Gertl said the whole village will be there."

Karl did not look at her. "Not me." He picked up a piece of bog and turned it over in his hands.

"Why not? You live in the village."

"My father won't allow me to go." Karl kicked some bog pieces off the wagon.

Anna shook herself. "Stop it. The stuff is flying in my face. Karl, it's Rita and Arnold's wedding. You have to come."

"Father said absolutely not. He's not going to let me go to the wedding of some traitor and socialist or something like that. Anyway, it's got something to do with the war, and I can't go."

"But the war is over. The Major said so. And Rita is no traitor. She is nice. I tell you what, I'm going to run in and ask your father if you can come."

61

Karl jumped off the wagon and gave Anna a shove, knocking her down. She jumped up to examine her bleeding knee. He stepped towards her and pinned her against the wagon. "If you talk to my father, I'm going to hurt you," he shouted, "I don't want to go to some dumb wedding."

"Let me go, you are hurting my arm." Anna jerked away.

"Erika is coming home next week with her baby, and Inge has to leave. She can't stay here anymore," he shouted. "Why don't you just go back to the city?" He turned and ran into the house.

Anna tried to wipe the dirt off her knee. "What is the matter with him? "A thin girl with long braids jumped off the wagon and came to look at Anna's knee. "We are all coming, but not the Schultzes. Karl's father is really mad."

Anna glanced at them. This didn't make any sense. But then she remembered that farmer Schulz and farmer Munster did not like each other and how they had shouted in the kitchen that day. Anna rolled her eyes and turned to her sister. "Let's go back to the Munster farm, Inge, so we can try on your new dress." She took Inge's hand. They started down the road.

Inge looked up at her with fear in her eyes. "Do I have to leave? Are we going back to the city?"

Anna put her arm around her waist. "Maybe you can live with me at the Munster farm. That would be nice, we'd be together again."

"Oh Anna, I want to be with you. Farmer Schulz, he shouts a lot. He doesn't like me."

"Inge, of course he likes you. He just fights with the Munster's. You know, grownups, they are that way. Hey, we are going to be in the wedding, and I am so excited. You will look so pretty in your new dress."

The next day, with the wedding behind them, Anna went back to Karl's farm. He told her he was sorry and that he really didn't want them to go back to the city. Anna smiled, poked him playfully on the shoulder and said that they were friends again. "The funniest part of the wedding was when Arnold and Rita kissed. And the pastor told them to do it." She snickered. "But I know they have done it before. I didn't tell Mrs. Munster. She would have called Rita names again. But, when we went swimming at the Burghof Mill Lake, they were hugging. I saw them kiss, lying on a blanket in the grass."

Karl just bent down to pick up a rock and threw it across the creek.

A few days later Anna and Inge snuck back to their secret hideout, the hayloft at the Schulz farm. Anna wanted to tell her what had happened this morning at the Munster farm. It was cozy up here. On a nice day with a breeze blowing through the rafters it felt fine. And nobody knew that they were up here.

"I really liked the wedding, Inge. Did you see them kiss?"

They both giggled. It was strange that people wanted to kiss.

"I can't imagine kissing a boy on the mouth." Anna shook her head and made a face.

"Me either." Inge puffed her lips. "It would be icky, yuck."

"I want to tell you a secret, Inge."

"A secret?" Inge's green eyes grew round.

"Come, sit close by me. Yesterday morning Mrs. Schulz came over to our farm. We had just finished breakfast and -- Promise you won't cry?"

"I won't." Inge scooted closer. "I want to be with you. Mama said we will be safe together."

"We will, Inge, we will. That's what I was going to tell you."

"So when, when can I go home with you, Anna?" she wailed.

"If you cry, I won't tell you anything." She shook her finger at her sister, then she put her arm around her and pulled her closer.

Inge sniffed up her nose and wiped her eyes. "I promise I won't cry."

"Mrs. Schulz said that Erika and her baby are coming home this weekend."

"Yes, Karl told me. I can't wait to hold the baby. Do you think Erika will let me?"

"I'm sure she will. But anyway, Mrs. Schulz told us they need the room now, and they can't keep you any longer."

Inge sniffled, but she didn't cry.

"And then Mrs. Munster said they needed the rose room too, my rose room, Inge, because Rita was moving in." Anna felt like crying, but of course, she didn't.

"Where will we go? Is Mama coming to get us?"

Anna shrugged. "Mrs. Munster said she has talked to Mrs. Kunkel, you know, the woman in the grocery store down the street across from the school? The store where we have bought candy, remember? She said the Kunkels would take us for a while and they were going to help them out, like giving them food. I asked Gertl later and she said the grocery store is closed because they had nothing to sell, so the Kunkels could use their help. I swear I was right there when they were talking. But I was not listening because Gertl said she would wash my ears with green soap if I listened again." She reached down and picked up a piece of hay.

"So, I won't be here to play with the baby." Inge's voice quivered.

"Of course, you can play with the baby, Inge. We will come to play with Karl and the others like we always do. If you cry, I might cry too, so don't, please."

Inge nodded, but then she cried and sobbed.

Anna rocked her back and forth. "You know Mama's radio heart is listening now, and it makes her sad when we cry, and she can't be here with us." She stroked her sister's hair. Inge stopped and wiped her face with her sleeve.

Anna tried to suppress a sob. "At least we will be together." And then she told her. She just had to. She didn't care if Gertl got mad at her. "You know what, Inge? The Major has visited Mama. She is getting all better in the hospital. And he is going to take us to her for a visit. We are going to see Mama." She stood and jumped up and down.

Inge squealed. "I am going to see Mama. I am going to see Mama! When are we going to see her, Anna? I want to go right now." She tugged on Anna's blouse.

"I don't know, but soon." Anna bit her lip. "Gertl told me that it's a secret. Mrs. Weller said not to tell anybody."

Inge sat down again." I'm scared. I don't want to go to the Kunkels. What if they don't like me?"

"I am sure they will like you, Inge. I saw Mr. Kunkel at the wedding, and he stinks, but that could be just at the wedding. I am so glad, Inge. We will be together again. I'll be there with you every night."

Inge leaned against her and hid her face in her blouse.

Anna stood up and brushed pieces of hay from her skirt. "Let's go play now. I promised Karl we would help him look after the geese."

They played war games in the fields. Anna made them call the enemy the Tommies instead of the Ruskies. That was fine with Karl and the others.

And later Inge and Anna picked flowers. They had such pretty flowers here in the meadow, little ones, but in many colors, bright yellow, red, purple. Inge said she wanted to give her flowers to Erika for the baby.

Anna didn't want to leave her sister behind, but she had to go back to the Munsters. She hugged Inge and waved as she headed down the road. When she came to the curve in the road the small figure was gone.

At the Munsters', Anna gave her flowers to Gertl, who smiled and put them in a cup in the center of the kitchen table. And at supper, she told everybody that Anna had picked the flowers for her.

After supper, Anna didn't really feel like doing anything, so she decided to visit Yanka. The dog was tied by the front door again and looked so sad. She sat down in her usual spot on the step and Yanka rolled over so Anna could pet her belly.

"Yanka, I am not going to live here anymore. They can't keep me because Rita is moving in. I promise I will come back to pet you. I am sort of scared because I don't know the Kunkels. Do you think they will like us?"

Yanka licked her hand, like she always did. Her doggie mouth curved into a smile.

"You know what? This is a secret, but the Major is going to take us to visit my mama." She buried her face in the dog's fur. "I'll miss my rose room. It's like waking up in a garden every day. But I will be with Inge again. I have really missed her."

She sat there with Yanka until it was almost dark. The wind had died down and the evening dew made her shiver. She snuggled closer to the dog. Somewhere a cow mooed.

She whispered in Yanka's ear. "We are going to visit my mama."

CHAPTER 9
Army Field Hospital

Nurse Lisbeth was helping Annemarie from bed into a wheelchair. "Doc Hartmann has also ordered crutches." She opened the windows to let in the late May air.

"Wonderful. I'll be dancing soon." Annemarie grabbed Lisbeth's hands and bobbed her head to imaginary music.

"That's my girl." Lisbeth swung the wheelchair around humming one two three, one two three to an old waltz melody.

Later she came back and handed Annemarie a box. "Special delivery from my friends in high places." She laughed. "Open it!"

Annemarie sat and looked at the box in her lap. What was Lisbeth up to now? You never knew if this was part of the day's joke. She picked up the box and shook it. Slowly, she removed the cover and stared at its contents.

"What, you don't like it?" Lisbeth cocked her head. "Sorry, I couldn't find any red yarn."

"Oh my God, Lisbeth, I love it." Annemarie pulled a set of polished wooden knitting needles and several balls of yarn from the box. "Oh my God, they're beautiful. Anna likes blue, and the pink and white I'll use for Inge." She stretched her arms up for a hug, almost toppling the wheelchair.

67

"Whoa!" Lisbeth threw up her hands. "Slow down. I'll wait to see the results of your handiwork. Have fun." She waved and turned to leave.

"Thank you, Lisbeth, thank you so much." Annemarie beamed and held up the yarn so that her bed neighbors could see. Annemarie turned to the woman next to her. "Strange, no Fuehrer speeches. It is so quiet in here. I can even hear the birds singing."

The woman nodded. "Somebody finally had the guts to turn the damn radio off."

Annemarie picked up the blue yarn and cast on. A few minutes later she stopped her stitches. The silence, interrupted only by the murmurs of her fellow patients, seemed eerie. She began humming a tune she remembered from grade school. *The morning is my pleasure. I ride in the quiet hour through the fields and meadows onto the highest hill to greet Germany, our homeland from the bottom of my heart.*

Suddenly, the soaring sound of an opera choir broke through the tranquil morning:

> *Freude schoener Gotterfunken Tochter aus Elysium*
> *Wir betreten feuertrunken*
> *Himlischer Dein Heiligtum.*

Eyes swimming, Annemarie dropped her knitting, sat still, and listened. For reasons she did not understand, tears streamed down her face, and she began to sing the glorious words along with the other patients.

The music stopped abruptly, and the voice of Doc Hartmann sounded. "Jawohl, that was Ludwig van Beethoven's *Ode to Joy*. Very appropriate for today, you think. Thanks to Corporal Willie Bergman, our radio tech who wired the music for me. I promised to fix his leg so he can walk out of here. I admit, I raided the commander's record collection to treat you to the most beautiful music ever composed."

There was a pause and then cheers arose from every bed.

"And now to the announcement: THE WAR IS OVER!"

Cheers again. "THE WAR IS OVER," he yelled even more loudly. "Scream, kick, jump, kiss your neighbor. Just try not to hurt anyone."

Annemarie laughed, wiped her eyes, and joined her neighbors' chatter. It sounded like a schoolroom after early dismissal.

"Listen up," Doc Hartmann's voice continued. "As new information is available, I will announce it. There could still be sporadic fighting in some places, so stay put and enjoy our hospitality until we get further orders."

The buzzing in the ward continued for hours, the euphoria lasting until late into the night.

Lisbeth had told Annemarie that this field hospital was a sanctuary in the midst of the storm. The military had cordoned off access for years. These facilities had been relatively safe and were locally defended by a military contingent. Lisbeth told her many times how lucky they were to have escaped the daily bombing raids and the struggles to stay alive outside the compound.

"There may be a God, or we have a guardian angel to protect us," Annemarie told Lisbeth later. "And I think you are an angel and so is Doc Hartmann if there is such a thing as a male angel."

Lisbeth chuckled and rolled her eyes.

"I hope Alfred has a guardian angel," Annemarie said, grimacing as Lisbeth removed her bandages.

Lisbeth cleaned the wound and rewrapped it. "Where did you say he was again? At what front?"

"Somewhere in France, I think. Yes, somewhere in France, I'm not sure."

Lisbeth's face turned pale. She leaned to hug Annemarie and left the room without another word.

Annemarie sat up, fingering her knitting. Did Lisbeth know more of what was going on in the country, since she was close to the hospital top brass? Did she know more war news than she was telling? She never mentioned her private life. All she ever did was joke about "friends in high places" and Annemarie did not ask. But she knew that Lisbeth was not a Nazi.

Annemarie woke the next morning to rain pelting the windows. *The war is over.* Doc Hartmann's joyous words still hung in the air. It meant that the soldiers would soon come home. She had not heard from Alfred in over a year. Was he wounded? He could be a prisoner of war. Thank God that he was not on the Eastern front, where returning wounded had reported that Russian soldiers killed all those who were not able to flee. Her stomach turned into knots, but despite her worry, she pictured Alfred walking through the door and a rush of feelings came over her. She didn't doubt that he would love her even if she could no longer walk. With Alfred by her side, she could face losing her right leg as Doc Hartmann had implied.

After breakfast arrived, Lisbeth wheeled in a serving cart filled with pudding, cigarettes and beer. She announced to the room, "Compliments of Commander Herberger, so everyone can partake in the war's end celebration. And don't ask me questions, please. I don't have any more information than you do." She shrugged. "Commander Herberger has left, and I don't know what's happening, when this installation will be closed, where you will be transferred, which ones can go home and how you might get there. I'm just an inmate here like the rest of you, I give up." She pulled a white handkerchief from her pocket and waved it at them.

Annemarie smirked at her macabre humor. She stared at the pudding and wondered where they got the sugar to make it. Even during wartime, when they survived on cabbage and potatoes, the elite seemed to live well. She shook her head.

Lisbeth popped open a beer bottle and raised it to the sky. "Enjoy the treats, friends, but only one beer for those who are well enough to get up and walk. Orders from Doc Hartmann. Celebrate, but not too much. And please don't die on me today in case you had such intentions. Prosit!"

"Prosit." Annemarie joined the choir of voices booming through the room. In her mind, she could still hear Beethoven's *Ode to Joy*.

Joy, fair sparks of gods, Daughter of Elysium,
Drunk with fiery rapture,
Goddess, we approach thy shrine
The magic reunites those whom stern custom has
parted,
all men will become brothers under thy gentle wing.

No more propaganda. No more dark, pulled shades, no roaring of planes approaching to drop their deadly loads, no more explosions. No more wounded. Real coffee. Her children would come home, and she would make them vanilla pudding. She raised her bottle, "Prosit, Lisbeth."

She hoped Alfred was celebrating too.

CHAPTER 10

Three weeks had gone by since Doc Hartmann announced the end of the war. Annemarie had heard nothing more about the closing of the hospital, but rumors were constantly circulating. The patient in the next bed said, "The British are taking over, pulling patients from their beds and arresting them."

"I don't believe that. Lisbeth would have told me." But Annemarie bit her lip. She pulled out her knitting and held it up. "I've finished two hats. All I have to do is add a pompom." She began to knit.

The woman looked around nervously. "I heard that about the British from the nurse who picked up our lunch trays on Sunday, the tall thin one," she whispered.

"You can talk now, nobody is listening. Remember? The war is over." Annemarie held up the blue hat. "This will look good with a white pompom, don't you think?"

The woman fell back on her pillow. "My house is gone, my parents are dead, and…" she heaved, covering her face with her hands.

Annemarie's eyes welled up. "I'll ask Lisbeth about the British. She has friends, she knows people."

Later that day, Annemarie asked Lisbeth about the latest rumor that the hospital was running out of food and supplies. And one of the patients, a young-looking soldier, said, "The staff is abandoning ship, getting out while they still can."

Lisbeth walked around carrying a load of sheets. She set them on a table in preparation for stripping beds and changing the linens. "Don't believe anything you hear." She helped Annemarie into a wheelchair. "When I find out something, I'll make sure you're the first one to know." She started to remove sheets from Annemarie's bed and announced to the whole ward, "Anyone who doesn't like it here can leave. But I wouldn't advise it. It's grim out there, folks, survival of the fittest, and most of you wouldn't have a chance." She glanced around the room. "But from what I hear, some trains are now running, and I'll be glad to find out which ones if you want to know."

It was so quiet in the ward Annemarie heard the breeze moving the curtains.

"Today, we have pudding. So let me know if you want vanilla or--" she checked the food cart– "or vanilla."

Annemarie clapped and a few others joined in. Someone shouted, "Chocolate," and a lone Heil Hitler sounded from somewhere.

While Lisbeth was passing out pudding, Annemarie sat in her wheelchair knitting furiously, trying to keep her anxiety at bay. She was working on the third hat, one for Doc Hartmann. He had mentioned he liked to ski.

"I have not heard from Major Rudi about the children," said Annemarie when Lisbeth came back to her section. "What if he did not make it back to the village? They won't find me after I get sent to another hospital. And no letter, no word from Alfred has arrived." She sniffled and pressed her knitting to her face.

Lisbeth handed her a dish of pudding. "Look on the bright side. You're safe, you've got plenty to eat, and you have a roof over your head."

Annemarie nodded and sighed. "I don't know what I would do without you, Lisbeth, I really don't." She shook her head and looked at Lisbeth, teary-eyed.

73

"Come on, let's see if you can move a little better on your crutches," the ever-practical Lisbeth replied.

Annemarie had tried walking with the crutches several times before, but had given up, disheartened with her slow progress. "I'm having a hard time. It hurts if I hobble on my left leg." She sat down and huffed. "Tell me, how will I be able to take care of my children like this? I can hardly stand on my feet, let alone carry a bag or fix a meal." She rubbed her injured leg. "I have no place to live, no furniture. How am I going to climb up three flights of stairs to my parents' apartment?" She covered her face with her hands.

Lisbeth put an arm around her. "You are putting the cart before the horse, Annemarie. It's a gradual process, but you will get better. Look at that soldier." She pointed at a bed at the other side of the room. "He lost both legs and part of his arm. And next to him, Max has a severe brain injury. We don't know if he'll ever be able to go home. And over there, poor Bruno, he's blind. It's a miracle he survived. I found out his entire family perished in a firebombing, but I haven't told him yet. I'm waiting for an aunt to get here."

Annemarie glanced at Bruno, feeling ashamed.

Lisbeth looked at Annemarie. "See, you don't have it so bad. You have children who need you, parents who will take you in, and a sister. Lighten up, Maedchen." She patted her on the shoulder.

Annemarie smiled through her tears. "I just can't help it, Lisbeth. But I'll make it. I know I will."

Lisbeth handed her a handkerchief. "say it with me. 'I will dance again.' Come on, say it."

"I will dance again," Annemarie repeated. "I will dance again." Her voice grew louder.

An hour later, Lisbeth came back from her other rounds, a big smile on her face. "You have a visitor."

"Oh my God, another one?" Annemarie gasped.

74

"Yes, my dear. A Mrs. Friedrich Bowman announced she wishes to see you." She grinned wickedly. "Your sister has come to the rescue. Let me go and escort her in."

Annemarie felt weak from practicing with the crutches and maneuvered back into her bed. She put her knitting aside and folded her hands on top of the covers.

"Margarete, over here." She beckoned her sister over from where she stood in the doorway. "How did you find me here?" she exclaimed, reaching to hug her sister.

Margarete waved a paper in the air. "I received this from the military administration, locating next of kin of wounded civilians. I don't know why they did not send it to our parents. What do they expect me to do with this?" Margarete squinted around, flaring her nostrils. "The smell is sickening in here." She laid the document on Annemarie's bed and took a small flask of Eau de Cologne from her purse and sprayed behind her ears. "I hope I don't catch anything." She glanced around. "Is there a chair anywhere? I need to sit down. It was an ordeal to get here on the train."

"Margarete, please. This is an army field hospital, not the Hotel Atlantic." Annemarie swung her arms and knocked a water glass off her nightstand.

Margarete let out a shriek and started to wipe her skirt. The white feather on her hat bobbed as she brushed.

"It's only water, Margarete," was all Annemarie could muster. She pointed to the hallway at the other side of the ward. "There are some chairs in the nurses' lounge."

"Never mind, I'll just stand. She brushed the skirt again. It matched her white patent leather heels and her white hat. "They whistled at me and yelled profanities when I walked in." She smoothed her hair under her hat. "Women are not respected nowadays."

Annemarie clenched her teeth. "These men have not seen a beautiful woman in months, or even years. They

75

probably think you are a film star or a general's wife." Why had Margarete come here? As always, she made everything about herself-- her inconvenience, her suffering. Like her mother had said, "Don't turn to your sister for help." She closed her eyes, wishing Margarete would leave.

With sudden concern on her face, Margarete bent close to her sister. "Kittie, you look pretty bad."

"For God's sake. I was bombed and almost died," Annemarie whispered, her eyes filled with tears.

"Oh Kittie, I am sorry. I'm just so upset about everything. Father is not doing well. He's cranky all the time, and Mother is getting worse and wasting away. And you are here. I can't do it all. I have my own family to take care of, you know." She lit up a cigarette and took a deep drag.

"Stop calling me Kittie. I'm not ten years old anymore." Annemarie's voice grew sharp. "You are checking on Mother and father, right? I've heard that there is no food, and the old folks can't go out and barter for it." She looked for a reaction in Margarete's face.

"Like I said, I have my own family to take care of. I can't walk that long way to their place all the time. The streetcars and subways are not reliable and when they run, they're full of stinking, dirty people who drag anything on the trains with them. It's disgusting. You could get robbed by that dirty mob. They don't stop at anything and there are no police around." She sighed and took another puff. "No, I can't go through that very often. But I did give Mother a bottle of oil not too long ago, for cooking, you know. Friedrich had brought me several bottles from the ship."

"I'm so relieved that their building escaped the bombing," Annemarie replied and mustered a smile.

"Well, at least I don't have to be out there scrounging for food with the mob. Friedrich always brings back a good amount and then I have my sources through the shipping company. Friedrich makes sure they keep me supplied with necessities." Margarete smiled. "I've even gotten coffee, and of course, my cigarettes and the Cognac and I need that for my digestion." She wagged her cigarette.

Annemarie sat up in her bed, hoping her outrage didn't show on her face. She took a deep breath. "Sorry, my leg hurts all the time," she moaned and rubbed her leg.

"You may lose that leg." Margarete puffed and blew circles that floated towards the window.

"I know. They told me. But I'm not going to let it happen. I might have to be in here for some time, and they will transfer me to another hospital." She swiped at her face. "The rumor is this hospital will be closed. Can you help me find out, please, Margarete?"

Her sister flipped her cigarette with an outstretched arm. "Ah, you know they'll find you some other place." She glanced at her watch. "Look, Kittie, I've got to hurry to get back to the city. The last train is supposed to leave at 4:30 and I have to walk all the way to the station. You have to fight the crowds to get on, let alone to get a seat. All those people, they smell." She grimaced and looked around for a place to put out her cigarette.

Annemarie handed her the empty pudding dish. She watched Margarete stub out her cigarette. "Could you take Inge and Anna, Margarete? Just for a short while. They are in Burghof with farmers, but I don't know really what's happening there. I have not seen them since the bombing." Her eyes filled with tears. "If you can just take them now, I will work out something else. I'm trying to get out. The crutches might work if I try harder." She reached for her sister's hand.

Margarete withdrew the hand and tapped out another cigarette. "What about Willie's folks?" She inhaled and blew the smoke out through her nostrils. "They are the children's grandparents. And in that small town, they can get food from the farmers, I'm sure. So, what if they never liked you." She checked her watch again. "I can't. I just can't take them, Kittie, it's too much for me, and it would ruin my marriage."

Annemarie sank into her bed and closed her eyes.

"You look so pale and thin. Don't they give you enough to eat in here?" Margarete blew more smoke and the gray cloud floated towards the window.

Ignoring that, Annemarie said, "Please, you must tell Father and Mother I am alive and that I will be home soon. Will you at least do that for me?"

"Of course, I will tell them."

"Could you also ask Mother to let Mrs. Dummersdorf know where I am? She is a friend. She lives on the fourth floor of the apartment building where I lived, remember? And please, Margarete, look after Mother and Father. I know they won't ask, but they need you. Take some food to them. I will take over as soon as I get out, I promise." She covered her face with her hands and sobbed silently.

Margarete patted her on the head. "Of course, I will. They are my parents too. But now, I have to hurry to the train station. Get well soon, for the sake of your children."

As Margarete passed Lisbeth on her way out, she said, "I think she's asleep."

Lisbeth looked at her askance.

"And if you want my opinion, she's too thin. You have to increase the amount of food, add some meat and milk, things that stick to her ribs."

Lisbeth looked after her, stony-faced.

"Rude people even in here," Margarete threw over her shoulder as she left.

Lisbeth walked over to Annemarie's bed. "There's one I would have no qualms sending to a work camp," she muttered. "Pompous bitch."

Annemarie opened her eyes. "I heard that," she said with a faint smile.

"You know, Maedchen, we are the lucky ones here in the hospital. We don't have to endure the battles of freedom out there like poor Margarete. So, we are going to concentrate on getting well, dancing and making it through the next few months."

Annemarie nodded and wiped her eyes. "She won't take my children, Lisbeth. But at least my parents are alive, thank God. I just have to hurry to get out of here. I'll never forgive myself if something happened to them and I was not there." She bit her lip to avoid crying again.

"And that witch won't take care of them, right?" Lisbeth growled.

"She brought them one bottle of oil once."

"Ludicrous." Lisbeth placed her hands on her hips." I think we have to send her to hell with gorgeous Willie's parents."

Annemarie had to laugh.

"All right." Lisbeth clapped her hands. "This calls for a celebration, another picnic. It may well be our swan song. So, shall we live it up?" Then she said out loud to herself, "Yes, Lisbeth, let's do that!" Then to Annemarie, "Rest for a couple of hours and I'll see what I can come up with."

Annemarie nodded and rolled over on her side.

"And no Witch Margarete nightmares. That's an order from your nurse." Nurse Lisbeth smoothed Annemarie's covers and left.

It was dusk when Lisbeth returned. She helped Annemarie into her wheelchair and pushed her outside to their favorite garden spot. "Tonight, you might see that shooting star." She looked at the sky. "I'll be right back with our goodies." Lisbeth turned and stepped back inside.

Annemarie sat like a lump, still numb from the encounter with her sister. But she was more determined than ever to get out of here to help her parents and bring her children home. She could live with her parents. They could make do with one room. She had no furniture to move, and all three of them could sleep in one bed. That was her plan, and it gave her some peace of mind.

And then she saw a shooting star.

Lisbeth returned, wheeling a serving cart. She pointed to the liver pate, Tilsit cheese, and pumpernickel and fruit tarts. "Look here." She held up a bottle of Champagne.

"Oh, Lisbeth, you must have raided the commander's pantry. All for me?"

"Yes, girl, all for you." She opened the bottle. The cork flew off with a loud pop.

"God, I hope that didn't alarm anybody. It sounded like a shot."

"No more shooting. We are now celebrating and preparing for our future. I see light at the end of the tunnel. Only a small light, but it's there." Lisbeth poured the Champagne into two flutes.

"Real glasses, I'm impressed." Annemarie smiled. "You know that I saw a shooting star and I made a wish? Now I need another one, I have so many urgent wishes. Do you know that this is the first Champagne I've ever tasted?"

"Cheers to a bubbly Champagne future."

Annemarie giggled. "And for you too, Lisbeth. To good friends."

Lisbeth was unusually quiet as they sat sipping Champagne and nibbling on pumpernickel with liver pate.

Annemarie licked the liver pate off her fingers. "You know, Alfred could be home any day now. I hope he can find me. I mean, I'm no longer in Burghof and I'll be in another hospital soon. His mother has my parents' address, so he could contact me through her. But I have not heard from her in a long time either. She was somewhere in the east, near Poland. Who knows if she made it out alive?"

"They say love will find a way, I'm sure," Lisbeth said thoughtfully. "Where did he live before you met him?"

"He lived in the city, Hamburg, where I lived. He had a wife and a daughter and owned a machine shop. His family perished in one of the first fire bombings." She paused and stared into the darkness. "When he came home on leave, all he found was rubble. A neighbor digging in the ruins told him that everyone had gone into the bunker where they had safely waited out air raids before. But, this time the bombers used some type of incendiary bomb. There was no escaping. Nobody could get away from the raging fireball. Thousands burned up; he was told. After that, Alfred never went back to the city."

Lisbeth refilled their glasses. "Do you like the Champagne?" she asked softly. "This is the best there is. The Commander had excellent taste." She clicked her glass against Annemarie's.

Annemarie took small sips. "I like it. It tastes so light, so sweet… bubbly. I think I could get used to it."

I met Alfred in Burghof, at Braun's tavern," she continued." You know that's where we went almost every night. I was, excuse me I *am* young, and all the young soldiers at Braun's were hungry for life. Everybody wanted to have fun, dance, laugh and love, not knowing if it would be their last chance. And I was happy that we were safe there, that we had a roof over our heads, and that the children liked the country."

Lisbeth nudged the cheese plate towards her.

"One time I took the train to visit my parents, to take them some food -- sausage, bread, cheese, you know. I saw the horrors unfolding there. The hordes of people who had no place to live, lost their families." She sighed. "I knew we were blessed to be where we ended up.

"I helped the farmers around the house and in exchange, they fed us. The Munsters' two sons are on the front, so Mrs. Munster and I had a lot to talk about. She liked it that I listened. She was in constant fear of getting that telegram-- you know. So, it all worked out."

"Tell me more about Alfred," Lisbeth interrupted. "You said you fell for him the first day you saw him?"

"Oh God, yes, I did. He didn't seem like the others. He was quiet, smart, warm. He looks nothing like Willie. He is just a plain man, with wavy brown hair and warm brown eyes. I just knew he was the one. Mostly, we sat and talked. We went on long walks. It was like we had known each other for years."

"So, you didn't get pregnant." Lisbeth grinned.

Annemarie smiled and bent towards her. "Lisbeth, this was real love. I don't know how to explain it. We spent every minute together that he was able to get away. We danced at Braun's, we went to the lake and swam, and one night, we even skinny-dipped." Annemarie giggled.

Lisbeth raised her eyebrows, chuckling.

"But nobody saw us. Only the moon smiled at us." Annemarie paused, remembering that moment, sipping Champagne. "And that's when we made love the first time, at the lake. We used his shirt as a blanket. It was heavenly." She threw back her head and laughed.

"He was so romantic, Lisbeth. He didn't rush things, you know. He touched me and kissed me and finally I knew what lovemaking really was." She closed her eyes. "He has to come home, Lisbeth. He has to. We got engaged."

"I hope that was a shooting star you saw and that you get your wish," Lisbeth said softly.

Annemarie composed herself. "We laughed so much. I think I was able to help him a little bit over that terrible loss of his family. We have already planned our future. He's going to enlarge his machine shop, which is hopefully still standing, and I will help him run it. I have never done office work, since I worked as a salesclerk in a department store, but he said he would teach me. If it wasn't for that goddamn war, we would be living a wonderful life now."

"You can still have that life. Don't give up. Maybe we will all have a normal life again. It is hard to imagine now when I see these soldiers around me here. Life will never be normal for most of them again, never. Compared to them, we don't have it so bad after all, do we?" Lisbeth raised her glass.

Annemarie lifted her own glass and offered a toast to Alfred. "And he loves children. Inge and Anna adore him. He's just like a kid when he plays with them."

"So, you want more children?"

"Oh, yes. We want to have two more, at least one boy. Oh, I can't wait to see him again."

Lisbeth poured the rest of the Champagne into their glasses. "I hope that happens."

"I'm so happy when I talk about him, I get carried away. I've been rattling on. Prosit! To you, Lisbeth, to your future." Annemarie toasted. "Do you have a pen and paper? I want to give you my parents' address since I don't know where we will be living. But I want you to visit Alfred and me. I want him to meet my best friend, Aunt Lisbeth, who helped me make it through the dreadful time in the hospital, who always gave me hope. You can stay with us when you come, as long as you want," she declared.

"Oh, Annemarie you are such a wonderful dreamer and I do hope that the shooting star will make wishes come true for you." Lisbeth rose and opened another bottle.

Annemarie laughed, "Lisbeth, what about Doc Hartmann's orders?"

"Tonight, he'll forgive us. In fact, I think he's not even here. He went to visit one of the German hospitals to work out arrangements for the transfer of patients.

"There'll be an official announcement tomorrow. They will be telling us about the timetable for the closing of this hospital and the plan for moving the patients."

Annemarie set down her glass, the Champagne dripping over her hand. "So, it's definite? We are moving *now*. So soon?"

"Oh, you didn't know. I should have told you sooner. Yes. They plan a quick, orderly transition and then the British will take over these barracks."

"Lisbeth, I really want to go home. I can manage, I really can," Annemarie pleaded. "My parents, my children."

Lisbeth shook her head. "I don't think you are ready to leave the hospital. But that's up to Doc Hartmann. I will try to find out where you will be transferred and let you know tomorrow." She dug in her pocket and handed her a paper and a pen. Please write down your parents' address. I promise I will visit you."

"Where will you go?" Annemarie asked with a lump in her throat. "To the same hospital where I'm going? Will you try to find your family? I never asked you about them. I am sorry, Lisbeth, I should have."

"Don't worry, forget it. We'll catch up when I visit you and Alfred." She stared into the night. "I'm not sure where I will go. These are German hospitals, so I have to see if I can get in with them. I don't have any papers, no documents for my nurses' training. It was all lost when I fled. So, we'll see."

"Oh, Lisbeth." Annemarie tried to raise herself out of her wheelchair and stretched out her arms. "You are crying," Annemarie said as they hugged. "My angel with the big heart."

Lisbeth stood back and poured the last of the Champagne.

Annemarie laughed. "I could not walk a straight line even with two legs." Then she pulled out a box she had tucked under her lap blanket and handed it to Lisbeth. "Open it."

Lisbeth gasped. "This is the box I gave you." She laughed and lifted the cover.

"Well?" Annemarie couldn't wait to see her friend's face.

"Oh, Annemarie, how beautiful." She took out the scarf and wrapped it around her neck. "How did you know that blue is my favorite color?" She caressed her face with the scarf. "It's so soft."

"Well, a friend of mine gave me the yarn…" They both laughed.

"You are quite a girl, Annemarie. I will always think of you when I wear this. And when I visit you, we'll have real coffee, and I'll bake a cake for you. You didn't know that I could bake, did you? My father was a baker. I will tell you more when we get together and teach you how to bake some special fancy cakes."

Annemarie looked at her friend, amazed. This was the most Lisbeth had ever talked about herself. "You know, I was really afraid of going to a new hospital. But now, I think I can do it. I will think of you and ask, 'What would Lisbeth do?' And that will make me laugh."

CHAPTER 11
Burghof Village

Anna ambled through the back door swinging a bunch of carrots by their greens.

Gertl looked up from the pile of chopped vegetables she was adding to a steaming pot on the stove. "Looks like they were ready to be pulled."

"Hm, it smells so good in here." Anna rubbed her belly. "What are you cooking?"

"Pot roast." Gertl wiped her hands on her apron and stepped to the table. "Sit down, Anna. I'm going to fix you something to eat."

"Oh, yum. Can I have a piece of molasses bread?"

To Anna's surprise, Gertl came up and kissed her on the forehead, then stepped to the sideboard and returned with the plate of molasses bread. She sat down next to Anna, who began eating, molasses dripping down her chin. "I have to take you to the Kunkels' house today, you know, the grocery store down the road." She studied the girl's face. "Can you get your things together or do you need help?" In a softer voice, she said. "Promise that you won't be angry with me."

Anna dropped her fork, pushed her plate away and stared at Gertl. "You are sending me away? Why?" She covered her face and started to cry. "What have I done wrong?"

Gertl sighed. "Nothing." She pulled Anna onto her lap. "I want to tell you a secret," she whispered in her ear.

"Rita is going to have a baby." She brushed the moist strands of hair from Anna's face.

Anna stopped crying and stared at her. "We're going to have our own baby, like Karl's sister Erika?"

"Yes, Anna, we are going to have a baby of our own at the Munster farm. Your rose room will be the baby's nursery. You can help Rita get it ready and she is counting on you to come over and play with the baby."

Anna pressed her face in Gertl's blouse, hiding her tears. After a moment, she turned. "My rose room. It's my rose room."

Gertl stroked Anna's hair. "We hope it will be a baby girl and I heard that they'll name her Gretchen."

"Oh, our own little baby." Anna threw her arms around Gertl. "I want it to be a little girl so she can wear pretty dresses like my doll Elise." She jumped up and down. "I can braid her hair like I do for Inge. I know how to braid pigtails." She jumped off her lap and clapped her hands. "I like that name, Gretchen. I can't wait to tell Inge. When is Gretchen going to be here?"

"Oh, that will be several months. Perhaps she'll be a Christmas baby." Gertl slipped her arm around Anna. "Come with me, I have a surprise for you."

They walked down the hall to Rita and Arnold's room. She opened the door and pointed to a small white suitcase. "This is for you. Open it."

Anna had never owned a suitcase. She kneeled on the floor pushed the clasp and the cover popped open. "Oh, how pretty. Oh, and more." She pulled out a white lace-trimmed nightgown, a pair of fluffy white slippers and a red blouse. "Red is my favorite color." She turned and hugged Gertl. She stepped in front of the mirror holding up the white nightgown.

"You look like an angel." Gertl smiled. Then she helped Anna pack her things. The suitcase was only half full when they were finished.

"All my other things burned up." Anna sight. "But now I have this pretty suitcase, my very own. I will keep it forever, Gertl."

"Let's hurry back to the kitchen. I don't want the vegetables to burn. And I made some pudding for you. When Inge comes, I'll take you to the Kunkel's."

"You make the best pudding." Anna licked her spoon. "Can Yanka come with me? She is so lonely here, nobody pets her." She put down her spoon, tears welling up.

"Yanka has to stay here and guard the house, Anna. But you go and tell her 'I'll come back and visit.' And I promise to keep an eye on her. You know I slip her bones and leftovers when Mrs. Munster isn't looking." She grinned. That was their secret because Mrs. Munster wanted to give the leftovers to the pigs.

"Look, there's Karl." Gertl pointed to the garden. "He's bringing Inge." When they came into the kitchen, Anna could tell that her sister had been crying.

"She wanted to stay and play with Erika's baby." Karl stomped his foot, turning to Inge. "Erika said you can come over every day and visit the baby. I've told you for the hundredth time now." He raised his eyebrows in desperation.

"I baked some molasses cookies yesterday," Gertl said. "Here." She handed one to each of the children.

Karl turned to Anna. "I have to watch the geese again later, so come on over." He grabbed the cookie and dashed out of the door.

"Where are your things?" Gertl asked Inge, who stood there in the red checkered dress her mother had made from curtains. It looked cute on her with a blue apron over it.

"Erika gave me the apron," she said and puffed up her chest.

88

"Did she braid your hair too?"

"Yes, she did, because she had pigtails when she was little." Inge beamed and flipped her pigtails. "Now I look just like Erika."

Gertl nodded and patted Inge on the shoulder. "Are these your things?" She picked up a brown cloth sack and opened it. "Is that all you have? What about socks, underpants, pajamas, child?"

Inge shrugged.

Anna answered for her. "Her things are upstairs in the loft, Gertl. Maybe they didn't all burn up."

"I'll ask Jake to go up there and see if anything is left. But I doubt it. That fireball probably consumed everything."

"What do you mean, *consumed everything?*" Anna didn't understand. "My doll Elise is still up there too. She has to come with me to the Kunkels."

Gertl puckered her lips. "Hm, Inge, you need some clothes. Kunkels won't have any because they never had children." She shook her head." I'll talk to my friend Eva. Some of the clothes from her youngest daughter might fit you. Oh my, what is this?" She pulled a small rag doll out of the bag.

Inge grabbed the doll and clutched it to her chest. "That's Pepita. Erika gave her to me." The doll had big button eyes, black wooly hair and a colorful outfit, like a gypsy dress in the fairy tale books.

Anna looked at the doll admiringly. "Oh, she's cute, Inge. Maybe Pepita and Elise can play together."

Gertl stuffed everything back into the bag. Then she took a bunch of the cookies, wrapped them in paper and placed them in the bag. "You can have those later," she smiled, "but don't eat them all at once."

Jake met them at the door carrying her doll, and before he could speak, Anna grabbed it from his hands.

"What do you say?" Gertl nudged her.

89

"Thank you, Jake." Anna hugged him and Gertl grinned, handing him a cookie and picked up Anna's suitcase. "Let's go. I'll take you to Kunkle's' now so I'm back in time to make dinner."

Less than ten minutes later they arrived at the Kunkels'. Gertl stopped her bicycle with her feet and lifted Inge to the ground. Anna climbed down by herself, relieved to get off the wobbly bicycle. Gertl leaned the bike against the porch rail, took the children by the hands and went up three small steps to the front door of the store. Anna stared at a large picture of a cow with a bell around her neck displayed in the store window.

Mrs. Kunkel met them at the front of the store and motioned them to come to the side door. They walked through a narrow yard with chickens running all around and passed a small barn next to a garden. "These are just like the beanstalks and the berry bushes we have in our garden at the farm," said Anna. She let go of Gertl's hand. She wanted to show Mrs. Kunkel that she was older and not afraid like her little sister, who clung to Gertl.

Mrs. Kunkel stood on the step to the back door, her arms crossed in front of her belly squinting and blinking her eyes repeatedly. She was shorter than Gertl and chubby, her hair twisted in a big bun. A large yellow pin protruded from the bun. Anna had never seen anything like that and wondered if it would fall out when Mrs. Kunkel bent down.

"Hello, Mrs. Kunkel." Gertl smiled at her. The woman nodded and squinted some more.

Anna felt Gertl's hand on her shoulder nudging her towards Mrs. Kunkel.

"This is Anna. She will be six in a few days."

Mrs. Kunkel bent and reached to pat her on the head. Anna took a step back, her eyes fixed on the woman's hair, waiting for the pin to fall out.

"And this is Inge." Gertl unwrapped Inge's arms from around her legs. "How old are you, Inge? Tell Mrs.

90

Kunkel." Gertl pulled her towards the woman. But the child struggled and wrapped her arms around Gertl's leg again.

"Well, she's only four and a bit shy." Gertl took Inge's hand.

Mrs. Kunkel squinted several times more and mumbled something which Anna did not understand.

They followed the woman into a small hallway, where she opened a door on the right. She switched on the light. "When the store was open, this was our storage room, so it's not been used in a while." Her eyes twitched. She pointed at Anna. "Put your things on the chair over there. Guess we need some place for your clothes. Maybe Mr. Kunkel can find a chest of drawers." She scratched her head. "Since it's only for a short time, it'll do."

Anna looked around. The small room had only one bed, which was covered with a grey blanket with frayed edges. A wooden table sat pushed against the wall. Anna placed her suitcase on the chair next to it. The chair, painted green, was chipped and scuffed. Anna thought it might be old like some of the chairs people had given them for the loft at the Munster farm. A big window covered almost the entire wall above the table. The window was cracked and patched and missing a pane in one corner. Several boxes were stacked next to the table. A wheelbarrow leaned against the far wall like the one in the Munsters' barn. The olive-green linoleum floor showed worn patches. Anna thought of her beautiful rose room at the Munster Farm. This small, stuffy room smelled strange, like pepper. "It smells funny in here." She took Inge's hand. Her sister had not said a word.

Mrs. Kunkel ignored them.

Gertl shifted from one foot to the other. "It's just for a short time." She wiped her eyes with the back of her hand. "Their mother will come and pick them up as soon as she gets out of the hospital."

Mrs. Kunkel nodded, and a brief smile appeared on her thin lips. "Only for a short time, that's what I promised Mr. Kunkel."

They returned to the kitchen, which was nothing like the large kitchen at the Munster farm. Everything seemed small in this house. With the kitchen table against the wall, a stove on the opposite wall and open shelves next to it, they had to walk single file to get to the chairs around the table.

Anna eyed a large pot on the burner. "Mrs. Munster always has molasses on the stove."

"You are not on a farm here, child," Mrs. Kunkel said in a sharp tone. But then she smiled. "Do you like molasses?"

"It's my favorite."

Mrs. Kunkel shook her head. "We don't have any molasses. But I have some strawberry jam I made myself from the strawberries in my garden."

Anna didn't know what to say. She thought that she might like strawberry jam, but it wouldn't compare to molasses.

Gertl rose and squeezed by the table. "I have to go back and get the food ready for supper." She patted Anna's shoulder as she backed out of the room. "Bye bye, girls." She winked. "Don't forget to visit Yanka." Anna saw her pull up her apron and wipe her eyes.

The children followed her outside and waved until the bicycle disappeared around the bend.

Anna and Inge sat on the steps that led up to the store. "We can still go to our secret hideaway at Karl's farm." Anna put her arm around her sister.

But Inge pouted. "I don't like it here. I want to go back to see Erika." She hid her face with her apron.

Anna pulled her close, but her sister shook her off. "I want my mama," she cried.

Mrs. Kunkel appeared at the door. "Girls, come help me feed the chickens," she called.

Anna helped Inge up and they followed Mrs. Kunkel to the small barn. The chickens came running, cackling loudly. She opened a barrel and took out a wooden ladle.

"This is what you do. You spread their food around and they'll come and eat it. Here." She handed the ladle to Inge, who finally smiled, spread the grain around and watched the chickens scurry to pick it up.

"You may do this twice a day, in the morning and in the late afternoon." Mrs. Kunkel's lips spread to a brief smile. "The chickens like you." She patted her on the head. "They'll lay some extra eggs for you."

After dark, Mrs. Kunkel handed the children each a slice of bread with strawberry jam and walked them to their room. "We turn the lights off early here. It is time for you girls to go to bed. I'll come back later and check on you." She closed the door.

Anna lifted her suitcase and set it on the table. "You can put your clothes here on this chair." She helped Inge pull her dress over her head. She popped the clasp of the suitcase, pulled out her white nightgown and slipped it on. "Gertl said I look like an angel in this." She turned to her sister.

"I don't have a nightgown," Inge said, standing in her underwear.

"Don't worry. Nobody can see us here." They climbed into bed, which creaked with their every move. "We have to share the pillow, there's only one." They cuddled under the blanket.

Inge sniffed and pulled the blanket off her face. "It smells like horses."

Mrs. Kunkel came in and said, "Good night, children," drew the curtain covering the long window, and switched off the light, plunging the room into total darkness.

Anna sat up. "I wonder what's behind the curtain." She climbed out of bed onto the chair and hoisted herself onto the table. She lifted the curtain a bit, trying to adjust her eyes to the darkness. "It's not the outside, it's the grocery store, Inge. It looks sort of spooky."

Later Anna woke up when Inge tugged on her arm. "I have to go pee." A streak of moonlight lit her face where she sat up.

Anna squinted and looked around, trying to remember where she was. "Can you wait till morning?"

"No, I've got to go now," her sister whined.

Anna sighed, helped her out of bed and they tiptoed to the door, she opened it and they stood in the dark hall. Inge held her hand between her legs.

The kitchen door opened, and Mrs. Kunkel stood in the doorway, her hands on her hips.

"I can't find the toilet and she has to pee."

"It's over there." Mrs. Kunkel pointed at a door on the left.

But Inge had peed on the floor. Mrs. Kunkel threw up her hands and stared at the puddle. "Oh, God in heaven." She wrung her hands. "We have to clean this up quickly before Mr. Kunkle comes home." She took a step towards Inge. "Mr. Kunkel won't like this." She shook her head.

Anna took her sister's hand and pulled her towards the toilet. She couldn't find the light switch and left the door open. Inge sobbed.

On the way back to their room they passed Mrs. Kunkel, who kneeled on the floor holding a rag. She dunked it into a bucket and looked up at them. "Don't do that again," she grumbled. "No telling what Mr. Kunkel will do."

"I want my mama," Inge sobbed. Anna pulled her sister back into the bedroom. She helped Inge out of her wet pants and draped them over the chair. Getting back in bed, her sister clung to her, whimpering. "I won't do it again, Anna."

Later that night, Anna woke up to a man's voice shouting at Mrs. Kunkel, who screamed back at him. Anna pulled the blanket over her head. "Please, please don't tell him what happened."

One week later, Anna celebrated her sixth birthday back at the Munster farm. Gertl had baked a birthday cake with whipped cream on top and the number six outlined with berries. Rita gave her a doll dressed in a white blouse with puffy sleeves, a red vest and colorful skirt. "She looks just like you, so pretty."

Anna held her to her chest. "I'm going to name her Rita."

Rita nodded. "I brought her from Poland just for you." She bent and gave Anna a hug.

Anna pressed her face into Rita's skirt. "OH, I wish Mama were here." When she looked up, she saw Mr. and Mrs. Kunkel coming in the door. He was a big man with a red face and a black beard. He always wore a knife in a sheath on his belt and often pulled it and waved it in the air. The children were afraid of him. He was holding a bottle, weaving and singing. He stumbled towards Anna, bent and patted her on the cheek. Anna took a step back because he smelled funny. Gertl had told her that he was a boozer, whatever that was.

Rita stepped in. "Otto, please leave her alone. You've had enough, I think."

He turned around and grabbed her arm. "No Polish floozy is going to tell me--"

Swiftly, Farmer Munster came from behind and put his arm around him. He swung the big man around and motioned to Rita's husband, Arnold, to get hold of Mr. Kunkel's other arm, and they hustled him out the barn door.

Later, Anna went out to visit Yanka and gave her a big piece of birthday cake. The dog snapped it up, licked Anna's fingers and rolled over to get her belly rubbed.

Inge came out and sat next to her on the step holding up a bag. "Extra birthday cake." She waved the bag, smacking her lips.

Than Mrs. Kunkel pushed through the barn door. "Let's go. We don't have all night," she hollered, and pulled Anna up the step. Yanka growled, the hair bristling on her neck. Mrs. Kunkel kicked the dog, who yelped, then barked, straining on her chain. Anna fell on her knees and Mrs. Kunkel pulled her away.

Inge cried. She had wet her pants again.

CHAPTER 12

Anna and Inge were playing in the Kunkels' yard with two girls who lived across the street next to the school. Their father was the village teacher. "School starts soon, and you'll be in class with me," the tall girl with the ponytail said and threw a ball to Anna.

"I'll be going to school," said Anna, "but we'll be back in the city by then."

"In the city?" The girls stopped and stared at her.

"My mama is coming to get us when she comes home from the hospital. The major said so, right, Anna?" Inge put her arm around her sister.

"Yes, he said Mama is getting better and he'll take us to visit her."

A sudden frenzied screeching stopped their play. Anna dropped the ball. "Look, Mr. Kunkel is chasing a chicken. Oh no, now he caught it." She quickly took Inge's hand.

Mr. Kunkel held the chicken by the neck while it screeched and flapped wildly. He slammed it on a tree stump next to the barn, swung an axe, and the body of the chicken fell and began to run.

Inge shrieked and ran into the house.

Anna covered her eyes. When she looked up, she saw the chicken still running away without its head. "No, no," she cried. Blood dripped off the stump. Mr. Kunkel cussed and called the chicken names, ran and caught it again.

She stepped behind the older girl to avoid seeing the blood. "What is he doing with the chicken?"

"You pluck the feathers off and then you cut it up and make chicken soup," the girl said.

The other one rubbed her belly. "Oh, fried chicken, that's my favorite."

Anna turned and ran towards the front yard. "I am never ever eating chicken again. Never."

The girls laughed and ran around her, making squawking noises, singing "We like chicken, we like chicken."

Later, when they visited the Munster farm, Anna asked Gertl, "How could the chicken run without a head?"

Gertl shrugged. "It's a reflex. The chicken's legs still want to run away."

That was the weirdest thing Anna had ever heard. She thought Gertl was making fun of her because she was a city girl. Later, in the yard, Anna told Karl about the chicken.

He laughed. "I've cut the heads off chickens. You're a sissy and a baby." She pushed him. "Sissy," he said again. "City kids don't know anything." He jumped, around, swinging a big stick.

Anna pulled Inge behind her so she didn't get hit.

"And you know what? I'm going to help kill a pig." He swished the stick back and forth across his throat.

Anna stepped back. "Why do you want to kill a pig?"

"To eat it, dummy." He laughed. "You eat bacon, don't you?" He kept swinging the stick.

"I like bacon." Inge answered, smacking her lips.

"Not me." Anna crossed her arms and frowned. "I'd rather eat molasses."

Karl whistled, stabbing an invisible pig.

That night at dinner, Mrs. Kunkel smiled and filled their bowls with chicken soup. Big bubbles of fat and pieces of skin floated on the top. Anna gagged. She jumped up and ran outside. Mrs. Kunkel called her to come back.

"I am not hungry." Anna leaned on the side of the barn, trying not to throw up. "My tummy hurts."

Mrs. Kunkel waved at her from the back door. "You come back in here at once." She bobbed her head so hard that the big hairpin fell out of her bun and rolled on the floor. "Now see what you have done," she shouted and knelt to retrieve the pin.

Sobbing, Anna squeezed by her to the table. She sat there and closed her eyes, so she didn't have to look at Mr. Kunkel.

"This is good chicken soup." Mr. Kunkel leaned towards her. "People are starving and would give anything for a bowl of this soup!" He shook his fat finger at her.

Anna stared at her bowl. "My stomach hurts. I can't eat it," she whispered. "I'll throw up."

His face turned red and he hollered, "You ungrateful child." He stuck his finger in her face. "You should be glad that we feed you." He drew the knife from his belt and waved it around. "Why don't you go back to the city and starve. That's what brats like you deserve."

Anna burst into tears.

"Go to your room," Mrs. Kunkel shouted, her thin lips quivering. Anna jumped up, inched by Mr. Kunkel and ran to the bedroom.

Inge was already there, sitting on a chair, rocking back and forth, holding Pepita. "I want Mama to come and get us," she whimpered.

"Shh." Anna put her finger on her sister's lips. "I don't want them to hear us."
She took her by the hand and pulled her onto the bed.

Then they heard Mr. Kunkel's booming voice. "I'm not keeping these spoiled brats here in my house. We can rent this room out for good money. There are refugees waiting in line, ready to pay."

"It's only for a short time," Mrs. Kunkel pleaded.

"Get those brats out of here," he yelled. The thud of a chair tumbling to the ground echoed through the house.

"You just go to Brauns' and get drunk. That's where our money goes, Otto, booze." The sound of a metal pan hitting the floor followed her shrill voice. "If the Nazis were still here, they'd put a stop to your boozing." A door slammed and there was silence.

The children lay in their bed, barely breathing. Anna stayed there a few minutes more, trying to decide what to do to make Inge feel better. She got up and opened the door a slit. It was dark in the hall and kitchen. "They've gone."

She pulled a pink blouse and a navy skirt from the bag of clothes Mrs. Weller had brought over. "You will look so pretty in this, Inge." Anna held up the blouse. "Let's try on some of these clothes." She moved the chair in front of the chest of drawers, helped Inge dress and climb up.

Inge tried to brush the wrinkles from the skirt, a slight smile on her face. "Can I wear this when we visit Mama?"

Later, when they went back to bed, Anna began to tell stories to cheer up her sister. Stories about children who could fly and go wherever they wanted, who were invisible so nobody could hurt them. After Inge fell asleep, Anna sighed and put her hand on her hungry stomach.

They woke to loud banging, and Mrs. Kunkel screaming, "No, stop. Don't do that, you are hurting me." Scared, but curious, Anna crept from bed, slowly opened the door and peeked out. The Kunkels' bedroom door was open with the lights on. She tiptoed along the wall down the hall and stopped behind their door. She gasped and covered her mouth. Mrs. Kunkel was lying on the bed and Mr. Kunkel was on top of her, holding down her arms. He had on a shirt but no pants. His bare bottom stuck up in the air. Anna stood still. She didn't know what to do.

Mrs. Kunkel groaned and screamed, "No, let me go," and he grunted and said something. Having a big fat man on top of her, no wonder she was screaming. It must hurt her, being squashed like that. Mrs. Kunkel tried to fight him off and then a glass fell off the nightstand and crashed to the floor.

Anna ran back to her room and closed the door. She held her breath, her heart pounding, praying to God that they had not seen her. "Quick, hide under the blanket, Inge." she jumped into bed and held the pillow over their ears. "If he comes in, pretend you're asleep." She put her arm around her sister.

In the morning, Anna's stomach was growling, but she did not dare to leave the room. Finally Mrs. Kunkel opened the door and told them to come and have breakfast. She looked like she always did. Anna could not see any blood or wounds on her. She smiled and even made scrambled eggs for Anna. She didn't mention the chicken soup.

Anna and Inge were sitting on the steps of the Kunkels' store when they spotted Karl walking towards them. Anna jumped down the steps to meet him.

"Come with me, I want to show you something," Karl said, and started running back down the road. She waved her sister to go back to the house and trailed after Karl. She couldn't wait to find out what he was up to.

He led Anna to the far end of the Schulz's barn. Piercing screams were coming from a big double door. He reached and grabbed her by the wrist.

"No, Karl, let go of me." Karl laughed and pulled her into the barn, shutting the door behind them.

It was horrible, worse than the burning houses in the city. Farmer Schulz and his farmhand, Ben, were trying to catch a big pig that was screaming and trying to get away. When they had it cornered Ben grabbed it by the ear and pulled it to the center of the room.

Anna twisted and turned, trying to escape Karl's grip, all the while watching, fascinated, as Ben hit the pig over the head with a big ax. The pig screamed and screamed. He struck it several times and it fell to the ground. Then he took a big knife and slit its throat as farmer Schultz held its head over a long trough, blood streaming from its throat.

Anna screamed and fought harder. She was glad that Inge had not come along. Karl laughed and tightened his grip and twisted her arm behind her back. She covered her eyes with her free hand. "Let me go! I'm going to die." The pig finally stopped screaming.

"It's dead," Karl pronounced. "They're going to make sausage from the blood." Anna's stomach churned. They dragged the pig over to a trough that was filled with boiling water. Then they scraped the hair off the pig's skin. Anna never heard of a pig having hair.

She closed her eyes. When she peeked a little later, they were dragging the pig to the wall and hanging it on a big hook, head down, blood still dripping.

"Now they are going to take out the guts and cut it apart," Karl explained.

While he was watching them, Anna jerked from his grasp and ran out the door. She didn't stop until she reached the Munster farm.

Gertl was leaning over the table kneading bread. She had opened the top button of her blouse and drops of sweat ran down her cheeks. The big iron stove glowed red and the air in the room was sweltering.

Gertl wiped her hands on her apron and touched Anna's forehead. "What happened to you, Anna, are you sick?"

Anna shook her head and buried her face in Gertl's apron shaking, sobbing.

Gertl stroked her hair, waiting to find out what had happened. "Come sit down, Anna. Would you like me to fix you molasses bread?"

"Oh no, no, I can't eat a thing, Gertl. I hate Karl." She told what he had done and how the pig had screamed and screamed.

"That was nasty of him. I am going to scold him and tell his father," Gertl promised.

"I will never eat meat again, I swear," Anna proclaimed. "Not in my entire life." She sat there watching Gertl kneading the dough on a large wooden board. "Gertl," she finally spoke, "Mr. Kunkel tried to kill Mrs. Kunkel last night."

Gertl put down the dough and crossed her arms. "What? What are you talking about, Anna? Were you listening again?"

"No, I swear I was not listening," she told what had happened. "I went into the hall only because I was scared."

At that moment Rita walked in. She gave Anna a hug and pulled two bars of chocolate from her pocket. "One for you and one for Inge."

Gertl held her hand over her mouth, smiling. "Anna, tell Rita what you just told me."

Anna repeated her story, adding the part about Mr. Kunkel having no pants on and his big white butt sticking in the air.

Gertl and Rita burst out laughing. When one stopped, the other started again. Finally, they stopped, wiping their tears from their eyes, gasping.

"Are you laughing about his big naked butt?" Anna asked.

The two women held their mouths and began laughing again.

Anna did not think this was funny. "I was really scared because I'm afraid of Mr. Kunkel. I didn't know what to do to help Mrs. Kunkel."

Although Rita could barely talk, she reached out and touched Anna's shoulder. "Next time just stay in your room, Anna. They were playing a game, that's what couples do."

"Does Arnold hurt you when you play that game?"

Gertl turned and started kneading the dough again. Still chuckling, Rita stepped to the sideboard and returned with a cup of coffee.

Anna stuck out her lip and stomped her feet. Why were they making fun of her?

"Don't worry, Anna, your mama can explain that game to you when you are older," Rita said in a gentle voice.

Finally, Gertl took a deep breath. "Go see Yanka now. She's been waiting for you. She told me you haven't been here to pet her in two days. And, before you leave, stop in and take home some fresh bread and molasses."

Anna went outside and was greeted by Yanka, her bushy tail wagging, jumping up to greet her. Sitting on the step, petting her, hugging her, Anna wished she could take Yanka home to keep her safe.

CHAPTER 13

At suppertime, Anna told Mrs. Kunkel she had a bellyache and could not eat. Mrs. Kunkel didn't get angry. "Never mind, we'll eat later." She always seemed more agreeable when Mr. Kunkel wasn't home. She told the children to sit down because she had something special to tell them. "Mrs. Weller stopped in this afternoon. Her brother-in-law, Major Rudi, will come tomorrow morning and take you to visit your mother."

Inge and Anna jumped up and down and danced around the kitchen.

Mrs. Kunkel smiled and pulled Anna close. " You must look nice when you see your mama. So, I want you girls to take a bath." Her nose twitched. "When was the last time you had one?"

"Erika gave me a bath once," Inge said.

Anna remembered when Gertl had poured hot water in a big metal tub outside and let her wash up but she didn't remember when.

"We have a bathtub here in our house, and I have already heated the boiler. It should be ready soon. So who wants to go first?"

Anna watched as Mrs. Kunkel placed more wood into the bottom of a tall metal barrel. Soon hot water ran into a huge tub. It. was so big that Inge and Anna both fit into it. Anna splashed some water on her sister. "Do you like this?" Inge squealed and splashed right back. They stayed in the tub until the water was almost cold.

"I can't wait to tell Mama," Anna said as she helped dry off her sister.

Back in their bedroom, Anna told Mrs. Kunkel that she wanted to wear the wedding dress Rita made, but the woman shook her head. "You have to put on something more practical, child."

Anna crossed her arms. "I'm not wearing the curtain blouse."

Mrs. Kunkel blew a noisy breath through her nose and stomped out of the room.

The next morning, Anna woke up early. She turned and shook her sister. "Inge, Inge, get up. We are going to visit Mama today. We have to get ready." She pulled out the red blouse Rita had given to her and a dark blue skirt from Mrs. Weller's clothes. Most of the clothes were too big for Inge but they fit Anna perfectly.

Inge picked a white dress with pretty red flowers. Anna thought she looked like a little princess. Mrs. Kunkel had told her yesterday she didn't know how to braid Inge's hair, but Anna did. "Erika showed me how," she had told her. "I put a little red bow on each braid, and she really looks like a doll. Mama will smile when she sees her."

When they finished dressing, Anna took Inge's hand and they walked into the kitchen. Mrs. Kunkel was sitting at the table writing something. She looked up, then glanced at her watch. "Children, what are you doing up this early? It is six thirty in the morning."

"We don't want to be late," Anna said. "Can we sit on the steps outside to wait for the Major, please, please?"

"You can't sit outside this early in the morning. "She squinted and adjusted her glasses." Go back to your room until breakfast."

Anna hung her head, took her sister's hand, and trudged back to the bedroom. "Do you want to play dolls?"

she asked. Inge shook her head, picked up Pepita and hugged her.

Anna glanced at the white suitcase under the table, packed in case they might stay with their Mama, but she was afraid to ask Mrs. Kunkel about it.

After breakfast, she stole a glance at Mrs. Kunkel. "When is Major Rudi coming to get us?"

Mrs. Kunkel picked up the coffee pot and refilled her cup. "He said he'll pick you up sometime this morning. I don't know exactly when. Go and feed the chickens." She picked up her cup.

Anna dawdled in the doorway. "What if the Major comes by and doesn't see us?"

"I said go, feed the chickens." She grabbed Anna by the shoulder and shook her. "Your arguing makes me angry; you hear?" She released Anna and picked up her coffee again. "Why can't you be a good girl like your sister?"

Inge ran out the door to the barn, came back with a ladle and began spreading grain for the chickens.

Mrs. Kunkel yelled from the window, "Don't forget to go to the toilet before you leave."

Anna leaned against the doorframe with her arms crossed. "I don't have to go."

Mrs. Kunkel put her hands on her hips. "You help your sister and then you use the toilet. Or you stay home, you understand?" Her shrill voice vibrated through the quiet house.

Anna hung her head and followed orders.

Finally, at nine o'clock, they sat on the steps of the store and waited. Two people on bicycles passed by. And then they saw the Schulz wagon with Ben sitting up front, who shouted "Whoa," and the horses stopped. "You want to come along? I'm going to the moor." He swung his whip and motioned to them to hop on the wagon.

"No, we are going to visit my Mama," Anna shouted.

"Tell her I said hello." He made a clicking sound and the horses started to trot on.

Soon after, they saw the shiny black automobile pull up in front of the house. Major Rudi climbed out, but he didn't look like the Major because he did not wear his soldier uniform. He smiled at them and went to talk to Mrs. Kunkel, who stood in the doorway and handed him an envelope. He nodded and shook her hand, then held his hand out to Anna to shake. "You are Anna, right?"

She jumped up and down. "Can we climb in?" She took his hand and pulled him towards the vehicle.

He opened the back door to let her in. "And this is your little sister, Inge." He patted Inge on the head and lifted her into the backseat where Anna already waited.

Anna had never been in a car. She held Inge's hand because her little sister might be scared.

"Your Mama is a nice lady," Major Rudi said as he turned the key in the ignition and started to drive off.

Anna looked out of the window as they passed Munster farm and then drove by the Schulz house. She wished Karl could see them, but the car went by the farmhouse and soon they left the village behind. She remembered the big red barn and what had seemed hundreds of black and white cows grazing, some standing close to the fence chewing and looking at them. She had never seen a cow before then and Mama had told them they give the milk she bought in the store. They had walked down this country road from the train station to the village, and Mama had had to stop frequently, winded from pulling a cart with their belongings and Inge sitting on top of it.

Now Major Rudi asked, "Are you excited to visit your mama?"

"Yes. I can't wait. I have so much to tell her. I just had my birthday party, you know. I'm six now. And I have never ridden in an automobile," Anna slipped to the edge of her seat so she could see him. "I like it. It's shiny and smells good."

"I want my mama," Inge burst out, then buried her face in her sleeve. She didn't even look out of the window.

Anna scooted closer to the glass. "Look at all the cars, Inge."

"Damn it, a convoy." Rudi's voice sounded hoarse. "Don't say anything. Keep quiet. If they stop us and ask you something, don't answer. Understand?"

Anna moved even closer to Inge and held on to her hand.

They pulled to the side of the road and the Major rolled down his window. A soldier walked up. He had a gun and wore a flat cap and said something Anna could not understand. Rudi kept pointing at them in the back seat, repeating that he was taking them to the hospital to see their mother. The soldier stuck his head in the window and looked at them. Inge started to cry. Anna smiled and waved.

The soldier smiled and waved back and motioned the Major to drive on. Rudi let out a deep breath of relief. "That was a close one. I guess he has children, too."

They drove on and didn't see any other cars, just big military trucks rumbling by and lots of people walking along the road carrying sacks, bags and backpacks. Some pushed carts and wheelbarrows. Anna wondered where all the people were going but was afraid to ask.

They drove and drove. The major did not talk any more.

Then Inge whined, "I have to pee."

Anna turned to her, worried. "We can't stop now. Can you wait till we get to the hospital?"

Inge shook her head.

"Inge has to pee right now," Anna announced, tapping the Major on the shoulder.

He stopped on the side of the road, got out and opened the back door. "Hurry, tell her to hurry."

Anna scrambled out, pulling her sister along. "We have to hurry, Inge." They slid into the ditch, and she helped Inge pull down her pants.

The Major stood smoking a cigarette and looking up and down the road. "Hurry, girls, we've got to get to the hospital and back today."

When Inge was done, Anna helped her back into the car and they drove on. In moments, Inge had fallen asleep.

Finally, they turned onto a smaller road and Anna could see a group of buildings surrounded by a tall fence. The gate stood open. The Major pulled through and stopped in front of the largest building of the compound. "Wait here. I'll be right back."

Anna shook her sister. "We are here, Inge, at the hospital. Wake up. We're going to see Mama."

Inge sat up and looked around. All they saw were a few automobiles, large trucks and a big tank. The tank looked gigantic and scary, looming over the other vehicles. Anna put her arms around Inge. "Maybe it is guarding Mama's hospital."

The major appeared at the door of the building, waved back and shouted, "Stay there," then walked around the corner and disappeared. Anna craned her head. She did not see anyone, nobody at all.

Inge whimpered, "Let's go see Mama now." Anna didn't know what to say. Why did they have to wait out here? Why couldn't they go inside?

After what seemed a long time, the major came around the side of the building. He walked slowly, opened the car door and climbed back into his seat. He turned the car around and crept out of the compound. "I promised her, I promised her," he murmured, then said louder, "Your mama is no longer here. All the patients have been moved, nobody knows to where." He pulled to the side of the road and dropped his head onto the steering wheel. "The British have taken over the place. I can't believe this." he pulled back onto the road.

"No. Go back, she's there," Anna wailed, waiting for him to turn around. She rolled the window down and squeezed her upper body through the narrow space. "Mama! Mama! "she screamed, waving with both arms, her face full of desperation. The car picked up speed and she slumped back into the seat, sobbing. "Mama," she whimpered feeling her heart had been cut out. She pulled her sister close, cradling her head.

"Damn Scheiss. I'm too late. I can't believe it." The Major turned around briefly glancing at the children huddled in the corner of the backseat. "Damn," he shouted again, and the car lurched ahead as he stepped on the gas.

Anna held Inge tight as they slid onto the floor. She grabbed the door handle and they crouched in a huddle.

"When we come to the next town, we will stop and try to find cookies. I know a bakery there. You like cookies, don't you?" The Major turned and looked at her.

Anna stared at him in disbelief and tried to suppress her sobbing.

Inge cried, "I want my mama."

CHAPTER 14
Beversen Regional Hospital

Annemarie sat in a wheelchair on the third floor of the Beversen Regional Hospital where she had been transferred. Rain peppered the tall window next to her bed. The moist air in the ward felt heavy, laden with stench of disinfectants and too many patients crowded into one room. Annemarie wiped pearls of perspiration from her forehead. She had pushed her own blanket to the side, but even the thin cotton hospital gown stuck to her like a second skin. The constant throbbing in her leg made it unbearable to sit in the wheelchair for long. Why hadn't it gotten better? She waited for the nurse to come with her pain medication. But it might be an hour or longer. She tried not to take too many pain pills. They made her drowsy and upset her stomach.

She sighed, drew Alfred's letter from the envelope and unfolded it for the twentieth time. It was dated October 1944, nine months ago. Alfred's mother had enclosed his letter with one of her own. She said that she had not heard from him since early December when she had received a brief note that his leave had been cancelled. She wrote that his unit was to replace one totally decimated by the Americans. Annemarie bit her lips, trying to hold back her tears.

His mother also wrote that she was planning to flee to the West if she still could, because the front was moving closer every day. The Russians were advancing rapidly with refugees fleeing ahead of them and reporting stories of soldiers raping and killing in a frenzy of revenge. She closed with, *My dear Annemarie, I am so glad you and Alfred shared happiness and I hope to see you and your sweet children again if that is God's will. I pray that He will forgive those who are committing such crimes against their fellow human beings. I will pray for Alfred that he may return to us safely and that the war will end soon.*

Annemarie folded the letter, placed it into the envelope and stared into space. Then she picked up the single sheet, its edges ragged as if it had been torn from a pad in a hurry. Slowly, she unfolded it. *My Liebling Annemarie.*

Every day, she let those words in Alfred's clear, calm handwriting gather and carry her away.

Gently, she smoothed the rumpled paper.

My Liebling Annemarie,

A day does not go by that I do not think of you. I hear your laughter and that helps me to endure this hellish place. It is unimaginable what misery the war is inflicting on the population here. They have no place to escape to and are suffering and watching their villages blown up, their livelihood destroyed, and their families killed. They are the innocent victims, pawns of the war, sacrificed for victory. It drags on and on, killing and maiming with no end in sight.

We are losing a lot of men in this fight against the Americans, who are advancing relentlessly. I am the only one left of my original unit. All the rest are wounded or killed. And for what? I don't know why we are fighting anymore, why a merciful end is not declared. All I ever wanted is to be home with you, to sit in the garden and watch my children play.

I have some good news too, my Liebling Annemarie. I have been granted a leave and hope to hold you in my arms on Christmas. That is, of course, if we can hold this town, if we don't get overrun, if I don't get shipped to the hellhole where the front changes every day, and if I can stay alive. So, a lot of ifs, but my love and longing keep me going, hour by hour, day by day. You are my only ray of hope here, Liebling.

I don't know if Mother is still alive. We heard that the Russians are advancing west at a fast pace and that they are unstoppable.

I hope you keep safe and please hug and kiss Inge and Anna. My Christmas wish is that my home leave will come through and St. Nicolas brings me back to you, my Liebling.

Your love and husband (almost…!)
Alfred

She had already learned from his mother's letter that his leave had been cancelled. The first few times she had read it, she'd cried herself to sleep. But finally, her tears had stopped and she tried to think only of his safe return. She could not allow herself to think of him shipped to the frontlines from where, he said, most did not return.

"I haven't seen my children in I don't know how long," she said to anyone who might be listening. "The Munster's and Gertl love children. And Farmer Schulz is the town's mayor and will keep them safe." She glanced around, but no one was paying attention. "Oh, if only Lisbeth was here." She pulled a handkerchief from the night table and blew her nose. She thought back to that morning, the rush of transferring the patients to regional hospitals, to the last sight of her friend being swallowed by the crowd. This was after Lisbeth had hugged her and said, "Always remember, we are survivors."

The staff here appeared frenzied. The hospital was understaffed and that was probably why the nurses were harried and impersonal. She missed Lisbeth, oh and Doc Hartmann and his crazy jokes, the flirting and the special attention he had lavished on her. She kept the hat she had knitted for him in the drawer of her night table. And his promise of a dance date was unfulfilled.

She folded Alfred's letter, kissed it and replaced it in the envelope, then reached for the crutches leaning against the wall by her night table and carefully started to stand. "Au," she shrieked, clutching her leg, the crutches slamming to the floor. She fell back into the wheelchair. Determined, she managed to get up again and started to take small steps, hobbling down the center aisle of the ward. Each step shot a bolt of pain up her leg. She cringed, struggling to hang on to the crutches, huffing like a swimmer doing laps.

"I will get out of here," she shouted, looked around at the other patients, smiled belatedly, and raised one of the crutches. People began to smile back. They waved and told her that she was doing much better than the day before.

"Thanks." Annemarie grimaced. She leaned on her crutches, trying to throw kisses at them. "Yes, ladies, I'm going to walk out of here and go home."

The ice was broken, and she had transformed a place where every patient had been suffering alone into a group of caring people. "I'm going to give them a little bit of Lisbeth and spread some laughter and fun around here," she murmured. Today was a new start and she felt more alive, ready to fight.

A chair partially blocked the aisle and as she tried to maneuver around it, she looked up and almost fell backwards. "Martha! Martha Dummersdorf!"

In front of her stood a stout woman with bushy red hair beneath a big green hat boasting two colorful feathers. She was clad in a brown raincoat and rubber galoshes and carried a large, worn handbag.

"Annemarie, let me look at you." Martha reached to help steady her. "I am so glad I finally found you." She followed her back to her bed and helped her into the wheelchair.

"How in the world *did* you find me, Martha?"

"Your sister stopped by after she visited your parents and told me she had seen you at a military field hospital and that you were wounded."

"Yes, when she came there, I made her promise to tell you where I am."

Mrs. Dummersdorf bent and planted a kiss on Annemarie's cheek. "Oh, Annemarie." She wiped her eyes and shook her head. "I tell you, it's a miracle that I made it here. You have no idea how bad things are."

"Did she tell you anything about my parents? I am so worried, Martha."

"Not much. She just said their health is not good and that she had brought them some food. I should have asked more questions." She lowered her eyelids. "But you know, Mrs. Friedrich Bowman doesn't make conversation with folks like me."

Annemarie clasped Martha's arm. "At least your parent's house did not get bombed and they have a roof over their heads."

"Yes, the whole block on that side of the street is still standing. But across the street, everything got bombed to rubble. It doesn't make any sense. Mrs. Gellert-- you know her, she lives two buildings down from me -- said her husband told her the Americans and the British dropped over six hundred tons of bombs on our neighborhoods when they were already negotiating for surrender in April. He works for the city. I think he's a fireman, so he found out about it. You won't recognize the place, Annemarie. It looks ghastly and you don't even know where you are."

Martha had always talked a lot and it was hard to get in a word. Annemarie had known her since she was a child, and she and her mother had always laughed after Martha Dummersdorf had visited, for even then, she had talked non-stop.

116

Annemarie bent towards Martha, trying to hug her. "I am so glad you came. I feel so helpless here in the hospital. I should be looking after my parents, bringing my children home." She threw up her arms in frustration.

"Annemarie, I saw you hobble on those crutches. Believe me I don't think you'd be much good at home. There is hardly any transportation. You can't get anywhere unless you bully your way onto a train, and that's if one is running. There are thousands of homeless families, wounded, sick, blind, and dangerous people roaming the streets, looking for shelter, scrounging for something to eat." She shook her head, her lips tight. "They find bodies on the streets every day because so many are too weak to carry on."

Annemarie covered her face and started to sob.

"Now, now, Maedchen. It'll be all right. It'll get better. It has to." Martha pulled a handkerchief from her bosom and handed it to her.

Annemarie pressed the handkerchief to her face, inhaling the dear, musty smell. "I am sorry, Martha, I just can't help it. I feel so overwhelmed."

"We all do, dear. Believe me. I have not heard from Bernhard. I know that he's alive, but he was wounded and is in a hospital some place down south."

Annemarie reached for her hand. "Oh, I am so sorry. But at least he'll be home soon, right? That's good news, isn't it?"

"Yes, guess I'm lucky. But I'm just waiting. Seems like we're always waiting for something good to happen, to make our lives normal again."

"Normal. If that isn't a joke, ha, ha," Annemarie mocked. "Normal, like being wounded, having lost everything, no place to live, not being able to walk --I can't believe that life will ever be normal again." Then she told Martha what had happened to her in the village, the

117

bombing, and the burning of the farmhouse and how she ended up in the hospital.

"Unbelievable." Mrs. Dummersdorf shook her head. "The last day of the war those bombers had to shoot at you. What sense did that make? I guess we will pay for this war for the rest of our lives." Martha fumbled in her bag, brought out another handkerchief and wiped her eyes.

Annemarie took that chance to interrupt her. "Martha, I need your help. I found out that Inge and Anna are still in the village of Burghof, living with some of the farmers who took them in after the bombing when I was taken away to a field hospital."

Martha's eyes dropped in sympathy.

"For a long time, I heard nothing and had no idea what had happened to them. But then a major who was stationed in the village came and visited me. He told me that the farmers were caring for my children. He promised he would bring them to me, but I never heard from him again." Her eyes welled up. "I have not seen my children since I was wounded."

"Maybe he hasn't been able to find you," Martha speculated. "Margarete had received a notice from the military about the closing of the field hospital and said that you had been transferred here. But I'm sure the major or the folks in the village wouldn't know. Now that the military is no longer in charge, I've heard that the British -- the Allies -- are occupying us and there's not much communication between any official government offices. Just rumors flying around. I don't know what will happen next." Her sad eyes drifted to the window where they seemed to be tracking the raindrops down the glass.

Mrs. Dummersdorf turned back and slowly wiped perspiration off her face and pushed up the sleeves of her blouse. "Oh, it sure is hot and humid in here."

Annemarie touched Mrs. Dummersdorf's arm. "Yes, it always is." She brushed the handkerchief over her

118

face. "Martha, if you can do this for me I will be forever grateful. My children are so little, only six and four years old, and I don't know for sure if the farmers are taking care of them. If you could somehow go to the village of Burghof and tell them their mama is getting better and will come to get them soon. Just tell them I love them and…" She lowered her head, unable to go on.

Martha dabbed her eyes. "Whoa. You've got me crying now. Annemarie, please." She gave a little broken laugh. "But let's make a plan. You know me. I'm not one to sit around and wait for things to happen. Everyone on the block calls me a tough old gal."

Annemarie smiled through her tears.

"I'll think of something," Martha continued. "I have to tell you though, traveling anywhere is almost impossible. Trains run infrequently, and if one runs, people swarm over it like wasps. Everybody is so desperate. They try to go outside the city and barter with the farmers. And they have to watch that the British don't catch them when their convoys pass."

Annemarie stared at her, eyes moist, pleading. Waiting.

Martha patted her on the shoulder. "But, where there is a will, there's a way. I will ask Walter Mueller. He used to work with Bernhard at the main railroad terminal. He helped me get the ticket to come out here. He's an official, so he can muscle his way on board, and he even got me a seat."

Annemarie nodded. "It's wonderful that you can still find friends willing to help."

"Well, he has known Bernhard for twenty-five years, and he knows me. I don't care if he joined the Nazis, at least he's alive. The Allies haven't gone after him. I guess they need him, since he's one of the few who knows how to run the place. All the big-wig Nazis took off,

119

disappeared before the war was over. They knew it was the end, so they took their loot and ran."

"Some people felt it their duty to stay on and keep things going, I guess," Annemarie said.

"Yes, and Walter is one of those dedicated to the railroad. It's his life. I hope Bernhard can work for the railroad again when he comes home. They're going to need engineers, people with experience, especially when there are hardly any able-bodied men left.

Annemarie leaned to hug her friend. "You are an angel."

"All right, then. I'll try my best to get to Burghof and find out about your girls." She wiped her face again and took off her hat, smoothing her hair back. "It may take me a while, but Walter may be able help again."

"I wish, I could offer you some water or something before you leave." Annemarie tried to scoot up in her wheelchair, to shift her weight from her injured leg. "But the nurses here are too busy. I'm sorry."

Martha gave her an understanding nod. "It's all right. So, how long do you have to be in here? What's the diagnosis?"

Annemarie shrugged. "I don't know. I haven't talked to a doctor but two times since I've been here. I wish Doc Hartmann was here. He is the one at the field hospital who helped me so much. All I know is that the wound on my foot is not healing. It's swollen and probably infected and there could be nerve damage. They've even mentioned amputation." Her lips quivered. "Doc Hartmann promised he would help me keep my leg." She sighed. "I hope I can convince the doctor here avoid amputation and let me go home."

"So, it looks like you might be in here a while then. You know, that could be a blessing in disguise. I can't see you fighting your way out there on crutches."

Annemarie clasped her hands. "Oh, I'm strong, a survivor, like Lisbeth said. I have no choice; I have to go home." She wiped her face with her sleeve. "Did you know that Willie died in '43? It's a long sad story like so many. But since then, I have met a wonderful man. His name is Alfred. You'll like him. He has a machine shop in the city, and we are getting married as soon as he comes home."

Mrs. Dummersdorf asked, "Where is his machine shop? What part of town?"

"In Barmbeck. You can get there easily on the subway, so you can visit us because we owe you so much, Martha, and I want to thank you."

Mrs. Dummersdorf's face took on a careful look. "So where is Alfred now?" she said hesitantly. "Is he wounded or a prisoner of war somewhere?"

"I don't exactly know. Last I heard was in December from the front in France. But by now he should be on his way home. And if he is a prisoner of war, it could take a little longer. I'm sure the Americans would let him go, don't you think? He is just a soldier, not a high-ranking officer, so I can't see why they would keep him."

Martha nodded. "Could be. You never know these days and without transportation maybe he's stuck someplace. No news is good news, right?" She stood up and arranged herself, taking a moment to get her hat on just right. "Well, I'm glad I found you, and I'm going to see what old Martha can do to find out more about your children." She glanced at her watch. "Oh my, it's late. I've got to be on my way. There is only one train going back. And if I miss that, I could be stuck here till who knows when. It's a twenty-minute walk to the station." She peered out the window. "Good, the rain has stopped." She caught a quick breath and continued. "With that crowd fighting to get on the train you never know what you encounter until you are actually on. But I don't blame them, people are desperate."

I WILL DANCE AGAIN

"I will walk you to the door," Annemarie said, struggling out of the wheelchair and reaching for the crutches. "See, I can walk." She grimaced and followed Martha through the aisle. Her lips were tight as she leaned against the exit, waving good-bye.

CHAPTER 14
Burghof Village

Today was Rita's birthday and Anna helped Gertl bake a cake. She showed Gertl the surprise she had made for Rita, a drawing of baby Gretchen in a crib with pigtails and red, chubby cheeks.

Gertl nodded, holding up the picture. "How pretty. She'll like that."

"And" Anna said smiling, "I'm going over to the meadows by the Schulz farm to pick flowers for Rita." She sighed. "I wish Mama were here. She could sew a pretty dress for baby Gretchen."

"There'll be plenty of time, Anna. Remember, Rita said that Gretchen won't be here until Christmas. Oh, that's Yanka barking. Go see who is there." Gertl picked up the cake and carried it to the pantry.

Yanka barked and howled, then barked again. Anna knew that she only did that when a stranger was there. She ran through the barn to the front door and plunged into the arms of a woman standing ten feet out of reach of the dog.

"Gertl," Anna squealed, "it's Mrs. Dummersdorf!"

Anna brought the woman to the kitchen through the garden because Mrs. Dummersdorf acted afraid of Yanka, who kept barking, pulling on her chain.

"Once she gets to know you, she is very sweet," Anna explained, but Mrs. Dummersdorf shook her head, looking over her shoulder as they walked around the house.

Mrs. Dummersdorf shook Gertl's hand. "I was Annemarie's neighbor and I have just come from the hospital where she stays, and."

"You saw my Mama!" Anna interrupted, tugging at her sleeve. "I want to see her. Can we go visit her today?" she shouted, jumping up and down.

Mrs. Dummersdorf stepped inside and looked at Anna. "Your mama wants to see you too, Anna, she's very excited." She put her arms around the child and squeezed her. Then she sank into a chair at the kitchen table and closed her eyes for a moment. Anna sat next to her, holding her hand.

"I have just made some coffee, Anna. I think Mrs. Dummersdorf wants to rest and visit for a while," Gertl said, and turned to the pantry, returning with a steaming china pot and two cups.

"Oh, the delicious aroma of coffee, I haven't had that in a long time," said Mrs. Dummersdorf. "I've been traveling since five o'clock this morning. I was lucky to get on the train through a friend who works for the railroad."

"Rita gives us coffee and chocolate too," Anna said, and scooted her chair close.

Mrs. Dummersdorf put her arm around Anna. She had often taken care of the children when they lived in the city. "I was able to take my bicycle on the train and that's how I got here to the village. I doubt that I could have walked all that way from the train station. It's too far and I am too old for that." She pressed her lips together.

Gertl asked, "Would you like a sandwich?"

"I have not eaten since last night." Mrs. Dummersdorf's voice cracked. She leaned back and rubbed her neck.

Gertl cut up some sausage, ham and cheese and several slices of bread and placed the plate on the table. Anna watched as Mrs. Dummersdorf ate every bite.

"Food is scarce in the city. We often go without," said Mrs. Dummersdorf. "I have not had meat in weeks." With her finger, she scooped the crumbs from her plate. "Thank you so much."

Gertl nodded and refilled their cups.

Mrs. Dummersdorf kept rubbing Anna's back. She cleared her throat. "If you people have some extra food— anything. Meat, cheese, eggs, bread-- anything, I would be very grateful if you will sell it to me." She leaned forward, her eyes pleading with Gertl. "I'm not asking for a handout. I brought some jewelry that I can give you." She wiped her eyes. "It's hard to find even potatoes. I stand in line for hours and then they run out before I get to the front. It would be easier if my husband were home. He might get some things on the black market." She threw up her arms. "But he was wounded and is in a hospital somewhere in the south. God knows when he'll come back."

Gertl reached for her hand. "I will check with Mrs. Munster. I'm sure she will help you. We all like Annemarie a lot and we are so sorry that she was hurt."

Anna listened spellbound as Mrs. Dummerdorf told Gertl all about visiting Mama, how she was already walking on crutches, and that she had asked her to find Inge and Anna. And that she missed them so much and couldn't wait to see them again.

"It's been hard on Annemarie not knowing what happened to her children." Mrs. Dummersdorf bent, pulled a handkerchief from her bag and wiped her face.

Gertl told her that the children were living with the Kunkel family down the street now because Rita and Arnold had moved in. She turned to Anna. "Sweetie, would you run over to the Schulz farm and fetch Inge, please? You told me she went there to visit with Erika and the baby, right?"

Anna did not move, just fidgeted with her hands. Gertl stood up and pointed to the door.

125

Anna puckered her lips and jumped off her chair, knocking it to the floor. Gertl shook her head and Mrs. Dummersdorf bent and righted the chair.

Anna darted out the door and ran down the road. She found Inge in the Schulzs' garden with Erika, sitting in the grass playing with baby Maria. "Inge, Inge, come along. Mrs. Dummersdorf is here." She grabbed her sister's hand. They ran back to the Munster farm.

"My, you've grown, Inge, since I last saw you." Mrs. Dummersdorf picked up Inge and twirled her around. "You are a big girl now."

Inge squealed. "I want to visit my mama."

"Yes, Liebling, I'll take you to see your mama, I promised her. And, a promise is a promise, right?" She pulled the child into her arms and hugged her again.

Anna looked up at her. "We went to visit Mama with the Major, but she wasn't there." She looked at her feet, shuffling them back and forth.

"As I said. I promised your mama that I will find you and bring you to her," she repeated and reached to touch her on the cheek.

Mrs. Dummersdorf set Inge on her feet and stood up. "Now I would like to visit the Kunkels. Annemarie wants to know who's been taking care of her children." She put an arm around each of the girls. "And then, on my way back, I will stop by and see about any extra food." She thanked Gertl for the coffee and sandwiches, grasping her hands, shaking them vigorously.

Gertl smiled and said once again that she would ask Mrs. Munster about the food. "Anna, will you please take Mrs. Dummersdorf to Mrs. Kunkel's house?"

"But it's Rita's birthday." Anna frowned. "I want to give her my present and have birthday cake with her."

"We will have cake when you come back. Mrs. Dummersdorf has to stop here later and pick up some things. I'm sure that Rita will wait for you."

"Promise?" Anna held out her hand.

"Promise." Gertl nodded and shook it.

They stepped outside where Mrs. Dummersdorf's bicycle leaned against the barn. "Inge can sit on the saddle in back," Mrs. Dummersdorf said, "but you'll have to walk, Anna. I'll walk with you. It's not very far, is it?"

"No, we walk there all the time." Anna hopped and skipped alongside the bicycle.

When they arrived, Mrs. Dummersdorf stood her bicycle against a tree next to the store.

"Mr. Kunkel smells," Anna blurted. "Gertl said he's a boozer."

Mrs. Dummersdorf stopped and pulled her closer. "Has he ever tried to hurt you?"

"No, he just yells a lot at Mrs. Kunkel. Oh, he tried to kill her once, but Gertl and Rita said they were just playing games. You know, he was on top of Mrs. Kunkel and he did not have pants on."

Mrs. Dummersdorf's jaw dropped, her mouth opened and she clutched Anna's shoulder.

Anna bit her lips. "I really wasn't looking."

Mrs. Dummersdorf shook her head. "All right, children, let's go in and talk to Mrs. Kunkel. We can tell your Mama everything when we go see her." She stopped. "Oh, look at all the chickens."

Anna stepped out ahead. "We have to go in through the side door."

"I wish I could catch one of these chickens." Mrs. Dummersdorf sighed. "Wouldn't that make a feast." She followed Anna through the yard.

"Mr. Kunkel can catch one." Anna stopped then and put her hand over her mouth, thinking about the bloody, headless chicken.

127

Inside, Mrs. Dummersdorf told Mrs. Kunkel who she was and that she had been at the hospital and visited Annemarie. Mrs. Kunkel stretched out her hands. "Come, come, I am so glad to see you. The children have been waiting so long." She motioned them to follow her into the kitchen and had Mrs. Dummersdorf sit down at the table. She told the children to go to their room. Reluctantly, Anna took Inge's hand and led her to their bedroom, leaving the door open so that she could listen. Inge sat on the bed wide-eyed holding her doll, Pepita.

Mrs. Kunkel's voice drifted down the hall. "Ever since the Major took the children to see their mother and she was not there; Inge is crying a lot. She's also wetting her bed now, not every night, but a lot. That's hard, you know. I have to wash all the time and my husband doesn't understand. He thinks she's doing it on purpose." Anna heard every word but couldn't make out Mrs. Dummersdorf's reply.

"This was going to be just for a short time," Mrs. Kunkel went on." We agreed to help out because they had no place else to go, the poor things."

"Do you think you can keep them just a little longer, until their mother can come and get them?" Anna heard Mrs. Dummersdorf say in a louder voice and held her breath to make sure she didn't miss a word. "Annemarie is still in the hospital, but she's using crutches now. She hopes to be out soon."

"Well, I don't know, my husband wants to rent out the room." Mrs. Kunkel's voice had turned whiny. "We have a hard time making ends meet since we don't have a farm and with the store closed, we don't have an income. It's not been easy."

Anna took a few steps closer towards the door.

"I understand." Mrs. Dummersdorf's voice grew a bit louder. "But at least you've got chickens and a garden. You have no idea how bad it is in the city. Thousands are without a place to live. They've lost everything in the bombing raids, and every day we have to struggle just to find something to eat. I'd give my wedding ring for one of those chickens."

Anna's mouth dropped open. If Mrs. Dummersdorf was going to take home a chicken, she wondered if she would know how to kill it, yuk. Anna shuddered. She turned to Inge. "She wants to take home a chicken," she whispered.

Then she heard a door slam and the booming voice of Mr. Kunkel. Anna quickly stepped back, keeping the door open only a slit. Hands over her mouth, she turned to Inge. "Mr. Kunkel has come home."

"This is my husband, Otto," Mrs. Kunkel said. "This lady is a friend of Annemarie's from the city. She came to visit the children."

"About time somebody shows up here," he snapped. "We need the room to rent out. There's a long waiting list, and lots of folks have no place to live. They're refugees, you know," he hollered in a hoarse voice, his words slurred.

Anna turned once more to Inge. "He's been boozing again."

"Calm down, Otto. The lady said Annemarie is still in the hospital and asked that we keep the children just a little while longer."

Anna heard Mr. Kunkel's fist slamming the table like he had done many times before. She jumped back and sat next to her sister. "We need the room and the money. We can't feed city kids here any longer. I've told you before, that's how it is. This is my house. Take them kids to their grandma or some other relatives. We take care of our own."

"Where are you going?" Mrs. Kunkel shouted.

"When I get back, I want those brats gone, you hear me?" A door slammed.

129

Inge trembled and Anna put an arm around her shoulder. "We're going to visit Mama, Inge. We will. She promised." But her sister hid her face in Anna's chest.

They heard steps and Mrs. Dummersdorf pushed the door open and stepped in, her face blazing. "Let's pack up your things, children. Do you have a suitcase?" They quickly stuffed their clothes into the white suitcase. "Is that all you have?" Mrs. Dummersdorf asked.

Anna nodded, "All except our dolls, Pepita and Rita."

Mrs. Dummersdorf closed the suitcase and looked up. Mrs. Kunkel stood in the doorway, her eyes twitching, her arms at her sides. Strands of long gray hair had worked loose and hung down into her face. Anna thought she must be sick.

Her face flushed, her hands shaking, Mrs. Dummersdorf told the children in a calm voice, "Tell Mrs. Kunkel thank you and say goodbye, girls."

Anna took a step back, her eyes darting from Mrs. Dummersdorf to Mrs. Kunkel, who muttered something Anna did not understand. She curtsied and said thank you. Inge clung to Mrs. Dummersdorf, hiding her face in her skirt.

"All right, then." Mrs. Dummersdorf picked up the suitcase and pushed past Mrs. Kunkel, into the hallway and out the door with the children in tow. She stopped briefly, eyeing a chicken that fluttered out of her way. In the yard, she took her bicycle, hung the suitcase on the handlebars and they walked towards the road.

At the Munster farm, they rounded the house and entered through the kitchen door because Mrs. Dummersdorf was still afraid of Yanka. Anna could tell because she led them in a big loop around the dog, who was tied up out front. Anna opened the kitchen door and ran to Rita, who was sitting at the table with Mrs. Munster and Gertl. "Happy Birthday. I wanted to pick flowers for you but--" Gertl laughed, shook her head and caught Rita's chair, which had tilted backwards.

Panting, Mrs. Dummersdorf bent and sat the suitcase down. "I'm taking the children home with me. They can't stay at the Kunkels' house." She straightened herself, clasping her hands together. "I don't know how, but I'll do it somehow, for Annemarie."

"Please, sit down." Mrs. Munster waved at the empty chair. "Would you like some coffee and cake?"

Mrs. Dummersdorf ignored her. "Mr. Kunkel demanded that the children leave at once. He was obviously drunk." She took some deep breaths. "Oh, the poor woman." She shook her head.

Still cuddling in Rita's lap, Anna watched her.

Gertl stood and scooped up Inge and sat down and gently rocked her.

"God, I have to get back to the town to catch the train," Mrs. Dummersdorf went on. "Only one is running and it leaves at four-thirty."

Mrs. Munster stood and took her by the arm. "Sit down and have a cup of coffee and cake. Gertl has packed some food for you to take back." She pointed at a big sack by the door.

"Thank you. Thank you so much," Mrs. Dummersdorf said in a broken voice. "I am so sorry, but I'm sure we'll miss the train if we don't leave now."

Mrs. Munster looked anxious. "How are you folks going to get to town and the train station? That's quite a way from here."

"We'll have to walk. I can't get both children and their things on my bicycle," Mrs. Dummersdorf said.

Rita ate her last bite, scooping whipped cream with her fingers. "You know what? Gertl and I both have bicycles. Why don't we take Anna and Inge to the station? That'll be my birthday gift, to take my little friends to the train." Her eyes welled as she turned and emptied her cup.

"I want to see baby Gretchen," Anna whined. "You promised I could play with her." She clung to Rita.

"You will, sweetie, you will. You and Inge and your Mama will come to visit us. And in the summer, you come and stay as long as you like. Our new house will be ready by then." Rita cupped Anna's face in both hands and kissed her on the forehead. "And you know what? I will wrap a big piece of cake for you and Inge, something to eat on the train. And you each get a cherry."

Mrs. Dummersdorf searched in her voluminous handbag and pulled out a small box. "This broach belonged to my mother." She offered the box to Mrs. Munster. "Please take it as payment for the food."

Mrs. Munster waved her away. "No, we are doing this for Annemarie. Put that back. You might need it later. Please tell Annemarie that we hope she gets well soon and to come and visit us." Anna had never seen Mrs. Munster do anything like that, ever. Then she came to hug Anna and Inge.

Rita and Gertl left to fetch their bicycles. Mrs. Dummersdorf led the children out to the barnyard, stopping for the food bag on the way. Rita had Anna climb on the back of her bicycle, and Gertl adjusted the saddle of her own bicycle and then lifted Inge up behind her.

"Thank you. Thank you so much," Mrs. Dummersdorf called back and waved at Mrs. Munster. She started to peddle, balancing suitcase and bag on the handlebars.

It took almost an hour for them to arrive at the train station. The train was already there. Rita and Gertl waited with the children while Mrs. Dummersdorf went inside the station. It took a while, but when she came out, she held up her arms, waving two tickets in triumph.

"At first, the man wouldn't give me these because I did not have any money and he said that there was no room." She stopped, laughing, still waving the tickets.

"So how did you get them?" Gertl asked, shaking her head in disbelief.

"I gave him one of the hams. I hated to part with it, but it worked. I don't know what I would have done if the man had said no." She let out a deep breath. "Thank you so much, I am very grateful for all you've done. I'm sure you will hear from Annemarie soon."

A horn blasted and Mrs. Dummersdorf pushed the children towards the train's door where a cluster of people had gathered. They climbed up the narrow metal steps. Mrs. Dummersdorf was able to garner a seat on one of the benches and sat down, pulling Inge on her lap. Anna crouched in front of her legs and sat on the white suitcase. She stood up and craned her neck, trying to look out the window. Seeing Rita and Gertl hop on their bicycles she began to wave. She kept on waving long after the two figures got so small that she could no longer see them.

The train slowly rumbled out of the station. Anna slumped down on her suitcase, buried her face in her hands. She felt Mrs. Dummersdorf's hand on her shoulder.

"What's wrong, dear?"

"I forgot to tell Yanka goodbye."

CHAPTER 16

It was hot and smelly on the train and crowded with people who seemed to have been traveling a long time. Mrs. Dummersdorf stared straight ahead, dozing, her head bobbing with the rhythm of the wheels. Anna sat wedged on the floor between the benches, straddling her suitcase. Feet encroached on her space from both sides and the sack of food resting between Mrs. Dummersdorf's shoes pushed into her back.

"It smells like poop," Anna whined. Mrs. Dummersdorf just snorted and leaned to the side.

Anna's eyes wandered around the compartment. She noticed an old woman sitting across from them. The woman had straggly hair and one side of her face was red and purple. She peered at Anna with huge, dark eyes set deep in her wrinkled, sunken face. Anna thought she might be a witch, and she was afraid of witches because they could put spells on people. But then the woman smiled and reached to pat Anna on the head with her gnarled, bony hand. "You are pretty like my daughter," she said in a raspy voice, smiling with a toothless mouth.

Anna tried to squeeze closer between Mrs. Dummersdorf's legs, hugging her knees.

Next to the woman sat a man who had a bandage covered with rust-colored spots, wrapped around his head. "Blood," Anna whispered, cupping her mouth with her hand. He mumbled words but Anna couldn't understand. She raised her head a bit and noticed that one of his pant legs was folded up and there was no leg there. He held

134

onto two crutches and rocked his head back and forth, mumbling. In a hushed tone, Anna said, "My mama has crutches too." But the man didn't respond.

Mrs. Dummersdorf woke up from her nap and turned to Anna. "When we get off the train you and I will have to walk home. Inge can ride on the bicycle. It will be a long walk, Anna. But you're a big girl, right? You can do that?"

Anna nodded "When are we going to be there? My legs hurt. They are all squashed up."

"Soon. We should be there soon." Mrs. Dummersdorf straightened and pulled up Inge, who had fallen asleep and almost slipped off her lap. Inge woke, wiped her eyes and rested her face on Mrs. Dummesdorf's blouse. Anna craned her neck towards her sister and whispered, "I think that woman over there is a witch."

Inge did not pay attention. Finally, she said, "I wanted to go and say goodbye to Erika and baby Maria."

Anna reached for her hand. She had a lump in her throat because she had not said good-bye to Karl and the other children and, of course, Yanka.

After a while the train's horn blasted as it rumbled into the city's main railway station.

"We are here, children." Mrs. Dummersdorf set Inge down. "Anna, when we get off, take Inge's hand and do not let go of her. I have a lot to carry and need to get the bicycle from the back of the train." She stood up and smoothed her skirt, bent and rubbed her leg. "I want you to stay together where I tell you and wait for me. Anna, are you listening?"

Anna nodded. People got up and started pushing towards the narrow exit doors. The man with the missing leg and the crutches didn't seem to notice that the train had stopped. The crowd shoved and elbowed her, and Anna worried that she might lose Mrs. Dummersdorf. The platform filled with people as far as she could see.

Hundreds or thousands, Anna thought. They moved like a gigantic centipede towards the center station's great hall. She grabbed Mrs. Dummersdorf's skirt and tried to hang on. Everything was unfamiliar and dark, and deafening noise swallowed their words. Mrs. Dummersdorf handed her the white suitcase while she herself schlepped the big sack with the food.

Anna huffed, dragging the heavy suitcase along. "Wait for me. I lost my shoe," she cried, trying to grab it before it got kicked away. She stopped, groping for her shoe, but the crowd pushed on and she fell down. Somehow, she found her shoe. "Wait for me," she hollered, waving the shoe over her head.

"Hurry up," Mrs. Dummersdorf shouted. She had sat down on a bench in the center of the platform, protecting the food bag next to her and Inge on the other side. "You and Inge sit here and wait for me to get the bicycle. Do not move, you hear me? Put your arm around the food sack. Keep it between you so nobody can snatch it." She got up and disappeared in the crowd.

"Don't move, Inge, we have to watch the food and my suitcase," Anna yelled in Inge's ear. Her sister sat, her eyes closed, trembling. It was getting dark, and Anna reached to grasp Inge's hand, holding on tight.

Finally, Mrs. Dummersdorf returned with her bicycle. She lifted Inge onto the rear saddle, hung the suitcase and the food sack on the handlebars and started pushing the bicycle towards the station exit. She took big, hurried steps and Anna could barely keep pace. She was tired and asked if they could stop and rest, but Mrs. Dummersdorf told her no, they had to get home quickly because it was not safe to be out after dark.

There were lots of people on the street pushing carts, riding bicycles and carrying sacks and bags. Anna wondered where they were all going on this dark evening. She squinted. "Why are the streetlights not on?"

"There is no electricity." Mrs. Dummersdorf answered.

"Where are all the houses?" Anna asked.

"Gone," Mrs. Dummersdorf said. "Hurry, we don't have time to talk now. We have to get our food home." She walked faster and Anna had to run to keep up with her.

Anna stopped. "That man in front of us just fell down." Mrs. Dummersdorf pulled her aside and dodged around the man.

"What if he's dead?" Anna turned back to look at him.

Inge whimpered, her hands clutching the saddle.

"Anna don't talk until we get home," Mrs. Dummersdorf shouted. "I'm not going to say that again." Why was Mrs. Dummersdorf so angry? Anna looked up at her but kept quiet.

Finally, they turned into a side street and stopped in front of a tall apartment building.

Anna remembered the house because her family had lived in the basement apartment before they were evacuated to the village of Burghof.

"Hold the door, Anna, so I can get the bicycle inside. And you and Inge wait here."

It was pitch dark in the hall and Anna was scared. Inge leaned into her and pulled her skirt over her face to make herself invisible.

"Can't we turn on the lights?" Anna pleaded.

"Child, there is no electricity now. Wait here while I carry the bicycle upstairs. Then I'll come back and get you." She closed the outer door of the apartment house, and Anna held Inge's hand, listening to her heart beating and the clanking of the bicycle Mrs. Dummersdorf was dragging up three flights of stairs. Anna was sure somebody would come and snatch them, maybe the Russians or the British.

"Mama," Inge whispered."

Then they heard footsteps coming down and Mrs. Dummersdorf appeared and waved them to come up. She picked up Anna's suitcase and the big food sack and huffed as she schlepped them up the stairs. Anna hung on to her sister's hand to make sure she kept up. Poor little Inge, afraid of the dark, stumbled up, step after step.

On the third floor, they turned right and stepped into an apartment. Mrs. Dummersdorf locked the door behind them. "Stand still." She picked up a candle, lit it and set it on the kitchen table. She emptied the food sack from the Munster farm onto the table.

The children sat down and looked around in the flickering candlelight.

Mrs. Dummersdorf handed each a glass of water and a slice of bread. "I'm sorry, I don't have any milk." Inge's bread had sausage on it and Anna's cheese. Anna stuffed a piece of cheese in her mouth and mumbled, "I'll never, ever eat meat again." She thought of Gertl fixing her a crusty slice of molasses bread and looked at Mrs. Dummersdorf, whose face was grey and tired.

"Why don't you want to eat meat?" asked Mrs. Dummersdorf.

Anna stuck out her lip. "A boy at the farm made me watch them kill a pig. And it squeaked and screamed and tried to get away. And blood dripped from its head." She shivered.

Mrs. Dummersdorf reached over and touched her cheek. "Poor little girl." Then she led them down a narrow hall to a small room and opened the door. "There is only one bed. I hope it's big enough for you. Don't worry we'll talk about everything in the morning."

Anna helped her sister undress and they crawled into the bed. They fell asleep before Mrs. Dummersdorf stopped back in to bid them good night.

The next morning after a breakfast of bread with blueberry jam, Mrs. Dummersdorf told the girls to go play

138

outside. Anna and Inge hopped down the three flights of stairs, laughing at the noise from their feet echoing through the hall.

"Look, Inge." Anna pointed. "Oma and Opa live down the street!"

"Can we visit them?" Inge asked anxiously.

"Sure, I'll ask Mrs. Dummersdorf," Anna replied, scanning the old neighborhood. "Look at all the empty spaces and piles of stone." She stared at the ruined walls and a doorway of what had been a tall building. "Remember Norbert Meier lived in the house across the street? That building is gone. Do you think Norbert jumped out of the window? Or could he still be down below in the cellar?"

Inge shuddered and moved closer, grasping her hand.

To Anna's delight, most of the children they had played with before being evacuated were still there, happy to see them. But nobody knew what had happened to Norbert Meier.

"I bet he jumped out of the window and ran away," Anna speculated. But as they played in the ruins and slid down the hill of rubble, she still wondered aloud if Norbert was down below in the air raid cellar. She couldn't get that thought out of her head.

"He couldn't be buried down there, because there's no air left to breath." One of the boys pointed out.

"How do you know that? He could be in a little corner down there waiting for us to get him out." Anna stooped, trying to peer through a crack in the concrete.

"My mom told me you need air and there is only gas down there. All the air burned up," the boy stated with authority.

Anna thought about Norbert being down there, knocking on the door screaming that he was hungry.

At supper that night Mrs. Dummersdorf had told them that it was very dangerous to play in the ruins, the basement and the walls could collapse and bury you, that there could still be live ammunition down there and it could explode. But Anna's fascination had grown, and she now told the other children about the live ammunition, whatever that meant.

"Bombs, grenades, stuff like that," the oldest of the boys explained, "and maybe a bunch of dead bodies too."

Of course, Anna did not do what Mrs. Dummersdorf said but kept on playing in the ruins. They scraped and loosened bricks from the walls and collected them in piles. A boy pointed at his pile. "You can sell these to people who want to build a house. My papa told my mama that people get money for the bricks. I'm going to sell mine and get a bicycle."

"I want a bicycle too so I can visit my mama." Anna counted her bricks. "Look, I have twelve already. I wonder how many I need to get a bicycle." Nobody knew the exact answer. "I think maybe one hundred bricks. That sounds like a lot." Anna kneeled and pounded and scraped dirt off the bricks. "Come on Inge, help me get more bricks. We could buy a train ticket to visit Mama if there aren't any bicycles. Sit by our pile and watch them so nobody steals any." In the excitement, she had forgotten all about Norbert below in the cellar.

The next morning, though, she remembered and asked if they could dig a hole to make sure Norbert wasn't down there starving. Mrs. Dummersdorf shook her head. "Remember, I told you not to play in the ruins. Besides, it's raining today. Why do you want to go outside? Stay in your room and play a game."

"No, we want to play outside." Anna did not wait for an answer but grabbed Inge's hand and stormed out the door. At the ruin they were joined by other children

watching a man and a woman piling bricks into an old
wheelbarrow.

"Those are my bricks," Anna yelled, and stepped
closer to the man. The other children flocked behind her,
awaiting the outcome of the confrontation.

The man looked up. He had a deep cut across the
side of his face with dirt crusted all around and a gray
military cap on his head. "Get lost, or I'll shoot you all."
He stood up and took a step towards her.

"You can't steal my bricks!" Anna repeated.
"Stealing is wrong, you'll get punished."

The man grabbed her by the arm and jerked her
closer. "Look, you brat, I told you to get lost or I'll shoot
the whole bunch of you." He shook her and she screeched
and felt a thousand needles shoot through her arm. The rest
of the children scattered. She heard Inge crying and saw
her sitting in the middle of the street holding a bloody knee.
The man shook Anna again, pushed her and finally let go of
her arm.

The woman, scrawny and wearing a babushka,
stepped over and gawked at her. She waved her finger in
Anna's face. "Run away, girl, or he'll hurt you."

Anna scrambled to Inge, who still sat holding her
bloody knee. A couple of the boys had moved to a safe
distance and were throwing stones at the man, who kept
piling bricks into his wheelbarrow. While Anna was
brushing the front of her dress and wiping Inge's knee, she
heard a loud pop and saw dirt flying.

"Run, Anna, he's shooting at us," one of the boys
yelled. She pulled Inge up and ran until they reached their
apartment building and slipped into the hallway and up the
stairs.

Inge ran ahead into the apartment. She panted, her
dress dirty and blood dripping down her knee onto the
kitchen floor. "The man stole our bricks."

Mrs. Dummersdorf set down her coffee, turned and stared. "Didn't I tell you to stay away from those ruins? I should spank both of you. That's what your mama would do." She put her hands on her hips. "Look how dirty you are. You have to wear that dress again tomorrow, Inge. I can't wash before then."

In spite of Mrs. Dummersdorf's words, Anna continued. "But we had twelve bricks already, and we're going to sell them and get a train ticket to visit Mama."

Mrs. Dummersdorf's face flushed, and she pounded the table. "Go to your room right now. I don't want to see you again until supper, you understand?"

Pulling a bawling Inge by the arm, Anna walked down the hall and closed the door behind them. She looked for a towel to wipe off Inge's knee but could not find one and was afraid to leave the room. So she used the corner of their bed sheet and then folded it under the mattress.

That evening at bedtime, Anna spun a story for Inge about two girls who were invisible and went to a store and took bread and molasses and eggs and nobody could see them. And then they had big sticks and scared the mean people away and collected their bricks. "How much money do you think we will get for our bricks?" she asked Inge.

"One hundred marks," Inge replied holding up all her fingers. "Yes, one hundred Marks for me and one hundred Marks for you, Anna."

That night Anna dreamed she rode in a car like the one the major had, and they were driving to see their mama.

The next day at dinnertime, Anna asked, "When are we going to visit Mama?" She fidgeted with a spoon, dropping it to the floor. "What if they've moved Mama away again and she isn't there when we visit?"

Mrs. Dummersdorf didn't answer, but said, "Children, tonight we're going to have something special, potatoes with cabbage. Mrs. Gellert gave them to me." She

142

held her head and groaned softly.   "Oh God, I don't think I can do this much longer."

Up to now, Mrs. Dummersdorf had fed them only gravy made from flour, water and salt and poured it over the potatoes. But the children liked it.

"I do miss the food we had at the Munster farm," Anna said between bites, "especially the scrambled eggs Gertl made for me. I guess they don't have chickens in the city."

Mrs. Dummersdorf stared at the window, her eyes sad.

Anna looked at Mrs. Dummersdorf, making her own eyes big and full of expectation. "Can we visit and take some food to Oma and Opa? The tall boy who lives in their building told me they have nothing to eat. Oma is so thin, he said, and she coughs a lot. They won't eat much, just one potato for each of them, please?"

Mrs. Dummersdorf nodded and started to cry. She pulled Anna onto her lap and smoothed her hair. Anna did not know why she cried. Because of the potatoes? But then Anna had to cry, too. Inge just sat there, holding her doll, Pepita, talking to her and calling her Baby Maria.

CHAPTER 17

Mrs. Dummersdorf stood in the pantry placing a jar of strawberries into a bag. "Children, today we are going to visit your grandparents."

"Inge, we're going to visit Oma and Opa," Anna shouted jumping around, clapping her hands. "Can we bring them potatoes?"

"Yes, Anna, we will bring them potatoes and beans." She patted Anna on the head. "Here, you may give a glass of strawberries to your grandma. Mrs. Gellert got it from the farmers."

Anna took the glass, and she and Inge ran ahead of Mrs. Dummersdorf. In a few minutes, they reached the apartment house where their grandparents lived. Anna stretched on her toes to ring the doorbell. "Remember, Inge, the third button from the bottom. They climbed up three flights of stairs and Anna banged on the door with her fist. Mrs. Dummersdorf tried to pull her back.

"Come in, it's open," Grandma called.

When Anna pushed the door open, she was met with the pervasive odor of old tobacco. She rushed into the small kitchen where her grandmother sat on the old brown sofa wedged between the window and the stove. There was barely room for Anna to squeeze through. She held up the strawberries. "These are for you and Opa."

Grandma smiled and put the jar on the table, then took the bag of potatoes from Mrs. Dummersdorf and set on the floor. "Come here and give me a kiss." She opened her arms and pulled both girls to her. "It's so nice to see you again. I have missed you." Grandmother was thin with short gray hair and not much taller than Anna. Her face and hands were wrinkled and dotted with brown spots, but Oma had long ago assured her that they didn't hurt. She set Inge next to her and kissed her on the cheek.

Anna planted herself in front of Grandma. "We were on the farm, and I know how to shell peas. Gertl showed me."

Mrs. Dummersdorf put her arm around Anna and moved her aside. "We brought you some food, not much, but I hope it helps a little." She smiled at the old woman. "The children live with me right now. I visited Annemarie in the hospital. She is getting better and could be home soon." She bent and touched Grandma on the shoulder. "I wish I had some coffee or tea for you." She sighed. "It'll get better, it has to. And if I get some eggs and butter from Mrs. Gellert -- you know her? She lives two houses down from us. I will bring you some. Her husband goes out to the farms and barters."

Anna's grandmother smiled and nodded. "That's nice of them." She turned to Anna. "Can you help me up? I have a present for you and Inge," she pulled herself up, one hand on the table and her other arm around Anna's shoulders, and walked over to the cupboard, rummaged through a drawer and handed Anna a necklace made of shiny red beads.

"Your mama made this when she was in school." She smiled, took the necklace and placed it around Anna's neck.

"And for you, Inge, here is the matching bracelet." She put it around Inge's wrist.

"Did Mama make that too?" Inge asked in her thin little voice.

"Yes, Inge, she did, and I know she wants you to have it. Look how pretty the color shimmers."

145

Inge jumped up and kissed her grandmother and Anna left the kitchen to look at herself in the large, oval mirror in the hallway.

"Come look, Inge," she called. "It glows in the dark."

Mrs. Dummersdorf shifted her feet and wiped her face with a handkerchief. "As I said, Annemarie thinks she will be home by Christmas. She told me so when I visited her." She smiled at the old woman. "So, make sure you eat and stay strong." She picked up her purse from the table. "I promise we will be back to visit and bring you more food."

Anna's grandmother nodded and sat back down on the worn brown sofa next to the iron stove. She coughed, and spit something into a handkerchief. "My other daughter, Margarete-- you remember her -- brought some cigars for her father. She knows he likes to smoke." she sighed, "I wonder where he's gone to." She looked around vaguely. "He must have gone out. I wish Margarete would get us some bread and butter, maybe meat or coffee. She told me that her husband brings her coffee from his trips." She stopped and looked at Mrs. Dummersdorf, a slight smile fleeting over her thin lips.

Mrs. Dummersdorf shook her head. "I understand. Annemarie told me that her sister doesn't have much sense when it comes to the realities of life." She glanced at her watch and sighed. "I guess we'd better go…"

Anna slipped onto the sofa next to Grandma and put her arms around her. "Can you read us a story? Remember the book you said belonged to Mama? The one about the girl who became a princess?" Anna cuddled closer. "You know what? I have a dog in the village. Her name is Yanka. And when I talk to her, she really listens, well, only when I pet her belly, of course." Anna's eyes filled with tears. "I miss Yanka so much and she is waiting for me back on the farm. She won't know why I have not come back."

146

"I'm sure she is fine, Anna. She will be there when you go back to visit. Dogs are smart. They understand." Her grandmother eased the hair from Anna's face. "I had a little dog once. Her name was Princess."

"Where is Princess now?"

"Oh, that was a long time ago, when I was a little girl. Dogs don't live as long as we do."

"I wonder how long Yanka is going to live. I want to visit her this summer. Rita and Gertl said I could. It's really not much fun in the city and I miss Karl and the geese and shelling peas. I know how to do it, Oma."

Her grandmother smiled and squeezed her. "You are as smart as your mama, Anna. And Inge is as sweet as mama." She patted Inge's hand.

Inge clung to her grandmother's hand. "When is Mama coming home to get us?"

The old woman stroked her hair. "Soon, Inge, she'll be home real soon."

Mrs. Dummersdorf stepped closer and turned to the door. "We have to go now, children. Give your grandmother a kiss and tell her we'll come back again."

"I want to stay." Anna clasped Grandma's arm and stuck out her lip.

"Grandma is tired. She needs to rest now." Mrs. Dummersdorf walked back to the table. "I will put these things in the pantry for you. I'll see if I can get you some butter and meat." Then she led the children to the door. Anna turned and waved, and her grandmother rose shakily, holding onto the table and waved back with a trembling hand.

The next day, Mrs. Dummersdorf announced that they were going to get a rabbit. Anna and Inge squealed. A bunny rabbit, cute and fluffy with big round eyes, thought Anna. "We'll call it Teddy." They walked down the street past their grandmother's building to a tall, wooden fence with a big gate. It was always locked. Anna knew because the boys she played with had tried to open it but were scared off by the fierce barking of the dog inside.

Mrs. Dummersdorf knocked on the gate and called for Mr. Grossman. Inge hid behind her as the watchdog barked and snarled. An old man in a tattered jacket limped out with his walking stick and opened the gate. Anna stared at rows of cages, stacked three high and filled with rabbits.

Inge wrinkled her nose. "They stink."

"Shush," Anna scolded. "You want him to give us a bunny, don't you?"

The man told Mrs. Dummersdorf that he had to live here in the barn so nobody would steal his rabbits.

Anna heard the dog barking again. "Can we pet your dog?"

"Oh, no." The old man shook his head. "Wolf is a watchdog. He comes out at night to guard the rabbits. He'll attack anybody who tries to come in here." He chuckled. "He only likes me." He opened a cage and took out a small white rabbit. "Here, you can hold him." He handed the rabbit to Inge, who squealed with delight.

"He is so soft, Anna, feel him." She held up the rabbit.

"Can we keep him, please?" Anna pleaded. "We can fix up a box and let him live on the balcony."

"No." Mrs. Dummersdorf shook her head. "The rabbits have to stay here until they get big enough."

"But you said we would get a rabbit." Anna kicked some rocks down the path.

"Yes, child, our rabbit will be ready tomorrow afternoon," Mrs. Dummersdorf answered, looking at the list she had taken from her purse.

Inge cried as she handed back the little white rabbit.

The man removed a big gray rabbit from a cage and showed it to Mrs. Dummersdorf, who nodded, "Yes, that one. It has some meat on its bones."

"All right then," the man said, "Come back tomorrow afternoon and it will be ready."

"I like the white one better," Inge whined.

"We can't afford to feed it, sweetie, and one big rabbit will last us almost a week if we are frugal." Anna did not understand. She was also sad that she hadn't been allowed to pet the dog. She knew that if she talked to Wolf and petted his belly, he would like her just as Yanka did.

The next day, Anna asked when they would get the rabbit, but Mrs. Dummersdorf said to wait, and to stop pestering. So the children went outside to play in the ruins with their friends and forgot all about the rabbit.

On Sunday, Mrs. Dummersdorf had invited the Gellert's for dinner. The children watched quietly as everyone filled their plates with potatoes, green kale and pieces of roast.

"How did you get the rabbit?" Mrs. Gellert inquired. "It's delicious. I have not had good meat like this since before the war." She smacked her lips and her husband nodded in agreement as he ladled another helping onto his plate.

"I bartered for it," Mrs. Dummersdorf answered between bites. "I crocheted a hat and scarf for the old man to keep him warm this winter." She smiled, looking happy with her bargain.

Anna put down her fork and looked around the table, her heart sinking. "Where is the rabbit?" she asked, afraid of the answer.

"Right here, on the table, our first meat in six weeks." Mrs. Dummersdorf smiled and patted herself on the chest. "We are so lucky to have food, especially meat." The Gellert's nodded in agreement.

Anna looked at them all, her lips quivering as the grownups cut off more pieces.

Mr. Gellert slapped his round belly. "I wish I had a beer with this."

Anna jumped up from the table.

"Where are you going, Anna? You have not touched your food." Mrs. Dummersdorf's voice rose.

"I think I'm going to be sick and --" she rushed out of the room, barely reaching the toilet, where she threw up, tears streaming down her cheeks.

Two days later, when they sat around the table eating breakfast, Mrs. Dummersdorf announced, "Girls, I have good news." She waved a letter she was holding

Anna liked it when Mrs. Dummersdorf was happy and could almost forgive her about the rabbit. "Are we going to visit Mama?" she asked.

"No, sweetie, this is *my* good news. My husband, Bernhard, is coming home. He will be here by the weekend." Anna looked at her, confused. Where was he coming home from? Mrs. Dummersdorf laughed, and then she cried.

Anna didn't know what to make of Mrs. Dummersdorf's announcement and that she could laugh and cry at the same time. Was she hurt? "Can we go and play?"

Mrs. Dummersdorf seemed not to hear her. "We will have to be really quiet when he gets home. He was hurt in the war. They told me he has seizures. "

Anna looked at her. She was afraid to ask more. Worried that Mrs. Dummersdorf would cry again.

"Go out and play now, children. I'm going over to Mrs. Gellert to tell her the good news."

Relieved, the girls put on their shoes and skipped down the stairs.

On Saturday, Anna and Inge met Mr. Bernhard Dummersdorf. He was a tall thin man and one of his eyes twitched frequently.

"Why do you wiggle your eye all the time?" she asked him.

He gave her a quizzical look. "I was hit in the head by shrapnel and darn lucky that I'm still around. I lost a bit of my brain, but, hey, it beats being six feet under." He laughed.

Anna stared at him. She liked Mr. Bernhard because he was smiling but she didn't always know what he was talking about. Also, they could no longer play inside now and had to be quiet all the time so he could sleep.

One day when Anna came home, she saw Mr. Bernhard falling to the floor, kicking and knocking around, flailing his arms and legs. She was so scared she could not move. "Is he going to die?" she whispered to Mrs. Dummersdorf.

"No, Maedchen, he is having a seizure. He's sick." She kneeled to hold his head.

And then, Mr. Bernhard stopped moving, lay there quiet for a while, and she helped him up and led him to their bedroom.

"Inge, come here, I want to tell you something," Anna shouted.

Mrs. Dummersdorf rushed back to the hall, took Anna's arm and shook it. "No shouting, Anna. No loud noises. It makes Mr. Bernhard sicker." Her face was flushed. "You children get on my nerves sometimes." She rubbed her neck and closed her eyes.

Anna slowly backed away and took Inge's hand as the younger girl appeared.

"Just go outside and don't come back until dark. Mr. Bernhard needs to sleep. I told you girls, didn't I?" Mrs. Dummersdorf waved her finger at them.

Anna stared at her.

151

Mrs. Dummersdorf stepped closer. "Do you understand?"

"Yes," Anna murmured and opened the door and bolted out, dragging her sister behind her.

"I am afraid. She doesn't like me anymore, and I am hungry," Inge whimpered, trying to keep up. They stayed out until dark. When they came upstairs, they tiptoed to their room, scared to wake up Mr. Bernhard and afraid to ask for food.

After they were settled in bed, Anna turned to her sister. "Imagine two girls, the princess and her friend, flying through the air to the sun. It is warm and the sun shines brightly. When the man opens the gate, a lady who looked just like Rita takes the girls by the hand and fixes them a warm, cozy bath and then they sit at a table full of bread, eggs, apples, molasses, and even chocolate." After a while, Anna stopped her story, since Inge had fallen asleep.

The next morning at breakfast, Mrs. Dummersdorf smiled. "I have train tickets. Mrs. Gellert got them for me." She stood up and put her arms around Anna's shoulder." Tomorrow, we are going to see your mama."

Anna jumped up but Mrs. Dummersdorf put her finger over her mouth. "Remember, he is resting."

Anna hugged her sister a lot that day and they went outside to dance around. "We are going to see Mama!" they chanted. "We're going to see Mama!"

CHAPTER 18
Beversen Regional Hospital

Annemarie rested in her wheelchair next to the open window. The early November wind brought a chill into the room, but she breathed in the fresh air, trying to escape the stuffy, disinfectant-laden air in the ward.

As many times before, her thoughts were in the village of Burghof. Did Inge and Anna have warm clothes? Did any of her belongings survive the fire? Where would they find sweaters, boots and coats for the winter?

Annemarie turned to Ellen, the patient in the next bed. "My little Inge catches colds easily, and I always have to remind her to put on her coat." Ellen had been wounded when the house she lived in collapsed and she ran out into the street, where debris hit her. Annemarie had befriended her and enjoyed her positive outlook and sense of humor. "Major Rudi, who had been stationed in the village of Burghof, visited me in the army field hospital," Annemarie went on. "He told me the children are staying with the farmers there. They have plenty of food and are doing fine." Annemarie grasped the arms of her wheelchair and pulled herself up, shifting the weight off her injured right leg. "I should be there with them. I feel so guilty, you know." She took a deep breath and wiped a strand of hair from her face. "They are so young. They need their mother, especially Inge, who is only four. I know she doesn't understand. I dreamed last night that she was standing in a field all alone crying, 'Mama, Mama'." She reached for a glass of water and sighed. "I wish this was beer." She

153

raised the glass. "Cheers, to the Allies, to the Kaiser, to Hitler and to the British, to the whole lot who put me here." She waved her glass and took a drink.

"I never had children, but I don't think I could make it through the war like you. You are a brave woman." Ellen stretched her arms towards Annemarie. "I wish I could get up and give you a hug."

Annemarie rolled the wheelchair around her bed to Ellen, bent as far as she could and reached to hug her. "Thank you, Ellen. I'm so glad you are my bed neighbor." She leaned back and wiped her eyes with a corner of her gown.

Ellen looked up at her with soft eyes. "At least your children are in a safe place. And the war is over, so things should get better soon. And you are young, Annemarie. You will heal quickly and go home soon."

Annemarie raised skeptical eyebrows, but she nodded. "I hope so." She rolled back to her own bed, picked up the glass and took another drink.

Ellen rested her head back on her pillow. After a while, she said, "My mother told me they are forecasting a very cold winter. Everybody is worried about getting enough coal. The only people who have any are the ones who can get out at night and steal it from the open cars parked at the railroad depot. Parents even send their children out to take what they can get."

"People are desperate, how else are they going to survive?" Annemarie replied. "But I sure wouldn't let my girls go out at night. They could get hurt."

"Yes, and the police and even the MPs are dangerous. I'm sure they have shot quite a few people."

Annemarie shifted uncomfortably in her chair. "So, when will you be discharged? Do you know yet what you're going to do?"

"I'm going to move in with my mother. Luckily, her building is still standing. She lives in a one-bedroom apartment, but we will make do. The doctor told me I won't be able to do a lot until I can get some rehabilitation and who knows if that's even available? But I've got my mother, and my sister lives on a farm, so she's been getting food, thank God."

"Good for you. At least you won't go hungry. You are lucky."

Ellen barked a laugh. "Yes, lucky, I guess, considering that I can't use my right arm and need crutches to walk."

Annemarie picked up her glass and took another sip of water.

From the far entrance came a piping little voice. "Mama, Mama." Anna came running down the aisle and flung herself into her mother's arms.

"Oh my God, Anna!" Annemarie reached out, spilling water over her child. She squeezed her close, then held her by the arms and stared at her in wonder. Anna scrambled onto her lap, snuggled down and wrapped her mother's arms around herself.

Then she squirmed and pushed back on her lap to look at her mother. "Mama, I'm six now and Rita gave me a suitcase," she blurted, indifferent to her damp clothes. "And we gave Oma potatoes and strawberries, too."

Then Annemarie saw Martha Dummersdorf walking towards her, holding Inge's hand. Inge looked so small, so forlorn, wearing a jacket at least two sizes too big, dragging her doll. Annemarie gently sat Anna down and reached for her youngest daughter, pressing her to her heart.

After a moment, Inge beamed and held up her doll. "This is Pepita. Erika gave her to me, and I got to play with baby Maria."

"Oh, my little one," Annemarie whispered brokenly. Then she gently tugged on one of her pigtails. "Do you think Pepita will want another dress?"

"Yes, please Mama, she does." Inge smoothed her doll's dress.

"Well, Mama will work on that, Inge. When I come home, we'll sew a pretty dress for her." As Anna hopped onto the wheelchair beside her, Annemarie grimaced as pain shot up her leg. Ignoring the ache, she ran her hands over Inge's hair. "I had braids like that when I was little." She kissed her on both cheeks.

Anna tugged on her mother's arm. "I braided them. I do it all the time. Erika showed me how."

"Well done. You are my big girl. I'm so proud of you, Anna." Annemarie smiled and patted her knee.

"We want to stay with you, Mama. We don't want to go back there," Anna announced, and slid out of the wheelchair. "We don't want to go back because Mr. Bernhard has seizures. He falls down all the time and we can't be inside." Anna puckered her lips, nodding vigorously.

Annemarie stared at Mrs. Dummersdorf, who stood a few steps away. "I am sorry, Martha, they are so excited." She reached out to her.

"I understand." Mrs. Dummersdorf touched Annemarie's shoulder, then turned to Anna and Inge. "Children, can you sit on Mama's bed and be quiet for a moment? Mama and I have to talk."

Ellen... quiet till now, sat up in her bed, then motioned the girls over, maneuvering herself into her wheelchair. "Come here, I will read you a story,"

This is my friend, Ellen," Annemarie said. "Go on now." she gave them each a kiss and urged them towards her neighbor.

Turning back to Mrs. Dummersdorf, Annemarie asked, "So Martha, tell me, what's going on? Are they both living at the Munster's? Can they keep them till I get out?"

Mrs. Dummersdorf shook her head and began to fill her in on what had happened. She fidgeted with her hands and looked at the floor. "The children could not stay at the Kunkels'. I'm sure you agree. So, I decided to take them home with me. I didn't know what else to do, Annemarie, I really didn't. And it has been hard." She crossed her arms and continued in a muted tone. "We don't have enough food. We barely make it from one day to the next."

Annemarie stared at her. "Oh my God, Martha." She briefly closed her eyes trying to suppress a sob. The farmers couldn't keep her children. Poor little Inge and Anna had been shuttled off to the Kunkels. Everybody knew that the man was an alcoholic. He spent more time at Braun's pub than at his store. How could she have thought everything was all right? She slumped, almost sliding out of the wheelchair. Then she grabbed the side rails and pulled herself up, reached for the water glass, but it was empty. "Why? The Major said the farmers were keeping them. He told me they were fine. He said not to worry." She shook her head. "Why couldn't they stay with them for just a little while longer?" She stared at Mrs. Dummersdorf, tears streaming down her cheeks.

"Annemarie, I told you that the Munster's needed the room for Arnold and Rita. And Erika, the Schulz's' oldest daughter, had a baby and moved back home." She spread her hands, palms up. "They meant well, Annemarie. They are good folks, really. And Mrs. Munster told me it was just for a short time. They thought you'd be home sooner."

"I am sorry, Martha," she choked out. "This is all so overwhelming. I had no idea, no idea." Annemarie was sobbing so hard that the wheelchair rocked back and forth.

Mrs. Dummersdorf took her hand. "We are alive, and you know how kids are. They live day to day. They 've been playing with their old friends. I am doing the best I can, Annemarie. But I've reached the end of the rope. Since Bernhard came home, he needs me all the time. He has seizures day and night. I'm going to need the room the children are in, so he has a quiet place." She wrung her hands.

Annemarie nodded, dabbing her eyes.

"And it's getting cold out now. The children can't stay outside all day." She raised her arms and let them drop.

"Oh my God, no." Annemarie's voice was rising. "They can't be out all day. Inge catches colds and you don't want Anna to get pneumonia again."

Mrs. Dummersdorf took a couple of steps back. "And now, Inge has started wetting the bed. Not every night, but still, it's a real hardship, you know. I have to do everything by hand and then there's no electricity most of the time, so I have no hot water. It's all so hard, Annemarie. I wish I could tell you everything was wonderful."

Annemarie sighed and said more quietly, "I am so sorry about Bernhard, Martha. I hope once things are normal again, he can get some medical help." She bent towards her old friend and gazed into her eyes. "You have done so much for me. I don't know how I can ever make it up to you."

Mrs. Dummersdorf stared past Annemarie out the window, her face drained. Annemarie knew that this had been hard for her to say.

Martha turned back. "The problem isn't so much the children, Annemarie. They are good girls, and no trouble. It's everything else. It's every day the same fight, the worries to find something to eat and now, with winter almost here, I need coal, anything to keep the stove on at least part of the day. Bernhard can't walk around nights and climb on coal trains, so that leaves me. Everything is up to me." She shook her head and her shoulders slumped. "You know I'm a strong woman. I thought I could do it, but I'm wearing out." She took a long breath. "I do get some help from the Gellert's, you remember them? They live at

#75 on the fourth floor.   She used to be a seamstress, and he's a jack-of-all-trades. I always wondered what he really does-- you know what type of work. He can charm the pants off anybody, especially the women. He's good-looking, you know. Blond, wavy hair, well built." She smiled. "And there are hardly any men around anymore that aren't old or wounded or damaged goods, you know what I mean."

Annemarie gave a shaky laugh. She straightened herself. "You know Martha, we are survivors. We've made it this far. And I really do believe things will be normal again, someday, hopefully before I'm ninety-nine."

"God, I could really use a good cup of coffee now." Mrs. Dummersdorf lifted her face and stuck her nose in the air as though she was breathing the decadent aroma.

"I've got some water. Oh no, that's gone. How about some vanilla pudding? I didn't eat it at lunch." Annemarie held up the bowl.

"No, no, give that to the children." Mrs. Dummersdorf fiddled with her wedding ring. "Annemarie, we have to find a place for Anna and Inge. I have no choice. I hope you understand."

Annemarie sat twirling a strand of her hair, trying to get her thoughts together.

"Maybe we should try your sister Margarete again," Mrs. Dummersdorf went on. "This is an emergency. I'll tell her that you'll be home soon, maybe by Christmas. That's only six weeks from now. Surely, she could take them until then."

Annemarie leaned back and rubbed her neck. "I guess you can try her, what do we have to lose?"

"All right, I'll go there and take the children with me. I don't see how she could say no. But just in case-" Mrs. Dummersdorf raised her eyebrows- "just in case Mrs. Bowman gives us the high horse, what about your husband's parents? Don't they live in a small town on the Baltic Sea?"

"Oh, God, I'd hate it! I'd hate to ask them for anything." Annemarie raised her arms like a shield. "They never liked me."

"But Inge and Anna are their grandchildren, for God's sake, the only thing they have to remember Willie by, his own flesh and blood!" Mrs. Dummersdorf shouted, then quickly glanced around to see if anybody paid attention. "Surely they will care and do the right thing."

Annemarie sucked in a whistling breath through her teeth. "I guess it's worth a try. Maybe I'm wrong. Maybe they have changed. Perhaps Willie's death has mellowed them." She tried but could only muster a faint smile. "I've got to get out of here, back with the children. And it scares me that my parents are not doing well. They are probably starving. Oh, I could wring my sister's bejeweled neck. I think I will."

Mrs. Dummersdorf reached and patted Annemarie's hand. "Now, now. It'll all work out." She sat down on the side of Annemarie's bed. "I admit, I have been preoccupied with keeping Bernhard and the children alive, but I feel really bad that I have not visited your parents again. I promise, I'll go over there, maybe tomorrow. I will try to get them some food from Mrs. Gellert. You know she and her husband go out to the farms and barter things she sews."

"That sounds like a good idea, better than stealing food,"

"You know what he sells? Bras. He sells brassieres to the farmers' wives. They can't buy them anywhere, so Mrs. Gellert measures the ladies and goes home and sews the bras to order. And then he goes back on his bicycle and delivers them."

Annemarie winked at Martha. "I wonder what else Don Juan delivers to the farmers' wives."

"Well so far no farmer has gotten him with his pitchfork." They laughed. Annemarie pictured Mr. Gellert delivering a D bra. "I think one day his wife will kick his Asch. She's the jealous kind. I wonder if he makes the ladies try them on." Annemarie laughed so hard, that her ribs hurt.

Mrs. Dummersdorf picked up her purse and rose.

Annemarie glanced around the room. "Where are the children? Oh, my, look at that." Ellen, in her wheelchair, was taking Anna and Inge around the ward, stopping at each bed to visit.

Mrs. Dummersdorf cleared her throat. "Annemarie, we have to get back soon. The train situation has not improved much. And when we get to the station, we have a long walk home. I will visit your sister and Willie's parents, and I promise to check on your mother and father." She bent down and hugged her friend. "Things will get better. It can't get any worse. First, they bomb us and now they starve us. But like I said, things can only get better." She turned and called the children to her.

Annemarie opened her nightstand and pulled out a piece of paper and a pencil. She wrote down an address and leaned back trying to remember the house number. She handed the paper to Martha. "This is the address of Willie's parents. It just has to work out. Only one month, that's all I ask for. I'm sorry. I just feel so helpless." She wiped the tears that had started again.

The girls ran back up to them and Anna said, "Look, Mama, we got candy and a book, and the lady down there gave Inge a little stuffed bunny rabbit." Anna happily spread the gifts on the bed.

"How lovely," she said to Anna, "I hope you thanked the nice people. I have something for you too," Annemarie opened the drawer of her nightstand again and pulled out the hats she had knitted. "Here, the blue one is for you, Anna. And the pink and white hat is for Inge. Try them on. I want to see how you look."

"I like my hat. It's the best one I ever had." Anna leaned over and kissed her mother on the lips.

"Me too, the best hat I ever had," Inge repeated after her big sister, pulling her hat over her ears.

Annemarie took out the red hat she had knitted for Doc Hartmann and handed it to Mrs. Dummersdorf. "And this one is for you."

"Oh, how beautiful. I can really use a warm hat," she said, a big smile spreading over her face. "What a clever pompom. Thanks, Annemarie, thanks a lot. I will use this hat every day." She turned to the children. "Girls, give Mama another kiss and say goodbye. We have to hurry to catch the train."

Anna pressed her lips together as Annemarie put both arms around her and pulled her close, feeling the tension in her daughter's small body. "You are my big girl, Anna, so take good care of your sister." Her words turned to a whisper as she pressed her cheek to Anna's. She lifted Anna's head and saw the tears pooling in her eyes. She gave her another kiss. Forcing a smile, she bent and kissed Inge, who hung on to her knee, sobbing.

Mrs. Dummersdorf stood there, her arms hanging at her sides, her chest heaving.

Annemarie forced a smile as she held her children." Take all your gifts, girls, and do what Mrs. Dummersdorf tells you. I will be home and get you soon, perhaps by Christmas." She released them. "Thank you, Martha," she whispered, and pressed Mrs. Dummersdorf's arm.

Martha nodded with trembling lips. "I've got Willie's address in my purse." She opened her bag to double-check. "Auf wiedersehen, my dear friend."

Annemarie watched them walk down the aisle of the ward, Inge still sobbing, holding Martha's hand, and Anna marching straight ahead, never turning back.

I WILL DANCE AGAIN

Annemarie sat in her wheelchair, unable to cry any more.

CHAPTER 19
In the City

"Girls, change into clean clothes because we are going to visit your Aunt Margarete today," Mrs. Dummersdorf announced as she spread strawberry jam on slices of cornbread.

Anna jumped up, stuffing her piece into her mouth. "Oh, great, we can play with our cousins and their dolls."

Mrs. Dummersdorf shook her head, pulled a towel off the rack and wiped the table. "Go on now and get ready. It's a long walk."

Anna pretended to swoon. "Our cousins have so many dolls. I wish I could have just one of them. Inge, you remember when we were there for Renate's birthday?"

Inge shook her head.

"I can't wait. It will be so much fun." She walked her sister to the bedroom. "Come, I'll help you get dressed."

Anna picked the dress Rita had made and helped Inge into it, then led her back to the kitchen. "We are ready," she said, posing Inge in front of Mrs.Dummersdorf.

Mrs. Dummersdorf ran her hand over her chin. "Children, it's very cold outside. Go put on something warm. And, oh--" She pointed at Anna. "Let me see your hands. Maedchen, your hands are dirty. When did you last wash them?"

Anna and Inge stood there; eyes cast to the floor.

"You two need to bathe before we visit your aunt. Oh my God." Her face reddened. "You have not had a bath

164

since you've been here. What's the matter with me? I've been so busy with Bernhard." She raised her arms in a helpless gesture. "This can't go on. Something has to be done, I hope, today."

Inge wiped her hands on her dress, then held them, palms out. " Clean!"

Mrs. Dummerdorf had to laugh. "Oh, Inge, child, I guess you can't help it." She put her arms around the small figure. "I think there is some warm water left on the stove. Let's get you two undressed. I'll find some soap."

Anna stuck out her chin. "I am six years old. I can wash myself."

"No, I will wash you. This bar of soap is the last one we have."

Anna pouted, but Mrs. Dummersdorf did not pay attention. She poured warm water in a metal tub and set it on a chair in the middle of the kitchen.

Anna took off her clothes. "I'm cold," she complained, shivering as she wrapped her arms around her body.

"Oh, don't be such a sissy. Let's just hurry and get this over with." Mrs. Dummersdorf wiped Anna's face and swiftly rubbed her back and front with a wet cloth, leaving a small puddle around her feet.

"Here is a towel. Go dry off and put on something warm. Hurry, we haven't got all day."

Then she pulled Inge over to the tub and washed her, dipping the cloth into the water and dripping it down the child's scrawny body. "You are entirely too thin," she sighed. "I have to see if I can get hold of some cod liver oil."

Inge whimpered, shivering.

"Here." She wrapped a towel around her. "Let's find something warm for you too. I think I saw a sweater in your bag." She picked her up and carried her to the children's bedroom. "You are as light as a feather."

"I'm big and strong," Anna proclaimed, twirling around in the fancy dress with the big bow in the back. "Rita made this for me. I wore it to her wedding,"

"Anna, I told you it is cold, it's November. We have to walk forty-five minutes." She rummaged through a pile of clothing heaped on the chair and handed Anna a blue wool sweater and a pair of gray slacks.

"These are ugly." Anna threw the clothes back in the pile. "My cousins will laugh at me. These are boys' pants."

"Put them on and not another word from you. We have to leave in five minutes." After she got them into their coats and the hats Mama had knitted, she said, "You look very nice." She nodded approvingly. "Your cousins will be envious that they don't have pretty hats like these. Wait by the door. I have to tell Mr. Bernhard that I'm leaving."

She stuck her head into their bedroom while the girls waited by the apartment door."

"And you're going to do something about the children, right?" They heard Mr. Dummersdorf say.

"Yes, dear. I am going to talk to her and see if she can take them."

"What about their things?"

"Oh, we can take care of that later."

Anna whispered to Inge, "Did you hear that? Do you suppose she's going to leave us there?"

Inge shrugged.

Mrs. Dummersdorf came back to the door. The children looked at each other.

Mrs. Dummersdorf locked the door behind them, and they started down the three flights of stairs. An icy wind whipped through the streets. They walked past blocks of ruins with only one or two houses standing. Debris, twisted metal and rocks littered the sidewalk and they had to maneuver around large chunks of concrete.

Anna stopped. "I am cold. When are we going to be there? My legs are tired."

Inge stopped too, and sat down on a piece of concrete, pronouncing that she could not walk another step.

Mrs. Dummersdorf grabbed her by the arm and tried to pull her up. "Come along, Inge, we have to hurry."

Inge pounded her heels and screamed, "I want my mama. A group of women stopped and gawked. Mrs. Dummersdorf's face turned red. She glanced at the bystanders, picked up Inge and carried her. Anna had to run to keep up. Angry gusts slapped their faces. Anna shivered and dragged her feet.

"If you stop again, we will turn around and you will not play with your cousins," Mrs. Dummersdorf scolded.

So, Anna pulled her hat over her forehead and tried to keep pace as they hurried past the bystanders, who looked at Mrs. Dummersdorf with suspicion.

"How long do we have to --" Anna started.

"I don't want to hear another word from you until we arrive at Aunt Margarete's. Not one word," Mrs. Dummersdorf barked. She shifted Inge to her left hip, and they trudged on through the icy wind.

Finally, they reached the apartment house where Aunt Margarete lived. Unlike the dingy, dark hallway of their building, the foyer was spacious, blue and gold tiles gracing the walls, and marble steps led to the first floor. Anna examined the odd-shaped nameplate on the door. "*Captain Friedrich Bowman,*" she sounded out loud.

Mrs. Dummersdorf pointed to the plate. "That's an anchor. Your uncle Friedrich is a ship captain." She set Inge down and rang the doorbell. Anna listened in amazement as a choir of bells and chimes echoed through the hallway. She had never heard such a sound.

Finally, Aunt Margarete opened the door, her eyes widening in surprise. She did not say hello. "Take off your shoes," she said to the children, blocking their entry, "and don't touch anything. I don't want my oriental vases broken."

Anna removed her shoes. Inge scooted behind Mrs. Dummersdorf, trying to hide from that stern lady. Mrs. Dummersdorf bent and helped Inge out of her shoes.

Aunt Margarete beckoned them in and pointed to a big brass coat stand. "You can hang your things here."

Mrs. Dummersdorf extended her hand. "I am Martha Dummersdorf, a former neighbor of your sister Annemarie. I have visited her in the hospital, and she asked me to talk to you."

Two girls rushed down the hall, one of them hugging Anna in such a hurry that she almost lost her balance. "Anna, come let's go and play," Cousin Renate piped. She took Anna's hand and pulled her down the carpeted hallway into the girls' room. Inge and her younger cousin, Trina, followed, ignoring Aunt Margarete's scolding about the oriental china.

Anna sat down on the floor in Renate and Trina's room and looked at the dolls and stuffed animals that lined the shelves. A huge dollhouse took up one corner. It was three stories high, furnished with little tables, beds, a sofa, and windows that actually opened. "Let's play with that." She scooted over to the dollhouse. After they played for a while, Anna hugged her cousin. "Maybe we get to stay with you."

Renate hugged her back. "Then we can play together every day. You want to play dress up?"

Anna watched in wonder as Renate opened her closet and pulled out dresses, blouses and skirts. There were ten or maybe fifty dresses, blue, yellow, red and even a silver-colored one. Anna picked out a red dress. It fit her perfectly, and she pranced around the room, curtsying at imaginary onlookers, feeling like a princess.

"You can keep it," Renate offered. "I don't really like red. I've never worn that dress." She wrinkled her nose. Anna hugged her and kept the red dress on as they pulled out more clothes and spread them on the bed. Finally, Renate slipped into a silver taffeta dress. It was floor-length and shimmered in the light.

Inge came up and tugged her arm. "I am hungry."

"Let's go get something to eat," little cousin Trina said and led them across the hall to the kitchen. "We want a snack," she piped, looking at Aunt Margarete. The four girls slid around the bench in the breakfast nook by the window. Trina picked two bananas from the bowl on the table and handed one each to Anna and Inge.

Anna held hers to her nose and sniffed it. It was yellow with brown spots. She did not want to admit that she had never seen such a strange-looking fruit. Inge took a big bite of hers and spit it out, coughing, pieces of banana falling down her sweater.

Trina and Renate laughed and pointed. "You have to peel it first," said Trina. She showed Inge how. "Now take a bite."

Anna was glad she had waited and pretended that she knew what a banana was. She peeled hers now and tasted the delicious sweetness for the first time. Inge, close to tears, handed her the other banana.

"Oh, come on, Inge, it tastes good." Anna smiled.

"I was just about to have my mid-day coffee," Aunt Margarete said to Mrs. Dummersdorf, whom she had seated at the table in the middle of the kitchen a few feet from the girls in the breakfast nook. "Real Arabica coffee beans." She poured them into a coffee grinder and started cranking the handle. "My husband brings them when he comes home from his trips." She bent closer to inhale the aroma.

The sound of the grinder reminded Anna of playing with Oma's grinder, scaring her sister and waking Opa from his afternoon snooze. Anna smiled, thinking of Oma shushing her. Then Anna noticed the chairs covered with pretty blue-and-white checkered pillows that matched the kitchen curtains.

Mrs. Dummersdorf leaned towards Aunt Margarete. "How did you get your hair done? Most beauty parlors are gone or closed. Your hair looks beautiful." Anna stared at Aunt Margarete, who was taller than Mama. Her dark blonde hair looked like it had just been curled. Every strand, every curl lay in place like she was going somewhere nice. She wore a grey dress-up dress and white pearls. Mrs. Dummersdorf shook her head, looking amazed. Anna put down her banana peel and looked at Aunt Margarete some more.

Aunt Margarete turned to Mrs. Dummersdorf, who sat up straight and fluffed her hair. "My neighbor on the third floor fixes my hair once a week." She smiled, then cast her eyes regretfully down. "She used to own a beauty shop, but it is gone now. Hit by the last bombing raid just a few days before the war ended. What a shame. It was the best beauty shop around here. The Major's wife went there, and I saw a famous actress there once. What was her name?" Aunt Margarete wrinkled her brows trying to remember. "She played in both films and the theatre."

Mrs. Dummersdorf nodded absentmindedly and fidgeted with her beads.

"Her mother lives with her now," Margarete continued, "and she also supports her sister's family, who had to flee from Berlin. It is very crowded in her place. I don't know how she copes with it every day." She sighed. "I pay her with food-- cans of vegetables, flour, margarine, whatever I can spare." Margarete picked up the pot and started to make the coffee.

Anna and the other girls had started coloring pictures. "I like the princess. I'm going to color her dress red, like mine." She held up the paper.

"I want that picture," Inge shouted, reaching for the one Trina had. "I'm going to color the pretty flowers."

Aunt Margarete turned to them. "Children, keep quiet. Mrs. Dummersdorf and I are trying to talk." She glared at Anna, still in the red dress, then turned back to her coffee-making. Inge let go of Trina's picture and scooted close to Anna, scowling at Aunt Margarete's back.

Mrs. Dummersdorf held up her cup. "How lovely. I have never seen such beautifully decorated china." She turned the cup, admiring he pink roses and delicate stems.

"It's Rosenthal, the original pattern. My husband gave it to me on our wedding anniversary." Margarete carefully placed the coffee pot on the table. "I have a set of six cups and saucers and, of course, the creamer and sugar bowl." She handed the sugar to Mrs. Dummersdorf. "All those little roses are hand-painted."

"Nice. Very pretty." Mrs. Dummersdorf gingerly placed the bowl on the table. She straightened herself on her chair. "Uh, Mrs. Bowman, the reason I came today is that I, that-"

"Friedrich just brought me a bottle of Cognac, very good, French, of course," she interrupted. "I know you'll like it." She stepped over to the fancy, mahogany hutch, opened the side door and took out a bottle.

Mrs. Dummersdorf's mouth dropped open.

Anna stopped coloring and scooted to the edge of the bench to get a better look.

"This is my secret little liqueur cabinet. I like to enjoy a drink when I have company." Margarete giggled and brought two small glasses from the cabinet, filling them with the golden liquid.

Mrs. Dummersdorf picked up her glass and took a sip. "My friends won't believe me. Real coffee, a Rosenthal cup and now, real French Cognac." She put down her glass.

Aunt Margarete's mouth curved into a benevolent smile. "I am glad I can share. I know you are not used to this." She took sip of her own Cognac.

171

Anna had finished her picture and began squirming in her seat. She saw that Aunt Margarete had refilled their glasses and noticed that her cheeks were getting red.

Margarete went on about her husband's trips, mainly to the Far East, and that he was gone weeks at a time. "So, I am left to do everything here, run the household, take care of the children." She sighed. "It's all up to me." She picked up her glass again and drained it. "Drink up, we need a refill. Cognac tastes even better after the first or second glass." Margarete refilled their glasses.

Anna wondered if Aunt Margarete was a boozer like Mr. Kunkel. She put her hand on Inge's arm and moved closer to her.

"I really shouldn't, I haven't eaten much today, Mrs. Captain Bowman. It's been a long time since I had a drink." She pushed away the glass.

Margarete left for the pantry and returned with a metal tin, which she opened and held out to Mrs. Dummersdorf. "From England. They're very good. Take one."

Anna stopped coloring again and watched Mrs. Dummersdorf take a cookie.

"Oh, delicious," Mrs. Dummersdorf said, and crunched that cookie, then helped herself to another. Anna's mouth watered. Mrs. Dummersdorf pushed a strand of hair from her face and cleared her throat. "The reason I came today is, I went to visit Annemarie at the hospital." She drained the last of her coffee and licked a crumb off her thumb.

Margarete wrinkled her nose. "Yes, it I so sad. It is a horrible place, that hospital, so crowded. And it smells. It made me gag. I was afraid that I would catch something."

Mrs. Dummersdorf rose. "About the girls," she said behind her hand to Margarete, dropping her voice and glancing around at the children to see if they could hear.

Anna quickly looked away.

"I can't keep them any longer because my husband just returned from the front and..." she fluttered her fingers to show the seriousness of his condition and began pacing up and down.

"Mama, can we have some cocoa?" Renate piped up.

"Don't shout, Renate. That's impolite." Aunt Margarete waved at Mrs. Dummersdorf apologetically. "She knows better." She rose and fixed a pot of cocoa, the chocolate aroma filling the kitchen. At this, Mrs. Dummersdorf sighed and sat back down. Aunt Margarete took the steaming pot to the breakfast nook and filled a mug for each child.

Anna saw Mrs. Dummersdorf slide her hand into the cookie box and get a handful and slip them into her purse.

Aunt Margarete looked at Anna disapprovingly. "Be very careful so you don't spill on that dress. Those spots will not come out. And that is a new dress."

The cocoa tasted so good. Inge asked for more. Anna picked up the pot with both hands and filled Inge's mug. Inge swung her feet and bumped the table leg and some cocoa splashed on the wooden table.

"See, I knew you would spill," Aunt Margarete scolded. "Renate, get a rag and clean up the mess." Renate made a face and stuck out her tongue as she went to the sink. Anna covered her mouth, waiting for Aunt Margarete to shout like Mr. Kunkel always did. But Aunt Margarete went and sat back at the table, picked up her glass and drank more Cognac.

After they finished their cocoa, Inge leaned against Anna and dozed off, her thumb in her mouth. Anna watched her cousins color while she listened to Aunt Margarete talk about what her husband might bring back from his next trip.

Mrs. Dummersdorf drummed her fingers and glanced at her watch. "Oh my, I have to get back, my husband is waiting." They both stood up and she turned to Aunt Margarete and took a deep breath. "Annemarie has asked me to visit your parents and bring them some food," Anna heard her say. Mrs. Dummersdorf turned to the children. "Anna and Inge, go get your coats, I'll be right there."

Anna didn't move.

"Do you have any food you can spare, like bread, butter, flour, meat, anything to help them survive? They are starving, and too old to go out and barter."

Anna stared at Mrs. Dummersdorf. Barter. What was that?

Aunt Margarete went to the pantry and returned with a large paper bag, which she handed to Mrs. Dummersdorf. Then she turned around, her eyes fixed on Anna, still in the red princess dress. "You should not take things that don't belong to you."

"But Renate gave me this." Anna turned in a circle to show her aunt how pretty the dress fit her. She smiled at Aunt Margarete. "Red is my favorite color."

"Take that off at once and give it back." Aunt Margarete took two steps towards Anna, her face drawn into a fierce frown.

Cousin Renate came in from the kitchen and pulled Aunt Margarete's arm. "Mama, I want her to have it," she screamed. "I hate that dress. I will never wear it." She stuck out her lip and stomped her foot.

"Go to your room," her mother shouted, "and you, young lady, take off that dress at once." She glared at Anna again, her hands on her hips. "We don't steal in this house."

Anna ran over to Mrs. Dummersdorf and clung to her.

"Calm down, Margarete, she is only a child." Mrs. Dummersdorf stroked Anna's hair and helped her take off

174

the dress. She walked into the playroom, found Anna's clothes and helped her get dressed.

As they walked down the steps and reached the outside door, they heard Renate screaming, her mother shouting back, her voice echoing through the foyer.

"She gave me the dress. I swear I didn't steal it. I did not." Anna whispered through her tears. "And Renate has so many dresses, she doesn't need them all."

On their long walk home, Inge asked Mrs. Dummersdorf if she could have hot chocolate when they got back to the apartment.

"Child, I don't have any cocoa," Mrs. Dummersdorf said. She stopped and opened her bag and handed each of them a cookie.

"Are these from Aunt Margarete?" Anna asked, grinning. I saw what you did."

"Yes, Anna, you caught me." Mrs. Dummersdorf dropped her head in pretend guilt. "I stole them."

Anna giggled again and bit into the cookie.

A cold November wind surged through the deserted streets whistling through the ruins. Mrs. Dummersdorf pulled up her collar. "God. It's getting cold. What are we going to do this winter? Hurry, children. We need to get home before dark." She glanced around as though expecting ghosts to appear from the ruins.

"Can we visit Aunt Margarete again?" Inge asked. "I want more hot chocolate."

"Perhaps when your mama is home you can visit again," Mrs. Dummersdorf answered, rolling her eyes towards Anna, who shook her head in disapproval.

"Aunt Margarete is mean," Anna mumbled, "I'm never going back to visit her. Never, never." She walked briskly, taking big steps, holding her head down against the wind.

When they arrived back at the apartment, Anna heard Mrs. Dummersdorf tell Mr. Bernhard that she was so

175

mad she could choke Mrs. Bowman, that cold, heartless witch. She shouted that she would never go back there even if she had to starve to death. Anna didn't want to listen anymore and went to their room, taking Inge with her. Inge sighed and crawled up onto the bed and was asleep immediately. But Anna stayed by the door and continued to listen. Mrs. Dummersdorf talked so loudly that she could hear every word. "I had to shame her into giving me food for her own mother and father, Bernhard," she shouted.

"Calm down, Martha. You don't have to go back there," Mr. Bernhard said his voice soft and dark. "So, what about the children?"

"You should have seen her liqueur cabinet," Mrs. Dummersdorf went on. "We drank French Cognac. It's not fair. I don't know what to do."

"You are getting too upset, Martha. But about these children, they are not ours. We have to think of our own family. This can't go on. They have to go. We have done enough."

Anna gasped and covered her mouth. She slid down the bedroom wall and crouched on the floor, her eyes filled with tears.

"Of course, *she* wouldn't take them, that selfish witch," Mrs. Dummersdorf went on. And Anna wondered if Aunt Margarete was really a witch.

CHAPTER 20

"Burr." Anna pulled the blanket back over her head and cuddled up to her sister. "It's cold in here. I'm not getting up today."

"Girls! I've called you twice now." Mrs. Dummersdorf's voice boomed over them as she pulled the covers off with a swift tug. "Get dressed. We are going to the Baltic Sea to visit your grandparents." She turned towards the door. "So, hurry up or we'll miss the train."

"But we don't need to take the train. "Anna climbed out of bed, shivering, and searched for her clothes.

"Put on something warm," she heard Mrs. Dummersdorf holler. "The wind will really be blowing at the ocean."

"Hurry, Inge, we're going to see the ocean," Anna said, confused as she scrambled into her wool sweater and trousers. When they were both dressed, they hurried to the kitchen. Grandparents? The ocean? She stared at Mrs. Dummersdorf across the table.

Inge frowned at the cornbread on her plate and pushed it away.

"Try a bite, Inge," Mrs. Dummersdorf encouraged. "I spread strawberry jelly on it, the jelly Mrs. Gellert got from the farmers. You liked it, remember?" She pushed the plate back in front of the child.

Reluctantly Inge picked up the bread and took a bite.

"We don't need to take a train. Our grandparents live here, down the street," Anna repeated, licking jam off her lips.

Mr. Bernhard, who had joined them for breakfast, looked up. "You are a smart girl, Anna. But these are your other grandparents, your father's parents. They live up North near the Baltic Sea."

Anna turned to him. "My father, does he live there too?"

"No, he's gone in the war," Mrs. Dummersdorf answered and started to clear the table. "But now we need to hurry to catch the train, so get on your coats and hats."

"What's the Baltic Sea?" Inge asked.

"It's a big ocean up north." Mr. Bernhard spread his arms to show how big it was. "There are lots of ships there in the harbor. They catch the fish for us." He stood and walked towards the hall, patting Inge on the head as he passed.

Anna wanted to ask him more about the ships and the fish, but it was too late.

"I'll see you later, dear," he called to his wife and waved at the children. "I sure hope they'll keep them. That sea air will be good for them, and they'll get plenty of food." He winked at Anna.

"I will be back as soon as I can." Mrs. Dummersdorf kissed him on the neck. Then she went to get their coats and hats from the rack, handed Anna hers, and helped Inge into her sleeves.

It was a blustery December day. Anna did not see any of her friends. It was too cold to play outside. They hurried down the street, turning left on Osterstreet, the road leading to the train station. Inge whined and Anna pulled the hat over her sister's ears.

Half an hour later, they arrived at the station just as the train's whistle blew and it had started to slowly pull away. Mrs. Dummersdorf heaved, trying to catch her breath after she had jumped on the platform, pulling both children into the compartment, which was already bursting with people. "Damn," she said under her breath. There were no empty seats in this compartment. People carrying sacks and large backpacks filled the entranceway. Mrs. Dummersdorf edged in between them, pulling the girls with her. They ended up wedged against the window.

Anna coughed, holding her sleeve over her mouth. "Pheu, I can't breathe." She wheezed and leaned against Mrs. Dummersdorf, who was holding Inge's hand. "I want to sit down," she whined, shivering in the drafty train, the damp, clammy air making it seem colder than it actually was. The faint smell of cabbage and unwashed bodies covered everyone like a blanket.

"There are no empty seats, girl. Hang onto your sister and lean against me." Mrs. Dummersdorf put her arm around Anna and glanced at the woman beside them. Stuffed into the walkway like sardines in a barrel, they swayed with the rhythm of the train.

Anna pushed herself free of the woman's bulky coat sleeve and peered up at Mrs. Dummersdorf. "Can we go swimming in the Baltic Sea?"

Mrs. Dummersdorf shook her head and managed a smile. "It's winter, Anna. It's way too cold."

"I don't want to go if we can't swim," Anna grumbled.

Mrs. Dummersdorf ignored Anna's complaint.

After an hour, the train made a stop in a small station, where most people got off. Mrs. Dummersdorf pushed open a compartment door and spotted an empty bench. Anna slid onto the seat next to the window. "Look, cows." She wiped the condensation off the glass. "They look just like the cows on Karl's farm." She pressed her face against the window. "I wish we could go back to the farm. I want to see Gertl and Rita, and the baby, oh, and poor Yanka, too." Tears began leaking from her eyes.

179

"Shhh." Mrs.Dummersdorf pointed to Inge, who had fallen asleep. "We'll be there soon," she said softly and put her arm around Anna.

When the train pulled into the next depot, Mrs. Dummersdorf picked up Inge and carried her down the narrow metal steps to the platform. They climbed out and Anna looked around for the ocean but did not see it anywhere. They walked down streets covered with round stones. "These are cobblestones," Mrs. Dummersdorf explained. "That's how they used to build streets in the Middle Ages."

Anna sniffed. "It smells fishy." She braced against the stiff sea breeze tugging at her coat.

"We are close to the ocean. You will see it soon." Mrs. Dummersdorf searched her bag and came up with a piece of paper.

"What's that?" Anna asked.

"That's the address of your grandparents' house."

They walked through narrow streets lined with small houses, many with painted shutters, some looking like gingerbread houses. Anna stumbled as she gawked around. There were no ruins, no rubble. "Look at all the pretty houses, Inge. They look like Cousin Renate's dollhouse."

"Yes, they are pretty." Mrs. Dummersdorf said. "The planes didn't bomb towns up here." She stopped in front of a small brick house with white shutters and three stone steps leading to a big brown oak door with a black iron number eight in the center panel. She checked the address on the paper. "Here it is. This is the house." They climbed the steps and Mrs. Dummersdorf knocked on the door. Anna jumped up and down, excited to meet her new grandparents, but Inge clung to Mrs. Dummersdorf's hand, her big eyes filled with fear.

A tall, blonde woman opened the door. She had freckles all over her face and greeted them with a big smile. Anna smiled back and curtsied.

Mrs. Dummersdorf extended her hand and introduced herself. "These are Willie and Annemarie's children and they have come to visit their grandparents."

The woman smiled down at Anna and Inge. "I'm your father's sister, your aunt Regine. Please come in." She stood aside and invited them into the hallway. They followed her through the narrow hall into a formal living room crowded with furniture. The girls sat down on a plum-colored, overstuffed sofa, and Mrs. Dummersdorf perched on a nearby chair. Anna let her fingers glide over the delicate crocheted doilies on the side arms and inhaled the rich aroma of the furniture polish.

A tall, thin woman in a black dress with a white collar entered and Mrs. Dummersdorf rose quickly. They shook hands. "I am Willie's mother," the woman said, her voice dry and without emotion. Her gray hair was pulled on top of her head in a small bun, her pale face dominated by a large, bony nose, steel-gray eyes and thin lips that barely moved when she spoke.

Anna stared at her. She looked nothing like her Oma back in the city.

"My name is Martha Dummersdorf and I am an old neighbor of Annemarie's. This is Anna.
Anna, get up and greet your grandmother."

Anna stood, smiled, and curtsied. Beside her, Inge tugged on Anna's sleeve. Anna glanced down. "Oh, and this is my little sister, Inge."

The tall lady looked at her with piercing grey eyes.

Mrs. Dummersdorf turned to Inge. "Go say hello to your grandmother."

The little girl trembled before the stern-faced lady in the black dress and didn't budge.

Mrs. Dummersdorf placed her arm around Inge. "She's only four, and a bit shy. They've been through a lot since Annemarie got bombed out and wounded." She paused and looked inquiringly at Mrs. Peterman.

"Would you like a cup of tea?" this strange grandmother asked, and called, "Regine, make some tea for us."

A little red-headed boy peered through the doorway then disappeared. "That's Willie, Regine's youngest." The woman smiled briefly. "And he has a sister, Ursula, who is eight."

Mrs. Dummersdorf folded and unfolded her hands. "Perhaps the children can go and play, Mrs. Peterman. I need to talk with you and give you a message from Annemarie." But Anna and Inge made no move to leave.

Presently, Regine arrived with a tray of blue and white cups, a round, full-bellied teapot and a glass bowl filled with cookies.

"I'm hungry," Inge whispered, eyeing the cookies.

The tall lady frowned. "Go fix something to eat for these children, Regine, and then find Ursula and Willie and ask them to play with their cousins."

Anna was glad to leave with Aunt Regine. Inge held onto her hand and whispered, "Grandmother looks mean."

"Be quiet," Anna shushed, quickly pulling her sister out of the room. They followed Regine into the kitchen, a large, warm room with painted ships on the wallpaper.

Anna noticed a steaming pot on the stove. "Is that molasses?" She licked her lips.

Regine laughed. "No, this is hot water. We don't have molasses, Anna, but we have honey. What would you like to eat?"

"Scrambled eggs." The words popped out of Anna's mouth before she could even think.

"Good. Let's find Ursula and Willie and you can eat lunch together."

They followed Regine up a flight of narrow stairs and found Ursula in her room sitting on the floor, surrounded by her dolls. The red-headed boy was in the corner drawing on the fogged window with his finger.

"This is Anna and her sister Inge." Regine put her arms around the girls. "They are your cousins."

"Are not," said the boy.

Anna cocked her head. "Are too."

Regine laughed a little. "Ah, now, Willie, be nice."

Anna turned her attention back to Ursula. She had freckles just like her mother and Anna liked her right away, especially when she handed her a baby doll.

"First, I want you all to come down and eat lunch," Regine said. "Then you can play." She kissed Ursula and smiled at the girls. They followed her downstairs to the kitchen, trailed by the boy.

Anna ate three slices of crunchy bread with piles of scrambled eggs and hot milk with honey. "This is so good, I never have enough to eat at Mrs. Dummersdorf's place in the city."

Regine patted her on the cheek. "You can eat as much as you want here, Anna."

"Can we have hot cocoa?" Inge asked.

"Yes, cocoa," the boy chimed in.

"Oh yes, cocoa. I wish we had cocoa, it's my favorite." Aunt Regine patted Inge on the head. "We have not had cocoa in a long time. How about more hot milk with honey? And later you can have pudding. I made it this morning."

Anna hugged her. "I like you." She snuggled her head into Regine's bosom.

Cousin Ursula pulled Anna away. "Come along. Let's go upstairs and play now." They scampered up the steps, leaving the boy to his own devices.

Upstairs, Anna studied her cousin. "Is this your room?" She could not believe that a child could be so lucky. It was huge, with white paneling all around the walls, bunk beds on one side and pink curtains on the window. A colorful braided carpet covered the center of the room. Anna admired the large, almost life-size doll house. It looked like a real house, even nicer than cousin Renate's doll house. "This is so pretty. I have never seen one this beautiful."

"Grandpa built if for me for my birthday last year." She scooted on her knees and opened the door of the doll house. "You can climb in, see?" She waved from the front window of the doll house. "Let's play with my dolls now." Ursula opened the roof and handed Anna and Inge each a doll.

Anna looked at the baby doll admiringly. "How many dolls do you have?"

"Five. Three baby dolls and these two, Lola and Maria. They are older and I like to dress them up. But I think they need a nap before we can dress them."

They had just undressed their dolls and put them to bed when an old man appeared in the doorway. Ursula pulled him into the room. "Grandpa, come play with us."

He smiled, "Who of you ladies is Anna and which one is Inge?"

Anna stood up and curtsied. "I'm Anna." She pointed at her sister. "And that is my little sister, Inge."

"Ah, you are Willie's children. How wonderful, pleased to meet you, I'm your grandpa." The old man shook hands and gave them each a piece of candy. He was tall like his wife, with a round belly, and his eyes sparkled. He had a bushy white mustache like St. Nick.

Anna liked her new grandpa. He sat down on the floor with them, and they played with a set of wooden farm animals he had carved for Regine's children.

Then Anna said," I want to see the ocean."

"Sure," he replied, "but it's too cold to be out by the water for long."

Anna jumped up, hugged and kissed him and tugged on his arm. "Let's go now, please."

"Just like your father. He loved the water," Grandpa murmured. The children rushed downstairs, Grandpa in tow, slipped on their coats, jumped off the steps and started down the cobblestone street, which sloped towards the sea.

"There's the ocean, see. There's the Baltic," Grandpa said as they got closer to the gray, churning water. "Your father loved the water. He was a captain on a ship." His voice had turned shaky.

Anna hung on his every word. Her father was a sea captain. She hopped and skipped down the street, trying to land on the largest cobblestone. The street ended at an embankment of rocks and the children climbed down some wooden planks and ran on to the beach towards the water.

"The beach is usually much wider, but the tide is coming in," Grandpa explained. "In summertime you can go swimming every day. And over there is the harbor, where the fishermen have their boats and go out and catch fish."

"Did my father catch fish?" Anna took his hand and swung their clasped hands back and forth.

The old man chuckled. "Oh yes, he caught lots of fish."

"And eels too," Ursula bragged. "They are like snakes. And we put them in a bucket and smoke them. They are yummy." She laughed and ran over to the dock and the girls followed her, forgetting all about the cold wind.

Anna gazed at a group of boats anchored in the protective cove of a small harbor. "Look at all the ships." The boats bobbed up and down with the constant splashing of the waves. "I want to go out on a boat," she hollered, "just like my father."

Her grandpa walked up behind her and she turned around and hugged him. "You come and visit us next summer," he said, "and we'll take you out on a boat."

"Maybe my father can go with us when he gets back." She looked at him wide-eyed. "Will my father be home by then?"

Grandpa stared at the sea and did not answer.

Inge came close then, licking her lips. "My tongue tastes salty."

"The salt air from the ocean does that," Cousin Ursula explained. "In the summer your whole body gets salty."

"We'd better get back. Your grandma will get mad at me for keeping you out so long in this weather." Grandpa pulled his gaze away from the water and looked down at them. He took Inge's hand and hurried up the street, back to the house.

Grandmother stood in the doorway, hands on her hips. "Where have you been, Richard? Mrs. Dummersdorf has to leave immediately, or she will miss the last train."

Anna froze in place. Grandmother was very angry. She grabbed Grandpa's hand and held on to it.

"So, why can't they stay and leave tomorrow?" he said, following her into the house, trailed by the three girls. He sat down and began taking off his boots.

"Well, that's nonsense, we don't have room for that many people," she said, raising her voice just like Mrs. Kunkel. Mrs. Dummersdorf had stepped out of the living room and they all stood crowded in the small, dimly lit hallway.

"Why can't they stay for a few days?" The old man asked. "They're so thin and pale. For God's sake, Irma, they're Willie's kids, his flesh and blood."

Anna looked at one, then the other.

Grandmother's voice cracked. "I say they're too much work and we don't have room." She pulled Anna

186

over to her and put her hand under her chin. "This one at least looks like him." She let go of Anna. "Maybe we could keep her."

"Irma, really now, I don't think you should --"

"Richard, I don't appreciate your comments," She pointed at Inge. "And that one, she doesn't even look like him."

Inge ran over to Mrs. Dummersdorf and grabbed her hand, "I want my mama," she sobbed and buried her face in Mrs. Dummersdorf's coat.

"Who knows?" Grandmother went on. "City women slept with many of those Nazis. City trash, that's what she is. I really don't know what Willie saw in her, I really don't."

"Girls, get your coats, we have to leave right now." Mrs. Dummersdorf's voice was grim. "Hurry, we have to run to catch the train." She turned and walked to the door, pulling Inge behind her. Anna ran after them. She didn't want to be left behind with her grandmother.

Grandpa stood on the front steps and waved. "You come back and visit us in the summer."

Aunt Regina, came out on the porch, and waved too, and Cousin Ursula shouted, "I'll show you how to catch eels."

Mrs. Dummersdorf walked so fast that Inge stumbled and was dragged along. Anna had to run to keep up. "Why was Grandma so angry?" she asked, trying to catch her breath.

"She is an old, bitter woman," Mrs. Dummersdorf replied. "Don't talk now, Anna, I get out of breath walking so fast."

"I like Grandpa, he's nice. He took us to the beach and gave us candy," Anna said. "He told us that my father is a fisherman, a sea captain and he catch lots of eels." But Mrs. Dummersdorf did not reply.

Soon they heard the train's horn blast, and they ran up to the platform. All the seats were taken by then and Mrs. Dummersdorf leaned against the walkway.

"Girls, sit on the floor by my feet. It will be a long ride to the city."

"My father is a sea captain. He has a fishing boat," Anna announced in a loud voice. But no one paid attention, and soon she fell asleep like her sister, tired from the fresh sea air and lulled by the monotonous rocking of the train.

CHAPTER 21
Beversen Regional Hospital

A doctor approached Annemarie's bed. She sat up straight, determined to get an answer about her release.

"Dr. Kronert," he barked, introducing himself without looking up from his chart. He pulled away the sheets, lifted her gown to look at the leg. "How'd that happen?" he asked, probing the partially healed wound in her right thigh. He unbandaged her thigh, which looked look like a big, rugged crater.

"Ouch." She cringed, "I was evacuated to a village near the city and the planes came and bombed the farmhouse," Annemarie explained. "It's a miracle that I was able to get out. I had to go down a lot of stairs and --"

"Wounded civilian," he interrupted, squeezing at the wound. She flinched. "Healing. You are one of the lucky ones. Many didn't make it." Finally, he looked at her face. "I've been at the front. There wasn't much left of most of 'em to fix."

She grabbed his arm but quickly withdrew her hand. "My fiancé is in the Ardennes. I have not heard from him since last December." She smiled nervously. "He should be home by now, but I guess it can take time."

"Not many left of those boys." He moved on to examine her foot. "They were outnumbered, sitting ducks in those trenches."

Annemarie raised her head, alarmed. "What do you mean, sitting ducks?" she asked as he removed the bandage from her foot.

189

He looked up briefly. "Superior air power. Nobody gets out from that alive." He busied himself with her wound, ignoring Annemarie who dabbed her eyes and began to sob silently.

"Can you feel this?" He poked various places around the wound. She grimaced and nodded.

He stood up straight and called over a nurse to replace the bandage.

Annemarie mustered all her courage. "When can I go home, doctor? I must get there by Christmas." She held her breath, her throat closing up.

"Not doable. Doesn't look good. Leg might have to come off."

She was shocked by his abruptness as he moved on to the next patient. She turned to the nurse who was bandaging her foot. "How rude and nasty of him. What have I ever done to that man?"

"He's military, an army doctor from the front. Guess they've seen so much, they get hardened. He's really not a bad man and is a very good doctor."

"I promised my children that I would be home for Christmas. They are waiting for me. A neighbor took them, but she can't keep them very long."

The nurse touched her on the arm. "Yes, it's not easy these days. Lots of children don't have parents left. Many died in the firebombing. Just be brave, it'll get better." She smiled and pulled the sheet and blanket over Annemarie's legs.

Annemarie's neighbor, Ellen, sat up and turned towards her. "She's right, at least your children have you and they know you'll be home soon," she said in a soft voice. "I will pray for you."

Annemarie pressed her lips tightly. "I'm not going to let them cut off my leg, absolutely not." She slapped her thigh and winced. "I just have to work harder with those crutches." She sank back into her pillow and crossed her arms over her chest. *They threw bombs at him, the doctor said. Just like they did at me.* The thought of Alfred languishing in a trench, wounded or even dead, was too much. She shuddered and pulled the blanket over her face.

Later that day she took Alfred's letter out of the drawer, hoping to seek comfort from his sweet words. But now, reading it again did not console her. Instead, his description of the hellish front, of being shipped out from where few returned-- those words seemed laden with doom. She wanted to find out more about the battles Dr. Kronert had mentioned but could not bring herself to ask.

The drizzly December day dragged her down even more. For the first time, she felt hopeless.

She fell into a restless sleep, with fleeting dreams of Alfred standing on that hill calling for her. And every time, as hard as she tried, she could not reach him.

She felt the blanket being moved off her face. "Wake up, Annemarie, you have a letter."

"A letter?" Annemarie opened her eyes and raised her head off the pillow.

There was Ellen, in her wheelchair, holding out an envelope. "Yes, a letter. A nurse's aide brought it in a little while ago, but you were asleep." A warm smile spread over her face. "Open it. Maybe you have some good news."

Annemarie smoothed her hair and took the letter. There was no return address. Her heart started to pound as she gingerly opened the envelope and pulled out several pieces of paper.

Dear Annemarie:

She knew immediately that it was not from Alfred. The writing was like someone had scribbled in a hurry, using a pencil, the words spread over the page in disarray. She lifted the last sheet. It was signed *Martha Dummersdorf,* dated a week ago. She waved it at Ellen. "It's from Mrs. Dummersdorf, my neighbor who has my children." She tried to smile but her lips quivered.

191

Dear Annemarie:

Sorry that I can't come myself, but Bernhard is sicker and has more and more seizures. I can't leave him alone. I hope you are *better and can come home soon. Inge and Anna really need you and they are excited about seeing you at Christmas. There isn't much here to be excited about. Cold, no coal or firewood, not enough food, and now rationing, which is a joke, since there isn't any food to be had even with the food stamps. It's a real fight to fill up the belly every day.*

Oh, there is food on the black market, but only if you've got something to sell that those shysters will take. The police are powerless and even the Allies can't tackle the black market. We did get some potatoes the other day, but those came from Mrs. Gellert. I told you they go to the farms, and she sews bras for the women, right? God, I never knew potatoes could be so delicious.

A smile crossed Annemarie's face. Potatoes, a delicacy. She shook her head, sighed and read on about the food shortages and the people who didn't have anything to sell or barter, starving, especially the elderly.

Annemarie put down the letter and took a deep breath. What about her parents? Was Mrs. Dummersdorf able to get food to them? Did she have enough food for her children? She stared out of the window and felt as gray and desolate as the winter day. She picked up the letter and resumed reading, hoping some good news was buried in the dismal report.

And now it's getting colder every day. Electricity and gas are rationed, and we have to make sure we don't use more than our allocation, or they will cut it off.

We do not heat our place unless it gets below minus ten, so we are cold all the time.

Coal is hard to come by. People go to the parks at night and cut down the trees and even the bushes. Can you imagine that? At least we're alive and have a roof over our head, and with the help of the Gellert's we have one meal most days. I visited your sister with the children, and they had a good time playing with their cousins. But, that woman, your sister, is inconsiderate, heartless, selfish. It's unbelievable. We had real coffee, English cookies, even French Cognac. She showed me all the food items she gets from her husband's shipping company. But I had to virtually shame her into giving me food for your parents. I wanted to strangle that woman. And she wouldn't keep Anna and Inge. I tried to explain to her. How, tell me, would taking in two small children for a month ruin her marriage? Her husband is gone for months. He isn't even there right now. And she accused Anna of stealing her daughter's dress.

I'm at my wit's end with Mrs. Friedrich Bowman. I'm not planning to see her ever again. It's too hard on my blood pressure.

As Annemarie read those words and thought of poor Anna, a tear dropped on the page and smudged the letters *Mrs. Friedrich Bowman.*

Just then Ellen's mother stopped in for a visit. She was a bubbly, gray-haired woman and she greeted Annemarie like she was her own daughter. "I am so glad that you and Ellen ended up in the same ward. Ellen talks about you all the time." She looked over at Annemarie.

"You don't look good today."

Annemarie waved the letter.

"Not much good news, I take it. Well, I brought some goodies. You know Ellen's sister is married to a farmer. Oh, did we try to discourage her then, and now it's a godsend."

She looked around the room and returned with a cart on wheels. "Here we go." She opened the large paper bag. "Bread, ham, butter, and - ah, a can of pears." She dug in her purse. "Here it is. I was worried that I'd forgotten the can opener. My sister cans fruits and vegetables. They are delicious. I don't know where she learned that, since we grew up in the city." She walked over to Annemarie's bed. "Come on, put away that letter for now and join us."

"Oh, look, here is a can of pickled herring, your favorite, Annemarie." Ellen waved the can at her.

This is like being with Lisbeth, Annemarie thought, and said, "I had a friend, a nurse at the field hospital, and we had picnics together. I really miss her." She gazed at them sadly. "I wonder where she is now."

"Well, they are short of nurses, so I'm sure she works at another hospital somewhere." Ellen's mother opened the can of herring and handed it to Annemarie.

"I have only three forks, so that'll have to do. I wanted to bring eggs, but they are hard to carry and fix, and I don't have coffee either. But I brought some tea. Is there a place where I can get hot water?"

"I think they have a hotplate in the nurses' lounge, and they might let you use it. "

Ellen's mother left for the nurses' lounge and returned with a pot of hot water and three cups. "Ellen will be home by Christmas. They told me that she'll be discharged on the twenty first of December." She looked at Annemarie. "What about you?"

"I'm hoping to be out of here by Christmas too, but the doctor has not agreed to that." A faint smile crossed her face. "I'm working on it. I'm an optimist. I told my children that I'll be there. And when you make a promise to your children, you'd better keep it."

"Well, that's great. We should have Champagne to make a toast." Ellen's mother raised her tea, and they clicked their cups together and cheered.

"To all of us. Home for Christmas," Ellen toasted, and they sipped their tea.

Annemarie was quiet as Ellen and her mother talked and made plans. Then she said, "Thank you so much for the picnic." She smiled and wheeled herself back to her bed.

I WILL DANCE AGAIN

She was anxious to find out what else Mrs. Dummersdorf had to report. She picked up the letter again.

Well, Walter Mueller came through again and got me three tickets for the train to Heiligenburg to visit Willie's parents. So, Inge, Anna and I took the train up there. What a charming little town. It looks like the war has passed it by. Willie's parents have a nice house. Willie's sister Regine is nice. And then I met Willie's mother. My God, Annemarie, she never smiled once the entire time we were there.

Annemarie shook her head and clenched her fist as she read Martha's words. Martha was an angel, trying to help, and she owed her friend a lot. She stretched, took a deep breath, and read on.

"She even claimed that Inge was not Willie's child. I was speechless and told the children to put on their coats, grabbed Inge and Anna and we left and ran to the station.

Annemarie took a handkerchief from her nightstand and mopped her face. More words were getting smudged on Martha's letter.

I have to hurry to get this letter to the post office today.

I'm at my wit's end, Annemarie. I need to put Bernhard in a separate room where he has quiet and can recover. And Inge's bed-wetting is getting worse. I don't know what to do, not let her drink at night, scold her, ask her, I don't know. Maybe she has something wrong with her bladder?

Here is what I did. I talked with Mrs. Gellert. You remember her. She lives two houses over from me. I told her that you would be home by Christmas. So, Inge and Anna are going to the Gellerts' now. They will have plenty of food there because of the bartering with the farmers. They only have a small apartment, so the girls have to sleep in a little attic room. You remember they live on the fourth floor? But for a short time, I think it will work.

Oh, before I mailed this letter, I visited your parents and brought them the food your sister gave me. Your mother told me that your father has died. Neighbors found him collapsed on the sidewalk. He had a stroke. I'm sorry, Annemarie. And your mother is not well. She is coughing a lot and I wonder if she has pneumonia. She asked about you, and I told her that you were coming home for Christmas. I wish I had coal for her, but we don't have enough either.

Write me, please. I will ask the Gellerts for some food for you. I assume you plan to live with your mother? It'll be your best bet, as there are no apartments to be had.

The Allies have confiscated a lot of the nicer ones, kicking more people out on the streets.

I guess they think that's what we deserve. I hope to hear from you soon.

Your friend
Martha Dummersdorf

CHAPTER 22
City of Hamburg

"The Gellert's live only two houses down the street, so you can carry these," Mrs. Dummersdorf said, and handed Anna her white suitcase and a large paper sack. "You're a big girl. I know you can do it." She herded them down the stairs and out the front door. "It's never this cold in December. In fact, I can't remember it being this cold ever," she lamented, pulling Inge's hat over her ears.

Anna looked up at Mrs. Dummersdorf and smiled, hoping it would cheer her up. But Inge was sobbing under her woolen hat, which almost covered her eyes. "Don't cry, Inge, Mama will get us at Christmas," she whispered. Inge pressed her lips together, trying not to cry. The three of them started walking down the deserted street. Anna did not see any of her playmates. Mrs. Dummersdorf huffed and puffed, carrying the large bag with Inge's belongings, a blanket and two pillows, which Mrs. Gellert had asked her to bring.

After they climbed up three flights of stairs, Inge sat down on the landing, panting and clasping her doll Pepita to her chest.

"Only one more flight. See?" Mrs. Dummersdorf pointed upward. The hall lights did not work, but some light filtered down from the attic windows, so they could see to climb the steps.

Anna pulled her sister up by the arm. "Let's go. It's cold out here and I'm hungry."

They heard the sound of a radio. A door opened at the fourth-floor landing and Mrs. Gellert called, "I've got breakfast ready." When they reached her door, she ushered them inside. She patted Inge on the head and took Anna's suitcase. "You can hang your coats here in the hall on these hooks that Emil made for my girls when they were your age. Let me show you where you will be sleeping."

The girls and Mrs. Dummersdorf followed her to a room at the end of the apartment   hallway. Anna squinted and looked around. The room had slanted ceilings, making it look even smaller than it was. There were no windows.

"When my girls lived here with us, they used this room as their secret hideaway," Mrs. Gellert explained cheerfully. "If we don't have electricity, which is quite often nowadays, it gets dark in here so you can leave the door open." She placed the suitcase and bags on the single bed next to the wall. "You can unpack after breakfast. There isn't much room, but you can put your things on those shelves." She pointed at the slanted wall. "It'll only be for a couple of weeks at the most, right?" She looked at Mrs. Dummersdorf, who gazed off to the other end of the room. "All right. Let's have breakfast now." They followed her to the kitchen.

The kitchen, the only heated room in the apartment, smelled like fried potatoes, reminding Anna of the Munster farm kitchen. Mrs. Gellert settled the girls around a rectangular white table laden with bread, butter, ham, cheese, two jars of jam and a tall glass of milk for each of them. Anna could hardly wait to eat. Her stomach was growling so loud that it sounded like there was a dog in there.

"Well, I have to get back home. All of you come visit me." Mrs. Dummersdorf kissed each girl on the cheek, waved at Mrs. Gellert and turned to the door.

"Wait, take this for Bernhard." Mrs. Gellert handed her a sausage. "See you later."

Anna and Inge sat looking at the table, unsure what to do next.

"Help yourselves, girls." Mrs. Gellert placed thick slices of white bread on their plates. "Here is some butter and jam, and we have sausage and cheese, too."

"Molasses!" Anna screeched, dipping her spoon into a brown earthen pot.

"Yes, molasses, we get it from the farmers. You like it?"

"It's my favorite." Anna ladled a glob onto her bread. "And scrambled eggs."

"I like scrambled eggs too. We don't have eggs right now, but we hope we can get some in a few days when Emil makes another trip to the farms."

After they'd eaten, Mrs. Gellert left the kitchen, and Anna jumped up and opened the cabinets. She saw several jars and cans and some items she did not recognize, plus two loaves of bread that smelled so good that she got hungry all over again. She could not believe how much food the Gellert's had in their pantry.

Then Inge got up and tugged on Anna's sleeve. "Let's go out and play."

Mrs. Gellert returned to the kitchen carrying a stack of dish towels.

"You have a lot of food." Anna smiled at her. "What is that?" She pointed at a big glass jar sitting beside the stove.

"Plums. They've been preserved so we can eat them later," Mrs. Gellert said.

"Can we go out and play now?" Inge asked.

"Put on your coats and hats. It's cold outside," Mrs. Gellert warned.

They scrambled down the four flights of stairs and soon met up with their friends, who were down the street playing in a partially collapsed basement of a ruin, building a house with broken bricks. Anna sat down for a bit, handing one boy pieces of brick.

"My father is a sea captain," she announced, and told them about their visit to the Baltic Sea, "He caught eels, lots of them." She looked around at the skeptical faces of her friends. They had never heard of eels. "They look like snakes," Anna explained. None of the children had ever seen a snake either, just in picture books. They seemed fascinated listening to Anna's tales, which made her feel very important.

After a while, Inge tugged at her sleeve. "I'm cold." Anna looked up, surprised that it was getting dark.

When they got back, Mrs. Gellert stood in the hallway, her hands on her hips, her face stern. "I was worried about you. Next time I want you to come home before night. Wash your hands and come in the kitchen to eat."

Mr. Gellert, a stocky man with wavy brown hair and a mustache, was already at the table when they sat down. They had met him at Mrs. Dummersdorf's place when the couple had visited for dinner. Anna remembered him eating that poor rabbit and didn't like him much.

"We have some good chicken noodle soup," Mrs. Gellert announced, filling their bowls.

"This is the last chicken we have, Emil, so you need to plan another trip soon."

"Yes, I know. You make the best chicken soup, dear." He grinned.

After a few minutes, Mr. Gellert put down his spoon and looked at Anna. "Why are you not eating your soup?"

"I can't eat meat." Anna pushed away the bowl.

"You can't or you won't?" Mr. Gellert sounded irritated. "You are lucky to have chicken soup, girl. Many other children are going hungry." His face turned red.

"I have a bellyache." Anna pushed away from the table and ran to the hall, where she stood, wishing she could have more of the molasses she'd had earlier. She was hungry. Should she go back and *try* to eat? She peeked around the corner.

Mr. Gellert was getting up to follow and she saw Mrs. Gellert also stood up and put her hands on his shoulders. "Just leave her, Emil, it's all right. These poor children have gone through a lot. They're only here for a week or two. No point in trying to change them." She massaged his neck.

He grunted. "Glad it's only for a short time. You know I was against taking them in the first place." He sat down and began eating his soup.

"I like the soup." Inge smiled." Can I have some more, please?"

"Now there's a good girl." He returned her smile.

As the temperature dropped outside, it was getting colder in the apartment. Anna and Inge climbed into bed early to keep each other warm under the feather cover Mrs. Gellert had given them. It took a while for Anna to go to sleep, as she was so hungry.

An hour later, Inge woke her. "I have to go potty," she whispered.

Anna too tired to get up, turned over and went back to sleep.

"I have to pee now, Anna," Inge cried louder.

Anna sat up. "Just go to the toilet, Inge. It's straight down the hall that way. She pointed left,   though in the dark, Inge couldn't have seen her. Anna lay back down.

"I'm scared. Come with me." Anna didn't want to get up. Besides, she heard a strange noise in the rafters and wondered if there were mice or bats up there. Karl had once told her that bats live in attics. She covered her head.

201

The next day when the children came inside for lunch, Mrs. Gellert confronted them. "Which one of you wet the bed?"

Inge started to cry.

"So why didn't you tell me?" demanded Mrs. Gellert.

Inge cried harder and did not answer.

"It's my fault," Anna said, "She woke me, but I was tired, and it was so dark and I was afraid of the bats." She put her arm around her sister.

"There are no bats in our house." Mrs. Gellert looked like she wanted to smile. "I would have lights on, but we have to save our electricity for when we need it. After this, I'll leave the bathroom door open for you." She hugged Inge. "There is nothing to fear here."

Her husband Emil stepped into the kitchen. "Except for the ghosts, of course."

"Oh, stop it, Emil." Her voice sounded irritated as he smirked and left the room.

Mrs. Gellert took the sheets from the bed and carried them to the kitchen. She put them into a big kettle on the stove. After they had boiled, she began washing them on a metal washboard. "Here, Anna, try this. I want you to see how much work this is." Mrs. Gellert didn't make her scrub for long. Then she said, "Now I want you to come to the attic with me up the next stairway." They followed her and watched her take out a key and unlock a large wooden gate.

"This is the room where we hang our clothes to dry, see how big it is? This attic goes over the top of the fourth-floor apartments." Anna saw some towels and clothing hanging on clotheslines crisscrossing the attic.

"You hold the basket, Anna, while I take my dry clothes off the line. Then we'll hang up the sheets."

"I want to help too," Inge whined.

"All right. You can fold the towels on the table over there." Mrs. Gellert showed her how.

That evening when they went to bed Inge pointed to the rafters. "Are there ghosts up here?"

"Of course not. Mr. Gellert was just trying to scare us," Anna scoffed. But when they lay quietly in that small, musty room listening, she was not so sure. She heard a creaking noise, sat up and stared at the open rafters. She held her breath and the noise stopped. And when Inge shook her and said she had to pee, Anna pretended she was asleep.

The next morning, after Mr. Gellert had left the apartment, Mrs. Gellert summoned the children to follow her to their room where she pulled the covers off the bed and waved a sheet. "What is this?" Her voice was shrill.

Inge started shaking.

"I have only two sheets for this bed, and one is in the attic drying. That can take days in the winter. What do you have to say for yourself?"

"I want my mama," Inge bawled.

Anna moved in front of her. "I think she was afraid of the ghosts."

"We have lived here for thirty years and have never seen a ghost," bellowed Mrs. Gellert. "There are no ghosts!" She crumpled the sheet in her hand. "Did you pee in the bed at Mrs. Dummersdorf's house? Maybe that's why she didn't want to keep you. We must wash this before Mr. Gellert comes back. He will be very angry if he finds out, especially since he didn't want you here in the first place."

Inge sat on the chair sobbing, clutching Pepita. "Mama," she whispered. "Mama."

At lunchtime, Mrs. Gellert did not mention the incident to her husband. Instead, she said, "I have the brassieres ready for Mrs. Grinderman, Emil. So, if you want to make a trip to the farm that would be great. I have a list, so the sooner you can go, the better. We are out of a lot of things."

After they ate cabbage and potatoes, Emil smiled at Anna. "You want to come with me to the farm tomorrow?"

Anna jumped up and down. "Yes, please, I want to go to the farm."

Mrs. Gellert frowned. "Are you sure, Emil? There is a lot of walking, and she is only-- how old are you, Anna?"

"Six years old. And I can walk. We walked a lot on our farm. Please take me along."

Mr. Gellert cocked his head and looked sideways at his wife. "She can be a good little helper, dear. You know what I mean. The Allied soldiers love little children, and they might let us pass through."

"Good thinking, Emil. And since we have more mouths to feed, we need extra food. Also, you should talk to Mrs. Grinderman's sister. She has not ordered any garments, but with this child along, she might mellow and consider it. Maybe she'll even give us some extra food." Mrs. Gellert smiled.

"All right, we'll go tomorrow morning." Emil looked down at Anna. "Now, you have to listen and do what I tell you tomorrow, understand? When we're travelling, don't say anything unless I tell you to."

"I won't." Anna bounced on her toes. "Do they have cows and dogs on the farm?"

"Of course, they do. Lots of cows," he assured her.

"And Inge, you stay home with me." said Mrs. Gellert, "You can help me bake Christmas cookies. Maybe we can send some to your mama. I don't have much sugar, but I have honey and molasses."

That night Anna lay awake for a long time, picturing cows, fields, dogs like Yanka, a garden and horses. Then she had an idea. "Wake up, Inge." She poked her sister. "Wake up."

Inge rubbed her eyes. "We have to go to the toilet now. Mrs. Gellert has no more sheets and she'll get really mad if you wet the bed again and then she won't want to keep us."

She pulled her sister out of bed, and they tiptoed along the dark hallway wall until they reached the toilet.

"See, it worked," Anna said when they were done. "No more peeing in the bed, you understand?"

Inge nodded and they both climbed back into bed and fell asleep.

CHAPTER 23

"Wake up, Anna. We have to leave." Mr. Gellert pulled her out of the bed. It was still dark outside. "Hurry, I'll be in the kitchen to grab a bite." He walked out and left the door open.

Then Mrs. Gellert came in wearing her red robe. "Let's see, Anna, we need slacks for you and a warm sweater, and your coat and hat. Do you have mittens?"

Anna shook her head and slipped into the clothes Mrs. Gellert handed her.

"Oh, I have a muff you can use. Come along." She walked into the hall. "Here, I found it." She pulled a black fur muff off the top shelf of the coat rack. "Feel how soft. It will keep your hands nice and warm." She looked at Anna's sandals. "I'm sorry. I don't have any shoes that fit you."

Anna smiled. She had always wanted a fur muff.

Mr. Gellert came out of the kitchen. "Come over here, Anna, I want to show you something." He held up a large belt with straps and pouches all around. "I am going to put this harness around your waist, under your coat." He bent in front of her. "We will pick up a lot of food and you can help me carry it." He strapped the harness on her and told her to put on her coat. "Nobody can see it. That's our little secret, so don't say a word to anyone."

"Yes, Mr. Gellert." Anna put on her coat, and it fit so tight over the harness that she had to suck in her stomach. She had a hard time closing the buttons.

.   "Here, eat before we leave." Mrs. Gellert
handed her a sandwich with Anna's favorite, molasses, and
she took big bites as she watched Mr. Gellert put on his
coat and a tall fur hat with flaps covering his ears. Daylight
began to streak in beneath the kitchen curtains and Mr.
Gellert unlocked the apartment door.

His wife pulled Anna close. "Do what Mr. Gellert
tells you and stay with him. Don't go off on your own. It
could be dangerous. Keep an eye on him, especially when
he's with the farm ladies." She winked at her husband and
handed him two packages wrapped in brown paper. "I hope
they fit."

He raised his eyebrows, grinned and slipped the
packages into one of the bags he carried.

Anna walked down the steps behind Mr. Gellert.
She stopped several times and tried to adjust her coat.

Mr. Gellert looked up at her. "What?"

"These bags hit my legs." She pulled up a coat flap.

"Don't be such a baby," he grumbled, grabbing her
hand and pulling her along. "You want to go to the farm,
right?"

"Yes, I do." Anna stumbled down the steps.

At the bottom stoop, he said, "Wait here,"
disappeared in the back of the foyer and returned with a
bicycle whose frame was rusty, the saddle discolored.
"Hold the door." Hampered by the harness that strangled
her like a sausage, Anna struggled, pulling the heavy door
open for him.

He picked up the bicycle and carried it out and
down the three steps to the sidewalk. He pointed to the
back. "Climb on the back saddle."

A gust of wind almost knocked Anna off her feet.
She shivered. "Is it far to the farm?" Her fingers began to
freeze. She couldn't stick them into the muff because she
had to use her hands to hang onto his back.

"We have a while to go until we get to the station. Then we'll take a train out of the city. And after that we have to bicycle a way to get to the farm." Two large bags were hanging on the handlebars, swinging in the wind as he peddled along.

When they arrived at the depot, Mr. Gellert scurried to the back of the train and hoisted the bicycle into an open car where people crouched on boxes, huddled together to keep warm. Then he lifted Anna up. She was so cold that her teeth were chattering. "We stay back here so nobody steals my bike," he grunted.

It was cold in the train and smelled like the cow manure Anna remembered from the Munster farm. She squatted on the floor and the train rumbled out of the station. Soon, she fell asleep.

After a while, she woke to Mr. Gellert's shouting, "We have to get off here." She sat up, rubbing her eyes. He handed her the bags. She jumped onto the platform, followed by Mr. Gellert, who carried the bicycle. The only building she saw was a small depot, surrounded by bare trees. She could not see houses or cows, just the lone road lined by trees that swung in the winter air and a ditch on both sides. It reminded her of the country road in the village of Burghof.

"Hurry!" Mr. Gellert pointed at the second saddle. She climbed on, wrapping her arms around him, and they joined a trek of people on bicycles, others walking on the road carrying backpacks and large bags.

"Are we going to be there soon?" Anna asked, leaning into Mr. Gellert's back to keep her face out of the biting wind.

"Soon. In an hour or so. We'll pass through one village and then we'll be at the Grinderman farm."

Mr. Gellert abruptly stopped on the side of the road while a convoy of military trucks approached and slowly passed them. He waved at the soldiers and smiled.

Anna smiled and waved too. "Are these Brits?" She covered her mouth with one hand and hung on with the other.

"Brits?" He laughed. "Yes, Anna, they are Tommies, British soldiers, a whole convoy of them."

"Are they going to the village to bomb the people?"

"No, no, there is no more bombing. The war is over. But we don't want to be stopped. We'll just keep out of their way." He pulled the bicycle back on the road.

"The thing is hurting my legs," Anna whined. Mr. Gellert did not seem to hear her.

Finally, he turned onto a dirt road and then into a farmyard. A big, brown dog greeted them, barking and jumping around the bicycle. They stopped at the farmhouse. It had a thatched roof and sat at the far end of the yard. She hopped off the bicycle and the dog ran over and sniffed her coat. She stretched out her hand and it licked her fingers. Next to the house, Anna saw a grey, wooden barn and across from it on the far side of the farmyard, several long, low buildings, like Anna remembered them from the Schultz farm where they kept the pigs.

"Remember, Anna, don't say anything unless I tell you to, do you understand?"

She nodded, shivering in the cold wind.

He leaned his bicycle against the house and opened a big green door, hollering, "Hello, it's Emil Gellert."

A short, heavy-set woman in a dark blue dress and a checkered apron appeared. She stared at Anna.

He put a hand on Anna's shoulder. "An orphan girl we took in."

Anna smiled and curtsied.

The woman smiled. "Come on in. She looks cold. Would you like some warm milk, dear?"

Anna nodded and took off her hat. They stood in a large, dimly lit barn just like the one at the Munsters'.

Farm implements lined the walls. The sweet smell of hay and a whiff of fried potatoes also reminded her of the Munster farm. She thought of Gertl's voice humming and singing in the kitchen.

Then a girl about Anna's age appeared and handed her a tall glass.

"Thank you. My name is Anna."

The girl turned and ran to the back of the house.

"She is shy." The farm matron smiled. "We aren't used to seeing city girls around here."

"Can I pet your dog?" Anna asked the lady.

"Oh, Rex? Sure, he loves to be petted." She turned to Mr. Gellert. "Poor little girl." The woman looked down at Anna. "How nice of you to take her in."

"Anna, go outside and pet the dog," Mr. Gellert said, put his arm around the woman and handed her two packages from Mrs. Gellert. "But stay in the yard, don't go anywhere."

Anna drained the glass and went back outside. She sat down on the stoop, hoping the recessed entranceway would shield her from the wind.

"Come, Rex, here, doggie," she called and to her delight, the big brown dog came close, sniffed her again and wagged his tail. She held out her hand and he licked her fingers again. He lay down and began to smell her cold toes.

"I miss Yanka. She's a dog I know. I miss everybody, my mama, Karl and my friends, Gertl and Rita." She wiped her eyes with her sleeve." Nobody wants us. I don't know what to do."

The door opened a crack and the farmer's daughter appeared again holding a plate with a sandwich. Anna thanked her, took the plate and bit into the bread. The girl ran back inside. When Anna saw that there was ham on the bread, she peeled it off and fed it to Rex, who swallowed it in quick gulps. Then she finished both slices of bread licking every crumb off the plate.

After what seemed a long time, Mr. Gellert appeared at the door followed by two women, each carrying two bulging bags and a basket.

"What a cute little girl. Poor thing." The younger woman handed Anna a cookie.

"Hurry now, Emil, I can't wait for my --" she stopped and looked at Anna "for my own new garments." She snickered and he slapped her on the butt.

"Let's see, Anna," Mr. Gellert said. "We'll hang the basket and the big bags on the handlebars. But you can carry some of these packages, can't you?" He didn't wait for an answer, unbuttoned her coat and stuffed the packages into the pouches arranged around her waist. He seemed happy, waving at the women. "I'll hurry back, ladies." He hung the bags on the handles of the bicycle and peddled out of the farmyard.

Anna pounded his back with her fist. "I can't move."

He ignored her. The bicycle was so loaded down that he seemed to have a hard time riding it, especially with Anna on the back saddle. He stopped. "We'll have to walk." She slid off and he started pushing the bicycle down the road. Dragged down by the heavy bags around her waist, Anna trudged behind him.

"Rex let me pet him. He liked me," she said. "But where are the cows?"

Mr. Gellert looked down at her. "In the barn. They keep them inside in the winter."

They joined people in ragtag clothes loaded down with heavy sacks, baskets and backpacks moving along the shoulder of the road like a gigantic snake in search of prey.

"Where are all these people going?" Anna asked.

"To the train depot. They're all going to catch the train back to the city. We'd better walk faster. We want to make sure that we get a spot on the train." He pushed the bicycle harder and took bigger steps.

"I'm tired. The bags are so heavy, they're hurting my belly," Anna whined.

Anna heard the sound of trucks approaching. Mr. Gellert stopped. "Oh, Scheisse," he shouted, and threw his bicycle and all the bags into the ditch.

"Jump, Anna, quick!" He pulled her down the embankment. "Lay down low so they can't see us." He pushed her behind some shrubs on the bottom of the ditch. The noise of the trucks grew closer and sounded like a train thundering by.

Anna was so scared that she hardly dared to breathe. "Are the planes coming to bomb us?" she whispered.

He placed his hand over her mouth. "Shh."

The trucks slowed, then stopped. Anna heard men's voices. Her heartbeat so hard that she was sure they could hear her. Something warm trickled down the side of the ditch over her hand and onto Mr. Gellert's arm. "Damn," he hissed between his teeth as Anna opened her eyes and glanced at him. "One of them pissed. Damn shit."

They huddled in the ditch until the trucks drove away. Finally, the roar of the engines faded. Mr. Gellert crept up the embankment to look. He slid back and hustled the bicycle up to the road and returned to retrieve the bags and the basket. He motioned Anna to crawl up but, loaded down with the heavy packets, she couldn't. He finally had to pull her up the side of the ditch.

"That was a close call, dear God, a close call." He took a deep breath and brushed off his jacket.

"Were they soldiers?" Anna asked as she tried to wipe the dirt off her coat.

"Yes, Tommies," he said, pointing to where the trucks turned left onto a side road. They don't like us to come out here and get food from the farmers. They think we're going to sell it on the black market, and that is *verboten*."

Black market? Anna didn't understand. People climbed from the ditch along the road as far as she could see, and the human convoy was on the move again.

Anna reached under her coat. "Ick." She looked at her hand. "Something sticky is running down my belly." She held her hand up to Mr. Gellert's face.

"Oh, damn, I hope it didn't all melt."

"What is melting?" Anna looked at her greasy, shiny hands.

"Open your coat," he ordered. "It's butter. I hope it will stop melting when the cold air hits it."

Anna could tell that he was angry. She was scared and didn't ask any more questions as she wiped her hands on her coat. The wind had picked up and the temperature was dropping. With her coat open, the cold wind tugged at the flaps and blew right through her sweater. She was freezing and tired and tried to keep her hands inside the muff. "I can't walk anymore," she whimpered.

"All right, let's see if I can push the bicycle with you sitting on the back." He lifted her into the saddle. He was a stocky, strong man and pushed on, as she clung to the handlebars, afraid that she might fall off.

Then Mr. Gellert pointed at a huge piece of military equipment hulking on the side of the road, partially blocking it. "Get off the bicycle, we have to walk around it," he hollered.

"It's a tank, I know." Anna looked up the black metal side dwarfing her small figure. "I saw one at Mama's hospital when we went with the Major."

Mr. Gellert maneuvered the bicycle around the hunk of metal. "Got hit, burned out, kaput."

"Are there dead soldiers inside?" Anna craned her neck but was too short to see down the inside of the tank.

Mr. Gellert did not look up as he lifted her back into the saddle. "Could be. But they'd be burned to a crisp, not much left after an explosion."

Anna gasped, remembering the explosion and fire at the Munster farmhouse.

It was past six when they reached the depot. Mr. Gellert muscled his way onto the train in the rear, lifting the bicycle and the heavy bags up into the open compartment. Then he pulled Anna up into the car, which was so crowded that she was lucky to find a spot on the floor next to the bicycle. It was freezing inside the train and Anna could see her breath. The stench of people mingled with the various odors of the food they had gathered. No one spoke. People leaned against each other, rocking along with the rumbling, rolling of the train. Crouched on the floor next to the bicycle, Anna fell asleep.

When they reached the city station, Mr. Gellert woke her. "Take off your coat so that I can get this harness off you. Looks like most of it melted, damn it." He tossed the coat back at Anna. "I'm sure the Missus won't like this." The tone of his voice frightened her. Exhausted, she trudged behind him as he pushed the heavily loaded bicycle through the streets on their long walk home.

Anna was so cold that even the fur muff did not keep her hands warm, and her feet felt like blocks of ice. It was eerily quiet in the city. The burned-out ruins looked like monsters ready to leap out of the shadows. Anna tried hard to keep up with Mr. Gellert, stumbling and taking two steps for every one of his. It was dark when they reached the apartment house.

"Go upstairs and tell the Missus to come down and help me with the bags." In a foul mood from the long, cold trip, Mr. Gellert pushed her towards the stairs.

"Can you turn on the light?" Anna asked, afraid of climbing four flights of stairs in the dark.

"There is no electricity, girl. Hurry, I can't stand here all night. You want to eat supper, don't you?" When she still hesitated, he shoved her towards the steps, and she fell on her knees. "For God's sake, Anna, don't be a baby. I'm losing my patience."

Slowly, she climbed step by step, clinging to the rail, fighting her paralyzing fear of the dark. Several times she stopped and sat on a stair, overcome by exhaustion. She finally dragged herself to the fourth floor and knocked on the apartment door. After the third try she heard footsteps and Mrs. Gellert opened the door.

She stared at Anna. "Where is Mr. Gellert?"

Anna pointed downstairs. "He wants you to come help him carry things."

Without a word, Mrs. Gellert walked past Anna, turned and started down the steps. Anna walked into the dark apartment hallway. She took off her coat, dropped it on the hall floor and went straight to the attic room. Inge was asleep and Anna climbed into the bed without undressing, cuddled up to the warm body of her sister and went to sleep.

The next morning at breakfast, Mrs. Gellert said, "We have very little butter." She was staring at Anna, who froze in the act of spreading butter on her bread.

Mr. Gellert slammed his fist on the table. "Look, woman, we had to jump into the ditch, or we'd have lost everything. The British would have it all now."

Anna stared at him in wonder.

CHAPTER 24

Anna dreamed that she lay stuck in the ditch unable to move, was covered with sticky syrup that ran down her belly. She wanted to scream but was afraid the British would hear her. Then two soldiers with big guns started climbing down the embankment and she felt wetness. She touched her belly, sure that it was blood.

"Mama!" she screamed. "Mama..." and woke up. She sat up. Her hand lay on the sheet next to her, which was warm and wet.

"Wake up, Inge." She shook her sister. "Wake up." She pulled off the covers.

Inge rubbed her eyes, looked around and climbed out of bed. "I have to pee," she murmured, shivering in her thin nightgown.

"No, Inge, you already did. The bed is all wet." Anna grabbed her sister's arm and forced her hand to touch the wet sheet.

"I didn't do it, Anna," Inge whispered between sobs, trying to get away from her sister's grip. "I didn't do it. I swear."

"Yes you did, Inge, and Mrs. Gellert will be very angry." She slid out of bed. "Here, hold this end of the sheet and help me dry it." She pulled the sheet off the bed and told her sister to stand at the far end of the room while she went to the other side, by the door. "Do what I'm doing. Swing the sheet up and down so it will dry."

"I can't." Inge let go of the sheet.

216

"Yes, you can. We have to dry this so that Mrs. Gellert won't notice you wet the bed again," Anna scolded.

For the rest of the night, the two girls stood in the dark, cold room, shaking the sheet up and down. Finally, in the early morning, Anna folded it back onto the bed and they climbed in, exhausted.

"My, my, you two must have been tired. It is ten o'clock." Mrs. Gellert stood in the bedroom doorway, her forehead wrinkled, but a smile on her face. "Breakfast is ready. Find something to wear." She looked at Anna. "Oh, all that good butter. What a shame." She picked up Anna's green sweater and slacks and examined them.

Anna did not reply, just walked to the kitchen and sat down at the table, reaching for the bread and molasses. She was relieved that she did not see Mr. Gellert.

"We made cookies." Inge pointed to a big platter on the stove overflowing with brown cookies.

Anna glanced at the pantry shelves, stacked high with food, cans and glass jars, eggs, bread and more. She ogled the eggs but did not dare to ask Mrs. Gellert to fix her some.

After breakfast, Anna quickly slipped into their room and made the bed, placing Rita and Pepita on the pillow.

Mrs. Gellert walked by and nodded approvingly. "That's nice. You made up your bed. I'm going into town with Mrs. Dummersdorf for a while, so you girls behave." She smiled and put on her coat.

"Where is Mr. Gellert?" Anna asked.

"He's out bartering," she replied, waving at them. "You can each have a cookie." She turned around and closed the door behind her.

Inge fidgeted with her apron and asked, "Do you want to go outside and play?"

"Nah, I'm too tired. My legs hurt." Anna sat at the kitchen table with her feet up on a chair. She wiggled her toes. After a while, she got bored and decided to take a closer look at the food in the pantry. "You know what?" She turned to her sister. "Let's take some food to Oma and Opa. They have nothing to eat. You heard Mrs. Dummersdorf tell Aunt Margarete."

Inge wrinkled her forehead, skeptical. "We have to ask Mrs. Gellert, don't we?"

"She'll never notice. We'll just take a few things. There's so much here." She picked up a can of pears, a loaf of bread, a jar of jam and two cans of beans. "We'll put them in our apron pockets under our coats, like Mr. Gellert did," she instructed.

Inge was still hesitant but did what her big sister told her.

"Here, let's take some cookies too, Oma likes cookies." Anna stuffed three cookies into Inge's coat pocket.

Slowly they climbed down the stairs, careful not to lose any of their loot. It was a gray, bitter day and a few snowflakes swirled in the air. They did not see any of their friends outside. Relieved, Anna took Inge's hand and they hurried down the street, across a boulevard and two blocks away to house number seventy-seven where their grandparents lived. Anna pushed open the big door of the apartment house and they entered the small dark hallway. On the right was the door to apartment 102, and on the left a large wall rack of metal boxes marked with names of the apartment dwellers.

"Maier, Braun," Anna read out loud and skipped the next one, which she could not spell. "Rebhorn, that's Oma and Opa," she pointed at the mailbox. "I know how to read," she had bragged to Karl back at the farm. "My mama taught me." Of course, Karl didn't believe her, but most of the other children did, and admired her.

Inge wrinkled her nose inhaling the damp, smelly air in the hallway. "I don't like cabbage."

Anna sniffed and held her nose. "It stinks."

The sisters climbed up the dark stairway and knocked on the last door on the right, which was slightly ajar. She pushed it open and called, "Oma, Oma. We have food for you."

Oma's voice came from the bedroom. "Come on in, girls."

They ran in and pushed open the bedroom door and hugged her.

Oma sat up in her bed, a few strands of hair hanging in her face, looking around, sleepily. "Oh my, I overslept, girls. You go into the kitchen, and I will be right along."

They backed up, closing the bedroom door, and crossed the small hallway into the kitchen. Anna rubbed her hands. "It's cold in here. I'm not taking off my coat."

Inge opened the door to the pantry. "Look, the shelves are empty."

Anna nodded. "Told you so."

Hurriedly, they unloaded the cans and bread onto the table. The kitchen was small, with a black coal-burning stove in the corner next to an old sofa pulled up to the table in place of kitchen chairs. A single window gave view of the drab apartment house balconies opposite a small courtyard. A cream-colored oilcloth with a red and black rose garland around the center covered the table. That cloth had been on that table as long as Anna could remember and she always admired it because the flowers reminded her of a garden she had seen in an old picture book. On the other side of the window was the door to the pantry and on the right of it a small sink with a large round metal bucket tucked underneath. Anna remembered that their mother had bathed them in that bucket.

They heard Oma's shuffling steps in the hallway.

Anna opened the kitchen door. "Close your eyes, Oma, and don't open them until I tell you to." Anna called.

Then Anna and Inge shouted, "NOW!"

"Oh, my, girls. All that food. How did you--"

"Look Oma, a jar of pears," Anna interrupted, and held up the jar.

"And bread and jam." Inge took them off the table.

"We don't have butter, but jam." Anna waved the jar up in front of Oma's face.

Then Inge repeated Mrs. Dummersdorf's threat, "You have to eat, Oma or we'll have to get you cod liver oil."

"You are my two angels." Her grandmother hugged them to her. "Just like your mama."

Slowly, she lowered herself onto the sofa, cut off a slice of bread and spread it with the strawberry jam.

The children watched her eat.

"Mama will be home for Christmas," Anna said. "And I went to the farm with Mr. Gellert yesterday. I got to pet a dog, but the cows were in the barn. And all the butter melted on my belly when we had to jump into the ditch because the British were coming." Anna bounced up and down on her toes. "And Mrs. Gellert was mad that we have no butter now."

Her Oma looked up, slowly chewing. "You went with Mr. Gellert to get food from the farm?" She raised her eyebrows.

"Yes, it was far away in the country, and we had to take the train and the bicycle, and I was very scared that the British soldiers would find us and bomb us."

Her grandmother shook her head in disbelief. "You are too young to be out there. It's dangerous. We have to tell your mama." She started to cough, her whole body shaking.

"Oma, are you sick?" Anna asked, scooting next to her on the sofa.

220

"Eat some more, Oma. That will make you better."
Inge took her bony hand.

"You girls better get back, so Mrs. Gellert does not
get worried. And I am going to go back and lie down for a
bit." She held onto the table, trying to stand.

"Oh, Oma, I forgot to tell you that our father was a
sea captain and he caught fish and eels."

"But I don't like my other grandmother. She's
mean," Inge said. "We are going back when it is summer
and we're going to swim in the ocean and go on a ship with
my other Opa."

The old woman smiled. "I am so glad that you girls
will get to swim in the ocean."

"Will you come along?" Anna asked, still bouncing.
"We'll all go, you, Mama, Inge and I and Opa."

She stroked Anna's head. "Sure, Kindchen, we will
all go." She started to cough again.

"Where is Opa?" Inge looked and suddenly asked.

"I bet he's out bartering for coal." Anna shivered in
the chilly, damp room.

Oma looked sad and patted her cheek. "He is up
there." She pointed to the sky. "But I will see him soon."
She took a big, checkered handkerchief from her robe and
wiped her eyes. "You run along now, girls." She slowly
turned from the table and shuffled towards the door,
grasping the furniture with her right hand.

"Can we come back tomorrow? Maybe Opa will be
here then."

Oma smiled sadly. "Of course, you can, Anna. Put
on your hats so you don't catch cold. And thank Mrs.
Gellert for the food. Don't forget, now." She leaned to hug
the girls.

" Oma, you're too skinny," Anna said. "I'm going
to ask Mrs. Gellert for that cod liver oil."

Inge giggled and buried her face in her Oma's robe, which hung on her frail body like the clothes on a scarecrow.

In the street, they hurried to their hiding place in the fallen ruins to meet up with four of their friends, who were there huddling close together to keep warm.

Anna jumped quickly back into her adventure from yesterday. "The soldiers were trying to kill us, but we jumped into a ditch. It was as deep as a house. And guess what, they didn't see us."

The admiring group hung on her every word. "Did they have guns?" one of the boys asked.

"Oh yes, of course, they were shooting all around us, boom, boom, boom. And, they had lots of tanks all coming towards us along the road. Tanks with huge cannons on them." Anna went on with her story, describing the dangers, the battle and how she escaped. She did not mention the butter melting down her belly.

When she looked up, they heard Mrs. Gellert hollering for them. She was bending over the railing on her fourth-floor balcony. Anna grabbed Inge's hand and they hurried up to the Gellerts' apartment.

Mrs. Gellert stood, her hands on her hips. "Where have you two been?"

"We visited Oma and Opa." Anna stuck out her lip.

"She was in her bed," Inge piped in, "and it was icy cold and -"

"I sent Mr. Gellert out looking for you." The tone of Mrs. Gellert's voice scared Inge and she started to sob.

"Next time you must tell me when you go someplace, you understand?" Mrs. Gellert stepped in front of Anna, shaking her finger in her face. "You are the older one, you should have known better."

Anna nodded, staring at her feet.

Then a door slammed, and Mr. Gellert came into the kitchen. "Damn it, where have you been?"

Mrs. Gellert stepped in front of him. "Emil, I've already handled it. They visited their grandparents."

"We brought Oma some food because she has nothing to eat," Inge spoke up, hoping to get back into Mr. Gellert's good graces.

Mr. Gellert's face turned red. "What food? Where did you get the food?"

The children did not answer, just looked at the floor. Inge got up from her chair to go and hide in their bedroom.

"You stay right here. Nobody leaves the kitchen," Mr. Gellert yelled, pushing her back into the chair. He stepped over to the pantry, checked the supplies and turned to his wife. "Did you take any of the food from here?"

She shook her head. "I thought you had taken it to barter. Remember, you said you would get me some butter and coffee."

He turned to the girls. "So, for the last time, did you take food from these shelves?"

"I wanted to give it to Oma because Mrs. Dummersdorf said that she doesn't have anything to eat and that she's going to die," Anna stuttered.

"So you stole food from us?" he yelled.

Anna cowered into the chair. "I gave it to Oma because she- she--"

"That's stealing. You stole food from us." He turned and grabbed up a large wooden ladle. "Come over here." His face had turned beet red and he swung the ladle over his head like a Viking warrior going into battle.

Anna was frozen with fear, unable to get up. Swiftly, he stepped over, drew back and hit her with the ladle. Anna shrieked and threw up her arms to cover her head as the ladle struck her over and over.

His wife jumped in between them. "Emil, that's enough!" She spread her arms in front of Anna. "What's the matter with you? She is six years old, just trying to help her grandmother."

The words stopped him mid-swing. He threw the ladle on the floor and stomped out of the kitchen, down the hall and out the apartment door.

Anna sobbed and held her head. Her sister was still crouched under the table.

Mrs. Gellert held Anna, who was sobbing loudly. "Next time, Anna, you ask me when you need food for your grandparents, do you understand? Will you ask me the next time? Look at me." She cupped Anna's chin.

"Yes, I will," Anna whispered, tears streaming down her face.

CHAPTER 25

Anna was exhausted and fell asleep immediately, but soon Inge woke her. She took Anna's hand and pressed it onto the wet mattress. "The bed is wet again, I don't know how it happened," she whispered. "I didn't do it, Anna, I didn't do it."

Anna slid out of bed and moaned. "Ouch, my arm hurts, and my head too. I can't help you dry the sheet tonight. Here, I will pull back the blanket and all you have to do is shake it up and down like before."

Four-year-old Inge stood in front of the bed and began shaking the sheet up and down, up and down.

"I'm cold, Inge, hurry, can you do it a little faster?" Anna shivered.

Inge let the sheet drop. "I can't do it anymore."

Anna picked it up and draped it over the chair. "There now. Maybe it'll be dry by morning. They climbed back into bed and fell asleep on the damp mattress.

Anna stirred and opened her eyes.

Mrs. Gellert was standing in the doorway. "It is ten-thirty, girls. Time to get up."

And then Anna saw that they had forgotten to put the sheet back on the bed. Alarmed, she looked at Mrs. Gellert, whose eyes were fixed on the sheet still draped over the chair.

"What is this?" Mrs. Gellert stepped to the chair, gathered it and held it up."Not again, you didn't wet again, Inge." She balled up the sheet and took it into the kitchen where she could look at it in the light from the window. "I

225

have no more clean sheets," she cried out. "And we have no soap either. I can't wash right now."

"What's going on, dear?" Mr. Gellert hollered from the bedroom, alarmed by his wife's crying.

Anna tiptoed down the hall and hid behind the open kitchen door.

"You have to go barter, Emil. I have no more soap."

"So, what is this? He came in the kitchen, not seeing Anna, who crouched even farther back behind the kitchen door. He grabbed the soiled sheet from her and inspected it. "How long has this been going on?"

"It started almost immediately after they came here. I went to ask Martha about it and she insists she told us that Inge wets the bed. But she swore up and down that the girl had only done it once or twice when she was with them."

"We took these children in and gave them food and a roof over their heads, and this is what we get in return," he shouted, swinging his arm. "We are going to fix this once and for all and teach that girl a lesson." He stormed out of the room.

Behind the door, Anna held her breath.

He returned, dragging a screaming Inge by her arms and slammed her onto the kitchen table. Holding her down with one arm, he pulled off her underpants and spread her legs.

He reached into the sewing basket and pulled out a needle and thread. Mrs. Gellert had been darning socks and left her sewing basket in the kitchen by the light of the window. "Do you know what this is?" He held up the needle and thread.

Anna began to shake, holding her hand over her mouth.

"I am going to sew you up, so you won't ever pee in our bed again." He hovered over her.

Inge kicked and screeched, but she was no match for the big man.

226

He bent down, pinning her arms with one of his and swinging the needle and thread in the other hand. Inge let out a scream so loud that the neighbor's downstairs hit their ceiling with a broomstick.

Forgetting her bruised arm, Anna ran into the kitchen and hurled herself at the man, hitting him with her fists and trying to pull him away.

Someone knocked on the door and Mrs. Gellert went to answer. Mrs. Dummersdorf barged into the kitchen. She stared at the child screaming on the table and at Mr. Gellert bending over her spread legs with the needle and thread.

He looked up. "I'm just teaching her a lesson. She has to learn not to pee in the bed." Inge stopped screeching, jumped off the table and ran to Anna, who pulled her down the hallway and into their bedroom. She shut the door behind them and held her trembling sister, who would not stop crying.

In the kitchen, raised voices. Then Mr. Gellert's heavy footsteps and the slam of the apartment door. The girls sat on the bed, listened, afraid to move, shaking in terror.

"I do feel sorry for them, but I can't cope with this, Martha," Mrs. Gellert cried.

Then Mrs. Dummersdorf's calm voice. "It's less than eight days until Christmas."

"But who knows if Annemarie will come home? You have not heard anything from her, right? What if she'll not be home for weeks or even months?"

"Let's keep a cool head and see what else we can do." Martha had lowered her voice so that Anna could barely understand her words. "Let me bring you a set of sheets, and I'll think of something."

"You'd better hurry, Martha, I don't know how long I can keep Emil calm. You saw him. I thought he was

227

going to hurt the child, I really did." Her voice trailed off and Anna could not understand what else she said.

Mrs. Dummersdorf shouted, "That was barbaric, hideous. You must keep him away from the children, you hear? And don't worry. I will come up with something, I promise, hopefully by tomorrow."

Anna heard steps coming towards the door. There was a knock.

"Can I come in, girls?" Mrs. Dummersdorf asked.

Anna opened the door and Mrs. Dummersdorf took her into her arms. Anna pulled away "Ouch, it hurts."

"What happened to your arm? And, good God, your face is swollen and black and blue."

"I fell off the stairs in the dark," Anna stuttered.

"You poor thing." Mrs. Dummerdorf hugged her gently. "You poor thing," she murmured again. Then she turned to Inge, who was crouched on the bed trembling, sobbing. She pulled the little girl into her arms. "It'll all be fine when your mama comes home." She stroked Inge's hair and held her, rocking her. Then she stood. "Girls, let's get dressed now and we'll go over to my place so we can put some ointment on Anna's head."

Inge stopped crying. "Me too, I want some ointment."

Mrs. Dummersdorf handed Inge her coat and stepped into the kitchen. "I am going to take the children with me to fetch some clean sheets," she said to Mrs. Gellert, who slouched on a chair, her elbows resting on the table. "You know what, I have a better idea." She snapped her fingers. "I'm going to pay another visit to Annemarie's sister and take the children with me. This time, she's keeping them.

Mrs. Gellert looked at her skeptical but composed. "What about their things?"

"Just pack it all up. I will let Mrs. Friedrich Bowman worry about that." She hugged her friend.

Taking her sister's hand, Anna felt a slight stirring of worry about going back to Aunt Margarete's.

Mrs. Gellert opened the pantry. "Here, take along some bread -- and what else? Some cheese and jam and a jar of molasses. Anna likes that. The children have not had their breakfast."

Thanking her friend, Mrs. Dummersdorf put the food into a bag and ushered the children out the door and down the stairs.

A few minutes later, they arrived at the Dummersdorfs' apartment. It was warm in the kitchen. Mr. Bernhard was not home. She fixed them breakfast and Anna ate her bread with molasses.

"Inge, eat, girl," Mrs. Dummersdorf urged.

But the child just sat there, hiding her face in her hands.

"We are going to have hot chocolate at your Aunt Margarete's today," Mrs. Dummersdorf said, stroking Inge's hair.

And then she sat Anna down. "And now, Anna, tell me what really happened to you. You didn't fall down the stairs, did you?"

Anna told her the truth. Mrs. Dummersdorf examined her arms and neck, and Anna cried out when she touched a lump on the back of her head. Mrs. Dummersdorf sighed and shook her own head. "Let's see if we can fix that." She went to her bedroom and returned with a jar filled with yellow ointment. "This will help with the swelling and it will take the hurt away too, Anna," she promised, rubbing ointment over the bruises. "You will feel better soon."

Anna wiped her eyes. "I didn't steal the food. I just took some to give to Oma. There is so much food in their pantry. I thought they wouldn't notice. I just took a little."

Mrs. Dummersdorf tilted up Anna's face and looked her in the eye. "You have a good heart, Anna. But you should have asked them first." Then she began to clear the table. "Girls, get ready. We are going to your Aunt Margarete's."

When they left the apartment house and stepped outside it had started to snow. Tiny flakes were floating down like a soft curtain.

Mrs. Dummersdorf looked down at Anna's sandals. "Oh, dear God. I wish I had some boots for you." She sighed and put her arms around each of the girls. "It'll be warm at Aunt Margarete's and you get to play with your cousins," she promised, bracing herself against the cold wind.

Inge finally spoke. "Anna, we'll get hot chocolate."

CHAPTER 26
Beversen Regional Hospital

Annemarie shuddered and pulled her blanket up against the cold and clammy air in the ward.

"They've promised some coal, but I've heard that people steal it before the trains ever get here," the nurse said, matter of fact. "Maybe tomorrow." She spoke without a smile or much hope in her voice.

Only eight days till Christmas. Annemarie stared at the tree that had been donated by the nearby village. It was decorated with stars made from straw. A few wooden toys crafted by the villagers peeked through the otherwise bare branches. On Sunday a group of local children dressed in red and green came through the ward singing carols. Afterward they handed out gingerbread cookies. Annemarie burst into tears when they sang "Silent night, holy night, all is calm…" Their voices, so pure, so full of promise, kindled memories of happier times.

She had wiped her damp cheeks and closed her eyes. Last Christmas she was waiting for Alfred to come home on leave. They were eager to plan their future, reopen his machine shop and most of all, get married. She remembered Mrs. Munster casting doubt, telling her she was living in a dream world. Annemarie had laughed and shrugged off the farmer's wife's doubts as the babbling of a bitter old woman.

Annemarie sighed now, thinking of Alfred's warm brown eyes, his hands so strong, yet gentle, caressing her, reassuring her that he would always be there. They were at

231

Burghof Lake, their favorite hideaway, lying on a blanket, surrounded by moonlight. She'd been engulfed by his scent of sweet tobacco and shaving cream, and he laughed when she accused him of wearing perfume. Now, when she reached out to touch him the moment slipped away. The war was over. Alfred had not come back. She was homeless, a cripple, and her children pawned off to unwilling neighbors, strangers who could barely fend for themselves.

The same stars lit up the winter skies. She wondered if he was out there looking at them, thinking of her. Annemarie wished she had some deep faith to comfort her. Her parents had never mentioned religion. Hitler, of course, was against it. He wanted to be the only one his people worshipped. If she believed in one thing, she was sure he was the Devil who'd come to destroy everything and everyone.

Ellen, the patient in the next bed, professed to be a Christian. She said one must forgive all sinners.

"Even the Russians?" Annemarie had asked her one raw day in early December.

"Yes," she replied. "You can't forgive selectively. God and Jesus forgave every sinner."

Annemarie had folded her arms over her chest. "Certainly not. I could never forgive a mass murderer or the soldiers who bombed our city, killed Alfred's family, almost killed me. Why did God not intervene and help the millions who suffered and died?"

Ellen tried to explain that this is not how it worked, but Annemarie could not accept that.

"Sometimes I wish I had faith like you Ellen, I really do. If faith would bring Alfred home, I would convert to any religion,"

"Perhaps someday you will understand." Ellen smiled. "I can't explain it. You can't say, 'I'll do this if God gives me that'. There are no promises or conditions."

Annemarie bit her lip. "Someplace I read, 'If it is to be, it is up to me.' I can't remember who said that, but I believe it. That's my motto."

She gazed on the Christmas tree, remembering Christmas when she was a little girl. They were poor and did not have much to give, but the excitement, the anticipation, the Christmas cookies they baked, the new mittens her mother had knitted, the blue rubber ball she loved to play with-- oh, and the pretty red coat her brother brought from one of his trips. But that seemed so long ago, unreal as though it happened in a novel she had read.

"Dr. Kronert has not been here in almost three days now," she lamented. "He has to sign my release papers. I have to get home, Ellen, I have to. Think of little Inge and Anna. I can't disappoint them." She threw out her arms. "You understand that don't you?"

Ellen slid off her bed and into her wheelchair. She scooted close to Annemarie's bed and took her hand. "God has a plan for us, Annemarie, and it will all work out in the end. You are a strong woman. I truly believe that your family will be reunited, and you will find happiness."

Annemarie sighed. Perhaps Ellen was right. Her life would turn around. In her heart, she still held out hope that Alfred would return home. Miracles happened, Ellen had said, and Annemarie tried to believe in miracles.

A nurse came by to check on their vitals.

"I really need to talk with Dr. Kronert," Annemarie said. "When is he coming back?"

The nurse shrugged. "I'm not sure. I believe he went out of town to visit his family."

Annemarie looked at her, alarmed. "Surely, he will be back before Christmas?"

The nurse shrugged again. "I'm just doing my job, Mrs. Peterman. I really don't know what Dr. Kronert's plans are."

233

"Do you have children? I have two little girls waiting for me to come home for Christmas."

"No." But here's a letter for you." she tossed the envelope at Annemarie as she left.

"Damn witch," Annemarie muttered. Somehow receiving a letter no longer caused her heart to pound. She felt like she was a hundred years old or even dead.

She turned to the back of the envelope and read the fine engraved print: CAPT. FRIEDRICH BOWMAN. Probably a Christmas card.

She waved it in the air. "From my sister."

Ellen's face lit up. "Looks like the postal service is still functioning. See, miracles still happen. Merry Christmas." She grinned.

Annemarie propped a pillow behind her back and tore open the envelope.

Dear Kittie:

It's almost Christmas and I am expecting Friedrich home any day. My girls are very excited to see their father and, of course, the gifts he will bring them.

I have some news for you too. One day last week, that awful woman, Mrs. Dummersdorf, arrived at my place. She had Anna and Inge with her. I can't

tell you how shocked I was, Annemarie. Anna had bruises all over her arm and on her head - Black and blue and swollen.

Annemarie shrieked and Ellen scooted over again and put her hand on Annemarie's arm.

"What is it, what does it say?"

"Somebody hurt Anna. She's got bruises." Annemarie burst into tears.

Ellen handed her a handkerchief. "That's awful. What happened to her?"

"I don't know yet." Annemarie read on, then stopped and dropped the letter in her lap. "Can you believe it? A grown man beat her with a wooden ladle because she had taken some food from their pantry and given it to her starving grandparents." She shook her head. "He called her a thief; said he would teach her a lesson for stealing. All she wanted to do is help her grandparents." She moaned and blew her nose. "And the irony is that he used her to go to the farm to get the food! My six-year-old daughter was out there, in danger."

Ellen looked at her with soft eyes. "What can you do?"

"Nothing much. I have to be grateful that these people took my children in."

"So, you forgive him?" A half-smile crossed Ellen's face.

Annemarie hesitated. "I'm not sure. Maybe. What choice do I have? But I'll never forget, never. I'm just glad my girls are safe now with my sister."

Ellen sighed, her hand making the sign of a cross over her chest.

"Poor little Anna. She's such a good girl, wanting to help her grandparents." Annemarie stifled a sob, picked up the letter and read on.

It gets worse, Kittie. Apparently, Inge is a bed wetter, since she did it at my house too. But the husband, a Mr. Gellert, got really angry when she wet the bed, I don't know how to say this.

He put Inge on the kitchen table, spread her legs and threatened to sew her up. He was even holding a needle and thread!

What barbaric person would do that to a child? Well, his wife made him stop, but he told her he was just teaching the child a lesson. How can that woman live with such a monster?

Annemarie stopped reading and told Ellen what she had just learned.

"Holy Mother of God, forgive those who have sinned," Ellen murmured as she painted the sign of the cross on her chest repeatedly.

Annemarie sobbed. "Where was your God when a little girl, only four years old, needed help?"

Ellen stroked Annemarie's hand and did not answer.

"Damn war, damn Hitler, damn everybody," Annemarie shouted. "I am not going to forgive the bastard. I have a score to settle with that Good Samaritan." Annemarie shuddered, unable to erase the horrible vision. She leaned from the bed and began to wretch.

Ellen wheeled herself into the aisle and to the nurses' station and brought back a nurse.

"I'm so sorry," Annemarie whispered as the nurse wiped up the floor.

"Do you want a sedative, something to help you sleep?" she asked.

Annemarie shook her head. There were two pages left. She picked them up.

Anna said that she had visited Mother. I think I told you that father passed away. I always told him that those stinky cigars would kill him. Stubborn old man.

"My father is dead," Annemarie moaned. "I knew he was not well, but I didn't know how sick he was."

Ellen patted her hand. "I know he is in a better place."

Annemarie sighed. "Maybe you are right." After a time, she picked up the letter again and read on.

Anna said Mother was in bed and coughing a lot, that it was very cold in the apartment. I did go and pick Mother up and bring her here. I got her to eat more and put on a little weight, but her constant coughing was too much. I could not get any rest, and finally, I had to take her back to her apartment. I left her some food and a bucket of coal. I told her to go see a doctor, but don't know if she did.

236

You know how stubborn she can be. I'm sure Friedrich will want to visit her, or bring her here for Christmas day, since he wrote that he might have a car at his disposal. A car! I have not seen one in this part of the city.

Annemarie shook her head. She was more determined than ever to get out of this hospital and go home. How could Margarete send her mother back to that cold apartment just because she coughed a lot?

I had to decide. That Mrs. Dummersdorf had the gall to just drop your children off here and leave.

Of course, I could not keep them. Where would I put them? I have my hands full with my two girls, especially Renate. She won't obey me at all. That'll change when her father comes home. And so, I had to find a place for Anna and Inge. They were here for three days, and Inge wet the bed every night. It was awful. There must be something wrong with her. Or could she just be obstinate? The new mattress in the guest bedroom is ruined. But never mind. It can be replaced but not before Friedrich comes home. And I really need it because he always sleeps in that room, since I'm used to my own bedroom.

Annemarie let her breath out in a huff. Quickly, she scanned the rest of the letter to find out where her children had been sent. She caught the word "orphanage" and stopped and turned back.

A woman I know works at an orphanage outside the city. She assured me it was a nice place. The children there have enough food and staff to care for them--

Annemarie crumpled the pages and threw them down.

"Are you going to be sick again? Shall I get help?" Ellen asked.

"I'm sick, but not like that. I'll tell you later." She couldn't even cry. She retrieved the letter and smoothed the pages.

Her daughter agreed to take them to the orphanage.
I told her to stop at Dummersdorfs' to get their
things.

Here is the address. Hopefully, you'll get this letter
in time to send them a Christmas card. If I don't see you
before, Merry Christmas, Kittie. And, keep a stiff upper lip,
as Father always used to say.

CHAPTER 27
At the Orphanage

"Don't be scared," Anna whispered, and put her arm around Inge. They were huddled on a bench, squeezed against the window in the overcrowded compartment as the train rumbled through the bleak winter landscape.

"I wanted to stay at Aunt Margarete's house," Inge wailed. "Where are we going now?" She hid her face in her sister's coat.

"I don't know." Anna glanced at the woman called Miss Irmgard, who sat across from them holding the bag with their clothes on the floor between her feet. Anna peered at her from the corner of her eye, pretending to look out the window. Miss Irmgard was tall and had a long ponytail and round, red cheeks.

Miss Irmgard leaned towards Anna. "You will like it at the orphanage. There are lots of children to play with and toys too, and swings," she said in a bubbly voice. "I work at the home and will be there to help you. We're going to have a big Christmas celebration and Father Christmas visits us. And if you girls have been good, he'll bring you sweets, and maybe a present. You are good girls, right?" she asked, sounding half-serious.

Inge hid her face and Anna did not reply. She thought of the food she had taken from Mrs. Gellert's pantry and wondered if Father Christmas had found out. And what was an orphanage?

"How does Father Christmas know where we are?" Anna finally asked the woman. "We've moved around a lot."

Miss Irmgard playfully waved her finger at Anna. "Oh, Santa knows everything. He has invisible elves that find out and tell him. And children who have been naughty will not receive a gift. They will get a whipping with a broom."

Anna puckered her lips and blew a whiff of air. "Mama is coming to get us. We'll be home for Christmas."

"But it's only a few days *Kindchen*. I think you will be with us for some time. But you'll make friends, and we'll sing Christmas carols. Do you know 'Oh Tannenbaum. Oh Tannenbaum, la la la.'"

Anna stared at her.

"I don't like her," Inge whispered in Anna's ear.

Anna put her finger over her sister's mouth. "Shh, don't talk."

Inge pulled Anna's hand away and cried, "Mama is coming to get us, she promised." She sat up straight to make herself look bigger.

Miss Irmgard pointed at Inge. "What's your name?"

"Her name is Inge," Anna said, "and she is four years old."

"You must call me Miss Irmgard." The woman nodded and pulled up the collar of her woolen coat. "We'll be there soon. Burr, it's cold in this train."

Half an hour later, the train came to a stop. People pushed and shoved their way to the exit dragging rucksacks and boxes spilling out on to the platform.

Anna searched around then looked at the woman. "Where is my white suitcase?"

" It's Miss Irmgard, Anna," she replied with a stern face.

"Where is my white suitcase, Miss Irmgard?" Anna's voice quivered.

Miss Irmgard held up the large sack she was carrying. This is all Mrs. Dummersdorf handed me. And it's heavy enough."

"I want my white suitcase," Anna cried. "Rita gave it to me." She began to sob.

"Mrs. Dummersdorf can bring it when she visits. I'm freezing, let's go. If we hurry, we'll get there in time for lunch."

"I want my suitcase," Anna said, trudging behind Miss Irmgard as they headed down the street.

They went past rows of tall apartment buildings, a few standing and many in ruins and rubble. Soon the buildings gave way to smaller houses with picket fences, trees and leafless bushes that glistened with ice.

"We are almost there." Miss Irmgard pointed at a white villa that appeared on their left. "Pretty, isn't it?" She pushed open the heavy, wrought-iron gate leading to a wide, tree-lined walkway.

Inge stared at the tall fence surrounding the villa.

Anna looked around as they walked down the path and up the broad stone stairway to a big double-door entrance. "Where are all the children?"

Miss Irmgard rang the doorbell and a woman in a white apron and cap opened. She bent and said, "Come in."

In the center of an enormous hall with a ceiling at least two stories tall, Miss Irmgard took off her coat. It was warm in the room and the smell of bread made Anna hungry. " This is Anna Peterman and her sister, Inge," said Miss Irmgard. She placed her arms around them.

The matron smiled at them. "I am Mrs. Gunther. Welcome, children." "Let me have your belongings and Miss Irmgard will take you to the lunchroom." She pointed at a glass double door on the other side of the hall.

Miss Irmgard took their coats and the sack of their belongings and handed them to Mrs. Gunther. "After lunch I'll show you the bedroom. And then you can play."

Inge held on to Anna's hand as they entered the dining room where they were greeted by a wall of voices, children talking, laughing, clattering their forks and spoons. Miss Irmgard led the way to a big kettle on a table across the room. "This is where you get your soup."

"I am scared." Inge's worried eyes scanned the rows of tables crowded with boys and girls of all ages. "What if they won't like me?"

Anna patted her back reassuringly. "Inge don't be afraid. I'll be here and I'll beat them up if they try to hurt you."

The woman at the soup station took a big ladle, filled a bowl and handed it to Anna. Pieces of chicken skin swirled around in the broth.

Anna gagged and held up her hands. "I don't want soup." But the woman handed her the bowl and a slice of bread.

Balancing their bowls, they followed Miss Irmgard to a table at the end of the room. Only two other children sat there, both boys about Anna's age. The room grew quiet as they passed through, and everyone peered at the newcomers. "This is Anna and her sister, Inge," said Miss Irmgard, "and this is Robert and Willie." She pointed at the boys.

Robert threw a piece of bread at Anna. "So, where're you from, your parents dead, blown up, poof, poof?" He smirked.

"We are from Hamburg and my mama is coming to get us for Christmas," Anna shot back. She shoved her bowl enticingly close to him. "You want this soup? I don't eat chicken soup."

"Oh yeah, I could eat three bowls. I'm hungry all the time." He pulled the bowl to him.

"And if you ever bother my sister, I'll fight you, Robert." She took a bite of her bread.

"You're a girl. Nobody can beat me, I'm the boss around here, you'll see. This is the table only the bad kids get to sit at, ha, ha, ha."

Anna looked around for Miss Irmgard, but she had joined the other grownups at a table at the far end of the room. She turned back to Robert. "You're going to get in big trouble if you mess with me."

His big brown eyes sparkled. "Oh, I'm in trouble all the time. My papa was a gypsy, and I am not afraid of anybody." He threw imaginary punches.

Anna grinned. She didn't know what a gypsy was, but she thought he liked her. He would never admit it, but she was pretty sure.

In a while a young tom-boyish looking woman with short-cropped dark hair clapped her hands and moved in front of the tables. "Children, finish up, lunch is over."

"That's Miss Birgit," he told Anna. "She's our sports teacher. I can jump the furthest."

"I'm no good at jumping and all that," Anna said wistfully.

"She'll show you, believe me, everybody gets to do it."

"Everybody under five line up behind me," Miss Birgit shouted, still clapping her hands. "The rest of you can go play." The smaller children formed a line behind her.

"The little children have to take a nap," he said, "but we get to play." He jumped up. "Want me to show you the fort we built outside?" He grabbed Anna's arm, trying to pull her along.

Miss Birgit walked by, pointing at Inge as all the younger children followed her. "Come along, little girl, join our choo-choo-train." She marched out the door.

Inge held on to Anna's skirt. "I don't want to."

At that moment Miss Irmgard appeared. "These two girls will come with me." She waved Robert away and picked up Inge. "Let's go see your bedroom now. After a nap you can play."

They walked through the large center hall, their steps echoing through the stone walls, and headed towards the biggest stairway Anna had ever seen. It curved around an entire wall and led to the upper floor. She touched the shiny wooden banister, letting her fingers glide around each of the beautifully carved rails. Miss Irmgard motioned to Anna to follow her. "Come along, I only have a few minutes before my break." At the top of the stairs they entered a big foyer, its walls lined with clothes hanging on rows of pegs. Several hallways fanned out from the foyer. They walked down one of them and stopped at a door marked with a large letter D. "You will be in room D. Remember, D like doll," Miss Irmgard pushed the door open. "Anna, over there, the lower bunk bed is your bed. And Inge, you will sleep on the upper bunk on the other side next to the window."

Anna counted six bunks lined against the walls with a group of square wooden cubbies stacked in the center.

"Everybody has their own cubby with each name marked on the side, here. See, here is Robert's name. And here, we're going to write Inge on this one." she pulled a pen from her pocket and wrote "Inge" on the side panel. "And yours, Anna, is right next to Inge's." She wrote "Anna" on the side panel of that cubby. "All the children in this room are older than you, Inge, but I thought you'd like to be with your sister. It might be a bit rough to bunk with the big kids, but with Anna there to help you, it should work out. We can always move you later if it doesn't." She patted Inge on the head.

"I want Mama," Inge sobbed.

"Oh, it'll be all right, *Liebling*. You'll feel better after your nap." Miss Irmgard walked with her to the bed across the room, then looked back at Anna. "You may go downstairs and play, Anna. The little children nap for one hour and then they come downstairs for playtime too."

Anna shook her head and crossed her arms. "I want to nap too. I'm very tired." She faked a yawn.

Miss Irmgard raised her eyebrows. "All right, but just today. After that you have to follow the rules. Now, don't forget, you are in D like doll." She turned and closed the door behind her.

"I'm scared. I can't climb way up there," Inge lamented, looking at the ladder by the upper bunk bed.

"All right, for now, you can sleep in my bed." Anna led her to her own lower bunk bed, climbed in and stretched out. "There is no pillow." She looked around. "And the mattress is prickly." After a moment, she sat up and peeked under the sheet. "Look, straw!" She pulled out a long piece and showed it to Inge.

Inge took the straw and turned it and studied it.

"Come, lay down." Anna pulled her into the bed and covered her with the blanket. Then she got up and walked around the room, checking out the other beds. "Look, I found a pillow." She picked it up and brought it to Inge, who took it into her arms and lay back down.

Anna could not go to sleep. After a while she walked over to the storage cubbies. She reached into Robert's cubby and pulled out dark green pajamas, a crumpled polo shirt and some slacks spattered with reddish-black stains. She found shoes made of wood, like those in a fairytale book. Clogs? Next, she pulled out a large, thick envelope. A name was written on it, but she could not read the fancy words. She glanced around, then opened the

245

envelope pulling out a heavy knife with a carved metal handle like a dragon.

When she heard steps approaching, she quickly shoved the knife into the envelope and the envelope into the cubby. Her heart pounded into her throat. The door opened and a young woman came in. "Time to get up, children." She turned to leave but spotted Anna. "Oh, there is just one of you?"

"There is me and my little sister, Inge, over there." Anna pointed.

The woman put her arm around Anna's shoulder. "I am Miss Eva, and what's your name?"

"Anna Peterman, and that is my sister Inge."

"Oh yes, you are the new arrivals Miss Irmgard brought this morning. Come with me." She pulled at Inge's blanket. "We must go downstairs now for our crafts hour. You will have fun. You each get to make an ornament for our Christmas tree." Her voice rose excitedly, her short curly hair bouncing.

Anna hopped on her toes. She had never made a Christmas ornament. She took Miss Eva's hand ready to run downstairs and join the other children.

Inge climbed out of bed and eyed Miss Eva with suspicion. "I want to go home."

"You will, Inge. I'm sure your mama will come and visit us soon. But first, come down and help us make ornaments for our tree." She took Inge's hand and they walked to the stairway leading down to the main hall.

Anna stopped halfway down and stared at the lights sparkling from a giant lamp that hung in the center of the hall.

"This is a magic chandelier," Miss Eva explained. It has over one hundred lights on it. I heard that it came from a castle many years ago. It's not lit often because we don't have enough electricity." She shrugged, and Anna decided she liked Miss Eva a lot.

"You don't look like Miss Irmgard," she said admiringly. "You're much prettier."

Miss Eva laughed, "I'm sixteen, the youngest teacher here."

"Is your Mama in the hospital too?" Anna asked.

"No, Anna, my mama is somewhere in the East, maybe in heaven by now. She stroked Anna's hair. "Let's find a place for you at the table and see what kind of ornament you want to make."

"So, where do you live?" Anna looked at her curls.

"Right here, Anna, with you and the other children. The staff has the third floor for those of us who don't have a home to go to." A faint, sad smile lit her face. She stopped at a table where several girls were working on their ornaments and pointed at a star one was holding.

The girl looked up and pushed a bunch of hair behind her ear. "My name is Veronika and my Aunt Lola is an artist." She had long red curls and lots of freckles.

Anna sat on the bench next to her, watched for a moment and said, "Will you help me?" The girl nodded and soon they were working on a star for Anna. Inge scooted in between them and put her thumb in her mouth.

In a while they heard music. A young man holding a large instrument appeared at the door. "Children, put your crafts away. We're going to sing." He pressed the white keys on the box and danced to the beat.

Anna stared at him, fascinated by the beautiful sounds.

"That's an accordion," Veronika explained as she placed her ornament and craft supplies into a small basket. She handed Anna a basket. "Here, I'll show you." she wrote "Anna" on the basket handle.

Anna and Inge followed her to the center of the hall where the man with the accordion sat at a piano.

"That is Hans, our music teacher," Veronika whispered, looking at him dreamily. "He sings too. He is handsome, don't you think?"

"Yes, he is," Anna agreed. "But he is old."

"Well, maybe he's a little old. Miss Irmgard told me he is twenty-one. She has a crush on him, but he likes Miss Emily." Veronika snickered and shaped a heart in the air with her hands.

"Attention. I want all the boys over on this side and the girls over here," Mr. Hans announced. "Remember which song we practiced yesterday, boys and girls?" He pounded the piano keys and the children started to sing "O Tannenbaum, oh Christmas Tree." They sang very loud and with great feeling. Anna covered her ears.

When Mr. Hans stopped, he announced, "Tomorrow we will all go out into the woods and pick our Christmas tree." Everyone started running around, excited at the prospect, while Mr. Hans looked on and smiled.

Suddenly an older woman Anna had not seen before appeared. She was short and round, her gray hair in a bun. "Hans, you are too wild. Children, quiet down. Form a line here and walk, not run, to the washroom."

"She is the head teacher, Miss Gertrud," Veronika whispered in Anna's ear as they followed the woman through a door, down a flight of stone steps into the basement where they snaked into a long room, brightly lit, with tall ceilings.

"As soon as the first group is done washing their hands the next group can enter," Miss Irmgard said, and began helping the children at the wash basin.

Anna waited in line behind Veronika until they could wash their hands. Under the sink, which stretched from one end of the room to the other, was a metal rail lined with towels. But when it was Anna's turn, the towel was wet, and she had to dry her hands on her blouse. Then she offered the other side of her blouse to Inge to dry hers.

Anna and Inge followed the others through a metal door and up a narrow stairwell, which spilled them back into the grand center hall. Anna shook her head, blowing out a rush of air. "I will never find that place again."

"Oh, you will, we all do, Anna. We go there every day, and once a week, we all go there to take a bath," Veronika reported matter of fact.

"How long have you been here?" Anna wanted to know.

"Oh, maybe one year, or two, I don't know exactly." Veronika pursed her lips.

"My mother is coming to get us for Christmas," Anna said, hoping that she and Inge would not be here for two years.

"Oh, so you'll not be here when Santa Claus comes?" Veronika frowned. "You'll miss all the presents and the sweets. My aunt Lola is coming to visit, and I hope I am getting a doll buggy. On Sundays we get to have visitors and I'm the only one who has a visitor every Sunday."

Anna did not know what to say. She took Inge's hand and followed the rest of the children back to the big dining room where the tables had been set for supper. "I don't eat meat," Anna announced, and all the children stared at her.

"We only get meat once in a while, sometimes on Sunday," Veronika said.

A tall boy with two front teeth missing waved at Anna. "You can sit by me. I'll eat your meat."

Anna followed the other children, who carried their plates to a table in the center of the room. Two large pots sat on the table and an older woman in a dark blue apron ladled a glob of food on each child's plate and handed each a cup of milk.

Veronika pointed at Anna's plate. "Potatoes and cabbage. We have that a lot, maybe every other day."

Inge frowned. "It stinks."

But Anna was hungry and dug in. "I like this." She pointed at her sister. "Inge, eat, it tastes good. You have to eat or else you'll get sick, and you won't grow up." This was what Mrs. Munster at the farm had told them many times. Reluctantly, her sister picked up her spoon and took a bite.

Miss Gertrud walked around, stopping at each table, watching. "You are entirely too thin," she said to Inge. "I'm going to put you on the list." She patted Inge on the head and walked on.

"What list?" Anna looked at Veronika, who seemed to know everything.

Veronica grimaced. "She'll get a spoonful of cod liver oil with her food because she's too skinny."

Inge put down her spoon. "No, I won't take cod liver oil." She threw up her hand, knocking over her glass of milk.

Miss Gertrud rushed over and yanked Inge off the bench. "We have no food to waste, do you understand?" She shook her. "Next time you spill, you are going over there." She pointed at a chair at the far end of the room.

Anna stood up. "She is only four years old."

"I did not ask you, so be quiet. We haves rules here, do you understand? Or do you want to go and sit in the chair?" she shouted.

Anna shook her head. The room turned quiet, and everyone stared at their plates. She reached for Inge's hand, and they did not speak again.

After dinner, Miss Gertrud told them they had an hour of reading time and Veronika showed them the books lining the shelves of one of the walls. "I can read these books," she announced.

Anna, who had to admit that she could only read a little bit, like her name and the names she had memorized at Grandma's apartment house, said, "Maybe you can teach me."

At seven o'clock Ms. Irmgard appeared and told all children under seven years to form a line and follow her upstairs. "Do you remember your room number?" she asked Anna.

"Yes, D like in doll."

"Good girl. Now you all put on your pajamas and then we will brush our teeth."

Anna, Inge and Veronika headed into bedroom D and saw Robert already there. Veronika went to her bed, then looked around. "Where is my pillow?" she shrieked. She spotted it on Anna's bunk, dashed over, grabbed it and hugged it to her chest. "This is mine. My aunt Lola gave it to me," she shouted, and pushed Anna.

"I am sorry, I didn't know, Veronika, I really didn't," Anna stuttered, sad to have offended her new friend.

"Cry baby, cry baby, ha, ha, ha," Robert, taunted, dancing in front of her bed.

Anna jumped towards him, glaring. "You wanna fight?"

"What is going on in there?" Miss Irmgard's voice interrupted. "No fighting, you understand?" She walked up and grabbed Anna's arm. "We don't allow fighting here."

Robert scurried to his bed and climbed in, pulling the blanket over his head.

Anna turned to her. "I have to help my little sister into her bed."

"No, you don't. You get in your bed, and I will help your sister. Where are your pajamas?" she asked Inge.

The little girl just stared at her, big-eyed.

The woman threw up her hands. "Oh, you are new, I forgot. I'll be right back with your pajamas. Don't worry,

251

little girl. She shook her hand at the children. "And no more noise from you."

Sometime later, Anna awoke and tried to sit up, bumping her head on the top bunk. She scooted to the edge and sat listening. "Mama," she heard faintly. "Mama." She climbed out of bed and tiptoed to Inge's bunk. Moonlight shone into the room and Anna was stunned to see what had happened to her sister. Inge hung squeezed between the straw mattress and the side of the upper bunk. Robert still slept in the lower bunk. Anna leaned over him, trying to push up the mattress, which was protruding through a gaping hole with Inge straddled across it. Anna looked up and saw that a slat holding the mattress had been pushed aside. She tried to move the slats farther to the side to free her sister, hoping she could do it without Inge tumbling down onto Robert. After several tries, she saw she was not strong enough. What to do next? She scrambled out and up the ladder and reached for Inge's hand to pull her up. But the slats separated farther, and both girls tumbled to the bottom bunk, landing on top of the sleeping Robert. Quickly Anna got free of the mattress and pulled Inge out. To her amazement, Robert was still asleep. Anna took a deep breath and led Inge over to her own bed.

"I don't know what happened, Anna, the mattress got big and swallowed me," Inge whispered.

"Don't talk now." Anna put her finger over her mouth. "We'll talk to Miss Irmgard in the morning. Climb in, you can sleep with me." They scooted into the narrow bunk and huddled under the blanket. The sisters fell asleep clinging to each other, surviving their first night at the orphanage.

CHAPTER 28
Beversen Regional Hospital

December 22, 1945, another gray and cold day following an endless string of them. Annemarie wondered aloud if there still a sun or if it, too, was broken and had vanished. She pulled the blanket up to her chin to ward off the chill.

Ellen smiled as she gathered her few belongings, ready to be discharged. "Of course, the sun will be back, Annemarie. Spring will come, praise God." She reached out and stroked her hand.

Ellen's mother, who had arrived to pick up her daughter, handed Annemarie a box. "Merry Christmas. Sorry I didn't have anything to wrap it in." She shook Annemarie's hand. "You will get out soon. All will be well. It's God's will, you'll see."

Annemarie bit her lip and shook her head, nodding, too emotional to speak. These folks were kind and willing to share what little they had. "Thank you, thank you so much," she was finally able to utter as Ellen's mother waved and started pushing her daughter's wheelchair down the ward, vanishing behind the double exit doors.

Annemarie felt as if her last friend had just gone away and she was left behind at a train station, alone, with a big lump in her heart. She sighed and began opening the box Ellen's mother had left and found two glass jars, one filled with jam and the other with pears. There was a ham and, a loaf of bread, home-baked, no doubt, since Ellen had told her that her sister lived on a farm. On the bottom she found a jar of herring and her eyes welled up. Ellen had remembered how fond she was of pickled herring. Where on earth did she find such a delicacy? "Yes, Ellen, I do believe in miracles, and you are an angel," Annemarie whispered, smiling.

"At least somebody is smiling." Dr. Krohnert appeared at her bedside, his voice dry.

"Dr. Krohnert," Annemarie said, "I'm so happy you are back."

"Compliments get you nothing from me," he replied, matter of fact. "Let's look at your leg."

Unfazed by his brisk demeanor, she pulled the blanket off her leg. "Dr. Krohnert, I want you to release me today. I urgently have to get home. I have no choice. My mother is gravely ill, and–" she pleaded, her face contorted with grief-- "I have two little girls. I promised them that I'd be there for Christmas."

When he did not respond, she started to cry. "Do you have children, doctor? Do you know what it feels like to have children who are now in an orphanage?"

"If I could solve everyone's problems in here, I would, believe me," he snapped. "But I can't. I am a soldier, here to do my job dispensing medical service and patching soldiers back together. If you heard about all the horror stories in here, you'd consider yourself lucky. Do what I tell you. Like I said that leg has to come off and then we'll talk about discharging you."

Annemarie sat up and shouted, "You are rude and heartless." She stopped to catch her breath. "You are an uncaring monster, just like the Tommies." She tried to push him away from her bed.

"I want you to sign my release papers now."

The doctor stepped back and stared at her. "You would have made a good soldier." He actually smiled. "But if I released you, it would be against my medical judgment and not in your best interest." He saluted her and walked away.

Annemarie sank back into her pillow. Why did he not understand?

The next morning the nurse handed her an envelope. "Congratulations!" she said. "You are being discharged." She raised her eyebrows. "How you did it is a mystery to me. Dr. Krohnert never allows a patient to influence his decisions, never." She smiled, a rare thing for this nurse, whom Annemarie had dubbed "the witch," and walked away.

"Oh my God, another miracle." Annemarie opened the envelope, tearing part of the form inside in her haste. *"I release this patient against my medical judgment,"* she read but did not bother to read the instructions for her wound care. So much for his wanting to amputate. Her hands trembled as she folded the paper and placed it back in the envelope. *Home.* She closed her eyes. *I am going home.*

The nurse returned with a bag of Annemarie's clothes. "This is all?"

Annemarie nodded.

"It is minus four degrees outside. All you have in here is a summer dress and a pair of sandals." The nurse stared at her.

Annemarie waved her hand. "I was wounded in May, and I've been in hospitals since then. And they bombed my apartment and all my things burned up."

The nurse shook her head and left. A few minutes later she returned. "Here are some trousers and an army coat and boots. They are too big, but they'll keep you from freezing to death. 'From one soldier to another,' Dr. Krohnert said to tell you. These are from a soldier who didn't make it." She sighed. "The doctor said, 'she deserves these.' I don't know what he is talking about. But he's the boss." She tossed the clothes onto Annemarie's bed and hurried away.

Annemarie pressed her fist against her mouth, afraid she would scream as she edged towards the side of her bed. "Oh, ah," she grunted trying to slide into the trousers. It took several attempts to lift her wounded leg. When she started on the boots, she moaned and fell back on the bed. It helped that the boots were several sizes too big, to accommodate her bandaged foot. But when she tried to place weight on that foot, she flinched at the sharp pain rising up her leg. The trousers hung loose even after she tightened the buckle to the last hole. After a brief rest, she wrestled her arms through the sleeves and pulled the bulky coat closed. She placed the envelope into its pocket and the grey cap on her head. It almost covered her eyes. She unloaded the box from Ellen's mother and stuffed the food into the empty bag the clothes had been in. Slipping the straps of the bag over her head, she reached for her crutches. After a few attempts to balance, she managed to stand and started to maneuver through the center aisle of the ward.

Clapping and sporadic laughter greeted her as she hobbled towards the door, fighting with her crutches, taking small steps with the huge boots. It took fifteen minutes for her to reach the front door of the hospital. An old nurse at the front desk glanced up from her papers and saluted. "Good luck, soldier," she mumbled and went back to her paperwork.

Annemarie thrust her body against the heavy door, struggling to hang on to her crutches. When she stepped outside the cold wind gust pushed her against the wall. Hampered by the long, heavy army coat, she sat down hard on the stone steps, and she tried to catch her breath.

She looked up and realized that she had no idea where she was. But every town had a train station, and she had to get there before dark. She scanned the area, trying to orient herself. Rows of leafless trees surrounded the hospital entranceway to a big open gate. Beyond the hospital compound a narrow road led towards the horizon. Despite the heavy coat she shivered.

A lone vehicle was approaching the hospital gate. An army jeep. It stopped at the bottom of the steps in front of the entrance door. A soldier leaned out of the window and waved at her. The big hospital door swung open behind her, and Annemarie recognized the woman rushing out. The nurse glanced at her briefly as she huddled there, smiled when she realized it was Annemarie and skipped down the steps holding onto her hat. She jumped into the vehicle, and it roared off. Moments later, the jeep returned, and the nurse leaned out of the window, waving. "Come on, hop in," she hollered.

Annemarie tried to stand and one of her crutches fell to the ground. The soldier stepped out, ran up the steps and handed it to her, smiling, talking in a language she did not understand. He wrapped his arm around her waist, took her crutches and helped her limp down and into the back of the jeep. He was young with red hair and a beret and wore a uniform she did not recognize as that of a German soldier. British?

The nurse turned around, addressing Annemarie. "We are taking you to the train depot. You can't possibly get there on foot in your condition. It's at least fifteen kilometers away on the other side of town."

Teeth chattering, Annemarie smiled, and fought the stabbing pain shooting up her leg. The two in the front seat were laughing and chatting in anticipation of their day together, she guessed. How wrong she had been, Annemarie thought. This nurse was a real person with a big heart. She was probably only hardened from her thankless job at the hospital, where she dealt with human misery day in and day out.

When the vehicle finally stopped at a small brick train station, the nurse stepped out, opened the door and helped her out of the jeep and into the depot. "Good luck," she said, handing Annemarie her crutches. "And make sure you dress that wound and have it looked after by a doctor." She saluted and climbed back into the vehicle.

Annemarie hobbled to the station platform. At least fifty people stood or sat huddled together, clinging to their belongings. Icy gusts whipped across the platform. She hobbled closer to the rails even though she had no idea when the next train would arrive. One thing she did know, she had to get on that train, no matter what. The pain in her leg was increasingly worse and she began to feel weak and dizzy, not having been on her feet in months, let alone out in the unforgiving cold.

Finally, she heard the train whistle and the locomotive lumbered into the station and screeched to a halt. The crowd surged towards the steps of the railroad compartments like a cloud of angry bees. People muscled their way ahead towards the door, shoving, pushing.

Annemarie did not know how she made it up the narrow, metal steps and into the compartment. She was out of breath, close to fainting but at least, in the train car there was no danger of falling. The wall of people held her up. All seats were occupied, people sitting on laps and on the floor of the compartment. Pressed against the window, clutching the bag in front of her, she tried to hang on to her crutches. The whistle blew and the train started with a jolt, jerking everyone back and forth. Annemarie closed her eyes, fighting the pain, wishing she could pull her leg out of the boot. But soon, the rhythm of the wheels helped her doze and drift away.

Suddenly, she startled. A man's booming voice called, "Tickets! Have your tickets ready for inspection."

"Oh my God," she said aloud, looking around. "They can't possibly squeeze through here and inspect tickets."

"If you don't have a ticket, you'll have to pay," the man next to her mumbled, fixing his eyes on the bag she clutched. Wearing a dirty military coat and cap, his face showing stubbles of a beard, he erupted into raspy laughter. "Soldier, you're a Freulein! Did you knock off some guy to get that coat?" He moved closer, obviously disgusted with the possibility. "You don't have a ticket, do you, ha?" He fixed his eyes again on her bag. "Got money to pay?" he barked.

She shook her head. "I was bombed and shot. I just got discharged from the hospital."

"Yeah, yeah." He pointed at her bag. "What've you got in there? I'll make you a deal. You get my ticket if you give me something for it." He started to finger the bag. She shrank back from the foul odor coming off him. "They're going to kick you off at the next station."

Annemarie sighed and pulled out the ham. "This is the best I have. The rest is just a couple glasses of fruit." She held up the ham, not sure he believed her.

"All right." He grabbed the ham, eyeing it with hungry eyes. "Haven't had meat in months, can't remember when." He dug into his pocket and handed her a ticket.

"Thank you so much, you are an angel," Annemarie whispered. "My friend Ellen is an angel too; she gave me the ham." She smiled.

But the man put the ham into a worn leather bag and sunk back into quiet stupor.

Two hours later, the train rumbled into the central station of the city of Hamburg. Annemarie recognized its vast hall and ornate ceiling. Home! She could not believe she had finally come home.

The human cargo spilled out of the train like an army of ants, streaming into the center hall and getting

259

swallowed by the crowds already there. Annemarie stopped to catch her breath. She had not been to the city since they were evacuated over two years ago, just before the final firebombing. Overcome with the desire to let go and sink into oblivion, she straightened herself and leaned on her crutches. She would see her mother. Bring her children home.

The huge hall of the central train station looked, like a scene from an old movie. Ragtag groups of people, men with canes, women wearing babushkas and children sitting on worn suitcases that were held together with belts and ropes. She realized, having been confined to a hospital for so long, she now was a stranger in her own hometown. Why were all these people here? Were they waiting for a train that might never arrive? Why did they not go home to their families? "Thousands are now homeless," she remembered Mrs. Dummersdorf telling her. "Refugees are surging into the city from the east with no place to stay and many die right on the streets." She recalled Martha describing the collapse of society. She shuddered. It was something she could not comprehend.

I have to get home somehow, she told herself and asked a group of women, "Do you know if the streetcars are running?" They looked at her suspiciously and huddled closer around their children.

Disheartened, she hobbled on towards one of the exits, passing a tall, framed mirror next to a window of what used to be a jewelry store. She stopped in her tracks stepped closer and lifted her arm in a salute and mumbled. *Good God, my own mother would not recognize me, this coat, these big boots.* Her high collar almost obscured her face, the large bag hanging down her front, her arms leaning on crutches.

She turned and hobbled away. She had to get home before dark, and that would be soon on this gray day. Stepping outside, she braced herself against the gusting wind. But she was not prepared for the landscape of utter destruction. Ruins stretched their grotesque remains into the winter skies. She hardly recognized the main street of her hometown. Shaken, Annemarie joined the stream of darkly clad people shuffling down the street carrying bags and pushing carts, seemingly oblivious to the destruction all around them.

She recognized St. Nikolai church, an empty hull now rising out of the rubble, its steeple missing. Exhausted, she sat down on part of a wall, her leg throbbing and her other foot hurting in the ill-fitting boot. The cold penetrated even the thick army coat. She began to have doubts whether she would be able to make it to her parents' apartment.

A man with a bushy beard came towards her. "What have you got in that bag, soldier?" He moved closer and looked at her menacingly. She raised herself up and swung one of her crutches, trying to swat him. He grunted and staggered past her. Though relieved, she had to move on. She remembered Martha telling her how people would prey on the weaker ones, steal their things or even murder them for a piece of bread. The veneer of a civilized people was gone, stripped away by this unforgiving war.

Driven by fear, she hurried on, dragging her injured leg. Blisters had formed on her fingers, which were frozen from gripping the crutches she had used only for short periods in the ward.

Three hours later, when darkness had swallowed the city streets and the columns of people had thinned, she finally reached apartment house number 77 where she had lived with her parents through her childhood. She did not recall how she'd gotten there, but somewhere along the way, a boy had pulled her bag off her arm, almost knocking her down. At that point, too exhausted to care, numb and frozen, she kept on going, driven by her will to survive for her children.

Drained of strength, she tried to push open the door of the apartment building. She fell on her knees and crawled inside, dragging her crutches into the dark hallway, which smelled of stale air and cabbage. Her parents lived on the third floor, and she willed her exhausted body to keep on, to slide up step by step on her rump, taking frequent breaks to rest. There was no light in the hallway, and it was quiet. Nobody came or left. Determined, she pushed on, one step at a time, until she finally reached the third floor. She leaned on a wall slumping and tried to stay up. All she wanted was to kiss her mother and fall into bed. Nothing more mattered. She had come home.

She rang the doorbell once, twice and a third time, and then flung herself against the wood, using a crutch to bang on the door. "Mama, it is me, Annemarie. Mama, open the door."

No sound came from behind her mother's door. But then she noticed that the door across the hall opened a slit, protected by a chain and she heard a woman's voice shout, "Who's there? Nobody is home." The door quickly shut again.

Annemarie stumbled over and knocked on the neighbor's door. "Frau Maier, it's me, Annemarie," she cried.

The widow Maier slowly opened the door and peeked through the slit from behind the chain. She squinted for what seemed a long time. Apparently, she could not decide whether this strange soldier could really be her neighbor's daughter, whom she had known since she was a child.

"Please, Mrs. Maier, where is my mother?" Annemarie cried, desperate, choked with emotion. "She is not answering."

The chain clicked against the door, which slowly opened. A candle flickered in the back. Mrs. Maier peered closer to see Annemarie's face, buried in the collar of the

262

army coat. "Oh my God, it really is you." She pulled her into the apartment.

Annemarie stumbled and collapsed in the hallway.

"Ach du lieber Gott." Mrs. Maier closed and bolted her door. She left and returned with a glass of water. Annemarie sat up and gratefully accepted it. "Can you get up?" Mrs. Maier, almost eighty years old and worn from the long hard war years, looked at Annemarie, sitting on the floor. She put her arms around Annemarie's shoulders and tried to prop her up. "Maybe if we take off that heavy coat," she suggested, shaking her head and calling out "Oh mein Gott." Together, they managed to remove the coat, and leaning on the old woman's shoulder, Annemarie hobbled to the living room.

"Here, lie down on the sofa, I'll bring you a blanket." Mrs. Maier hurried into her bedroom and returned with a big feather comforter. "You are frozen, girl, your teeth are chattering." She covered Annemarie with the soft featherbed. "Oh, your boots, let's take them off." She managed to pull off the left boot but when she tried to pull off the right one, Annemarie screamed.

"I was wounded, I just got out of the hospital, Mrs. Maier," she groaned. "Oh God, it hurts." she cried, her tears streaming down her face.

Looking concerned, Mrs. Maier studied Annemarie. "We should get that boot off before it swells even more." She wrung her hands, then hurried away, finally coming back with a large pair of scissors. "My dear Franz had these in his toolbox. Remember, he did shoe repair after he retired." She proceeded to cut into the boot.

Annemarie winced and let her tears flow freely. Her foot and leg throbbed, sending waves of pain clear to her hip.

Mrs. Maier cut the boot open halfway and gingerly peeled it back until she was able to free Annemarie's foot. "OH Gott oh Gott." She stared at the bloody bandage.

"That has to come off, it is draining." She shook her head and stared at Annemarie, wringing her hands again.

"Can you cut the bandage off?" Annemarie asked.

The old woman went to bring the candle closer. Reluctant, shaking her head, she took the scissors and slowly cut away the bandage while Annemarie moaned. "I don't have any bandages, but here is a clean towel, it will have to do." She lifted Annemarie's foot, gently wrapped the towel around it and covered her legs with the featherbed. She sighed and sat down at the table, her hands in her lap.

"My mother is not home?" Annemarie whispered, too weak now to raise her head off the pillow. "Is she at my sister's house?"

Mrs. Maier twisted her fingers together. "They took her to the hospital. I think she is very ill. You know, she got so thin. I think she came down with pneumonia. I'm not sure, I don't know what to say."

Too weak, too exhausted to cry more, Annemarie managed to ask, "What hospital?"

"Eppendorf Regional, I heard Mrs. Kraus from upstairs say. I do have her key. You know, your mama always thought you would come home." She smiled.

Annemarie did not reply. The last thing she saw before sleep overcame her was Mrs. Maier blowing out the candle.

CHAPTER 29
Hamburg, December 1945

Mrs. Maier stood by the sofa, peering down at her. "Annemarie, are you awake?"

"Annemarie raised her head off the pillow and stared at the woman. For a moment, she did not know where she was.

"I am sorry, I just wanted to make sure you aren't -- I mean that you are alive." Mrs. Maier attempted a smile. "It's eleven o'clock and I need to go to the store on Luther Street to see if they've received meat, eggs or any food I can buy." She shook her head. "When they get anything in, it's always sold out while I wait in line. It's hard, with my arthritis and bad knees, I can't stand in line very long." She sighed again and wrapped her arms around herself.

Annemarie watched her, the last hours coming back to her. "Thank you so much, Mrs. Maier. I finally feel warm under your feather comforter. I'm sorry I slept so long." She sat up, looking for her boots, then recalling that Mrs. Maier had to cut off her right boot because her foot was so swollen. "You helped me so much. You saved my life." Annemarie smiled at the old woman. "May-be I can wear a pair of my mother's shoes. I must go to the hospital. I have to see her." Annemarie's voice was strained with fear that she might be too late to see her mother.

"Here, these are to your mother's apartment." Mrs. Maier handed her a key ring. "It's the large one." Her wrinkled face showed concern. "Let me help you walk across the hall." She took the crutches and then helped her up. "Did you not bring a suitcase?"

"No, Mrs. Maier. I got robbed on the way here. A boy stole my bag and ran."

"What is the world coming to? So much sadness and crime. How could anybody steal from a cripple?" She shook her head looking chagrined and added, "I didn't mean-, I'm sorry. Forgive me."

"Please don't worry," Annemarie told her. "When I get food or coal, I will make sure to repay you for your kindness."

"Oh, it's no trouble my dear, I'm so glad you are home." She looked away. "I think your mother had no will left to live. All the terrible things that happened to her, you know," Mrs. Maier then turned to slowly make her way down the stairs, grasping the railing and mumbling to herself.

Annemarie hobbled the few feet across the hall and, leaning on her crutches, she opened the door to her parents' apartment as she had done a hundred times before. It was ice cold. The faint smell of tobacco still lingered, from thirty years of her father's cigars. In a strange way now, it gave her a sense of comfort. She took up her crutches and limped into the kitchen. The oilcloth with the embroidered roses around the edge still covered the table. Nothing had changed. Leaning onto the wall, she slowly walked to the pantry, stumbling, grasping the door handle. She opened the pantry and found two glasses of pears and a jar of strawberry jam on the otherwise empty shelves. Realizing that these were the items Anna had brought to her grandmother from Mrs. Gellert, she burst into tears. Her little, brave Anna. "I've got to pull myself together," she said out loud. She took a deep breath, picked up a jar of the pears and stepped to the sofa, dizzy from hunger.

With her last strength, she knocked the lid of the jar on the corner of the table, and it popped open. Her body shaking, she did not get up to get a spoon from the second drawer on the bottom of the sideboard she remembered so well, but brought the jar to her mouth and let the fruit slide in. The pears tasted sweet with a slight cinnamon tang, and she finished every drop.

She leaned back, pondering what to do next. Her leg throbbed. The towel Mrs. Maier had wrapped around her foot had slipped off the foot, exposing the open wound. The cold turned her fingers numb. But she had to get to the hospital today to see her mother. Every minute counted. She felt her mother reaching out to her, waiting, saving her last breath to see her.

The pears and sugar had given her a rush of strength, and she heaved herself up and, hopping on her good leg, holding on to the furniture, made her way into her mother's bedroom. A lump rose in her throat. She knew every piece of furniture-- the ornate oak chest she'd always hated to dust, the grandfather clock with the big brass pendulum her mother had told her was an heirloom from her grandparents, the bed with the oak headboard covered with the colorful comforter her mother had crocheted many years ago, and a nightstand with a pair of glasses and a water glass next to them, as though the owner had stepped out for a moment.

Annemarie fought back tears. She opened the large wardrobe that covered one wall. On the left, her father's jackets and trousers hung in a row as though he had put them there yesterday. On the right, her mother's clothes lined up in order - the velvet dress she had seen her wear only once, the blue summer dress with the puffed sleeves and the old fur jacket her sister had given to her mother because it no longer fit her.

On the top shelf were two of her father's hats and several hats she had never seen her mother wear. She opened the side door of the closet and found underwear, socks and sweaters and several pajamas in neat stacks.

Checking through these things, she felt like a girl again, digging in the closet the day before Christmas, trying to find what her mother might have hidden, and frozen with fear of being discovered. She leaned against the door jamb, crying silently. After a few minutes she selected a pair of her father's long johns and corduroy trousers, plus the fur jacket and a matching fur hat she discovered on the top shelf. The other side of the wardrobe contained bed sheets and towels stacked in neat piles. Her mother had learned neatness when she was in service as a housekeeper. Girls who came from poor families had no education and few choices other than marrying or working in servitude to the wealthy. But her mother kept a sense of humor and sunny disposition in the face of the daily fight to keep her family fed. Annemarie smiled while the tears streamed. Then she took a pair of thick, woolen socks her father had worn working as a longshoreman. They smelled a bit musty and smoky, but they would keep her feet warm.

She closed the closet and hobbled into the small, dark hallway. Her father's ornate walking stick and her mother's blue umbrella hung on a peg, and the black coat with the fake brown fur collar draped over a polished wooden hanger.

On the bottom of the wardrobe was a shoe rack. She picked up her father's worn work boots hoping to fit in her wounded foot without having to cut the boot. She looked around, undecided what to do about the open wound. It had to be covered before she could attempt to slide it into the boot. Then she remembered that her mother kept ointments and bandages in one of the dresser drawers.

She hobbled back into the bedroom, and slowly dressed in layers with the items she had selected. She laughed because she could hardly move her arms. Then she opened the dresser drawer and found everything just as it had been for twenty years– bandages and gauze, tubes of salves, bottles that smelled like chamomile. She didn't

268

know what the various ointments were, so she picked a large piece of gauze and a bandage and sat on the bed to wrap her wound, then slipped a sock over it to keep the bandage in place.

Luckily her father's boots had long laces she could adjust to fit her small feet and loosen around the swollen one. Back in the hallway, she stood in front of the full-length mirror mounted in the center of the wardrobe. Better than the army coat, she concluded. At least nobody would mistake her for a soldier. She nodded at her image in the mirror. "Not too bad." Her sister's fur jacket and matching hat looked rather impressive, but her father's trousers, bulging over his long johns, and the work boots, made her look ridiculous. "As if anybody cares," she said to herself. " At least I'll be warm."

Once more, she decided to seek help from her old friend, Martha Dummersdorf, who would know how to get to the hospital. She placed the apartment keys in her jacket pocket, grabbed her crutches and made her way into the hall, facing the daunting task of descending three flights of stairs. It was quiet again, and she wondered if the people were staying inside to keep warm or were just too old or sick to get out. She remembered that most of the tenants were elderly.

Annemarie slid her crutches down the stairway and clung to the railing, hopping down a step at a time. Even the noise of the crutches landing on the wooden floor did not rouse any of the neighbors. Were they afraid to open their doors? Was someone listening on the other side, anticipating a knock?

Annemarie's foot began to throb, the sharp pain travelling up into her thigh. But turning back was not an option. She had only one goal, to make it to the hospital to see her mother.

It was December 23, but she saw no crowds out shopping, no children waiting for Father Christmas, only a gray, cold sky and deserted streets. Slowly she limped two blocks down the lonely avenue, which looked grotesque with gaps between houses and ruins skirted by mounds of rubble. She paused at the corner at Werner's pub, now identifiable only by the big double entry door, partially open, leading to nowhere. She circled around a pile of debris, realizing that this had been Tilgers, a fancy ladies' clothing store where she had stood as a child, her face pressed against the window, admiring the dresses and blouses and wishing that she could own one. Had someone saved the beautiful clothes, snatched them before the building went up in flames?

She arrived at the apartment building where the Dummersdorfs had lived as long as she could remember. She stopped and sighed. Their apartment was on the third floor, too. She leaned against the entrance door, trying to catch her breath.

"Who do we have here?" A man's voice startled her, and she almost lost her balance. It was Bernhard Dummersdorf, a jovial smile on his face. "What a surprise, it's Annemarie." He stepped back to take a better look.

She tried to smile. "I just got home from the hospital yesterday. I am--" Overcome with exhaustion, she fell against the door.

He jumped forward and caught her. "Come on up, Maedchen, you need something warm to eat."

Without a word, she surrendered into the arms of the big man and slowly he helped her up the stairs, alternately walking and resting until they reached the third floor. "Look who I found," he hollered as he pushed open the apartment door. Martha stood speechless and gaped at the figure her husband was holding.

"Annemarie. Good God, you look - come in-- I'll make some coffee."

Bernhard guided Annemarie to the kitchen and she sank into a chair. "Let me take your coat and hat," he

270

offered. "We've been lucky to get some coal yesterday and keep the kitchen warm. Nice, isn't it?"

Grateful, Annemarie nodded. "I have to go to the hospital." She started to cry. "My mother is very ill. A neighbor told me she has pneumonia." She choked and could not utter another word.

"Now, now, don't do that." Bernhard helped her take off her jacket and hat. "We'll have some real coffee and a bite to eat, then we'll see what we can do." He motioned to his wife, who was already opening the pantry door to get the coffee.

"Oh my God, the aroma, real coffee. I think I'm going to faint." Annemarie smiled through her tears.

Soon, Martha poured the steaming coffee into porcelain cups with saucers, the ones she used only for special occasions. Against Annemarie's protests, she fixed a platter of ham sandwiches. "I don't have any cake," she apologized, "no flour or sugar, but the ham is really good, from the farm. Thank God for the Gellert's."

Annemarie did not reply but sipped the coffee as though it was Champagne. "I almost forgot how good this tastes."

"Eat, Annemarie, you look so thin. I'm surprised that Bernhard recognized you." Martha handed her another sandwich. "Eat first. Then you can tell me what happened."

Grateful, Annemarie ate, savoring each bite. Martha refilled their cups. "Compliments of Mrs. Friedrich Bowman." She laughed, then listened as Annemarie described her long journey to the city. Martha kept shaking her head. "Unbelievable! It's a miracle that you made it home. Somebody could have killed you for your clothes, or you could have frozen to death."

"Now, now, Martha, don't scare the girl," Bernhard interrupted. "Let's see if we can help her get to the hospital to see her mama."

271

Annemarie's eyes lit up. "I will be forever grateful."

"I think there is a train today going in that direction. It's only a couple of stops and then you have to get off at Eppendorf Station and from there it's just a short walk to the hospital." The old railroad man was in his element. He probably knew the schedule by heart, since Martha had told her that he met with his old comrades almost every day to find out what was going on.

"I don't have a ticket, I don't have any money, I have nothing, nothing at all," Annemarie said, wringing her hands.

"No problem, Bernhard has tickets for that train." Martha said.

Bernhard grinned. He looked at his watch. "You need to leave right now and hurry. There's only one train running, and it leaves at 2:30." He left the kitchen and returned with the tickets. "These guarantee you a seat. I don't know about the return train. There's only the one scheduled at 6:30, the last one for the day. If you miss that, you'll have to wait till tomorrow." He stood up and returned with Annemarie's fur jacket and hat. "Ask for Bruno at Eppendorf station and tell him Bernhard sent you. He'll help you get on a train home." He gave her a benevolent smile.

"You know what," said Martha, "I'll go with her. Look at her, so frail, on crutches. I think she'd be safer." Martha did not wait for his answer, just reached for her coat. "Look, Annemarie." She pulled a hat from her pocket. "Remember, you gave this to me. I wear it every day. It keeps my ears nice and warm." She slipped into her boots.

Bernhard returned and handed her a small paper sack. "Give this to Bruno."

Martha peeked into the bag. "This nice bottle of brandy? He'll like this"

272

"Like I said, ask Bruno to take care of you two."
Bernhard was the man in charge and his wife nodded,
though Annemarie knew she was worried that he would
have a seizure while they were gone.

She put her arm around Martha's shoulder, and they
slowly climbed down the stairs and walked to the train
station as fast as Annemarie could hobble. Her leg hurt so
much that she had to bite her lips, but she thought of her
mother and knew that she had to make it. The train arrived
already full, and more people clamoring to board. With the
help of Martha, resolute, strong and pushy, they managed
to get on, leaving behind a cluster of cursing, angry people,
some trying to hang on, some clinging to the steps of the
train as it left.

For a while, they did not speak but stood squashed
against the wall despite having seat tickets. No one made
an attempt to get up. People just stared at the floor,
oblivious to anyone else.

Annemarie finally broke the silence. "Anna and
Inge are in an orphanage."

"What! No, no," Mrs. Dummersdorf shouted. "I
can't believe it." Martha put her face in her hands. "When I
went there a second time, I was sure she would keep them,
her only sister's children, for God's sake."

Annemarie did not reply. She could not find the
words.

"She could not keep these two little girls for one
week," Martha kept on. "We had real coffee and English
cookies. And after the second shot of Cognac, I got up, told
her about Bernhard's seizures and that I was leaving the
children with her. She shoved back her chair and her face
turned red. Then I remembered how I got things done when
I was a Hitler Women corps leader. I told her she had no
choice, threatened her with retaliation, and said that I
would contact her husband's employer, the big shipping
company where Bernhard knew higher-ups. I think that did

it." Martha snorted. "Anna and Inge were coloring with their cousins. I stepped over to the table, kissed them each on the cheek, turned and stormed towards the door. She followed me. I said that you'd be grateful, waved good-bye and hurried down the stairs."

"You did all you could, Martha. I will forever be grateful to you and Bernhard. If there is a God, you will go to heaven." Annemarie attempted a smile. They spent the rest of the trip in silence.

"Lucky for us it's only a short walk to the hospital from here," Martha explained when they left the depot. She watched Annemarie grimace at every step.

Annemarie saw her notice. "I was discharged against doctor's orders. But I had to come home. You do understand, right? I received a letter from my sister informing me that my mother was at home, freezing and starving, coughing to death."

Martha shook her head.

"But let's not talk about that right now." Annemarie hobbled on, pausing between steps.

"Would it help if I put my arm around your shoulder? I can hold your crutches."

"I don't know, maybe." Annemarie sniffled and wiped her nose with the sleeve of her fur jacket. "Margarete would have a fit if she'd seen me do that. "She tried to smile. Martha joined her and soon her eyes filled with tears. "God will deal with her in his own way," Annemarie muttered. "That's what my friend Ellen would say."

"Yeah, maybe she'll be struck by lightning." Martha burst into bitter laughter again and Annemarie joined her, tears dropping onto her sister's precious fur collar.

Finally, they arrived at the hospital, a cluster of four-story brick buildings, and hesitated.

"I see people going in there." Martha pointed at a building with a large ramp leading to a double door. Annemarie hobbled up the ramp and into a wide hallway. A woman at the reception desk gestured to a row of chairs. She eyed Annemarie's crutches. "Are you here to check in?" She picked up a clipboard.

"We are here to see Mrs. Anna Rebhorn," said Martha.

Annemarie had slumped into one of the chairs. The woman at the desk, gave her a skeptical look, and checked the records on her desk then nodded. "Room number sixty-nine on the second floor. The elevator is on the right. You are lucky, we have electricity today."

"We have to hurry, Annemarie, we don't have much time for the visit. Remember, Bernhard said the last train leaves at 6:30." She helped her out of the chair as Annemarie grimaced in pain. They walked to the elevator. "God, I hate hospitals. They all smell the same and they are so bare and depressing, like sickness and dying." Martha covered her mouth with her hand. "I'm sorry, I'm just babbling, I didn't mean that. "she put her arm around her friend, guiding her through the hallway. "There it is." She pointed to a door on the right and pushed it open.

Annemarie scanned the long, rectangular room with its grey walls, the paint peeling in splotches. She could not believe how many beds were crammed into this ward. It was quiet. Perhaps the patients were asleep or sedated. She did not see any other visitors. The room smelled of disinfectants and the damp, sticky air made Annemarie cough. Heat boiled up from radiators lined along one wall.

"The odor in here is enough to make you sick," Martha murmured.

Annemarie focused on each bed, trying to find her mother, hoping that they were not too late. Then she spotted her in the last bed. "Mama!" She flung down her

275

crutches and hobbled the last few feet. "Mama!" Her
mother lay with her eyes closed; hands folded on her chest.

"Oh my God she is dead," Annemarie whispered.
"Mama?" She bent down and kissed her on the forehead,
tears dropping on her mother's face. "It's me, Annemarie."
She smiled shakily and stroked her mother's hands.

Mrs. Rebhorn opened her eyes. "Annemarie, I knew
you would come." She tried to raise her head off the pillow
but started to cough.

"Don't, Mother." Annemarie gently guided her
mother's head back to rest.

Mrs. Dummersdorf stepped up, holding the
crutches. "Hello Mrs. Rebhorn. Your daughter is here now
to take care of you. You get well quickly. She wants to take
you home." Martha looked around and realized that her
voice had echoed through the silent room. "I'm going to
find some chairs. I'll be right back," she said more quietly
to Annemarie, who had sat down on the side of her
mother's bed.

"Why didn't Margarete take you home?"
Annemarie asked, though she knew the answer.

Her mother opened her eyes and smiled.
Annemarie could not believe how frail she looked, her face
was so pale and sunken. "Oh, your sister, she means well,
but she can't help herself." Her words were barely audible.
" She is just like her father. He had a cold heart, not a
happy man, but not a bad man. We never went hungry."

"I know, Mama, I know. And we had happy times
too. I love you Mama," she swallowed hard.

"Annemarie, don't count on your sister for much.
She cares in her own way, but…" Her mother's voice grew
even weaker. "I don't know why." She gasped for breath.
"I tried my best, I really did…" Her eyes fell shut.

Annemarie touched her mother's cheek. "It doesn't
matter now, Mama, we are here together, and I will always
be with you." She choked on her words. "Look, I can walk.

Soon I won't need crutches." Annemarie slid off the bed and took a step, then turned back and slipped to her knees. "Don't leave me now." She grasped her mother's hands and brought them to her lips.

Mrs. Dummersdorf appeared with two chairs. "How is she? Is she…? She stared at the pale woman, then leaned to wrap her arms around Annemarie.

"I just showed her that I can walk and told her I will take care of her," Annemarie said, sobbing. She let Martha help her into a chair.

A nurse stepped by and picked up the chart from the end of the bed. "She is resting comfortably."

"I want to take her home," Annemarie whispered.

The nurse looked down at her. "Could you come with me for a moment?"

Martha helped Annemarie out of the chair, and they stepped away to the center of the ward.

The nurse held out a clipboard and pen. "I need you to sign these forms, so we know who is responsible for funeral arrangements."

Annemarie fell into Martha's arms. "No, she looks good, she--"

"I am sorry. She is gravely ill, she is too undernourished, and her body is too weak to recover."

Annemarie's voice caught. "Can't we give her food, or a pill to make her strong again?"

"It's too little, too late. She is too far gone. We're just keeping her comfortable, I'm sorry, it's in God's hands, but I think now that you have come, she will be ready to let go." The nurse looked at her with kind eyes.

"How long, how long?"

"She could go any time, probably tonight. Oh, meine Liebe, I'm so sorry. However, we need to fill out these documents." She held out the clipboard to Annemarie, but Martha took it and started writing. Then she held it for Annemarie, who signed without reading.

Then Martha filled in one last detail. In the line
"Responsible for funeral arrangements" Martha wrote: *Mrs. Friedrich Bowman. Relationship: Daughter.* She
handed the board to the nurse and walked back to the bed.
"We have to leave soon if we want to catch the last train
home."

"You go home, Martha, I'll stay here," Annemarie
murmured.

Martha sat down in the other chair. No words were
spoken. Finally, she said, "I'll leave you alone with your
mother now. I'll be down in the lobby." She hugged her
friend briefly and left.

Annemarie took off her boots and sat on the side of
her mother's bed. Moaning, she lifted her leg onto the
chair. It was oozing through the homemade bandage.
"Silent night, holy night," she hummed. It was the day
before Christmas Eve.

*"No sourpusses in my ward." Annemarie looked up
and saw nurse Lisbeth next to her bed, hands on her hips.
"You will dance again, Maedchen. Doc Hartmann is
waiting." Annemarie twirled around to imaginary music ...*

Annemarie startled when the nurse touched her
shoulder. "I must have nodded off, I'm sorry." She looked
up, not sure where she was.

"She's gone, Mrs. Peterman. Your mother passed
on." The nurse gently removed her mother's hands from
Annemarie's and placed them on her chest.

"Is she, is she?" Annemarie whispered.

The nurse nodded.

Annemarie cupped her face with both hands,
sobbing silently. Mutti I tried, I wanted to… She slumped,
gripped by pain overwhelming her.

The nurse stroked her shoulder then handed her a
handkerchief.

Annemarie straightened herself, slowly wiped her face and asked "What time is it?"

"It's almost five in the morning. The doctors will be coming by for rounds soon and the next shift of nurses should be here shortly." Her eyes focused on Annemarie's foot. "What is that?" She stepped closer, pulling at the soiled gauze.

"I was wounded and just got out of the hospital yesterday."

The nurse grimaced and peeled back the bandage. "You need to have this taken care of immediately. This wound is infected." She shook her head. "Who on earth let you check out of the hospital?"

"I had to come home to see my mother, I just had to, you understand. The doctor wouldn't let me go, but I insisted."

The nurse scratched her head. "You can't go home like this. The wound has to be cleaned and you need medication."

Annemarie shrugged. "I have two little girls at an orphanage waiting for me. I promised I would be home for Christmas."

The nurse patted her on the shoulder. "I have a girl and a little boy. They are with my parents because I have to work on Christmas. But we are planning to have a small celebration the next day, though God knows we don't have much to give." She sighed and straightened her shoulders. "Wait here, I'll be right back."

Annemarie sat there, feeling as though she had turned to stone. "I tried, Mama, I tried so hard to come," she whispered, and kissed her mother's cheek, so gaunt, was still warm. "You will be with Father and with Otto and -- you'll see your beloved Richard again."

The nurse returned. "Lie down on the side of the bed," she ordered. "I'm going to treat your wound and rebandage it for your trip home. It's against the rules but if we hurry, we'll be done before anybody gets here."

Annemarie lay down next to her mother and touched her hand. She had come home and made her mother happy. She drifted again, content in this knowledge.

After a few minutes, the nurse tapped her on the arm. "We're finished. Promise me that you will see a doctor. You want to be there for your girls, don't you?" The nurse looked at her with a stern face. "This is my Christmas present to you so I can feel that something good came of all this." She helped Annemarie off the bed, turned and was gone before Annemarie could thank her.

Annemarie looked up and saw Mrs. Dummersdorf. "I fell asleep in the lobby. I am sorry, Annemarie." Tears welled in Martha's eyes. "So sorry."

They embraced. Then Annemarie bent and kissed her mother on the forehead. "She is with my brothers now. She loved those two boys so much." Slowly, she pulled on her boots, carefully lacing them around the swollen foot.

Martha helped her into the fur jacket and handed her the hat. "Maybe we will be lucky and won't have to wait all day for a train."

Annemarie looked straight ahead as they walked out of the ward. "I have to arrange for her funeral. I don't know what papers I signed."

Martha waved her arm. "Don't worry. I wrote down your sister's name to be in charge of the funeral and everything else."

Annemarie gasped.

"No, no, it's the best thing for all of you. Margarete has the means to take care of everything. That's the least she can do for her mother. You are in no shape. And you have to get well for your children."

They walked to the depot in silence. Grains of snow were falling. Then the sun appeared on the horizon.

"That's my mother. She's in heaven now," Annemarie whispered.

They stopped in the station office, a small sparse room. Martha handed Bruno the bag with greetings and thanks from her husband. A huge smile spread across the man's face. "Merry Christmas," he shouted, "I wish I had something for you two ladies."

"Oh yes, Bernhard said you will help us get on the next train to the city." Martha smiled at him.

He checked the schedule. "Hm, not good. There might be a passenger train later this afternoon, but you can never be sure these days." Then it was as if he noticed their disappointed faces and Annemarie's crutches. "Let me see what else we can come up with." He gazed at his schedule again. "There is a freight train due, oh, in half an hour or so. Of course, they don't take passengers. But I'll see who is in the locomotive. If it is Karl, we'll be good. He's an old war comrade. You two ladies wait in here." He smiled and stuffed the bottle into his leather bag. "Nobody needs to see this." He laughed and winked.

Mrs. Dummersdorf reached and shook his hand. "Come visit us, please. Bernhard needs his friends now more than ever."

"How is he doing?" The man asked.

"Same. I keep thinking he's better and then he has another seizure. But you never know, we all hope for a miracle these days."

After half an hour, the damp cold began to penetrate even Annemarie's fur jacket. Then she saw Bruno had climbed onto the step of a locomotive. He waved, motioning them over.

They hurried to the platform. The engineer opened the door to the crew compartment and Martha climbed in, assisting Annemarie up the narrow metal steps. The man inside called to Bruno, "You owe me, remember." Then he smiled and waved. "Merry Christmas!" He saluted as the train began to pull out.

Martha put her arm around Annemarie. "There are still nice people out there who help their friends. We have to remind ourselves of that when we get bitter and lose hope. Now let's get you home and to bed."

Later when the train came to a stop, she took Annemarie's hand. "Let's go by my place so Bernhard knows I'm alive." She sighed. "We'll have breakfast and pick up some food for you." As they stood up from the metal bench and climbed out, they offered the men a Merry Christmas. They did not reply.

Noticing the indignation on Martha's face, Annemarie said, "Maybe they've lost their families."

"You are right. Who knows what burdens people carry these days?"

Slowly, they made their way back to Martha's apartment. The sun was shining, and a few people passed them, their faces glum as if they had forgotten it was Christmas. Annemarie's leg throbbed as they walked up the three flights to the Dummersdorf's apartment. Inside, she slumped into a kitchen chair, resting her head on her arms. Martha made coffee and ham sandwiches, but Annemarie barely ate. Then the door opened, and Bernhard stepped into the kitchen and pulled up a chair. Martha said, "Bruno appreciated your gift."

"He likes to have a little glass; you know what I mean." He smiled, looking satisfied that his plan had worked.

Martha gathered some food and placed it into a small sack. "It's not much." She shrugged.

"Oh, Martha, I owe you everything. I'll pay you back, I promise." Annemarie said.

"Nonsense, Maedchen." Martha shook her head vigorously. "We are neighbors. That's how it has always been. Who knows, I might knock on your door someday and ask for help. And now I'm going to walk you home and tuck you in."

"You don't really have to, Martha. I think I can make it."

"No, you cannot walk home alone. An order from Nurse Martha." She laughed and helped Annemarie into her jacket.

They walked down the street in silence. When they approached house # 77, Annemarie's tears started again. "She'll never come back here," she sobbed.

"Let's get you upstairs now. There are many people who lost their families, who lost their children, Annemarie. At least you have a roof over your head. And you have your children. Be thankful for that." She held on to Annemarie, slowly dragging her up the steps to the third floor.

"Oh," she cried out when they stepped into the kitchen. "You have coal! Not a lot, but enough to heat the place for now. You get yourself to bed, and I'll make a fire."

Annemarie limped to the bedroom and sat down on her mother's bed, fatigue overwhelming her. She pulled her mother's nightgown off the bedpost but could not bear to put it on. She took off her clothes and slipped on her father's pajamas and sank into the bed, which began to spin.

Martha stuck her head in the door. "I put the food in the pantry. Leave the doors open so the heat can spread through the rooms." She turned to leave. "Get some sleep now."

"Can you go to my sister's house and let her know that Mother has passed?" Annemarie called out.

"I'll do anything for you, but I promised myself that I will never set foot in Mrs. Friedrich Bowman's place again. You don't know what I have gone through with the woman. But don't worry, the hospital will notify her.

I WILL DANCE AGAIN

Remember, that's why I wrote her name on the forms.
Believe me, this time she won't be able to get out of it.
Now, rest and get better. And, I almost forgot, Merry
Christmas."

CHAPTER 30
At the Orphanage

Robert sat up in his lower bunk and pointed at the huge bulge hovering over his face. "What happened?"

Anna hopped out of bed and over to Robert to look. "So that's it. The boards under the mattress moved apart and Inge fell through the hole."

"I can fix that," Robert said, climbing up the ladder and dropping Inge's straw mattress down to Anna. "All you do is slide the boards over, see." He pushed the slats towards the middle so that they were evenly spaced. "Hand me the mattress." He reached down, took it, and placed it back on the slats.

"That's scary. Are all the beds like that?" Anna pulled the blanket off Robert's bed and lifted his mattress to take a closer look.

"That's how they are." Robert climbed down the ladder.

Some of the children snickered and one of the boys pulled his blankets over his head.

"It's the ghost, he comes out at night." Robert grimaced and turned towards Inge. "Boo."

Inge started to cry. "I won't sleep here ever again." She clung to Anna's arm.

"Oh, they will make you," Robert said. "We have to follow the rules here."

Anna cocked her head at him. "You can't scare me. There are no ghosts." She planted herself in front of Robert, her hands on her hips. "And stop scaring my sister." She stepped closer, glaring at him.

Miss Irmgard appeared in the door. "Children, put on warm clothes and form a line," she barked. The children scattered, collecting their clothes. "We're going out to pick a Christmas tree this morning," she added.

Anna and Inge looked up at Miss Irmgard. Their cubbies were empty.

"I will go downstairs to find some warm clothes for you girls." She shook her hand at Robert. "And no fighting or trouble, or you won't get to go with us to pick the tree."

Robert jeered at Anna. "You can't go, ha, ha, ha!" He ran around the cubbies, making faces.

Veronika put her arm around Anna and whispered in her ear, "He put the hole in Inge's bed. I saw him do it before. Shh, don't tell that I told you." She smiled at Anna, glanced back at Robert and whispered, "He's a gypsy. They're bad people, they steal, and his mother was a witch."

Anna's mouth dropped and she reached for Inge's hand.

Veronika shook her finger at Robert. "If you are nasty to Anna, I will tell Miss Irmgard and you'll be the one to stay home."

"You are a spoiled brat and a baby!" Robert jumped at her just as the door opened and Miss Irmgard stepped in. She grabbed his arm.

"What's going on here? Robert, are you picking on the girls?" He shook his head, and neither of the girls said a word.

Miss Irmgard handed a sweater to each Anna and Inge. "I could not find any long pants for you, Inge, but these were left at the office." She helped Inge slip on the trousers, shaking her head. "You are so thin, child, I can feel your ribs."

"We were bombed and everything burned up." Inge hugged Miss Irmgard, who stroked her head.

They all washed their faces and brushed their teeth, then formed a line that snaked to the hallway where the children's boots were lined up against the wall. The sports teacher, Miss Birgit, joined them as well as Mr. Hans, the music teacher, playing "Oh Tannenbaum" on his harmonica. Anna had never seen such an instrument. "I want to play that."

"You do?" Hans smiled. "Great, I'll see if I can find one for you and teach you."

Anna preened, basking in the envy of the other children.

Inge tugged on Miss Irmgard's sleeve. "I want my hat."

"You have hats?"

"Yes, my mama knitted them for us."

Miss Irmgard left to retrieve the hats. "I couldn't find any boots." She handed Anna and Inge each a hat.

Anna held up her sandaled foot. " These are the only shoes we have."

"Ha, ha, you can't go out with us," Robert hollered.

"Who can't go?" Mr. Hans dashed over to Robert, picked him up and threw him over his shoulder, laughing as Robert squealed. "Promise to be nice to these girls." Hans swung him around again.

"Yes, yes, let me down."

He set the boy down and ruffled his hair. "I think you want Anna to be your girlfriend," he teased, making Robert blush and dash away.

Anna glanced at Mr. Hans. "I like him," she whispered to Veronika, who looked up at the teacher with big eyes.

"I wish he was my boyfriend," Veronika said dreamily, "but he likes Miss Irmgard." She put her hand to Anna's ear. "I've seen him kiss her." The girls giggled.

287

"And" Anna said, pursing her lips, "he's old."

"You are right. We celebrated his birthday last July. Miss Irmgard told us he was twenty."

Anna raised her arm and pulled back a strand of hair tickling her cheek. "That's old, even older than Miss Irmgard."

"We need to find boots, it's too cold to go out." Miss Irmgard sighed. "Let me think." She puckered her lips. "I wonder if Anna can borrow Miss Karin's boots. She went home for Christmas. They'll be too big, but what else can we do?" She walked down the rack and returned with one pair of boots for Anna, but none for Inge. "Here, Anna put on these extra socks, that will help a little."

Finally, everyone was ready. They lined up behind Mr. Hans and followed him outside. He stopped, opened the big iron gates and children followed him out of the compound and marched down the sidewalk in pairs. Soon, they reached the end of the street and fanned out into the woods. Mr. Hans played his mouth organ and Anna, arm in arm with Veronika, and with Inge by her side, stayed close behind him. She did not know anyone who could play an instrument and was enthralled by the beautiful sounds.

"He also plays the guitar and the piano." Veronika smiled. " He let me play the piano once."

"You play music?"

"Yes, when my mama and father were home, I took piano lessons. Mr. Kunze came once a week and taught me."

"Can you play a song for me?" Anna put her arm around her friend.

"Maybe. We'll have to ask Mr. Hans." Veronika hummed along with the song he was playing.

"Is your mama coming to get you for Christmas?" Inge asked.

"No, they are… they can't come home. I don't know where they are. The soldiers came to our house and took them away." Veronika dropped her head and stared at the frost-covered duff.

Anna squeezed her hand. "Maybe they will be back soon and get you."

Veronika looked at the milling children. "My Aunt Lola, she's really old, like a hundred, comes every Sunday. She always brings me presents. Nobody else gets presents."

After the group had gathered in this wooded area, Miss Birgit told them to fan out and find the perfect tree. "Remember the rules," she shouted. "When I whistle three times, come back here."

Anna, Veronika and Inge stayed close to Miss Irmgard. Anna took Miss Irmgard's hand. "Are there witches in these woods?"

"No, Anna, there are no witches. Just in fairytales." A few minutes later, Anna stopped and pulled on Miss Irmgard's sleeve. "What is this?" She stood in front of a small, wooden cross with a helmet resting on its top.

"That's where a soldier fell and they buried him and placed his helmet on the cross to remember him by," the teacher explained.

"Was he dead?" Inge asked, her eyes wide.

"Yes, Inge, there was a lot of fighting in these woods in the last weeks of the war. And a lot of the soldiers, mostly young boys, were drafted and had to fight. And many got shot or blown up and they --" She stopped, alarmed, when she noticed the horror on the little girl's face. "They are in heaven now, Inge, with the angels." She patted her on the head. "The war is over, and now we are safe here in the woods."

"The Tommies bombed them," Anna explained. "I saw their big tanks with the cannons when I went to the farm to get food with Mr. Gellert."

The children looked at her, their mouths open. "They had cannons?" one of the boys asked.

Before Anna could reply, Miss Irmgard, who had gone a few feet ahead, shouted, "Children, come look at this tree." Everyone ran to see. It was a tall pine with branches stretching all around in perfect symmetry.

"Oh, it is beautiful." Anna touched a branch. "It wants to go home with us." Everyone agreed and they jumped around, touching the branches.

"I saw it first," one boy shouted.

"No, I did," another yelled.

"We found the tree, all of us did," Miss Irmgard said, and shouted, "Birgit, we found the perfect tree."

Miss Birgit appeared, parting the branches of two bushes, a group of children surging behind her. "Oh, that is the most beautiful tree I have ever seen. What do you think, children?" A chorus of voices rose, and a group of girls started to dance around the tree, singing "Oh Tannenbaum."

Soon, Mr. Hans and his group appeared. He stepped over and briefly put his arm around Miss Irmgard. "I agree."

Anna wondered if he was going to kiss her.

Then he said, "Shall we pick this one? What do you think, children?"

"Yes, yes, this one," everyone shouted. He took out his harmonica and played "Oh Tannenbaum" while the children sang along.

"Can the dead soldier hear us?" Inge whispered in Anna's ear.

"Yes, he can. He's not really dead, just not here. He's in heaven like Miss Irmgard said."

"Anna, my feet are cold," Inge whimpered, hopping from one foot to the other.

Anna bent and started to rub her sister's toes, which stuck from her sandals, unprotected from the biting cold.

Mr. Hans took a handsaw he had brought along. "Children, help me-- one two, one, two, one and two," he shouted as he pushed the saw through the tree trunk.

"One, two, one, two, one, two," the children joined him.

"All right, everybody gets behind me now. The tree is about to fall." When the tree was down, he asked Miss Birgit for the rope and wrapped it around the tree to keep the branches close to the trunk. He lined the boys up along the rope and shouted, "one, two, one, two, one two." They tugged at the large tree, slowly moving it along. Miss Irmgard stepped up to help.

"Men only," he shouted. "No girls allowed."

It took them half an hour to pull the big tree to the orphanage and finally through the big open gate. When they reached the wide stone stairway Hans shouted, "Stop, drop the rope! Boys, you did a great job. Thanks for all your help."

Anna was envious when Mr. Hans walked up to each boy and shook his hand. "Good work, thanks." He called each one by name.

Miss Irmgard walked in and looked around. "Children, line up behind me now to go to the washroom. Take off your boots and put them on the rack. Then clean up and meet me in the   dining room.

"I am hungry!" Mr. Hans shouted, surging ahead to the dining room.

"You'll have to sit at the trouble-maker table, Mr. Hans, if you keep shouting," Miss Irmgard said grinning and waving her finger at him.

"After lunch we each get to hang our ornament," Veronika told Anna on the way to the dining room.

"How do you know that?"

"That's how we did it last year. You wait and see. I made three ornaments. I'll show them to you."

"When is Christmas going to be here?" Inge asked.

"On the twenty-fourth of December. We get dressed up and sing Christmas carols, and then Father Christmas comes with presents." Veronika's face turned red with excitement. "You'll see. it's beautiful. They light the candles. Oh," she sighed, "I can't wait for my presents."

"My mama is coming to take us home for Christmas." Inge squeezed Anna's hand. "Right, Anna? She promised."

"Yes, she promised," Anna repeated.

"Oh, I will be so sad. I like you so much, I want you stay. You are my best friend, Anna." Veronika hugged her and stroked her hair. "You are the best friend I ever had." Her eyes filled with tears.

Anna hugged her back. "You are my best friend, too. I can't wait to see the ornaments you made. But mine is not done." She bit her lip. "Maybe you can help me finish it?"

Veronika nodded.

"Can we sit next to you?" Anna asked.

"Yes, but let's hurry so we can get in the food line first and find a table."

Anna looked at her plate. "What is this?" she bent and smelled the food.

"Potato pie, you'll like it."

Anna breathed a sigh of relief. "Thank God it's not chicken soup."

"Look, there is Mr. Hans at the trouble-table. Hurry, let's sit by him." Veronika nudged her.

"At the trouble-table where the bad kids sit?" Anna asked, slowing down to keep her milk from spilling.

Veronika hurried and sat next to Mr. Hans.

"Oh, you were bad too?" He shook his head like he was worried.

She nodded, looking happy.

Anna munched the potato pie, which she liked a lot. "Please find me a mouth organ. I want to learn to play a song for my mama, maybe 'Oh Tannenbaum'."

"I'm cold, Anna." Inge snuggled up to her rubbing her hands.

Veronika shivered. "They must be running out of coal again. Last year, we didn't have coal for a whole month. I wore my pretty fur jacket; the one Aunt Lola gave me. I was the only one who had a fur jacket." She smiled and glanced at the others.

When their plates were empty, Mr. Hans looked around the table. "Children, we are going to decorate our tree this afternoon and you will help me, will you, Inge?"

Inge stretched up her arms. "Yes, I can do it, I am big enough now."

"Of course, you are. You can be one of my elves. Then we will sing Christmas carols to make the tree happy to be with us this Christmas. I think it waited all year just for us, to come into our home and let us decorate it." He looked around. "And, if we have time before you go to bed, I'll teach Anna how to play the harmonica."

Veronika's mouth dropped open. "Can I come too? We can play another song on the piano." She put her arms around him

"What do you say, Anna?" he asked.

"Yes, she's my best friend, she can come too." Anna hugged Veronika. She had forgotten all about the pillow incident.

After lunch, Mr. Hans and some of the bigger boys - - including a surprised Robert went outside to carry the big pine up the stairway and inside the hall, securing it into an iron tree stand next to the piano. When he asked Miss Irmgard about Anna and Inge going home for Christmas, she shook her head, and for a moment, the funny man's face turned sad. "Damn war," he muttered, and left to look for a harmonica. Anna, who'd been standing behind Miss

Irmgard, felt her heart drop. But mama had said. And mama had never told a lie.

"Children! Listen," Miss Irmgard shouted. "Get your ornaments and sit on the floor around the Christmas tree. Miss Birgit will be there and help you hang them."

Anna pulled her sister close while she lined up behind Veronika and they all marched through the big glass doors into the center hall. They walked around the tree singing while Mr. Hans played the piano.

"Halt," Miss Irmgard called, and everyone sat down on the polished wood floor.

Anna had never seen such a big tree. It was taller than Mr. Hans and almost touched the chandelier. "Look, Inge, the lights above look like big white candles and snowflakes. See how they sparkle?" She pointed at the glistening crystal chandelier.

Inge squirmed, her cheeks flushed and her eyes round and shiny. "I want to hang my ornament now."

Finally, Mr. Hans spoke. "Children, who do you think should hang the first ornament? The oldest child?"

"No, no," the children yelled, "the youngest one."

He pointed at Anna and Inge. "How about asking our newest children to go first? Let's show them we are happy to have them."

"Yes," the children shouted.

Anna shoved her sister towards the front. "Get up, Inge, you go first."

Shy, but beaming, Inge walked up to the tree where Miss Birgit opened her arms and scooped her up.

"So, where shall we hang your ornament?" Inge picked a branch high up and Miss Birgit lifted her to hang her ornament.

"Well done, Inge." Miss Birgit put her down. The children clapped.

Then the rest took turns hanging their ornaments. Miss Birgit looked around. "Is there anyone who has not had a turn?" Several children pointed at Robert, who sat on the floor cross-legged, making faces.

"Come up front, Robert, let's hang yours." The boy shrugged his shoulders and did not move. Miss Gretel stepped over and looked at him. "You were not making faces at me, Robert?"

He shrugged again and shook his head. "Ornaments are stupid." He drummed his fingers on the floor.

A boy shouted, "He didn't make one, he cheated."

Anna, who was sitting in the row in front of Robert, quickly turned and slipped him one of her ornaments.

Robert glanced back at her, gaping, jumped up and sprinted to the tree. Everyone fell quiet.

"All right Robert, where do you want to hang your ornament?" Miss Birgit asked. He pointed to the top of the tree.

Before she could say anything more, Hans came and picked the boy up and set him on his shoulders.

"Pick any branch you can reach except for the top. That's for the angel."

Robert stretched and picked the highest branch he could reach, higher than all the other ornaments. "Mine is at the top," he shouted triumphantly.

Hans set the boy down. "Good job, Robert."

Robert sprinted back to his place and pulled on Anna's hair. She shook her head and pushed his hands away, but she was smiling.

On the other side, Inge tugged her arm. "When is Mama coming to take us home?"

"I don't know Inge. Shh, we have to sing carols now."

Miss Birgit turned the lights down and Mr. Hans started to play, guiding the children through the songs they had practiced. And then Miss Irmgard and the other staff walked around with baskets of cookies.

To Anna's delight, the supper that evening consisted of bread and molasses and milk.

"I hate molasses, it stinks like cow manure." The voice was unmistakably Robert's.

Anna stood up to see where he was sitting and waved at him. "Inge, go and ask if I can have his molasses bread and give him my milk."

A moment later, Inge returned with the bread. "He told me to tell you that you are a doll," Inge repeated. "Why did he say that? You don't look like Pepita or Rita."

Anna lowered her lashes and devoured her second slice of molasses bread.

After the children ate, they played for a while and Anna and Inge joined a group of girls with paper dolls.

Inge sat, sulking. "I want Mama to come now."

"Inge, it is not Christmas today. Wait till tomorrow. Maybe Father Christmas will bring her on his sleigh because, remember, she is sick, and can't walk."

CHAPTER 31

Saturday was always bath day at the orphanage. However, since tomorrow was Christmas, Miss Irmgard announced that they would all take a bath this evening.

"I don't like bath time," Veronika whispered in Anna's ear. "We have to take off all our clothes."

"All of us, together?" Anna stared at her.

"Yes, you'll see," Veronika replied, looking glum as they marched upstairs to their bedroom.

"Quickly now, put on your pajamas, Anna." Miss Irmgard was in a hurry. "Everybody ready? All right, line up, you know the rules."

The children from room D joined others emerging from their bedrooms, walking single file down two flights of stairs to the basement washroom.

"Now, starting with room A, children, take off your pajamas and wait in the hallway for your turn."

Anna's mouth dropped open. She stared at the children removing their pajamas and standing naked in front of the bath hall. "Oh my God, those are boys." Anna covered her eyes.

Veronika nodded. She leaned towards Anna and whispered, "Have you ever seen, you know what I mean, a naked boy?"

Anna shook her head, feeling her face burn.

"Seen what?" Inge interrupted. "Tell me too." Veronika snickered and Anna's face turned red and she looked at the floor.

Veronika nudged her. "Our room number D is next." She pointed to the open door where children from group C stopped two at a time, in front of one of the large bathtubs.

"Hurry up children, Miss Irmgard helped Inge out of her pajamas. Robert was first to take his clothes off. He showed no sign of embarrassment, jumping around, waving his arms to fight imaginary foes.

"Stop acting up, Robert. Do you want to go in back of the line?" Miss Irmgard's patience seemed to be wearing thin.

He frowned and stopped and stood still.

"I'd rather be dead," Anna whispered to Veronika, looking away.

"All boys have that," Veronika explained, pointing, even Mr. Hans."

Anna peeked, trying to hide that she was staring at the boy standing in the middle of all the naked children. She moved her arm over her eyes and stared at the floor.

"Your turn next." Miss Irmgard led them into the steamy bath hall and lined them up in front of the tubs. Staff members stood in front of each tub, lifted two children at a time into the water, and proceeded to scrub them.

"Soap got in my eyes," Inge hollered, and struggled with the woman trying to wash her. The woman swatted her on the bottom and Inge screamed.

Anna stood in the next tub, unable to help her. She, too, started to cry. She closed her eyes so that she did not have to look at naked Robert, hoping he would do the same, but he didn't. Finally finished, the woman lifted her out of the tub and handed her a towel. Quickly she wrapped it around her and followed Robert to the far end of the washroom. Miss Irmgard was there, helping Inge dry off and get into her nightgown.

Back in room D, Veronika slipped under her blanket and put her pillow over her face.

"I want a pillow," Inge whimpered.

Miss Irmgard picked her up, ready to lift her up to the top bunk above Robert's bed. "I wish we had pillows, child."

"No, no, I can't go there," Inge squealed, struggling to free herself.

"Can she sleep in my bunk just this one night?" Anna begged. "Please, Miss Irmgard."

"All right, but just this once," she relented, and Inge quickly scampered over and climbed into her sister's lower bunk.

Anna climbed the ladder to the upper bunk, her eyes half closed to avoid seeing Robert in the bed below.

"Be good. Remember that Santa Claus is coming tomorrow." Miss Irmgard switched off the lights and closed the door. Anna watched beams of moonlight streaking through the tall window. She tossed and turned, trying to get comfortable. Suddenly, her straw mattress gave way and she fell through to the lower bunk bed, on top of Robert. She shrieked and struggled to get out of the bed. The boy in the next bed woke up and started to snicker.

"It's not funny," Anna yelled.

Soon everyone was shouting and laughing. In an instant, the light came on and Miss Gertrud, the head teacher, towered in the doorframe. "What are you doing in that boy's bed?" she demanded, looking at Anna.

"I don't know. I fell through a hole," Anna stuttered.

"Speak louder, I can't hear you."

Anna repeated what she had said. Robert was snickering, making faces at her. She threw herself at him, trying to twist his arm, and managed to hit him with her fist.

"Enough." The head mistress's tone made Anna stop.

"You are both in detention." Anna started to cry. Robert just shrugged, having been there many times before.

And then Veronika spoke up. "He did it. I've seen him do it before."

Miss Gertrude stepped over and put her arm around her. "What is it, sweetie, what have you seen him do before?" Veronika started to sniffle.

"Don't cry, sweetie. Just tell me, what did you see him do before?" The woman cuddled her.

"He-" she pointed at Robert- "He pushed the slats apart so there's a big hole and that's how Anna fell through." She continued sniffling and eyed Robert defiantly. He stuck out his tongue.

"Is that true, Robert? Did you move those slats?"

He shrugged. "It was a joke."

"A joke! Anna could have gotten hurt. And" she turned to Anna, "what were you doing in the upper bunk? We assign those only to younger children."

"My sister is supposed to be up there," Anna wailed, "but she's only four and she fell through the hole yesterday and she was so scared that I asked Miss Irmgard if Inge could sleep in my bed and-" Anna wiped her eyes.

"All right," Miss Gertrude interrupted, and patted Anna on the shoulder. "You were just helping your little sister, were you? I will talk with Miss Irmgard. This room is for six-to twelve-year- old children and Inge is four, you said?"

Anna nodded. "But we have to be together. My sister is too scared to be without me."

"We will see about that. Now, Robert, you fix that bed so that Anna can go back to sleep."

Slowly and with obvious reluctance, he did what the head mistress demanded.

"And now, you come with me." She grabbed him by the neck and shoved him out the door, turning the light off with a firm "Good night." They heard her scold, Robert. "Santa Claus knows about this, and I am sure you will be punished. An older boy hurting a girl. Santa will be angry. There will be consequences."

CHAPTER 32

"Wake up, Anna, it's Christmas eve." Veronika pulled the blanket off Anna's bed.

Anna stretched, yawned, then came wide awake. "Oh, I had such a lovely dream, I almost didn't want to wake up." She climbed down the ladder.

Inge jumped around with a big smile on her face. "Mama is coming today. I can't wait. How long before it starts?"

They both dressed quickly and hurried down for breakfast. In the center hall, the children chattered excitedly about Father Christmas bringing presents.

A little later, Mr. Hans shouted, "Children, we have visitors coming this afternoon and we want to sing Christmas carols for them." He struggled, keeping them focused. Afterwards, Miss Gertrude announced, "I want you to look nice for Father Christmas, so dress up in your best clothes. Everybody back downstairs in the big hall at one o' clock. So, line up behind Miss Gretel and go to your room. Hurry! It's almost twelve-thirty." The children scampered upstairs to look for clothes to wear to the festivities.

Back in room D, Veronica asked Anna, "What are you going to wear?"

"Me? I want to wear the dress Rita made for me. It has flowers and bows, you'll see. It is the nicest dress I ever had." But I don't know where our things are.

They had not seen Robert. "He's in detention," Veronika explained. That's where he is a lot."

302

Anna made a worried face. "Will he get spanked with a broom by Santa?"

"Probably. Last year he did. He should know better. Why is he always so bad?" Veronika shook her head. "I don't like boys, except Mr. Hans."

Then Miss Irmgard came in with Veronika's dress. Anna gasped. It was the most beautiful dress she had ever seen, made of pink taffeta and decorated with velvet bows and little flowers around the hem.

Anna could not take her eyes off her friend. "Veronika, you look like a princess in this."

"My Aunt Lola gave it to me. She had a dress shop, but now she doesn't because of the war. She saved this dress for me." She twirled like a ballerina. "I can't wait to see what gifts she will bring me today, maybe a doll buggy and-"

"I can't wait for my mother to come," Anna interrupted. "You'll like her, Veronika, she's so pretty, and she laughs a lot."

Miss Irmgard stood in the doorway and looked at Anna. "Where is your sister?"

Anna glanced around. "I don't know. She was here a minute ago."

Miss Irmgard wrung her hands. "We have to find her. Go downstairs and look, and check the bathroom, too."

Inge would not go there by herself, Anna thought. She scurried down the steps to search, but Inge was nowhere. Anna went back upstairs.

"Does she have a special friend here; someone she likes to play with?" Miss Irmgard asked, her hands on her hips. Anna shook her head. Her sister always stayed close to her.

"Well, you look for her. I'm going downstairs to find something for you to wear." Miss Irmgard frowned.

303

"I want to wear my flower girl dress," Anna said before Miss Irmgard left. At Miss Irmgard's puzzled look, she explained that Rita had made her and Inge matching dresses when they were flower girls at her wedding.

"All right, I will go and look through your things for the dresses. And you, Anna, you go back around and ask the other children if anybody has seen Inge. It's almost four – visitors time."

Anna skipped down the steps, hanging on to the banister. She saw people gathering by the tree where benches from the dining hall had been set up. She turned left and stopped behind the tree when she saw the front door leaned partially open. Looking left and right, she ran out the door.

Snowflakes swirled through the bare trees. It was so cold that she could see her breath. She stepped off the narrow, ash-covered path leading down the steps towards the main gate and slipped on a patch of ice. She remembered that the older boys had helped Mr. Hans spread the ashes for the visitors. She brushed the ashes off her knee and squinted. And then she saw a woman, holding Inge's hand, slowly walking up the path towards the steps. "Inge," she shouted, "Inge," louder, rushing down the steps. Out of breath, she grasped her sister's hand and pulled her close.

"I found her standing by the gate." The woman stopped to catch her breath. "We have to get her a warm coat and some hot milk. She could catch pneumonia, poor child."

"I was looking for Mama," Inge whispered, shivering, her cheeks flushed from the cold wind.

The woman stopped, resting on her cane. "I think I'm the last one off the train. Everybody else was ahead of me. I can't walk well because of my bad knees." She climbed up the next step. "I am Aunt Lola, Veronika's aunt. What is your name?"

304

"Anna," and this is my little sister, Inge." Anna pulled Inge along, her teeth chattering. "We'll have to get dressed or we'll miss Father Christmas. And Miss Irmgard is angry because we couldn't find you." Anna coughed.

Inge sobbed. "Mama is coming and taking us home. She promised."

"I am sure she would come if she promised. Now we better get you inside," Aunt Lola said, patting Inge on the back. She rang the doorbell, and Anna pushed against the door.

The head mistress, Miss Gertrude, opened the door. "Miss Lola, please come in. We're glad to see you. Veronika is so excited." She motioned to one of the staff to help Aunt Lola take off her fur coat and hat.

"Inge!" Gertrude stepped back and stared at the girl.

"I found her at the gate," said Aunt Lola, "I think she's almost frozen."

The rest of the staff had gathered around. "Where have you been, child?" Miss Irmgard took her shoulder and shook her. "We have been looking all over for you."

Inge started to cry.

"She was looking for mama," Anna stuttered.

"You know the rules. No child is allowed to go outside alone, especially without a coat." She grabbed Inge by the arm and up the stairs and to room D. Anna trotted behind her.

"All our visitors are in the big hall waiting for the Christmas program, and we could not start because we were all looking for you." She kept on scolding. Inge sobbed more and did not say a word. "I was going to braid your hair and put in a pretty bow I made. But now we don't have time. Let's get you dressed and go downstairs." She helped the child undress and slipped the dress Rita had made over Inge's trembling body. "We should give you a hot bath, but there is no time. The celebration must start."

305

Miss Birgit stopped by. "You found her! Thank God." She looked at Inge. "Where have you been hiding, dear? We've looked everywhere." She kneeled in front of Inge and took her hands.

"I went looking for Mama. She is coming to take us home today," Inge whispered, pressing her face close to Miss Birgit's chest.

"Veronica's aunt found her outside by the gate. No coat, no hat, who knows how long she was out there." Miss Irmgard shook her head angrily.

"Oh, your mama is coming today?" Miss Birgit hugged Inge and patted her on the head.

Miss Irmgard poked her friend in the side and shook her head as if she were trying to be as inconspicuous as possible.

"Let's go downstairs now," Birgit said. You have to help us sing. Mr. Hans is waiting for you." She took the trembling child by the hand, and they walked down the stairs. Anna followed.

All the children had gathered on the broad stairway that circled down into the main hall. They filled the entire stairway. Veronika waved. "Come sit by me, I've saved you a spot."

Anna and Inge squeezed next to her, nudging others aside.

"Look at the tree. Oh, the candles are so beautiful." Anna pointed at the top of the tree. "Do you see the angel? Look how she sparkles."

Veronika jumped up and pointed. "There is my Aunt Lola." The small group of visitors sat on benches next to the tree. Mr. Hans stood by the piano on the other side.

The head mistress stepped in front of the tree and started her Christmas address. Excited, the children paid no attention, but joined to clap when the visitors did.

"Do you see your mama?" Veronika whispered.

"No, I don't see her." Anna squinted. "But she's short, maybe she's sitting in the back row."

Mr. Hans played "Oh Tannenbaum," turned and directed the children to sing.

Inge nudged Anna. "See the presents under the tree?" She peered through the railing.

Anna craned her neck. She saw several boxes, some with bows.

"How did Santa get inside to put them under our tree?" Inge asked.

"Psst, watch Mr. Hans," Anna whispered. "We have to sing some more."

"I can't wait to show Mama my dress." Inge kept on talking, seemingly oblivious to her sister's warning. Finally, she couldn't wait any longer. "Mama," she shouted, "Mama." She jumped up and down and waved frantically.

Miss Birgit came sprinting up the stairway, making her way through groups of excited children. She motioned Inge to her.

Inge strained her neck. "My mama can't see me up here."

Miss Birgit took her hand and they walked down the stairs through groups of children. "You sit here in the front row, so she won't miss you. But you must be quiet now. Nobody gets up to visit until after the program." Inge opened her mouth, but Miss Birgit shook her finger. "Not one more peep out of you. Father Christmas is watching."

Two girls sang a carol Anna had not heard before, but she thought they sounded like angels. Then a boy recited a poem about snow and the stars and little baby Jesus in a crib. Anna clapped wildly. She wished she knew a poem. Finally, they all sang "Oh Tannenbaum" and the visitors applauded. "This is so beautiful," Anna whispered to Veronika.

Then the head mistress announced cider and cookies was set up in the dining room. "Children who have visitors may now come down and join them. Visiting time ends at four." The children started charging down the stairs. Anna almost fell because they were all pushing and shoving.

Robert had reappeared, dressed in brown slacks and shirt. He led a bunch of boys running for the dining room. "Cookies and cider!" he shouted.

Anna nudged Veronika. "Doesn't he want to find his family?"

Veronika shook her head. "No, he never has a visitor. He's an orphan. They don't even know where he is from. I heard Miss Irmgard say that he's a gypsy."

"What's a gypsy?" Anna asked, but Veronika shrugged and rushed past her and into her aunt Lola's embrace.

Anna went looking for her sister and found her milling among the visitors. "Inge." She pushed through the crowd. "I'm here!" she shouted, finally catching up with her.

She reached for Inge's hand and pulled her close. "Let's stay together. She can't find us if we run around." They threaded their way through groups of visitors, scanning faces, asking if they had seen their mother. Most were women, clad in worn clothes, their faces looking lined and tired. Anna saw a man on crutches and missing a leg, his pants tucked up at the knee, a patch over one eye. For a moment, she felt sad, but today was Christmas. People exchanged hugs, smiles, and kisses and looked at the beautiful tree with misty eyes.

"Mama," Inge shouted again. Anna did not stop her. She didn't know what to do. They kept walking around holding hands. Anna bit her lip, trying not to cry. She stuck her head into the head mistress's office to see if her mother was there. The sisters finally stood by the door to the big hall, waiting.

Finally, Visitors began to trickle out, hugging and kissing children, crying and promising to visit again.

Veronika's Aunt Lola was the last one to leave. "Oh my, I hope I get to the train on time." She took her cane and was hugging Veronika but stopped when she noticed the two forlorn girls still by the door. She smiled. "Father Christmas gave me a small gift for each of you. I left them with Veronika. Well, I must go. I will see you next Sunday. Merry Christmas." She put on her fur hat, kissed Veronika and stepped out the door.

Veronika took Anna's hand. "Your mama didn't come?"

"Maybe she got lost, or the train was late," Anna said in a quavering voice.

"You know what? Let's ask Miss Irmgard. She knows everything." Veronika tried to pull her friend along, but Anna refused to move.

"I'll find her and be right back." Veronika ran to the dining room and came back leading Miss Irmgard by the hand.

Miss Irmgard put her arms around Anna and Inge. "Your mama wrote a letter. She said that she was still ill and could not go on a train, but she sent you something."

The girls started to cry. "She promised," Inge sobbed.

"Inge, she really wanted to come, but the doctor would not let her. He said she was too sick to leave the hospital. You see, she needs to get well first. You want your mama well, right? So she can come home to you?"

Anna nodded, but Inge was inconsolable.

"We don't hand out gifts until Father Christmas has come, but I'm sure, because you have been such good girls, he'll understand and make an exception. "Gently she pulled the girls towards the tree and picked out a large, brown envelope. "Here, let's read what it says:

'To Anna and Inge Peterman.' "Who wants to open it?"

Anna took the envelope and tore it open. It looked like a bunch of papers.

"Let's read your mama's letter first." Miss Irmgard had pulled an envelope from the bottom of the stack. She squatted on the floor and asked the girls to join her. She pulled Inge's hands away from her face. "Listen." She unfolded the letter and started to read:

My dear Anna and Inge:

This is a Christmas greeting from your mama. My wish is that you do not cry but have fun playing with this gift I made for you.

You are the only children who will receive such a special gift made by your mama. Father Christmas told me that you have been good girls and that I can be very proud of you.

Father Christmas says to be happy little girls, sing Christmas carols and play with your friends. I hope you like the gift.

You can pick names for the two paper dolls and cut out more dolls for your school class. Anna, you show yoursister how to do it.

I will see you soon and I'll be thinking of you! Remember, Mama knows everything, so no crying!

All my love to the sweetest girls in the world, Anna and Inge!

Your Mama

"Remember, Inge, Mama said not to cry," Anna reminded her little sister, who still did not believe that her mama was not coming.

Anna pulled the papers from the envelope and spread them out on the floor. "Oh, how beautiful. I love paper dolls. Look, there is the schoolhouse, oh, see the little desks and benches." She counted six and squealed with delight.

"What is that?" Inge asked, finally getting interested.

"Oh, that's the teacher. See? She has a book in her hand." Inge picked up the cutout, a doll with her hair in a bun and dressed in a long skirt.

"What shall we name her?" Inge asked.

"Let's call her Miss Irmgard." Anna looked up.

Miss Irmgard looked through the hand-cut figures and a classroom complete with benches, a desk for the teacher and a blackboard. "I would really like that. Your mama is an artist. Look how beautiful each figure is. One has little braids. Hm, she looks a lot like you, Inge, what do you think?"

Inge smiled and the girls started to play with their paper dolls.

Mr. Hans stopped by and said to Miss Irmgard, "We need you to help us get ready for Father Christmas's visit." He winked at the girls.

Anna and Inge were soon joined by other girls, who admired and played with their precious paper dolls. When some boys led by Robert came over, Anna gathered the dolls and quickly placed them back into the envelope.

"What is in there?" Robert asked.

"Give it to me!" one of the boys shouted and grabbed for it.

But before he could get it away from her, Robert jumped up. "Boy, you touch that envelope and you're going to fight me." He threw a fist. The boy turned and ran.

Anna watched all this in amazement then she asked, "Wanna see my new paper doll schoolhouse?" But Robert stuck out his tongue and dashed away.

"Children come into the hall now," called Mr. Hans. "Sit down on the steps like we do when we are singing, take the same places." Mr. Hans stood in front of the tree

311

wearing a big red hat. "Pretend I'm Santa's elf." The children hurried to take their places on the steps. "Listen. Do you hear what I hear?" He pointed to the front door and the children followed his gaze.

The sound of bells came closer. Anna froze in place. Father Christmas was really coming. She would see him for the first time in her life. She took Inge's hand. "Hear the bells, Inge? That's Father Christmas coming from the woods." Inge listened, her eyes wide and focused on the front door.

"Oh, the bells are getting louder. He's on the stairs." Hans said, dancing around. "I was good all year. Is there anybody who was bad, really naughty?"

The room fell quiet as the children held their breath, some shaking their heads and some hiding their faces.

Then a knock on the door. Mr. Hans rushed to open it.

"Father Christmas?" The children called, starry-eyed.

Father Christmas, in his red suit and his long white beard, raised his arm and waved, "Merry Christmas, children."

"Merry Christmas," the children chanted, led by Mr. Hans, who jumped up to sit on the sleigh Father Christmas had pulled through the door. Father Christmas swatted him with his broom and Hans jumped off, pretending to be scared.

A boy's voice piped up. "Where are the presents?"

Father Christmas sat down in a big armchair next to the tree and Miss Birgit, Mrs. Gertrud, Miss Irmgard and all the others walked around the tree and lit the candles. "Can you children sing a carol for me?" Father Christmas asked in his deep, gravelly voice.

Mr. Hans sat down at the piano and started to play "Away in a Manger," conducting the choir with one hand as he struck the keys with the other.

Anna and Inge sang their hearts out, spellbound by Father Christmas, the beautiful tree and the sack of presents on the sleigh. Next, they sang "Oh Little Town of Bethlehem,"" Silent Night," and then, Father Christmas waved his arms and spoke. "Have you all been good?"

"Yes!"

"Now, I know that some of you have been naughty--" he lowered his voice-- "and they will have to be punished!" He picked up a bundle of branches and waved it. "Is there a Mr. Hans here?" He looked around. The children grew quiet.

Mr. Hans stepped up. "Yes, Santa, that's me."

"Should he be punished?"

The children yelled "No, no, no!"

"All right, Mr. Hans, if you promise to be good and do what Miss Gertrude tells you, and if you stop flirting with the ladies, I will let you go this time."

The children screamed with delight, and Hans waved at them and dashed away as Father Christmas tried to swat him with the bundle of sticks.

"Is there anybody else who was naughty?" He looked around as a quiet chill spread through the room.

Robert hopped down the stairway and planted himself in front of Father Christmas. "I was."

Anna didn't dare to breath.

"You are Robert, I know, and you have been naughty at least-- refresh my mind, Mr. Hans, how many times has Robert been in trouble this year?"

"Oh, I don't remember, maybe once or twice."

Father Christmas faced Robert with a stern look. "I think it was a lot more times than that. He did some things that could have hurt another child, didn't he?" For once Robert did not say a word.

Hans looked alarmed. "But he has also been good, he helped and he--"

"Did I ask you to speak?" He waved the broom in Hans's direction then turned back to Robert. "Did you help Miss Irmgard gather firewood? And did you sweep the hall for Miss Gertrud?"

Robert nodded and looked uneasily at the other children, who were gawking at him.

"Well, in that case you will be spared the broom. Just remember, I know everything. So, be good, young man." Robert sprinted back up the steps, disappearing into the group of children.

One by one the children were called in front of Father Christmas to receive a gift he pulled from the sack. Inge was afraid, so Anna went with her. But she did not cry and Anna was happy when they each received a gift. Mr. Hans played "Oh Christmas Tree" and the children sang boisterously. Father Christmas waved as Mr. Hans escorted him and his sleigh out the door.

"Merry Christmas," the children shouted.

Then Miss Gertrude told them to come down and line up behind Miss Birgit and pick another present, this time from those under the tree.

The head mistress smiled, and said to everyone, "Thank God and a group of village women who baked cookies, made candy and somehow sent small gifts for each of you. And we can be thankful we had electricity most of the time. We've all had food, the villa survived the bombing raids and the fighting bypassed us, by the grace of God. Yes, times have been hard, but with God's help and the goodness of the farmers we were able to celebrate Christmas of 1945." She went around and shook the hands of her staff.

Robert devoured his cookies right away and was ogling Anna's bag. She smiled and handed him a cookie.

"What did you get?" Veronika asked Anna.

"Mittens. Look, blue ones." She slipped them on. "Father Christmas knew that Inge and I didn't have mittens."

"I got a scarf. Here, you take it." Veronika handed the knitted scarf to Anna. "My Aunt Lola gave me this. She touched the leopard fur scarf and hat she was wearing.

"Oh, that is beautiful," Anna gasped. "I like your aunt Lola, she is very nice."

Veronika smiled and pulled out a small box. "Here, she gave me this for you."

Anna opened the box. "Oh, how beautiful." She held up two silver necklaces each with a heart-shaped pendant. She placed one necklace around Inge's neck, then turned to Veronika. "This is the best Christmas I ever had, except…"

That night the children talked and laughed until Miss Irmgard pounded on the door. "Quiet, children, or I'll tell Father Christmas." The room grew still.

Anna waited until she was gone and tiptoed over to Inge's bunk. "This has been the best Christmas, and Mama knows that, and she is happy too." She pulled the blanket over her sister and tucked her in.

"No, it wasn't. Mama didn't come." Inge pulled the blanket over her head.

Robert raised his head. "It was pretty good."

"What did you get for Christmas?" Anna whispered.

"Another pair of mittens," he answered. "But I lost one of my old ones."

"Oh, and, Robert," Anna said, "Don't mess with Inge anymore. You know Father Christmas is watching, "Anna said and tiptoed back to her bed.

"I won't." His voice came muffled from under his blanket.

CHAPTER 33
Hamburg

Annemarie drifted in and out of consciousness, not knowing how long she had been sleeping. She dreamed of her little Inge running away from the orphanage, hiding in the woods, crying for her mama. But when she reached for her, it was Alfred waving as he turned and faded away in the fog.

She woke up drowsy, the flowers on the wallpaper floating in a circle. She turned to the window and the sky was still grey. "I'm home," she murmured, "and Anna and Inge now will come home." Her face crumpled. She wanted to hold them, shield them from harm, smooth Inge's hair, play paper dolls with Anna. Then she tried to brush away the nagging thought that perhaps Alfred was dead, she would never see him again. Was he trying to send her a message? She thought of her friend Ellen's words – "there is always hope. God will win and all will be well." In her dream, Ellen had appeared as an angel, smiling, waving for her to follow into a fluffy cloud. When the cloud floated away, she saw her mother in a beautiful garden with apple trees and holding a basket filled with apples.

She was burning up, her nightgown drenched. She was too weak to get up and check her mother's medicine drawer for a remedy. What if she never got well again, just slipped away? She wailed, "Why? Why? Answer me, somebody--" she tried to lift her legs to get out of bed but moaned, then screamed when she tried to step on the floor. She shuddered. "Where is your God, Ellen? Tell me?" Her

316

mother was dead. And she ill, bedridden, her children in an orphanage. Christmas day had come and gone, and she had not even noticed. She wanted to believe the orphanage was a good place, they had enough to eat. Did her letter with the paper dolls arrive there? Finally, she gave up on finding medicine, fell back onto her pillow and drifted in another dreamless sleep.

When she woke again, she heard noises--someone pushing and banging on the door.

She raised herself onto her elbows and waited. Steps sounded from the hallway, and she heard something dropped on the kitchen table with a thud. "Hallo, I'm in here," Annemarie called weakly.

"Oh my God, you scared me half to death." Her sister Margarete stepped into the room. Clad in a black coat, black dress and hat with black lace partially shadowing her face, she looked somber. "My God, Kittie, I didn't know you were here!" Margarete huffed, throwing up her arms. "When did you come home? No one told me. You should have come and told me. I could have brought you food. The pantry is empty."

Annemarie wiped her forehead with her arm and whispered, "Margarete, I was at the hospital when mother passed away. Mrs. Dummersdorf helped me home. I have been too ill to go anywhere since." She fell back onto her pillow.

"You were with Mother when she died? And no one told me. I would have come, of course, but I didn't know she was in the hospital." Her sister stared at her; face flushed.

"Margarete, you didn't even come and pick her up for Christmas." Annemarie fished under her pillow for a handkerchief. "No one came to Mother's apartment. Nobody checked on her." She blew her nose.

"Well, Friedrich did not get a car, and he's only home for a few days, and his parents-- you know I can't stand those people-- well, they came and insisted on staying with us. They just left yesterday." She stopped to take a breath. "Three days I put up with them. They slepped on the mattress Inge had soiled. I didn't care." She unclasped her patent leather purse and pulled out a silver cigarette case.

Annemarie sighed and closed her eyes. She really needed the bathroom.

"And then I received the notification that Mama had died." Margarete sobbed. "My mama. And I wasn't there to hold her hand when she died." She took a handkerchief from her purse and sobbed into it. "I will never forgive myself. I do wish you had told me." Annemarie's raspy breathing and Margarete's sobbing filled the quiet room.

Annemarie spoke softly, "I was ill in bed with a high fever, in bad pain. My leg is hurting so much now I can't even stand up. I have been alone here, too ill to go anywhere." She coughed, her body shaking. She reached for her leg, moaning. "Margarete, I know this won't make you happy, but you're going to have to help me to the toilet."

Margarete glanced at her watch, then stooped for Annemarie to wrap her arm around her shoulder. Annemarie clutched to her sister and started to hop towards the hall.

When Annemarie finally struggled back to bed, she said, "When were you going to come here to check on her? You left Mother alone for Christmas, with no coal and no food. An old, sick woman, your mother, alone. A neighbor had mercy and was somehow able to get her to the hospital. She would have died sooner if not for that Good Samaritan." Annemarie took several deep breaths, heaving, her face wet with perspiration. "Well, that's past now. I guess everybody has to do what they must." She fell back on her pillow, wishing this time that sleep would sweep her away.

Margarete stopped her pacing and glared at her. " So you think it's my fault that Mama died?" She stood, bobbing her head, her black veil billowing with every agitated breath.

"No, I did not say that, Margarete. I know you loved Mama just as much as I. It's just- it's the war, the damn war, my getting wounded and not being here to help. I was discharged against the doctor's orders. He said my leg has to be amputated, and now I'm believing he was right." She wiped her eyes, then covered her face with her hands. "And my children-- in an orphanage," she wailed, "and I have not heard a word."

Margarete lit a cigarette and laid the match on Annemarie's table. "Well, don't worry. My friend's daughter works there. She said they are doing fine."

When Annemarie did not reply, she continued. "When I have time and when I've gotten myself back together and after Friedrich leaves, I will go and visit them." She bent over her sister. "Are you all right, Annemarie?" She took her by the hands and tried to pull her up.

"No, I'm not. I feel so weak," Annemarie whispered. "Can you get me some water?"

Margarete hurried to the kitchen, her heels echoing on the wooden floor, and returned with a glass of water and a jar of pears. "This is the only food I found." She shook her head. "I will bring some when I get time. Kittie, you are literally starving." She opened the jar and went back to the kitchen to fetch a spoon, returned and handed it to her. "Here, eat this, it is better than nothing."

Annemarie took the jar and began to spoon the pears into her mouth.

Then Margarete started to pace again. "Kitty, the reason I came is, I just returned from Mother's funeral. There was no time, and not knowing that you were home, I had to make a decision." She raised her eyebrows and spread her lips in a smile. "Friedrich paid for everything. He thought the world of Mother. There was nobody there but Friedrich and me. It was really sad, but it being Christmas, we had no time to notify anybody. And with hardly any trains running, I don't know who could have come. Her neighbors are all old, and they wouldn't have been able to make the trip to the cemetery. We put her in the family plot next to Father. That's good, isn't it?" She stopped in front of the bed then turned and picked up her purse.

Annemarie had begun to cry silently, tears streaming onto her pillow.

"The reason I came here is to look through Mother's things, to see what I want. She promised me the grandfather clock. I hope you know that. It's mine, she told me so."

Annemarie lay there, her eyes closed, pain in her chest, fighting not to slip away.

Margarete continued, "Since we are the only two survivors, I think we should go through her things and just divide them all. That, I think, is the fairest way to do it." Margarete looked down at her. "You should go see a doctor, Kittie. I don't know if my doctor, Dr. Schlosser, will take you. He only admits private patients now since most people can't pay and the government health insurance is kaput. He has to survive too, I understand that."

Annemarie wiped her face with the sleeve of her nightgown, then propped up on her elbows again. "No, no, I will get better. I just need rest and food, that's all. If you could get me some food." She tried to reach for the water glass and Margarete picked it up and handed it to her. "Right now, I'm too ill to go out, but I've been so hungry…"

"I will see what I can spare. But we mustn't tell Friedrich. He would not approve of me giving away food that his company provides for their officers." She sighed and looked at her watch. "Well, I have to get back home. I'm still so upset about Mama's passing and the funeral. It was so sad to see her in that casket."

"Please, Margarete, stop. I can't bear it." Annemarie's elbows gave way and she fell back on her pillow. "Do we have to go through her things today? Can't it wait?" She attempted to wipe the sweat off her face. "What, Margarete, could Mama possibly own that you don't already have? What? Tell me."

Margarete had walked around the room and opened the door to the big closet. "As I said, we are the only survivors and they say things have to be divided equally, that's how it is done. I don't need any of the clothes." She opened the other door, and started pulling out sheets, making two piles. "Here, one bunch for you and one for me."

"I don't care. Take what you want." Annemarie lay back, too tired to care.

"Oh, this one might fit my guest room bed." Margarete held up a sheet and beamed. "You can keep all of the furniture except the grandfather clock, which, as I said, Mama promised to me. And I do want the figurines she has up there on the shelf. I think they are Meissen originals. You don't want them, do you?"

Annemarie reached for the headboard and pulled herself up. "I want the old cake server with the roses on it. And, I want the other clock, the small one on the dresser, and one of the figurines. Also, I do need the dishes in the kitchen."

Her sister looked up, blinking.

"I've been bombed, remember, and I have nothing. Everything is gone, Margarete. I am planning to live here. Mama said I could, and I need things when the children come home." Annemarie's voice had turned sharp.

Margarete's mouth curved up in a brief smile. "If you want to live here, you have to pay the rent. I think it's

280 Deutsche Mark per month. How are you going to come up with that?"

"I'm going to find work. Since I wouldn't expect you to give me the money." Annemarie crumpled her blanket. "I am sorry, I am very tired, and I feel nauseated. Please leave now." She fell back and pulled the cover up to her chin. "We can do this another day. I promise I won't run off with anything."

Margarete picked up the stack of sheets and stuffed them into a pillowcase. "You don't have to treat me like I'm here to rob you. Let's be civilized about this. Mama would not want us to fight over her things." She walked to the shelf and removed one of the Meissen figurines, wrapped it in a towel and carefully placed it in the pillowcase between the sheets. "This will always remind me of Mama and I need her strength now," she sniffled. "I hope you don't mean what you said after all I have done for you." She turned, picked up her purse and the stuffed pillowcase and left, the door slamming forcefully behind her.

Annemarie was too exhausted to cry.

The next day she heard Mrs. Maier at the door calling her name. Annemarie pushed herself out of bed, letting out a yelp when her foot touched the floor. She grabbed her crutches, hobbled to the door and opened it.

"This box was left here in front of your door yesterday evening. But I was afraid somebody would steal it, so I kept it for you." Mrs. Maier peered into her face. "You don't look good. I just made some lunch." She took the box to Annemarie's kitchen and went back to her own place, returning with a plate of food. "It's not much, but I actually got hold of some bacon. Mrs. Kraus upstairs got it through her son, the black market, you know. And the green beans are really good. Her sister canned them, she said. The potatoes are from my last ration. I was the last in line to get some." Mrs. Maier smoothed her apron and smiled.

Annemarie felt a rush of gratitude. "I promise, I will share with you when I have anything." She managed half a smile. "But it looks like you might have to wait a while."

Mrs. Maier waved her off and took the plate to the kitchen. She returned, put her arm around Annemarie and led her to the kitchen. "You better see a doctor, Annemarie. Doesn't your sister have connections? I remember that she is well off."

Annemarie laughed. For the first time in a long time, she laughed so hard that she almost lost her balance. "Not a chance, Mrs. Maier, not a chance, I have nothing to pay with. I can't even sell my body." Annemarie laughed again and the old woman laughed too, looking unsure that she should.

Annemarie took a knife from the drawer and cut the top of the box. Amazed, she pulled out a can of corned beef, English cookies, a jar of honey, a canned ham, a box that said MILK. She could not read the other words on the box. There were also bags of sugar, flour, and three cans of fruits and vegetables, and a bottle of Cognac! She almost fainted. Was she dreaming? Mrs. Maier smiled and offered to put the food into the pantry. "I will pick up the plate later," she said, and left.

Who had sent her this precious gift? Lisbeth? They'd lost contact since the military hospital closed. She examined the box and found an envelope on the bottom. The engraved address read, Captain Friedrich Bowman. Her sister? Perhaps she felt remorse and had sent this package. But to her surprise, the letter was from Friedrich.

Dear Annemarie:

I heard that you are ill. Margarete told me a lot, but you know her.

She said that you needed food, and I know she'll come through in her own good time. But I have instructed my secretary to pack a box for you and deliver it. There is only one condition: It must be our secret. Do not tell Margarete. You know how she is, stubborn old girl.

Get well, Annemarie, you know that we are very fond of you.

I'll be gone again, this time for three months. I am so sorry your mother died. What a kind, wonderful woman she was. She will be missed. Margarete is heartbroken.

Damn war!

Again, let this be our secret.

Kindest regards,

Friedrich B.

CHAPTER 34

When Annemarie woke again it was so cold in the room she could see her breath, and icicles glistened on the inside of the balcony door. How long had she been asleep? The last time she had eaten was when Mrs. Meier brought her food. She needed to get up and go to see Mrs. Dummersdorf. Maybe she could get her some medication. She wanted to be strong. Holding on to the headboard, she pushed herself on her elbows and dangled her legs off the bed. She tried to step on her left foot, but the throw rug in front of the bed slid away, and she tumbled to the floor. The pain made her see white.

There was a knock on the door, then a second, louder one.

"Anyone home? Open up." Another knock and someone jiggled the doorknob.

"I am here," Annemarie tried to shout, but could only manage a whisper. She heard Mrs. Maier telling the visitor that Annemarie should be in there.

"Hello, Annemarie, open up."

Annemarie crawled to the door, reached up and turned the key. "Lisbeth!" She gasped and crumpled to the floor.

"Good heavens!" Lisbeth dropped the bags she was carrying and stooped to peer into Annemarie's face.

"I fell. I have such pain in my leg. I can't even take one step."

Lisbeth placed her arms under Annemarie's shoulders and pulled her into the bedroom and back onto the bed. "God, it's colder in here than outside." She rubbed her hands. "Don't go anywhere, I'll be right back."

Oh, how Annemarie had missed her. The rock called Lisbeth had returned. Or was she a mirage, a dream? She stared at the figure. Lisbeth wore a brown fur coat with matching hat. Lisbeth set down the bags she carried and leaned over the bed. She was the nurse now, checking on a patient.

Annemarie grabbed her arm and almost jerked her off her feet. "I just wanted to make sure you were real." She attempted a smile.

"Well, I'm real, but I think you are a ghost. You look that white." Lisbeth opened her coat and took off her hat. She was a blonde now. She saw Annemarie looking and grinned. "Do you like it?" She smiled and winked. "Okay, I want to get some heat into this place. But first you need to eat." She pulled a metal thermos bottle from one of the bags. "Chicken soup." She poured some into the cap and held it to Annemarie's mouth. The soup was warm and tasted salty and Annemarie slowly drank it.

"We need to make a fire, but all I can see is a few bricks of coal. I need wood. Something to start it." Lisbeth looked around. " This bookcase, it's almost empty."

Before Annemarie could speak, Lisbeth had pulled the bookcase off the wall and broke off the back panel. The wood was old and gave way easily.

"My mother inherited that from her mother," Annemarie said weakly, but Lisbeth shrugged and hauled the wood into the kitchen.

Annemarie heard her cuss. The old cast iron stove was giving her trouble. Annemarie remembered how her mother had fought with that stove and a smile crossed her lips. That stove was older than she, one of the few amenities' poor tenement-dwellers had.

Lisbeth appeared in the doorway. "It's going to take time for the heat to spread into this room. Let's put you on the sofa in the kitchen so we can have coffee. We'll have a kitchen picnic." She smiled and helped Annemarie out of bed. "Don't you have a sweater or something?" She opened a dresser drawer. "This will do." She held up one of Annemarie's father's cardigans and helped her into it as if she was dressing a doll. Held up by Lisbeth, she slowly made her way into the kitchen and lay down on the old sofa next to the stove.

"Here, use this." Lisbeth handed her a pillow from the bedroom. She turned back to the stove. "Scheiss, no electricity again." She slammed the kettle on the burner. "Guess we will get hot water eventually." She blew a sharp breath. "You do want a cup of coffee, right?"

Annemarie nodded and sighed.

Lisbeth opened the pantry door. She pulled a bottle from the shelf and examined it. "Ooh-lala, Premium Cognac." She whistled. "Annemarie, you too must have friends in high places. This would get you a lot of coal and firewood."

"You won't believe where that came from." Then Annemarie told her about her sister's husband's secret package.

"So, why isn't your sister here to help you?"

Annemarie swallowed hard. "My mother died. I held her hand. I wanted to take her home, take care of her." Lisbeth handed her a handkerchief. In a halting voice, Annemarie told her what had happened.

"So, you've been here alone, and she knew you were ill?" Lisbeth scowled and wrenched the lid of the Cognac, pouring some into two water glasses from the sideboard. She picked up hers, smiled wickedly, and drank it, refilled it and held it up for a toast.

With wet eyes, Annemarie smiled and toasted. "To another miracle. You, Lisbeth, are the miracle."

"You are hallucinating." Lisbeth reached and touched her forehead. "I think you have a fever."

"No, Lisbeth, you are an angel, I am beginning to believe in God. Maybe Ellen was right." Annemarie fixed her eyes on Lisbeth's face. "You do look like an angel."

Lisbeth laughed. "Me, an angel! I've been called a lot of things, but no, not an angel." She turned and added coal to the fire.

Annemarie set her glass on the table. "I am feeling lightheaded." She leaned back, winced, and reached for her leg.

Lisbeth rose, the laughter gone from her face. "Let me see." She did not wait for an answer, took the blanket off Annemarie's lap and pulled up her pajama pant. "Doc Hartmann sure wouldn't have released you." She examined the wound in the foot. "Damn!" she shouted, and Annemarie almost jumped off the sofa. "You can be lucky you don't have gangrene."

Annemarie explained why she had left the hospital and retold her terrible journey home.

"You should have stayed there. It is a miracle you are still alive." Lisbeth rummaged through her bag. "I don't have any bandages with me, but here are some pills." She pulled out a small bottle. "I am going to heat more water and clean that wound. You do have soap, I assume?"

Annemarie shrugged and pointed to the sink.

"I need a pillowcase to cut and use as a bandage."

"In the bedroom closet if my sister didn't take them all," Annemarie said, her face red. "I had no choice; I don't know how I had the strength to make it home. But I was at Mother's bedside when she passed. That makes it all worthwhile. I couldn't let her die alone, Lisbeth. Had I come one day later, she would have been gone and I would never have seen her again." She winced as Lisbeth worked on her wound. "I have not seen my children. Some woman my sister knows took them to an orphanage. I broke my promise to bring them home for Christmas." She began to cry again. "Sometimes I wish I had died in the bombing."

Lisbeth disregarded her words. "All right, I've wrapped your leg. Tomorrow I'm going to come back and take you to a doc. He will dress it properly and give you some medication. And, since you have two children waiting for you, I suggest that you forget about dying." She went to the sink and washed her hands.

"Mrs. Dummersdorf said there are no clinics open and no doctors either."

Lisbeth smiled and waved her arm like she had a magic wand. "Well, remember, I have my friends ..." She opened one of her bags. "I brought you cake. Baked it myself." She opened a package and held up a pound cake covered with powdered sugar. She took two plates from the sideboard and cut generous pieces. She laughed, "Another miracle, finally the water is boiling." She poured it into the metal pot. Soon the kitchen filled with delicious coffee aroma.

Annemarie picked up the cup Lisbeth gave her, took a small sip and tasted the cake, then fell to eating. "This is the best I've ever had." She finally put down her fork and cleaned the crumbs off the plate with her fingers. "I don't know how people survive. I think my mother starved to death." Annemarie sighed. "I blame myself." She massaged the backs of her hands. "And you? What about you?" she asked, leaning closer to Lisbeth, who sat on a chair near the stove.

"I'm working, doing all right." Lisbeth smiled and checked her watch. "Look, I have to go. My driver will be here at four." She rose. "Eat the rest of the soup and take one of these pills two times a day. I'll be back as soon as I can to get you to a doctor." She emptied the bags and set the cake, bread and several cans of food on the table.

Annemarie gasped. "Your driver?"

"Remember girl, friends." Lisbeth slipped into her coat and hat. "Can you put coal on the fire? There is enough in the bucket to keep it going for a few days if you use it sparingly." She picked up the empty bags and waved. "Remember, we're survivors."

Before Annemarie could answer, Lisbeth was gone.

Annemarie lay on the sofa in the kitchen now comfortably warm. She had to pinch herself to know this was all real. Lisbeth's cake sat on the table and there was coffee left in the old metal pot her mother had used as long as she could remember. The pills Lisbeth gave her worked. Her leg had stopped throbbing. Annemarie pulled herself up by bracing the table and picked up her crutches. She hobbled to the front door, opened it and called, "Frau Maier?"

Her neighbor's door opened, and she stuck her head out. "Annemarie, what do you need?"

"Please come and have some coffee, real coffee." She smiled when she noticed the old lady inhale the aroma that was escaping into the hall.

"Oh, my, this reminds me of the old days." She stood, twisting her apron.

"Come in, sit down, let's have some coffee and cake. My friend Lisbeth baked it." Annemarie held onto the table and lowered herself back on the sofa. "Lisbeth is a nurse. I met her at the army field hospital." Annemarie smiled. "Do you believe in miracles?"

Mrs. Maier nodded. "I think God sends us miracles." Her hand shaking, she picked up a spoon and took a bite of the cake. "Oh, this is delicious. My mother used to make cake like this. With eggs and butter, oh, it is so good."

Annemarie smiled. This was the first time she had been able to do something for Mrs. Maier. "Cut another piece and take it home with you," she encouraged. "And take a jar of pears, too. I have two of them."

Two days went by, and Annemarie was able to get up and around on her crutches. Her spirit had returned, and she was making plans to visit her children. She had

330

managed to keep the fire going by adding just enough lumps of coal to take the chill off. Sleeping on the sofa and keeping the kitchen door closed helped extend the meager supply.

As long as she still had heat, Annemarie decided to take a sponge bath. She sniffed her armpit and wrinkled her nose. How long had it been? She hobbled to the sink, pulled the big metal tub over to the stove and poured water from the kettle into it. Sitting on a chair, she washed herself, dripping the warm water over her body. "Heavenly," she said aloud and closed her eyes as she ran the warm washcloth over her arms. A puddle formed by her feet, but she did not care. When the water started to cool, she wrapped the blanket around her and hobbled to the bedroom to find clean pajamas. It was ice cold in the room, and she hurried back into the kitchen, looking at herself in the hallway mirror on the way. Her father's pajamas hung on her scarecrow body, and the short hair framing her pale face made her look like a little boy. She stuck out her tongue at the image. She was ready to venture back into the outside world.

A few days later, Lisbeth announced her arrival with a firm knock and a loud "Open up, it's me."

"I'm so happy to see you." Annemarie reached to hug her with one arm. "I feel so much better. Those pills you gave me did wonders."

Lisbeth peeked into the kitchen. "Still warm in here. Good job, girl." She glanced at the water bucket. "Oh, we took a bath today. Good thing, because you are coming with me to see Dr. Lewis."

"But I'm much better now. I want to go and see my children." She smiled broadly at Lisbeth.

"No. I want you to get dressed now, right away. The driver is waiting. We have to hurry." She nodded her head.

"Put on something warm-- your father's long pants, a sweater anything. I wonder if we'll ever see spring again."

Protesting was useless. Nurse Lisbeth had made up her mind. Obediently, Annemarie checked in her parents' closet and pulled out a flannel shirt, Father's heavy work trousers and woolen socks.

"What about shoes?" Lisbeth asked.

Annemarie pointed at her father's work boots. "They are the only ones that fit over my swollen foot."

Lisbeth helped Annemarie into the fur coat and handed her the matching hat. "You should move to a ground floor apartment," she grumbled. Helping her down the last flight of steps, Lisbeth asked, "How on earth did you ever make it up there?"

"On my hands and knees, one step at a time."

The street appeared deserted. Every living thing seemed to be indoors or frozen. A lone military vehicle waited in front of building #77. A man in uniform helped Annemarie into the back seat.

"What kind of car is this?" Annemarie asked.

"Jeep," Lisbeth answered, and scurried into the front, and saying something to the driver which Annemarie did not understand.

She sat, mum for the whole trip. Coming down three flights of stairs had exhausted her and made her realize how weak she was. She peeked out of the window as they stopped at the gate of what appeared to be a military compound. A guard checked the driver's identification and saluted while they passed through. They pulled up in front of a big double door that turned out to be the entrance to a hospital. Lisbeth grabbed a wheelchair for Annemarie and whisked her through the hallway without creating attention.

In a waiting room a short, slim man with a mustache looked at Annemarie's foot. He asked her something and Lisbeth stepped in to translate.

"He needs to drain the wound and it's going to hurt," Lisbeth said.

After a painful half-hour, Annemarie was back in her chair with her coat on. The doctor spoke briefly with Lisbeth. She gave him a slap on the arm. He smiled and said something that made her laugh.

Back in the jeep, a tired and groggy Annemarie asked. "What language were you speaking?"

"English," Lisbeth answered without further elaboration.

The driver dropped them back at the apartment house, and Lisbeth helped Annemarie hobble up the three flights, huffing, stopping often, cussing under her breath. Back in the apartment, Lisbeth said, "Let's put you to bed now. Stay on the sofa where it's warm. I'm leaving the soup for you. Eat some."

"No, I feel sick to my stomach," Annemarie grumbled, but Lisbeth waved off her protest.

"You have to eat to get stronger. Doctor's orders. And keep taking the pills." Lisbeth picked up her coat and hat. "I'll be back to change the dressing."

As she left, Annemarie lay down on the sofa and drifted.

CHAPTER 35

"Thank you, Mr. Krause." Annemarie smiled at the big man and handed him a paper bag containing the bottle of Cognac.

He nodded, hitched up his suspenders, and surveyed her pantry for other items he might want, as his son, Karl, came through the door with two buckets of coal. He lowered his cap and sniffed. "I'll be interested in more Cognac, or any liquor. Of course, I never know when Karl can get more coal."

Lucky man, Annemarie thought. Karl, who had been a small-time Nazi thug, as her father had referred to him with disdain, had come home from the front -- her father had doubted that he'd served -- unscathed and was now in the black market. She shuddered. It was truly survival of the fittest, like in the Stone Age. Of course, the crooks and the scheisters always rose to the top, shedding their uniforms and their alliances, ruthlessly making their way up the local food chain. Her father would turn over in his grave if he saw her dealing with the Krause's.

"How about a couple of hams?" She held up the cans she had found in the box from Friedrich. "One more bucket of coal for both of these?" She hefted them in the air.

"What else have you got in there?" He rummaged through her box, came up empty. "All right, I'll take the hams and the coffee." He turned and yelled through the open door, "Karl, one more bucket for Mrs. Peterman."

Annemarie pressed her lips together. This was the nice coffee Lisbeth had left. But what choice did she have? She needed coal. If cutting down on food or giving up coffee is what it took, then so be it. She did hope that Lisbeth would return soon and bring her more soup.

"Do you want to sell that figurine, the one on the shelf up there?" Mr. Krause had walked into the hall and opened her bedroom door. "I'd take that clock too. The Tommies love those old pieces. I can get a lot for that."

"No! No, those are the only things I have left from my mother." Annemarie hobbled into the hallway, stopped in front of him and shut the bedroom door.

"Yeah, bad thing she died." He shook his head. "If her old man had not been such a damn socialist, she'd been better off."

Annemarie did not reply. She felt like kicking him in the balls, but she'd best keep her mouth shut if she didn't want to freeze to death. She curled her hands into fists. "Thank you, Mr. Krause."

"Well, if you ever want to sell that clock, let me know," he said as he left and started up the stairs to his apartment.

Annemarie closed her door with a bang and went into her bedroom. "Don't worry, Mama, he will never get your clock." Lovingly, she wiped the dust off the shiny wood. Then she shivered and hobbled back into the kitchen where she stared at her three buckets of coal and wondered what she'd do when she had nothing left to trade. Mr. Krause had mentioned old things. She decided to ask Lisbeth what else the Tommies liked. She couldn't think of anything more she had that anybody would want, but she had to find a way. Without heat, she could not survive this winter. Mrs. Maier said they hadn't seen such a harsh time since she was a little girl. When spring came, Annemarie would be stronger, go out and find work, bring her children home and start life over.

The electricity was out again, and she went to sleep early, snuggling on the sofa next to the warm cast iron stove. Perhaps this night, she would see Alfred in her dreams, feel safe and happy for a little while. She clung to the hope that he would someday soon come walking through the door.

"Hallo! Open up, it's me."

Annemarie was awake but still under the covers on the sofa. She glanced at her watch. Ten-thirty! Must be Lisbeth's pills that made her sleep that long. "I'm coming," she shouted and pulled herself up from the sofa. Sunshine streamed through the kitchen window and the sky was blue and cloudless. She hobbled into the hallway and opened the door.

A smiling Margarete greeted her and held up a bag. "I am bringing you food." She stepped into the hallway and took off her coat and hat. She shivered. "Don't you have any heat in here?"

"Only in the kitchen, come on in." Annemarie followed her sister.

"Oh, you've got coal." Margarete eyed the three full buckets. "How did you get that?" She squinted.

"I traded with a neighbor. The Krause's from upstairs."

"Them? God, I remember how father hated those Nazis."

Annemarie shrugged.

"But their son Karl is sort-of good looking. He always wanted to go out with me." Margarete grinned. "I actually did go out with him, but only once, because father would have kicked me out if he'd known."

"Hm, I always thought Friedrich was the only one."

"Oh, my dear Kitty, there's a lot you don't know about me. You were just a little child, spoiled by Mama, I might add." Margarete raised her eyebrows, nodding her head.

Annemarie had to smile. "Well, Margarete, how are you?" She did not wait for a reply. "You look better, must be the sunshine. Finally, it remembered us and has returned."

"Oh, but it's still just as cold out there, I'm glad I wore this sweater." Margarete turned around, modeling her gray sweater. "It's from Shetland sheep wool, very expensive. Friedrich gave it to me for Christmas. Here, touch this, it's so soft." She guided Annemarie's hand across the front of the sweater.

"Lovely," Annemarie said. "I'm so glad that he spoils you."

"Yeah, considering that he had to sleep in the guest room over Christmas." Margarete winked.

"You mean you never, you don't sleep together?"

"We do have two children, Kitty." Margarete gave her a benevolent smile.

Acts like I am still six years old, Annemarie thought, then said aloud, "I'd offer you coffee, but Mr. Krause took all I had."

"Oh, that's all right. Look what I have in here!" Margarete opened the bag and spilled its contents on the table. "More coffee. And a bottle of Cognac." She held up the bottle. "Do you really want this? It's from Friedrich's office, and they obviously don't know what you really need."

"Oh yes, I really want it." Annemarie snatched the bottle and held it to her chest. *Two more buckets of coal.*

Margarete looked at her sideways. "Since when do you drink?"

"Since I'm no longer twelve, my dear." Annemarie set down the bottle and picked up a glass of strawberry jam. "My favorite. Thank you so much, Margarete." She pointed at the cans of vegetables and fruits and bags of sugar and flour on the table. She reached for Margarete's hand. "You don't know how much I appreciate this."

"You can thank Friedrich. He said that we need to help. After all, we are family." Margarete's voice vibrated as if she was reciting a dramatic poem.

"A cup of coffee would really be nice." Annemarie picked up the package of coffee and examined it. "Is that real?"

"Of course, it's real. I would never have that imitation coffee in my house. You know that. Friedrich knows better than bringing me the fake stuff."

"You are the queen, Margarete, but would you mind making the coffee, please? The water on the stove should be hot. All you have to do is grind the beans." Annemarie picked up the coffee grinder.

"Oh, this coffee is already ground. I told Friedrich that's the only kind I want. While it brews, let's check Mama's wardrobe and see what else we might want to divide." Margarete put on the coffee and walked toward to the bedroom.

Annemarie shrugged. "Go on and look. If you want something, just take it."

Margarete was back within a few moments. "Well, there isn't anything in there except that other ballerina figurine."

"Which is mine and I'm keeping it."

Margarete sighed, noisily blowing the air through her nostrils. She got up and poured the coffee.

Annemarie brought her cup up to her face and inhaled the flavor. "My only vice." She took a sip. "A cup of real coffee."

Margarete opened a box of cookies. "These are very good." She took one and dipped it in her coffee. "They're from England." She handed one to Annemarie, then lowered her voice. "Kitty, I have something to tell you."

"What?" Annemarie took another sip of coffee.

"Yesterday I went to the orphanage to visit your children." Margarete pulled a pack of cigarettes and a lighter from her purse. She flipped the lighter and lit a cigarette.

Annemarie set down her cup hard.

"Friedrich asked me to go check on them, and I felt I owed it to you after the fight we had." She inhaled, then blew small circles across the table.

Annemarie waved away the smoke and placed her hands on the table to steady herself. "How are they? Is Inge able to cope?" She choked on her words. "For God's sake, tell me." She breathed hard, trying to keep her voice under control.

"I went with Irmgard, remember, my friend's daughter, the one who works there? I could never have gone by myself. Those overcrowded, smelly trains make me sick." She grimaced. "And then we had to walk a long way to get to the orphanage. It's too far for you to walk in your condition. Way too far." Margarete put out the cigarette on her saucer. "But it's a nice big villa in a beautiful park. I think it will be pretty in the spring."

"The girls will be home with me by spring." Annemarie's voice rose. Why hadn't Margarete told her she was going to see the children? She felt like shaking her sister.

"More coffee?" Margarete rose to refill their cups and continued talking. "Anna looked good. I think she has grown a bit. But she is getting in trouble a lot, the head teacher told me."

"Anna in trouble? For what?" Annemarie pushed away her cup, sloshing the coffee.

"She gets in fights with other children. I think she has a temper, Kitty. I noticed that when she was with me. She tried to take one of Renate's dresses."

"You are crazy. Anna would never do that," Annemarie shouted.

"Don't blame me, Kitty. You have not been with the children much, so you really don't know." Margarete got up and started to pace. "I'm having problems with Renate too. Maybe it's the age."

Annemarie's lips had started to quiver. "What about Inge?"

"They said she cries a lot. And she still wets the bed. And speaking of beds, Irmgard showed me their beds. You wouldn't believe it, Kitty, they have no real mattresses. Just straw sacks on wooden slats. Inge told me she has fallen through the slats down to the bed below. Apparently, they move apart. And, they don't even have pillows." She sighed. "It's only been a short time since the war ended. I think they are lucky to be in such a nice place. Many children don't have it that good."

Annemarie covered her face. She felt helpless, powerless and guilty.

"Oh, one other thing, Inge said that they all bathe naked together and that she saw a boy's 'dingy', that's what she called it. And Anna told me one boy who is always in trouble asked her if she wanted to touch his. But she was embarrassed and ran away." Margarete walked back and forth and shook her head. "I think it is unbelievable that they keep boys and girls together naked. I complained to the head mistress, I think her name is Gertrud. She looks like a Gertrud. She said they are just little kids and she didn't have enough staff, and that this was not a hotel. And did I remember there has been a war? That she was doing the best she could. And then she asked, "How about coming out here to volunteer or donate some food or clothes." She stopped in front of Annemarie. "She got quite nasty with me and told me that they had more important things to worry about, like getting coal and food and medication." Margarete threw up her hands. "I told her that bathing boys and girls together naked was immoral. And that woman said, 'Well, file a complaint, if you like.' I still get angry thinking of how I was treated." Margarete sat back down and picked up her cup.

"Anna did say that Father Christmas had been there," Margarete continued, "and that she adores the paper dolls you sent, that it was the best present she ever received. She also said she is learning to play the mouth organ, and she played me a Christmas carol."

"I made them a school and a teacher, all cutouts." Annemarie smiled despite her irritation, picturing her girls with the paper dolls.

Margarete placed a cookie on Annemarie's saucer. "Have one of these. They call them shortbread; I don't know why." Annemarie picked it up and stared into space as Margarete kept talking. "The place smelled bad and was cold. I think a lot of children get sick there. It's not the best place." She shook her head emphatically. "But they get enough food and I think the staff, mostly young people, are nice to the children."

"What can I do about it?" Annemarie said in a thin voice. "What, huh? Tell me."

"Well, don't blame me. I thought I was doing you a favor to go there. I think you could be a little more appreciative." She rose and brushed crumbs off her skirt.

"I am sorry. I am so frustrated. Maybe I should go there and take them home."

"Kitty, that's crazy. You are not well enough to travel, nor to take care of them.

"I could go to work."

Margarete laughed. "There is no work. Friedrich said the Tommies are dismantling our shipyards and what factories are left. Nothing is running. Only a few stores are open. Kuhnert, the greengrocer on the corner, is open again. But it's winter, so he doesn't have much, Mrs. Bauer upstairs said. It's much worse now than during the war, Kitty. You've not been out, you don't know."

341

"But things have to get back to normal. People must live, feed their families. How are they doing it?"

"The black market. It's everywhere. If you want my advice, leave your children in the orphanage, at least until you get back on your feet." Margarete rose and picked up her purse and hat. "I have to go. I left my children with my upstairs neighbors."

Annemarie sighed and sank back into her pillow. "Thank you, Margarete, and tell Friedrich how much I appreciate everything." And she did, despite her own frustrations.

CHAPTER 36

A week had passed. Annemarie was restless, anxiously awaiting the return of Lisbeth, her lifeline and the one bright light in her lonely existence. She'd promised she would come back, but in these uncertain times things could change in an instant. Was Lisbeth involved in some type of illicit dealings with the British? Perhaps they had discovered her previous connections with the Nazi brass and had arrested her. Don't be ridiculous, and *Hitler is dead.* But Mr. Krause told her the Tommies were rounding up people, accusing them of war crimes and shooting them.

She lay back her head and drifted. She saw Alfred standing in the doorway, smiling and reaching out for her. She pictured Anna and Inge in the blue dresses she had sewn for them. She shook herself. Where was Doc Hartmann now? He'd always made her laugh. The charming Doc had flirted with her more than with the other women. That brought a smile now. "We have a dance date," he had told her. Did he remember? After those thoughts, she sighed and looked over at her shrinking supply of coal. What else could she trade with Krause, that ass? "I won't give up your clock, Mama," she murmured.

Her mother had received the clock as a wedding present, and she guessed it to be over one hundred years old. But it still kept the time accurately, its pendulum swinging, in good and bad times. She wound it regularly, a loving ritual that made her feel close to her mother.

And the fragile Meissen figurine, a ballerina with delicate pink lace fashioned from shiny porcelain and

343

balanced on dainty red slippers - it reminded her of the princess from the Nutcracker opera her mother had taken her to when she was little. To keep these things safely out of the hands of Krause, she needed another miracle.

Lisbeth would know what else she could trade, what the Tommies might find valuable. Perhaps the antique bookcase? But now the back was missing. Would they even take furniture? She hobbled into the living room. Her father's armchair was old. She stepped over to take a closer look. The fabric, a medieval hunting scene, was faded and threadbare, but the frame, crafted of solid wood, with armrests beautifully carved depicting the head of a fox, looked old. Lisbeth might be able to tell her if this chair could be of interest to them.

She gazed through the ice-frosted pane of the balcony door, onto the empty street and thought of the happy times she had spent here as a child, having princess tea parties with her friends. They would sit around the little wrought-iron table which they covered with a lace cloth her mother had given them.

She stared at the deserted street and thought about her best friend, Lena, who had lived across the street on the third floor of the building that was now reduced to rubble. Only a lone window frame jutting into the sky. Ghastly.

Her gaze fell to the basement window where old Granny Muller had leaned out, shaking her fist and grumbling about the noise. But they had just laughed and kept on playing. Had Granny Muller survived? A black cross was posted in front of the ruin. Was she buried beneath this mound? Annemarie shuddered and turned towards the kitchen.

Then a knock on the door and the familiar voice. "Open up, Annemarie. Hurry. It's cold out here."

Annemarie dropped a crutch trying to hobble to the door. "Oh, Lisbeth, I've been waiting for you." The other crutch fell as they hugged.

"I can't always get away." Lisbeth helped her into the kitchen and onto the sofa.

"So, do you work for the British now?"

"Don't ask questions." Lisbeth went to the sink and washed her hands. "I am eating well, as you can see." She twirled around and pointed at her belly.

"You look the same to me, beautiful like a queen."

Lisbeth leaned to pull up Annemarie's pajama leg, took scissors from her bag and cut away the bandage.

"Well, it hasn't gotten any worse," she muttered, and proceeded to clean and dress the wound.

Annemarie waved a hand at the supplies she had brought. "Do they let you take these things home?"

"You ask too many questions." Lisbeth frowned up from beneath her brows, the nurse in charge not tolerating curiosity from her patient.

Annemarie flailed around for something to say. "I… don't have any coffee left."

Lisbeth fastened the bandage with a metal clip and smiled. "I brought some, and I'm hungry." Annemarie returned her smile. She must give up trying to figure out Lisbeth, a woman so real, so down to earth and yet so distant, so mysterious.

"That stove is barely going, and you are almost out of coal," Lisbeth said as she added water to the coffee pot on the burner.

"I have been trading with the Krause's upstairs," Annemarie explained. "I've given them Cognac, ham, whatever they will take. They like alcohol. One bottle is worth a whole bucket of coal." She watched Lisbeth empty her bag, hoping there would be another bottle. Lisbeth raised her eyebrows but did not reply.

"He said the Tommies like antiques," Annemarie went on, like old glass, figurines, things like that. I am desperate, Lisbeth. I don't have anything left except my

345

mother's clock and the ballerina, and I am keeping those. If I have to freeze, I will."

Lisbeth held a can of pickled herring under Annemarie's nose. "Recognize this?"

Annemarie laughed. "Just like the picnics we had at the hospital."

"And please, don't call me an angel. It's only pickled herring." She picked up the coffee pot and filled the cups.

Annemarie smiled. "Can I call you, my miracle?" She took a bite of her sandwich. "Corned beef, what a treat." Crumbs and pieces of meat fell onto her plate.

"I brought a couple more cans. I'm sure your Mr. Krause will trade them for coal. You can't get corned beef except on the base. They have it shipped in."

This was more than Lisbeth had ever volunteered. "Thanks. Do you know what else they might like? But I must get more coal, at least until spring." Annemarie wiped her mouth and looked at her friend.

"I'd like to get my hands on your Mr. Krause." Lisbeth's tone said he would not appreciate getting to know her. "What ever happened to neighborly help? You've grown up here, they know your family. Oh, I'd like to kick him in the ass, I really would."

Annemarie didn't doubt she'd follow through with her threat. "Right now, he is my only source for heat. What can I do? My father would kill the bastard with his own hands if he were here."

"I brought a bottle of brandy. That should be good for at least one bucket." Lisbeth's voice dripped with sarcasm.

"Can you take a look at my father's old armchair? It could be an antique. Do the Tommies take furniture?"

Lisbeth thought for a moment. "Let me check into that. I really don't know. But it's easier to get liquor. And I know somebody who has plenty of it." She smiled mischievously and touched Annemarie under the chin like a child. "And I think he would be happy to share some with you."

What was Lisbeth talking about? She could never figure this woman out.

"I have a surprise for you." Lisbeth stood and refilled their cups.

"A surprise?"

"Yes. A surprise. Don't you want to find out?"

"Of course, yes. I just don't know what to say."

"We have been invited to a party, a dinner dance at the club. I want you to come with us."

Annemarie stared. Had Lisbeth lost her mind? She hauled herself up from the sofa and limped to the center of the small kitchen, facing her friend. "Look at me! I am a cripple, scrawny, unable to walk without crutches, a mess. I don't have enough food and I barter with a Nazi for a bucket of coal."

Lisbeth stood up. "All the more reason to go. It doesn't have to stay this way. There are plenty of people who are doing well."

"Like you," Annemarie wanted to say, but she didn't. She just waved her hand, clutching the table with the other. "How, do tell me, how am I going to go out with you? I can't walk, I -"

"You are coming to the club with me, basta! Next Saturday, I'll pick you up at eight."

Annemarie stared at her.

"For God's sake, I'm not asking you to become a prostitute, if that's what you think." Lisbeth glared at her.

"I didn't mean that. I'm sorry, I really am." Annemarie fought back tears. "I'm just, you know -- I haven't been out, I am such a mess."

"Oh, phew, get over it. You are so naïve. Yes, you're a little thin, but you are young and beautiful. So, start living. Life is not going to be handed to you on a

347

silver platter." She pulled Annemarie into the hallway in front of the mirror. "Say, I am beautiful, I want to dance again."

Annemarie had to laugh. "I want to dance again," she sang, awkwardly twirling around the hallway, hanging on to Lisbeth's arm.

Lisbeth smiled. "That's my girl."

Annemarie scrutinized her image in the mirror and scowled. "But I have nothing to wear."

"No problem, I'll come early and bring something. You'll see, Cinderella, you wait and see."

Annemarie hugged her and whispered, "Thank you."

"Just wait for the real surprise." Lisbeth winked. "I will see you on Saturday."

"But wait," Annemarie said, and pulled up a sleeve. "Look at this, my skin is falling off. I've got something, I don't know what." She scratched her arm.

Lisbeth took her arm and looked at it. "I'll bring you some ointment. I think you are malnourished. So, eat! I keep telling you. Eat more meat, fat, and fruit. Don't give it all away." She took Annemarie's shoulders and turned her. "I'm going to get Herr Krause arrested if he keeps bothering you." Back in the kitchen, she handed Annemarie a thick slice of corned beef. "Eat!" She stepped back and glanced at her watch.

"Your driver is waiting?" Annemarie said, munching.

"Yup. Got to go. See you on Saturday, Liebling." She waved and went to the hall to put on her coat.

Annemarie heard the door slam but listened a while, hoping she would hear the Krause's come in. Her fire was almost out, the bucket empty, and it was getting cold in the kitchen. When she heard Karl Krause's loud voice, she hobbled to the door, opened it a slit. "Can you get me more coal?" She opened her door wider and held out the bucket.

The young man sized her up and whistled. Pompous ass, she thought, but smiled.

"Your father said he could use liquor and meat. I have a bottle of brandy and a can of corned beef. Could you ask him if he will give me two buckets for it?"

He squared his shoulders and smirked. "I don't have to ask my father. I make the decisions."

"Wait here." She limped to the kitchen and back and handed him the items.

He turned the can over in his callused hands. "Good stuff from England. We usually get only ham."

"Two buckets, then." Annemarie held up her bucket.

"All right, but just because you are so pretty." He transferred the brandy to the hand holding the meat and took the buckets.

She shrank back into her hallway.

"In the future, don't bother Papa, just ask me." He leaned towards her.

She nodded and smiled, backing away from his liquored breath. How could Margarete have gone out with that man? The next time she would make sure to catch old man Krause and avoid Karl. But he did return momentarily with two full buckets. Annemarie nodded her thanks, motioned him to set the buckets in the hallway, then quickly shut her door. One by one she dragged the heavy buckets through the hallway into the kitchen. Exhausted, her foot throbbing, she added some coal to the stove and sank into the couch. She thanked her mother, who had taught her to tend the fire. Yes, Mama, you always said," You will thank me someday," and you were right."

Soon, the old stove was glowing again, and Annemarie relaxed.

She lay propped on the sofa next to the stove, thinking of what Lisbeth had said. She was right, she always was. Annemarie drank the rest of the coffee. *I can't* *just sit here and wait. Wait for what? For Alfred? For my leg to heal. For times to get better so I can go out and find work? How long would that take? Months, maybe a year? And w*hat if Inge got sick, or they expelled her for bedwetting? And Anna, her little fighter, what if she got hurt? They could move her girls someplace else, and she wouldn't even know.

"No," she said aloud. She would do whatever it took to bring her children home. On Saturday, she would go to the club with Lisbeth. She might have to take extra pills to walk on her leg, but she had to survive. Alfred would understand.

CHAPTER 37

Saturday, late afternoon, the doorbell rang. Lisbeth stood in the doorway with a large paper bag, and something draped over her arm. "The driver is picking us up at seven-thirty." She smiled at Annemarie approvingly. "Looks like you've been eating, girl."

Annemarie laughed. She had to admit she was excited and a little nervous, thinking about going to a dance at the club, whatever that was.

"Unfold the sheet. I want to see the look on your face," Lisbeth urged.

Annemarie pulled away the sheet and held up a dress, speechless.

"Do you like it? Say something."

"Oh my God, it's beautiful! I have never seen such a lovely gown." She touched the dress. "Everything is burned up, there are no stores open. Where on earth did you find this?"

"As I've said before, don't ask. Let's just say a friend found it for me and he wants you to wear it tonight." She touched Annemarie on the shoulder. "Are you still with me? Let's see how it looks on you."

Not taking her eyes off the dress, Annemarie took off her sweater and her father's old wool trousers.

Lisbeth dressed her as though she was a mannequin in a store window. "Perfect!" She stepped back. "You look like a princess. Or better, a goddess. Come see." She took Annemarie's hand and pulled her to the mirror.

351

Annemarie stared at the girl in the shimmering, full-length gown. A darker shade of lace ribboned the V-neck and draped down to her waist, accentuating her delicate figure.

"Here, I almost forgot." Lisbeth handed her a silver necklace with a dark blue pendant.

"Where did you get--?" Annemarie stuttered.

"No questions." Lisbeth clapped her hands. "You look stunning."

"I don't have any shoes," Annemarie stammered, unable to take her eyes of off her reflection.

"Never mind, the dress will cover them. But I'll see if we can find something other than your father's work boots. So now let's fix your hair." She led a stunned Annemarie back into the kitchen.

"There isn't much you can do with my hair," Annemarie protested, but Lisbeth took a brush and rollers and a tube of gel from her bag. Annemarie watched her, amazed at how her hair became a shiny cap framing her face. Then Lisbeth pulled out a small satchel.

"What is that?"

"Makeup." Lisbeth opened another tube and squeezed out a glob of paste and spread it over Annemarie's face.

"Makeup? I've never heard of that."

"They have it in England. It makes your skin glow. And see, I found your favorite lipstick." Lisbeth waved it in front of Annemarie's face with a self-satisfied smile.

"My favorite lipstick? I've never owned one. Oh, now I remember. You found one for me at the hospital that day."

"Annemarie, you look beautiful. I think my friend will be pleased. Stay on the chair here, don't move. I will get myself ready and then we'll find shoes."

As Annemarie waited, she studied the dress, so perfect for her. This couldn't be real.

Lisbeth returned from the bedroom with the black fur jacket Margarete had given to Annemarie's mother. "This will look good with the dress." She handed it to Annemarie and nodded approvingly. "Maedchen, you look like one ritzy lady. Those boys will go crazy." She giggled, then held out Annemarie's mother's bedroom slippers. "The only shoes I could find. They are black and they'll be hidden under the dress." She lifted the hem and slipped them on Annemarie's feet.

Annemarie rose and took a couple of cautious steps. "I need my crutches. I'm sorry."

Lisbeth nodded. "No problem. Like I said, you will be sitting most of the time, and when you dance, you can hang on to your partner. And by the way, you like my dress?"

The salmon-colored skin-tight sheath with its plunging neckline was perfect for Lisbeth, accentuating her pale skin, full figure and blonde hair. Of course, she wore her trademark bright red lipstick.

Annemarie's gaze fell to Lisbeth's feet. "Oh my God, look at those shoes. Are you wearing silk stockings?"

"They are nylons. Nigel got them for me. He says I have sexy legs." Lisbeth grinned.

Annemarie had never seen high heels like that either.

Lisbeth checked out her appearance in the hall mirror. "Nigel has good taste."

Annemarie didn't dare ask who Nigel was. "Does he bring those clothes from England?"

"I'm not sure. Could be. Officers always get privileges. It's the same in all armies." Lisbeth shrugged and checked her watch. "We better go. The driver is waiting. She helped Annemarie up. "You might feel a little cold, but it's warm in the club and once you have some Champagne you won't feel a thing." She grinned as if enjoying Annemarie's perplexed expression.

Annemarie had a difficult time getting down the stairs while trying to avoid stepping on her dress. It was dark as usual, in the hallway. The electricity had been out since yesterday.

Steadying her friend, Lisbeth grumbled after each landing until they finally reached the entrance hall and she reached to open the door.

The driver jumped out and came to help Annemarie into the back. He whistled and made a comment in English, and she heard Lisbeth say something to him and he shut up.

Annemarie arranged her skirts and clapped her hands together in anticipation. "You speak English well, Lisbeth."

"Remember, I speak five languages, most of them fluently."

It was dark now and Annemarie had no idea where they were going. They passed a checkpoint and drove through a big gate and stopped in front of a brightly lit villa. Fragments of music and laughter drifted to the outside. The driver dropped them off and Annemarie followed Lisbeth up the walkway, trying to manipulate her crutches. She had taken one of Lisbeth's pills and did not feel the pain in her leg.

A tall, uniformed man opened the door, and ushered them into a large foyer with a ceiling at least two stories high. They had entered a fairytale world. They foyer opened into a ballroom with a large, crowded dance floor. The room was dimly lit and she could barely make out a long bar on one side and a sitting area, its tables lit by small lamps. The noise was deafening. People were talking and laughing and dancing to a live band set up on a stage at one side. A cloud of smoke floated over the room, engulfing everyone in a light haze. It reminded Annemarie of a film she had once gone to see with her sister at the UFA theatre downtown.

Lisbeth said something to the doorman who, saluted and disappeared into the crowd.

"Let's wait here." Smiling and waving at people passing by, she took Annemarie's arm.

A few minutes later, the man returned with an older man in uniform, who bent and kissed Lisbeth's hand. Lisbeth said something Annemarie couldn't hear for the noise. Then he turned and kissed her hand too, smiling briefly. This must be Nigel, Lisbeth's friend. He was distinguished-looking, with gray, short hair and a thin mustache. Annemarie guessed his age at around sixty. His eyes were dark, gray as steel, and deep lines marked his cheeks. Since people passed him and saluted, Annemarie knew he was important, perhaps a general?

He offered his arm, escorting each woman in turn to a table. She noticed that he walked with a limp and that an aide followed, carrying his cane. The aide helped Annemarie into a chair and reached for her crutches, but she smiled anxiously and slid them under the table. "The general," as Annemarie dubbed him, only had eyes for Lisbeth. Perhaps she was his private nurse, provided by the Germans to the occupiers just as they had given them houses and apartments -- after kicking the original occupants out on the street. That's what Mrs. Dummersdorf had told her. Annemarie smiled, trying to be part of the group, feeling awkward, since she could not understand a word.

After drinks were served, Lisbeth raised her glass to good times. Annemarie followed suit without knowing what they were toasting. She smiled and slowly sipped her drink. It was not Champagne. She had tried that before with Lisbeth. This tasted delicious, sweet and tangy. A waiter came with a large tray of mini sandwiches. They were piled high with roast beef, salmon and a liver-like paste. Annemarie watched the others and took two small ones and placed them on her plate. She picked one up and took a bite. It was delicious, and she helped herself every time the man came around with a new platter. She wondered if there was a way to take some home. Mrs. Maier would enjoy such a treat. But her dress didn't have pockets, and her mother's small purse was barely big enough for her keys and a hanky. She glanced around, then picked up a napkin and shook it open, and put it on her lap. Maybe when they left, she could take a few pieces with her. The abundance of food was incredible, and surely, they wouldn't notice.

Volleys of laughter drifted over from the bar. After a short break, the band members wandered back from their break. The general rose and bowed to Lisbeth. "Nigel and I are going to dance," Lisbeth told her. "David, our waiter, will bring you more drinks." And she and her general melted into the bobbing crowd.

Annemarie felt as though she was on another planet or in heaven. Maybe it wasn't even her. Maybe it was some other woman was sitting here, sipping a drink and feasting on these delicious sandwiches.

A man's voice brought her back to earth. "May I have this dance?"

She squinted up, then jumped out of her chair, "Doctor Hartmann!"

He caught her before she could fall. "Is that really you? Did I die and go to heaven?" She squeezed his arm, then touched his cheek.

"Ouch!" He held his arm."Please don't hurt me." They laughed and hugged, and Annemarie tripped and fell against him. "More hugs! How can I resist." He held her until she struggled. "You look stunning, like a princess." Then he laughed and held her at arm's length and gazed at her.

"I think you've had a few too many," she teased, but willingly followed as he took her hand and started for the dance floor.

Annemarie clutched his arm. "I can't stand without my crutches. I'm not sure I can do this."

He took her arms and placed them around his neck. "Yes, you can, just stand on my feet, little girl. We'll just do the slow ones." He put his arms around her waist, and they swayed to the music.

She looked up at him. "Are you sure I'm not too heavy?"

"You are lighter than goose-down. And, I have a reason to hold you close without getting slapped." He laughed. "There are a hundred guys here who would love to hold you, believe me."

Was it the music, or the drinks? Annemarie snuggled against him and closed her eyes. They danced, melting together, as though they had danced many times before. The scent of his aftershave brought a certain familiarity – it swept her back to when he had bent close and worked on her leg. When they had dubbed him Don Juan for wearing cologne, he would say, "Just for you ladies," and flash his irresistible smile.

"You are good," he murmured. He pressed his cheek against hers. They danced until the band took another break. Annemarie felt as though she was waking from a dream as Doc Hartmann guided her back to the table where he ordered more drinks and started a conversation in English with Nigel. Annemarie did not care that she did not understand a word because Doc Hartmann had taken her hand and held it under the table.

Lisbeth soon joined them and leaned towards her, whispering, "How do you like your surprise?" Lisbeth pointed at Doc Hartmann. "Don't tell me you were not surprised when he asked you to dance."

"Oh my God, more than surprised. He kept his promise. I hope I don't wake up and it is all a dream."

"You are the most beautiful woman here, Annemarie," said Lisbeth. "People have been asking me

357

about you all night long. They think you are sixteen, with that short pixie hair, ha, ha, ha." Then Lisbeth turned and said something in English to the men and they all laughed and looked at Annemarie.

"What? Do I look funny?" Annemarie touched Lisbeth's arm.

"No, Annemarie, you look so young, so innocent, a lovely irresistible German princess," Doc Hartmann said, putting his arm around her. "My princess. I want to hide you, and keep you safe from all these dirty, tough men." He pulled her closer.

"Who? What are you talking about?"

"Oh, believe me," said Lisbeth, "Annemarie, if you weren't sitting at Nigel's table, they'd be all over you. They'd be fighting over who would take you home."

Before Annemarie could reply, another round of drinks was served, and Doc Hartmann raised his glass and offered a toast in English. Lisbeth laughed and they all clinked glasses.

Lisbeth tilted her glass towards Doc Hartmann. "Just remember, you owe me."

His face turned serious, and he leaned over the table to kiss her on the cheek. "I know, Lisbeth."

Annemarie watched, smiled and finished her drink. She snuggled closer to Doc Hartmann. "I don't want this to end." The band played "Lily Marlene", and everyone sang along. Annemarie glanced at the people around them. Women, glamorous, with fur capes, their hair coiffed. Prostitutes? She had never seen one, so she wasn't sure. Most of the men were in uniform but they didn't seem to be regular soldiers. Probably officers. Maybe the ladies were their wives.

"Let's dance again, Liebling." Doc Hartmann helped her out of the chair and led her onto the floor. They danced cheek-to-cheek and she let desire carry her body away. Nothing mattered, just the two of them holding each other.

Suddenly she winced and grasped her leg.

"What is it?" He stopped, his arm firmly around her.

"I think the pills are no longer working. It's the first time I've been out," she grimaced as pain shot up her leg. Please, Liebling, will you take this schoolgirl home?" She smiled despite of the throbbing. She braced herself on a chair back and waited as Doc Hartmann retrieved her crutches and spoke a word to Lisbeth and the general.

The uniformed doorman brought a big black car to the front and Doc Hartmann helped her into the back, stretching her injured leg across the seat. He slipped behind the wheel and slowly drove out of the compound. When they reached the gate, the soldier saluted.

Annemarie leaned back on the soft leather. "This is not an army vehicle. It's so much nicer."

"It's mine, Liebling." Doc glanced back and smiled.

"You are a general too?" She giggled.

"No, I'm not a general. I'm the regional medical chief. I will explain another time."

She began humming "Lily Marlene", and he joined in as he drove through the deserted streets lined by ruins and mounds of rubble.

"This has been wonderful." Annemarie sighed. "A princess for one night, like Lisbeth said." She closed her eyes.

Presently, he stopped the car in front of house number 77, opened the rear door and leaned into the back to kiss her. "You are amazing, little schoolgirl." He took her face into his hands and gazed into her eyes then, gathered her up and helped her to stand. "Come, let me go with you up the stairs and put you to bed."

"Are you sure I'm not drunk?" She giggled.

"Oh, just a little." He lifted her, carried her up the stairs and unlocked the apartment door. "Three flights of stairs in the dark. How did you ever do it?" He shook his head and handed her the crutches. "We need to check out that leg and fix it." His voice was that of her doctor now.

"Shush," she whispered, and placed her fingers over his lips.

CHAPTER 38

Annemarie held her head to stop the room from spinning. Sunshine flooded the kitchen, and she closed her eyes. She held onto the table, trying to raise herself, and realized that she was still fully dressed. The blue gown shimmered in the sunshine. But it was cold in the room. *Scheiss. I have not added coal to the fire since last night.*

Her head was about to explode, and her leg felt as if a fiery dragon was chewing on it. I have a hangover. The drinks kept coming, oh God, my head, the room spun when she tried to move. She closed her eyes. Other than a beer or glass of wine to usher in the New Year or celebrate her father's birthdays, Annemarie and her family did not drink. They had no money to waste on such luxuries. She tried to focus on her watch. Twelve-thirty. Afternoon. She whimpered, wishing Lisbeth was there. She always knew what to do.

Slowly she forced herself to search for her crutches. To her surprise, they were on the kitchen table. Lord, she must have been really drunk. She turned to open the stove. Dead. Cold.

She heard a knock and hoped it was Doc Hartmann. A smile crept across her lips. But Mrs. Maier called her name. She fell back on the sofa. Oh, God, the room was still spinning, and she felt sick to her stomach. All those sandwiches, why had she stuffed herself like a child? She moaned and pressed her hands to her mouth.

The knock came again.

"I'm in here, Frau Maier," she called and forced herself to roll off the sofa and crawl to the door, dragging her leg. She opened the door. Mrs. Maier just stood there and stared down at her.

Annemarie tried to smile. "I can explain. My friend Lisbeth took me out to a club last night."

Mrs. Maier's mouth dropped open. The old woman kept staring at her there on the floor in a full-length formal gown.

"I know it sounds crazy. I'd had nothing to eat, and I went to a party. But it isn't what you think. We went to visit my old doctor friend from the military hospital. I am sorry, Mrs. Maier, I feel sick. My head hurts and my leg is throbbing and the fire went out…" She leaned against the wall to keep herself up.

"I can bring you some food," said Mrs. Maier. "I've cooked some chicken I received from Mrs. Krause." Mrs. Maier sniffed and blew, sniffed again. Annemarie realized that she smelled the English perfume and cigarettes from the party. Mrs. Maier mumbled something about smoke and bent to put her hand on Annemarie's shoulder. I've never seen such a pretty dress."

She thinks that I am a prostitute now, shacking up with the Tommies. Annemarie felt she would faint.

"It smells in here, really strong, like when your father smoked those cigars." Mrs. Maier shook her head, then gently took Annemarie's arm, and sniffed again as the ball gown billowed around Annemarie's legs. She raised her up and helped walk her to the kitchen. "Sit on the chair here, Annemarie. Where are your pajamas?" She looked around.

"In the bedroom. I wear some of my father's clothes because they keep me warm," Annemarie said in a small voice.

Mrs. Maier left and returned with the trousers and cardigan. "Are these the clothes?"

Annemarie nodded and took a deep breath. She noticed the smoke smell now. It made her stomach churn.

"It's getting chilly in here. I heard that you have been getting coal from Mr. Krause?"

Annemarie nodded.

"Well, let's get you back into these clothes and then we will make a fire." Mrs. Maier sounded like a mother speaking to her child. She helped Annemarie take off the gown and into the clothes then lie down on the sofa. The pain in her leg made her feel light-headed.

Mrs. Maier held up the dress, admiring the lace and the shiny material. "I had a beautiful dress when Herman and I were engaged," she mused. "That was in 1884 when I was just twenty." She smiled and draped the dress over her arm and left the kitchen. "I hung it in the closet," she reported when she returned.

"Oh, thank you," Annemarie whispered.

Mrs. Maier bent over the stove. "Where is your kindling?" She straightened, stepped close and felt Annemarie's forehead. "I think you have a fever."

"Don't worry about me. I'll be all right after I get over this … You are so nice, Mrs. Maier. If you need anything, just go to my pantry. My sister brought some food, and so did my friend, Lisbeth." She sank back into her pillow.

Mrs. Maier shook her head. "I don't need much, I'm old, I get by. But I need something to start your fire."

"I don't know. I don't have anything." Hung-over and exhausted, Annemarie couldn't think straight.

Mrs. Maier's eyes brightened, and she snapped her fingers. "I'll be right back. I think I have some old magazines and newspapers. Herman liked to read, and he saved them all. He always said you never know when they will be useful. He was a very smart man, my Herman."

Annemarie had to smile. The woman must be eighty years old, and her husband had passed away years ago, yet, she still loved and cherished the man.

When Mrs. Maier returned with a stack of magazines and newspaper Annemarie asked, "Don't you need them, yourself? After all, I'm the one who let the fire burn out." She watched Mrs. Maier, praying that the old stove would work. But her worry was needless. Mrs. Maier had the fire going in no time.

"That was magic. I can never get that stove to work so quickly," Annemarie said admiringly.

"You know how many years I have worked with a stove like this? Too many. You just get the hang of it after a while if you want to have heat and cook a meal." Mrs. Maier smiled. "Oh! I was going to bring you some chicken, I almost forgot."

Before Annemarie could reply, the old woman had left again. Tears rolled down Annemarie's face. Her neighbor's kindness was overwhelming.

Mrs. Maier returned, carrying a bowl. "I had some flour and made gravy. Amazing how you can make flour, water and salt taste good." She splayed her hands." So, eat, girl. It will make you feel better. But I don't have any vegetables."

"Thank you so much, I will. But first, I have to ask you for one more favor. My leg. It really hurts. I don't remember where I put my pills. Lisbeth gave them to me. She's a nurse, did I tell you?"

"Yes, you did, dear. Are the pills in a jar or a box or bottle?"

Annemarie said. "A small glass jar with a screw-on lid."

"Where do you keep your medicines?"

"I think they are in the first drawer of my mother's dresser."

Mrs. Maier hurried to the bedroom.

Annemarie heard her rummaging in the dresser drawer and muttering. Finally, the woman returned with three jars and gave them to her. "Do you remember which one it is?"

"The pills are small, a sort of greenish color. Ah, these are the ones." Annemarie held up one of the jars. "I know because the sticker is in English. I can't read what it says."

Mrs. Maier looked at her a little suspiciously.

"Don't worry, Nurse Lisbeth got them from her doctor. I recognize them because I never take pills, and these others are old bottles my mother had." Annemarie unscrewed the lid, her hand trembling. "Can I ask you for a glass of water?"

Mrs. Maier rubbed her hands over her mouth, still looking a little askance. But she went to the sink to fill a glass from the drying board. "I hope those are right, I never take any pills. I think they make you feel worse."

Annemarie shook out two pills and took the glass.

Mrs. Maier watched her swallow them. "Now, drink all that water."

Annemarie drained the glass as she was told. "I'll eat the chicken in a little while. Thanks again, Mrs. Maier. And please, take some food from my pantry, pick what you need."

Mrs. Maier waved her off. "Really, Annemarie, I don't need anything." Then she hesitated and looked at the two buckets of coal.

Annemarie smiled and said, "Take one." The old woman protested. "Please, take one" she repeated.

Mrs. Maier's face lit up and she picked up one of the buckets. "That will keep me warm for quite some time. I've learned how to be miserly." She beamed. "Get some rest, Annemarie, and don't forget to eat." She turned to the door, lugging the heavy bucket.

I WILL DANCE AGAIN

"You are an angel," Annemarie called, not sure
Mrs. Maier could still hear her.

CHAPTER 39

Other than tending the fire, Annemarie spent the next two days on the kitchen sofa. Her outing had been too much. Her pain was worse than before. Oh, but it was worth it. She had experienced life beyond her wildest imagination. "You are a princess," he had said, "if only for one day." She closed her eyes and sighed, reliving the moment.

After last night, things seemed different between them. She was sure that he must realize it too. Or was she just another of his conquests, young, naïve and defenseless against the charms of a successful doctor? She hoped Lisbeth would come again soon so that she could ask what she knew about this man. It was obvious that he circulated in that elite group of British officers and well-to-do people and lived a life most Germans could not imagine. Just as Lisbeth seemed to. How did she do that?

Of course, she already knew what Lisbeth's answer would be: "Go for it, girl. Hook him before some other woman does." Annemarie laughed out loud. Reminding Lisbeth that she was engaged would be useless. She knew where Lisbeth stood. Live now. You never know what tomorrow will bring. Annemarie wrestled with those thoughts. If she was honest, she had to admit that she wanted to make love with him and never have the next day arrive. He had aroused feelings she had not felt in a long time, not since that night at the lake with Alfred. Alfred. He still held her heart in his hands, reminding her of the promises they had made.

She heard a knock and grabbed her crutches, lifting herself up. "Who is it?" Probably Karl Krause.

"Doctor's house call," the voice answered. Annemarie burst out laughing and struggled to the door.

"May I come in, Mrs. Peterman?" Doc Hartmann smiled. He was carrying a worn leather medical bag.

Annemarie looked down at her old sweater and her father's trousers. "I-I'm such a mess." her hands fluttered to her uncombed hair.

"My little sparrow." He took her into his arms. "I came to take a look at your leg. No, no. It's against the rules to say no to your doctor." He helped her into the kitchen. "Oh, it's warm in here." He spotted the bucket of coal.

"Cost me two cans of corned beef." She laughed, then scowled. "Lisbeth brought them. I would have loved to at least taste it. She's my angel--" she drew the sign of a cross with her fingers-- "but now I am running out of things to barter with." She grimaced.

He set her down and sat beside her. His arms still around her, he pulled her close, then lifted the trouser leg. "All that dancing, I should have known." He shook his head, then dressed the wound in her foot. "Liebling, it's not healing. I know the best orthopedic surgeon and--"

'No, no," she pleaded and touched her finger to his lips. "Oh, but that night was heavenly. I will always remember it." She sighed and turned away. "I have coffee, a little left from the packet Lisbeth brought." She tried to get up, but he gently pushed her back, kissing her cheek.

"You just stay there, Liebling. I can make a remarkable cup of coffee."

She watched as he picked up her mother's old pot. "My mother has one of these." He smiled. As the coffee gurgled through, he brought two cups from the sideboard. "Mother didn't want me to get a big head. She taught me to do all the kitchen chores."

"I like the woman. She did a good job." Annemarie laughed and then caught herself. "I hope she is still -- I mean--"

"She's alive and well, thank you. And she still keeps me on the straight and narrow." He gave her a wry grin.

"Are you kidding? She'd need a shotgun to keep all the women away from you." She glanced at him sideways, and they laughed. For a moment she forgot that she was sitting here in her father's old clothes on a worn sofa in a tenement kitchen.

Someone banged on the door. "It's me, Karl! Need any more coal?"

Annemarie screwed her face into a frown.

Doc Hartmann went to the door.

"Oh, a gentleman visitor." Karl whistled from the hall.

"Dr. Peter Hartmann. I'm Annemarie's doctor. Can I help you?"

"Annemarie, you got anything to trade?" he shouted. "You still have my bucket."

Annemarie hobbled to the door. "No, I don't have anything. But I'm trying to find some antiques."

There was a dark stain on the lad's sleeve. "Blood?" Doc Hartmann inquired.

"It's nothing. I just got tangled in some wire."

"Barbed wire?" The Doc raised his eyebrows.

Karl did not answer.

"That can cause blood poisoning. Does it hurt?"

The man stared at him. "Yeah, a little, but it's nothing I can't handle."

"You mind if I take a look?" Doc Hartmann did not wait for an answer but reached to push the sleeve up Karl's arm. "Hmm, doesn't look good. I think you got an infection." He released his arm. "Here's how it is." He looked Karl Krause in the eye. "I'll fix up that wound for two buckets of coal."

Karl pulled back his injured arm. "One bucket, that's it."

"No deal. Good luck finding a hospital or a doctor when that infection spreads." Doc Hartmann stepped back and started to close the door.

"Two buckets then," the young man grunted.

Doc asked him to step into the kitchen and sit down. "This will hurt. I have to clean the wound. It's quite deep." Doc opened his bag. "Barbed wire will cause infection every time. I've seen lots of it in the soldiers returning from the front."

Karl Krause flinched as Doc worked but did not say a word until he was finished and walked him back out, giving him instructions on how to care for the wound. "All right, where's the coal? I can help you carry one of the buckets."

"No, I'll bring it down. Just tell her that I need my buckets back."

Annemarie stayed in the kitchen, overhearing their conversation. She could not believe that Karl Krause did not give Doc Hartmann any of his usual lip.

"All right," she heard Doc say, "I'll wait here for you."

And without further conversation, Karl returned with two buckets of coal. Then she heard Doc politely thank him. He carried them into the kitchen.

"You are one smooth operator," she said. "I'm impressed. I think you should run for mayor or general or some type of office."

He grinned, sat down beside her and bent to kiss her lightly on the mouth. "I got that from my father. He had to be a politician to live with my mother." He laughed out loud. Then he said in a serious tone, "Annemarie, I don't like that fellow. He is up to no good. Watch out, don't let him into your place again."

"I can take care of myself. I know, he's an asshole who never went to the front." She told him the story about her father's fights with the Krause family. "But I need coal, Doc, I have to stay on his good side."

"Damn, I shouldn't have fixed him up, just let the bastard croak."

She burst out laughing. "You are such a wonderful doctor. You'd have fixed up the devil or even Hitler, wouldn't you? And it worked. You got me coal."

"Are you going to call *me* your angel now?" He formed a halo with his hands.

"Well, should I call you, my Saint? Saint Hartmann, I like how that sounds."

He laughed. "You are funny, Annemarie. You remind me of the days when I was young and carefree and -
-"

"What are you talking about? You're not even thirty, are you?"

"I tell you, these war years, the soldiers, the stories I've heard, the sadness and the madness of it all, it gets to you. I am thirty-six, but sometimes I feel a hundred."

Annemarie studied his face and touched his hand. This was the first time Doc Hartmann had revealed his serious side.

He pulled her closer. "Doctors have feelings too, little sparrow. We are human. But we've been trained to do our job and we can't let our feelings interfere with that."

"In a way, you remind me of Lisbeth. She's all business, all nurse, but then her real personality comes out and the angel appears."

He took a deep breath and stroked her hair.

Annemarie snuggled into the curve of his shoulder. "I think Lisbeth saved my life. The care, the food. She has a way to lift me up, make me feel that I can make it. She

371

taught me how to survive." Annemarie swiped at her tears and slipped an arm beneath his jacket and around his waist.

"I fell for you the minute I saw you," he murmured, his voice growing hoarse. "It was a hectic, turbulent time after the war ended with the closing of the field hospital and the transfer of all the patients. I worked non-stop. It fell on me to do everything." He sighed. "And then I couldn't find you. You'd just vanished."

Annemarie sat up straight and pulled away. "Come on Doc, every girl, every nurse there, was in love with you. I heard a lot of stories about your conquests."

"Well, I was one of the few able-bodied around. He spread his hands, pleading. "Somebody had to do it. For the Fatherland." They laughed. "You have to admit, a little loving goes a long way when there is not much to live for." He leaned in to kiss her.

"So, it was your job to keep up the morale of the nurses, Dr. Hartmann? Admirable. Der Fuehrer should have awarded you a medal for your dedication."

He poked her gently. "Little witch. Why must you torture the man who loves you?"

"Did you sleep with Lisbeth?"

He stared; mouth open. "No, I did not. We are good friends." He reached for her. "If it weren't for Lisbeth, I might never have found you. You are right, she is an angel. Our angel."

Against her misgivings she smiled, opened her arms and gathered him in.

"You are so sweet, Annemarie so -- God, you're making me feel--" He abruptly pulled back and gestured towards the kitchen clock. "I need to get back. We've got several surgeries scheduled. They're going to declare me AWOL." He kissed her once, more deeply, and reached for his jacket and scarf. "See you soon, little sparrow," he said, standing. "I want you to come to my house for dinner."

She shrugged her shoulders. "If times were different, I would jump around with excitement. But look at me, here in the kitchen in my father's old pants. Sometimes I'm not sure if I should laugh or cry." She sighed shakily.

"Laugh!" he said. "That's what I like about you. I don't know how such a fierce fighter could be hidden in such a tiny, lovely body. You are trouble, Maedchen. Big trouble. You just don't know it. Or do you?" He bent and kissed her one last time.

She pushed him away. "Doctor Hartmann. Where are your bedside manners?"

"See? That's what I mean. You're playing with me. I wish I could stay. Damn, work gets in the way." He picked up his bag. See you on Saturday. I will pick you up at six, and I don't care what you wear. How about coming in your nightgown?"

"You wish. All right, I'll try to find something."

She listened to his footsteps running down the stairs. Then she hobbled to the bedroom balcony door and watched his big black car pull away.

Back in the kitchen, she bent and tossed two chunks of coal into the stove. Her leg had begun to throb. Why hadn't she told him?

She lowered herself to the sofa and thought as honestly as she could about this extraordinary man. Did she really love him, or was it something else? He had a car. He could take her to see her children. He was her only hope to get to the orphanage until her foot healed. She sighed. Why was she hesitant to ask him all this? She closed her eyes and tried unsuccessfully to picture Alfred. Should she feel guilty? But like Lisbeth said, go for it. What if Alfred did not come back, was already dead in a ditch in France?

"Oh." She grabbed her foot as bolts of pain shot up her leg. Holding onto the table, she pulled herself up and stepped to the sideboard, opened the drawer and took out the pill bottle. It was almost empty.

I WILL DANCE AGAIN

CHAPTER 40

Annemarie woke and glanced at the kitchen clock. Ten! Sunlight broke through the blue winter sky, engulfing the room. She tried to raise her leg and gasped from the pain. She reached and pulled up her right pant leg. "Damn." Her ankle was bulging over the top of the bandage, pulsating with waves of pain. Would it help to cut off the bandage? "No, I can't. What then?" she said aloud. It was only Tuesday, and Doc was not coming back till Saturday. Maybe Lisbeth would stop by soon. Annemarie clasped the table and gingerly scooted of the sofa, hopping on her good foot towards the sideboard. "Idiot, I'm an idiot," she sighed. "Why do I keep the pills in here?" She opened the drawer and took out the bottle. Now water. She looked at the sink on the other side of the room. Leaning against the sideboard, she slowly lowered herself to the floor and scooted. Pulling herself up the sink front, she picked up a cup and sniffed. Coffee. Oh, well. She filled it with water. She maneuvered back to the sofa and eased herself down. "I don't know what to do," she whispered. What if Doc was right and her leg had to come off? She opened the bottle and popped in a pill, washing it down with big gulps. Then she leaned back and closed her eyes, waiting.

A knock on the door and Mrs. Maier's voice aroused her from a dreamless sleep. When she raised her head, the room spun. She clutched the edge of the sofa and shouted, "I'm in the kitchen."

Mrs. Maier opened the door, carrying a coffee pot and a small tin. "From Mrs. Krause." She smiled. "Biscuits Karl got from a Tommy." She stepped to the sideboard and came back with two cups.

Annemarie pulled herself to a sitting position. "I feel a little dizzy." She held her head. "My leg hurt so much, and I took some pills." She attempted a smile.

Mrs. Maier nodded and filled their cups. "The sun looks so bright out there. I wonder if it has warmed up a little."

Annemarie took in the aroma and picked up a biscuit. "Real coffee. Mrs. Maier, you are such a wonderful neighbor. Mother always said so."

"Yes, I miss your mother. She always cheered me up. It's a shame, a real shame." She shook her head and fell silent. Then, "These English cookies are very tasty. Please take another."

"Oh, I will. I have not eaten today. So, what's Mr. Krause been up to lately?"

"Oh, that's funny. Karl Jr. said that your doctor friend operated on his arm without painkillers. Of course, we all know Karl, he likes to play the hero." They laughed. "And old Mr. Krause told me that a man he used to work with has just returned home."

"Home from where?" Annemarie asked, almost knocking over her cup.

"The front. His wife thought he was dead. She had been told that nobody survived when their unit was overrun by the Americans."

Annemarie's head jerked. "Where was he, I mean at what front? Did he say?"

"France, I think. Normandy. But the sad thing is that the wife has a boyfriend now and he moved in with her and they have a baby." She sighed and sipped her coffee. "You can't blame her. She didn't know."

Annemarie said, "And times are bad. She probably needed a man to find food and protect her." Maybe she shouldn't have said that. But oh! A soldier had come home from Normandy.

"They said he couldn't breathe, that he had been burned and his lung was hurt badly. Mrs. Krause said that it was not right that the boyfriend had moved in and that she didn't want her husband back, and –"

"Do you know where the soldier is now?"

"Mrs. Krause said he left the same day. He has a sister somewhere in the South and that's where he was headed. But you really can't blame the wife. Nobody came back from Normandy, we know that." Mrs. Maier wiped her face with her apron. "But it's so sad, that poor soldier. He fought for the fatherland and he's badly wounded and now he is not wanted at home." She sighed and gazed towards the window.

Arousing from her own thoughts, Annemarie said, "I wish I could have talked with him."

Mrs. Maier reached to place her arm around Annemarie. "Mr. Krause said the man could hardly talk; he could barely breathe. How could they discharge such a sick man? He belongs in a hospital, not out on the streets."

Annemarie swiped at her eyes.

"Well, as you said, there's always hope, but I don't know why people cling to any hope these days."

Annemarie looked into Mrs. Maier's eyes. "You said you believe in miracles, didn't you?"

"Yes, I do." She gave Annemarie a tremulous smile. "You are a good woman, just like your mother -- Oh, I heard from Mrs. Krause that Muller's corner store is expecting eggs tomorrow. I'm going early and will give some to you." She clapped her hands.

Annemarie's mouth watered. "Fresh eggs. It's been so long," she said

377

Mrs. Maier picked up her coffee pot and turned to leave. "Wish me luck."

Temporarily free of pain, Annemarie decided to check her mother's wardrobe for something to wear to the dinner. She sifted through housedresses, black or navy blouses and skirts and jackets. Why had they worn such drab clothes that only made them look older? Of course, they had lived through World War One. And they were poor and out of work. She remembered the game she and her mother had played. Sitting at the dinner table, Mother would pour tap water into glasses and have them toast to "Pearl of the Faucet," as if they were drinking wine.

Sitting on the edge of the bed holding one of her mother's dresses, she smiled. The dress was dark blue with flowers embroidered around the neck. She tried to remember when her mother had worn that dress. Oh, yes, at her sister's wedding, was it 1938? Overcome, she wiped her face with the corner of the bedspread, then slid off the bed, reached for the wardrobe door and returned the dress to the hanger. "Oh Mama, I promised that I would buy you the most beautiful dress." She bit her lip. She would never fulfill that wish.

Suddenly she thought of her sister. Margarete had a whole wardrobe of clothes, and she might let her borrow a dress. She pictured her sister's face when she told her that she was going out with a well-known doctor. "Oh, a doctor, Kittie. You must introduce me." Ha, ha. But her sister had not come by for a while.

Think. Annemarie sighed. Margarete was always quick to point out that she had no taste and didn't know how to dress.

Annemarie finally picked a white, short-sleeve blouse decorated with small blue daisies. She found a blue cardigan. That would look all right, especially if she wore Margarete's fur jacket over it. But she could not find a

378

skirt. Margarete was right. She didn't know how to dress. She sat staring at the wardrobe. Finally, she had an idea. She pulled a navy-blue dress off the hanger and picked up her mother's sewing basket and hobbled into the kitchen.

Spreading the dress on the table, she carefully cut off the top, leaving enough material to make a waistband to turn it into a skirt. When the skirt was finished, she leaned back and gazed at the patch of winter sky that showed between the drab apartment buildings. *I miss you Mama, If only I could have come home sooner*. She slid to the edge of the sofa and rose, glancing around for her crutches. It was pointless to think of what might have been. She limped to the sink to wash. But when she flipped the light switch, nothing happened. It was pitch dark now, so she hobbled back to the sofa.

If only Lisbeth would stop by tomorrow, she thought as she lay down. She wanted to talk with her about the feelings she had for Doc Hartmann. Could it be possible for her to love another man when her heart belonged to Alfred? When they danced she had felt his desire. Soon, she would not be able to resist. She still believed that Alfred would come home. But Dr. Kronert said that nobody survived the onslaught of the American forces that swept through France.

She tried to wiggle her toes, but her foot felt ice cold and feeling had not come back. She began to rub her calf. Days and days in this small kitchen had given the sad and bad thoughts time to invade her head and heart.

She wrangled off her covers, stood up and hobbled to the bedroom, feeling her way along the walls and furniture. Passing the balcony window, she stopped to watch a lone woman dressed in black, hurrying along the sidewalk, a small child tottering behind, stumbling to keep up.

Annemarie shuddered, thinking of her children lingering in the orphanage waiting for her. Margarete had told her she was too ill to take care of them. But other women did it. Somehow so could she. And if she had Lisbeth's help to bring them home, she could. Or, if she asked Doc Hartmann -- he had an automobile, which implied that he was influential with the new government. He wanted to see her again and he wanted more. Should she ask him, or would it be like using him? Could she do that? Margarete had said she was too naïve, and Lisbeth had told her to do whatever it took to survive. Could she, for her children, perhaps?

The street was now deserted. She shivered and drew the curtain. Her foot had begun to throb again. She turned back to the sofa and let it cocoon her.

As she was drifting off, she jerked awake. Booming voices, yelling and slamming doors. The neighbor's upstairs were fighting again. As usual, they were arguing over their daughter, who was Margarete's age, pretty with long blonde hair. Her father kept calling her a floozy, and that he would not tolerate her sleeping with the Tommies while she lived in his home. It always ended with the wife crying and him bolting out the door.

Annemarie pulled her pillow over her head.

CHAPTER 41

"Still needs to come off," Doc Hartmann muttered, bending over her leg. He looked up at Annemarie who sat propped on the sofa. "As I told you, I have a friend who's one of the best orthopedic surgeons around."

She shook her head and put her finger over is lips.

He reached up and tickled her belly.

"Hey, watch your bedside manners." She straightened her blouse.

"Now that I have your attention, let me tell you more about this doctor who owes me." He raised his eyebrows, noisily sighed and bent to replace the bandage on her foot. Then he slipped next to her on the sofa and put his arms around her.

"Maybe once I am eating better, it will heal." She laughed nervously brushing strands of hair from her face. "How am I going to take care of myself and my children with one leg, Doc?"

"Listen, Liebling. As your doctor, I tell you, the leg has to come off. You have developed a well, never mind. It's a wound that won't heal due to nerve damage."

"No, no" she screeched, "You promised to help me. Ellen said there are always miracles. Besides, how am I going to dance with one leg?"

He pulled a roll of bandages from his bag and wrapped it around her foot and up her calf. "For extra support this evening."

"With thousands of disabled soldiers coming home, they're developing orthopedic limbs that look so real that you can't tell the difference."

"I'm not sure, I can't think of it right now. It's hideous." She took a sharp breath.

Annemarie wiggled out of his arms. "What time do we have to be at the dinner?" She smiled. "It will take me a while to get dressed, since I have such an extensive wardrobe." She clutched the table and slowly rose.

"I am not giving up. I am just as stubborn as you, and I know that I am right. If you weren't so pretty, I would get mad at you. Patients never argue with me." He followed her into the bedroom. "Ugh, it's cold in here."

"Thank God for Karl, the coal man." She gathered her clothes and handed them to him, took his arm as they slowly walked back to the kitchen.

"Speaking of Karl the coal man, I'm going to see if I can find a revolver for you."

"No, no." She flung up her arms in protest.

He hugged her to him. "Just for emergencies, Liebling, just in case."

"You are a crazy man, Doc." Annemarie shook her head. "My mother always said that you catch flies with honey. And I do need more coal, at least for another month" she took his face in her hands, playfully patting his cheeks. "So, why don't you get me a bottle of cognac or whiskey instead of a gun?" She picked up the blouse. "And now, close your eyes so I can change."

He reached for her. "Do I have to?"

"Yes, sir, you do. I'm not one of your floozies from the club."

"Oh, jealous, are we?" He grinned. "All right, but hurry. I won't be able to keep my eyes closed for long."

"Maybe I need a gun to keep *you* in line." She raised her eyebrows, struggling into her outfit, and hobbled to the hallway mirror. "I'm not sure. What do you think?"

"You look like a schoolgirl." He came up behind and wrapped his arms around her waist.

"I look funny in this blouse and cardigan, don't I? All the ladies will wear fancy dresses, high heels and nylons." She sighed. "Maybe I should stay home."

"You are my princess, and you are coming if I have to carry you there." He picked her up and set her down again. "You are beautiful, Liebling, and you are young. And, you have me. Lots of women would love to trade places with you."

"I know that, Don Juan."

"Can I help it? I am just trying to keep everyone happy, help the war effort."

Annemarie shook her head and frowned at her image in the mirror.

Without a word, Doc helped her into Margarete's fur jacket, opened the door, scooped her up and carried her down the stairs. "Do you ever have electricity here?" He felt his way to the exit door.

"We do. It was on this morning."

"How do people live like this?" Doc grumbled. He helped her outside as the heavy door slammed behind them.

"Just as they always have. One day at a time." Annemarie could not resist a bit of sarcasm. "Welcome to the life of the other half of the citizens of the glorious fatherland."

Doc did not say anything, just guided her into the front seat of his car.

They drove through deserted streets. Annemarie stared out into darkness that seemed to swallow them.

He glanced at her. "What's on your mind, Liebling? Why so quiet?"

"Everything is so dark and grim. I wonder when it will end. What did our soldiers and the thousands of this city die for?"

"That's all in the past now. It's over. We survived, and we want to build a new life. That's how it has always been. Just look at history." He studied her face, his eyes soft and sad. "We can't make the dead come alive again, but we can become part of the new order, whatever that will be. I am joining those who are building for the future. And you can too, Annemarie."

She did not know how to answer, just tried to absorb what he had said.

"I didn't intend to give you a lecture. I just want you to know how I and many others feel." He patted her arm.

"I guess you are right. Once I asked Lisbeth why she was working for the Nazis, and she said, 'Would you rather be dead or alive? I chose to live.' A simple way to explain what you just said."

"You know, Annemarie, all I ever wanted to be a doctor, heal people, help them get well. I made up my mind early on that I was not going to sacrifice my dream for any government or ideology."

"But so many did not have that choice, Doc. They had to fight and die in some faraway land…" She thought of Alfred. All he'd ever wanted was to have a family and his machine shop.

Doc's hand reached for hers. As if he had read her mind, he said, "I want to have a family, build a clinic and practice, maybe be here in the city, or perhaps in a small town somewhere." He squeezed her hand. "Build a house for my wife, make her happy, go to the beach in the summer and grow old together."

She did not reply. Instead, she said, "Look, there are lights ahead. Where are we?"

"We are going to the home where Nigel lives. It's a big villa on the lake. Good food, grand drink and a good time to be had by all." He flung out an arm.

"Sounds good, I'm all for that. I'm starving. If they don't give me food, I'll attack. Here comes the wild German Freulein ready to take what she wants."

He laughed as they pulled up to a tall iron gate. An armed guard looked into the window, saluted and waved them through. They drove up a tree-lined drive and stopped in front of a white villa, its entrance illuminated by floodlights. Doc handed the car keys to a man in uniform and took Annemarie's arm as they slowly climbed the wide stairway to the entrance.

Annemarie stopped. "Wait, I don't have my crutches." Doc assured her that she didn't need them because they would be seated most of the evening. At the door, they were greeted by another soldier, who glanced at Doc's credentials and escorted them into the lobby.

The man took her fur jacket and hat. Annemarie stood awestruck, in a two-story-high foyer with a majestic marble stairway circling to the second floor. Tall windows hung with velvet drapes on either side of the stairway reminded her of some she had once seen in the state theatre. An oriental carpet muffled their steps, and an enormous chandelier illuminated the room in starlight smaller chandeliers flanked each of the windows offering intimate circles of light that glistened like candles off the gold and red wallpaper. How could there be gold in wallpaper? Annemarie wondered. Laughter and conversation drifted from an open French door leading into a smoke-filled room where guests were gathered.

Annemarie felt totally overwhelmed by the beauty of this house. She stopped and stared at a large painting of angels floating. Was this really a home? Did real people live here?

"Doctor Hartmann!" The voice of a woman brought her back to reality. "We worried that you would not come." The woman's ruby-red lips smiled, and she flung herself into his arms.

"This is Erika," Doc said as he freed himself from the woman's embrace. "And her friend, the beautiful Ursula." He indicated the redhead next to Erika.

"This is Annemarie," he said, and placed his arm around her shoulder.

Annemarie forced a smile. She had never seen such beautiful dresses. And yes, both women wore high heels and nylons. Nylons! She remembered Lisbeth mentioning that she had got them from London.

The blonde, Erika, was especially beautiful in her pink, skin-tight dress with a décolleté that made Annemarie wonder how she kept her big bosom from popping out. "We have missed you at the club, Doc. Where have you been hiding?" Erika chirped and cut her eyes sideways.

"Lisbeth!" Annemarie cried, turning to wave at her friend, who was emerging through the double doors. She felt awkward and wanted desperately to get away from these beautiful women.

Lisbeth joined them, gave Annemarie a hug and started talking to Doc. Annemarie leaned on Doc, struggling, he took her arm and supported her while they moved toward the double doors. Nigel appeared, looking impeccable and distinguished in his uniform.

Annemarie smiled and he nodded, saying words she did not understand. He guided them to a circle of high-backed chairs arranged near the gold-laced wall between the glittering chandeliers. A waiter appeared and offered them drinks.

"Oh, I like this. What is it?" Annemarie raised her glass.

"PIMMS," he answered.

"PIMMS is a drink they love in England. I had never tasted it before either," Doc said. "But it's very good, isn't it?" He toasted, laughing.

"Yes, it is. I could get used to this."

Lisbeth smiled at Annemarie and pulled Doc away. "Excuse us for a moment." Nigel followed them. As they left, he motioned the waiter to refill Annemarie's glass, turned and blew her a kiss. She picked up her glass.

This PIMMS tasted delicious. She wondered how much alcohol was in it. She was beginning to feel relaxed and bold at the same time. She glanced again around the large room. It was like a scene from an opera. Ceiling-to-floor windows covered almost an entire wall. The buffet was spread on a long table in the middle of the room. Based on the crowd milling around the table, she assumed that the food was excellent. Annemarie's stomach growled. Doc said they were going to a dinner, and she had envisioned sitting at a table being served roast, gravy, corned beef. Oh, she was so hungry. Piano music drifted through the room, and she closed her eyes. Then she rose and looked around for Doc Hartmann. Rude of him to leave her alone. He must know that she would feel uncomfortable, not knowing anyone.

A waiter appeared and refilled her glass. Since it was useless to look for Doc in the crowd, she decided to find out who was making that lovely music. She hobbled over to the piano, wishing she had her crutches. An elderly man offered Annemarie his seat. Gratefully, she accepted, and fell into the overstuffed chair next to the piano. Maybe Doc was right. Her leg was not healing. It was starting to throb.

She smiled at the piano player, a middle-aged, thin man with a gray beard and dark curls surrounding a bald spot. "You play beautifully. You should play in a concert hall where people will really appreciate it."

He looked up at her with dark, sad eyes. "I used to play in the city symphony." His voice softened. "It was before … before…" He stopped and looked around. "I am lucky to be alive and playing at all. My family would be starving if it weren't for Nigel's love of music." He shook his head and mumbled something.

"Is this your villa?" Annemarie asked.

"Of course not, miss. No, no. It was confiscated, like many houses around this lake and other parts of the city. The Tommies-the Allies- took these houses for their top brass. Nigel lives here."

"Really?"

"They kicked out the owners, who had to leave everything behind. It's a shame. But Nigel is a gentleman. He treats this house like his own home. Lisbeth sees to that. But many other houses and apartments they took are ruined by the soldiers. They break things, they get drunk at their parties, and they steal."

Annemarie's mouth dropped open. "What do you mean, they steal?"

"Just what I said, they take paintings, antiques, furniture. Old clocks, they really like those."

Before she could ask another question, he started playing again. Just like I, Annemarie thought. He's bartering, only with music instead of Cognac. She smiled at him admiringly. "What is this music called?"

"Gershwin." The pianist closed his eyes, leaning into the music. Annemarie had never heard of Gershwin, but it was so beautiful, almost bringing tears. She thought of her life, her children and Alfred. She closed her eyes and listened.

From behind her, she heard Erika's voice. "Good God, I wonder where Doc found that one, ha, ha, ha. The last one he brought at least had class. But this girl -- that outfit, the little flowery blouse. He must have rescued her from a bunker." The women laughed shrilly.

Still holding her glass, Annemarie jumped to her feet, wincing from pain, and turned toward the laughing women.

"Maybe she is good in bed," one hollered, followed by more laughter. "Yeah, ha, ha, ha, Doc must have found himself a virgin."

Annemarie hopped closer and grabbed Erika by the arm, almost losing her balance. "You want to know where he found me?" She glared at the women. "At an Army field hospital. That's were. Do you know what it is like to get bombed, burned, shot through the legs? I lost everything. We've been in a war, where have you been?"

The women stared at her, speechless.

"I suffered, and our brave soldiers suffered-- shot at, maimed, blinded and poisoned, all for the fatherland, for the likes of you." Annemarie's heart was pounding. She leaned and threw her drink into Erika's face. The piano man stopped playing and a circle of people gathered around them.

Then a familiar voice. Lisbeth's. "They are bringing in the main course, ladies, so, please, this way," She pointed towards the table in the center of the room.

Without a word, the women turned and left, the one called Erika, wiping her face.

"Don't mind them." Lisbeth smiled at Annemarie. "They've had too much to drink. And Erika, she is crazy for Doc." Lisbeth laughed. "It's a party, these things happen at parties."

Annemarie tried to compose herself. "Where do they get those beautiful dresses? Other people don't have food or coal." She felt deflated, like a schoolgirl called to stand in the corner. Why would Doc want to be with her? Just so he could show the others that he was able to get any woman he wanted. She attempted a smile, trying to push those thoughts away.

Lisbeth moved closer; her face unsmiling. "As I told you before, we all have two choices, my dear Annemarie, starve to death or decide to live and make it.

So, what's your choice going to be?" She turned and followed the crowd to the dining room.

Annemarie stood, hurt and shocked. Now her friend, Lisbeth, had shrugged her off.

Two arms reached around her, and she felt lips on the nape of the neck. "I'm sorry I was gone so long. Business, always business. Are you enjoying the music, Liebling?" Doc pulled her closer. "Alfons, here, he's a master. The best pianist in the world." He lifted her face and kissed her on the mouth. "Don't be sad. I promise I will never leave you again." He rocked her in his arms.

"I wish I had never come here," she whispered.

"Play something romantic for the lady," Doc said, turning to Alfons, who nodded, smiled and started to play. "When they Begin the Beguine."

"Feel a little better?" Doc stroked her hair. "You appreciate good music, like me. We'll have a piano if you like, and I will ask Alfons to teach you to play."

But Annemarie was inconsolable. Tears streamed down her cheeks.

"Liebling, you look like an angel when you cry." He kissed her tears away, holding her until the music stopped.

"You are not leaving?" Doc asked the piano man.

"Oh, no, dinnertime. We, too, must eat." He waved and walked towards the big banquet table.

"Let's get ourselves something to eat, Liebling. Nigel is known for his excellent kitchen." Annemarie stared at him. "He cooks? The General cooks?"

"You are smiling now. Good. And, no, Nigel does not cook. He hires a chef. And like the piano man says, we all have to eat." He gently pulled her up and put his arm around her waist. Slowly, they walked over to the buffet table. He steered past it to a small group of round tables marked RESERVED and pulled up a chair.

"Have another drink." He motioned for the waiter. "I will bring you a desert." He left, and soon returned, balancing two plates.

"Beautiful china." Annemarie let her fingers glide around the gold rim.

"Rosenthal. A very old, valuable set." Lisbeth soon joined her at the table and Nigel followed. A uniformed aide pulled up a chair for him.

Annemarie felt someone nudge her good leg. She reached under the table and found Doc's hand on her knee. "Smile," he whispered in her ear.

Annemarie bit into a thin slice of dark bread piled high with roast beef. "Oh, this is so good, the best I ever tasted." Then she smiled and toasted towards Nigel. To her surprise, he smiled back.

"The former chef of the Intercontinental Hotel, one of the best chefs in the world cooks for him," Lisbeth translated, and patted Nigel's hand.

After a time, Doc got up. "Would you like some more? This is the best meal I've had in a long time." He winked at Nigel and said something that made the General laugh.

While Doc went to fix them a plate of desserts, Annemarie asked Lisbeth for directions to the toilet.

"Wait." Lisbeth stepped around the table, putting her arm around her and helping her along. "Doc says that the leg has to be amputated." Annemarie looked at Lisbeth. "A good friend of his is the best surgeon in the city. I would accept his offer." She paused at the restroom door and studied Annemarie's face.

Annemarie did not answer, just went in and closed the door. Choosing to ignore Lisbeth's words, she surveyed the room. She could not believe her eyes, a chandelier in here. The wallpaper was gold-lined, and the soap dish looked like marble. Next to the toilet was a short porcelain sink on a stem. Since there was a regular sink against the wall, she wondered why they had a second, freestanding one. This toilet reminded her of one she had admired when she had gone to the opera with her Hitler Youth Group.

Lisbeth was waiting when she emerged. "Doc is crazy about you, Annemarie. I have never seen him like this. Who'd have thought that little Miss Prim and Proper could land the most sought-after man in town?" She took Annemarie by the arm.

Annemarie stopped and stared at her friend. "Oh, you too?"

"I'm not joking. The man is in love with you. He'll take care of you; he's got a future. Get your leg fixed and bring your kids home."

Annemarie burst into laughter. "You are out of your mind, Lisbeth. We could never last."

"All right, no arguing here, no more serious talk. Tonight, is strictly pleasure." Lisbeth pulled her along. "You pretty little thing, use that sweet mouth of yours for what a man will enjoy. No lectures on the war or anything else."

They arrived at their table, where another waiter was serving coffee and brandy. Annemarie looked at the dessert plate, then at Doc. "Is this all for me? It will take me three days to eat all these sweets. I guess I could wrap some in a napkin and take them home for Mrs. Maier."

Lisbeth gave her a look of alarmed disapproval.

"A joke, just a joke." Annemarie started in on her cake, then ate a delicious moist pastry that tasted like caramel pudding. "Out of this world, truly delicious. The hotel chef made this?" She asked Nigel.

He nodded, pleased.

Annemarie noticed that Lisbeth was staring at her, looking very happy. "Why do you keep looking at me?"

"I am imagining you in a white wedding dress with Belgium lace--"

"Lisbeth, stop it." Annemarie smiled, but she did not think it was funny. Doc said nothing, but he caressed her hand under the table.

It was past midnight as they drove back to Annemarie's apartment.

"You know, I really meant it when I said I wanted to wrap up some cake for Mrs. Maier," Annemarie murmured. "All that food, so much for everybody – chocolates, wine, roast beef, cream puffs. How come these people have everything while eighty-year-old Mrs. Maier is barely eating, and many people are starving?"

Doc smiled. "There's a lot you don't understand, little sparrow. You've been tucked away like Rip Van Winkle."

"Dr. Hartmann! You are making me angry now. For your information, I have been on my own all throughout the war, taking care of two children. And I'm surviving."

"Sorry, princess. I didn't mean to insult you. But I like it when you get angry. I just meant that you haven't been out and around lately."

She cut him off. "I haven't moved in the right circles, is that what you are saying?"

His face turned serious. "Annemarie, so much has happened since the war ended. The Allies have taken over and are running things now until a new government can be established and--"

"I am not stupid, Doc, just let's say, uninformed and poor. Yes, poor. From the wrong side of town."

Doc put his arm around her. I love you just the way you are." He nuzzled her neck. We can talk another day. We'll have lots of time to talk."

"I'm cold." She shuddered. "I hope spring will come soon. It has to, even in 1946."

He pulled the car to the curb and stopped next to a streetlamp. "If there were lights in this lantern, I'd call you Lily Marlene." He opened the car door, helped her out and pulled her into his arms. He leaned on the lantern post and drew her closer. Suddenly, she no longer felt the cold. His lips searched for hers, hungry, demanding, and she gave in.

Then she pulled back. "I can't." She tried to push him away. His arms did not release her. She was afraid. It had been so long since she felt such overwhelming desire. "No, I can't, I mustn't." She managed to free herself.

"Why not, what is it?" His voice was hoarse.

She started to sob. "It's Alfred. I saw him last night in my dreams. We are engaged. He's in Normandy, but he promised he would come home." She shivered.

He stroked her hair. "Normandy," he murmured, shaking his head. He pulled her close again and held her gently.

After what seemed an eternity, he pressed his cheek against hers and whispered, "I hope you will fly again, little sparrow, and may your dreams come true." She felt the pounding of his heart.

She stepped back, searching for her crutches. "I am so sorry. I do care about you, more than you know."

He kissed her on the cheek, turned to the car and pulled out the crutches. When they reached the door of apartment house 77, he picked her up and carried her through the dark hall up the stairs. "You will always be in my heart. Take care, little sparrow." He helped her open the apartment door, handed her the crutches, and quickly turned away.

She stood in the doorway, crying silently, listening till his steps faded.

CHAPTER 42

A week had gone by since the breakup. She kept hoping Lisbeth would come. Lisbeth always knew what to do. And every day she waited for a letter from Alfred. No letter arrived. The occasional footsteps in the hall were never Lisbeth's. Weighed down by despair, she didn't bother to get up, but the thought of her children kept her from giving up. Annemarie stared at the kitchen clock and counted the hours till dark, hoping for the return of the dream where she saw Alfred standing on a hill reaching for her.

But even that dream now eluded her. Had it been a farewell? Over and over, she played it through, looking for meaning. When they had fallen into each other's arms, it had seemed so real that she could feel his heart beating. But probably he lay dead in a ditch, or field hospital or a prisoner camp. She stared at the empty coal bucket and huddled deeper into her blanket. She had long ago taken the last of Lisbeth's pills and throbs in her leg would not let her sleep.

Suddenly, the door creaked open, and Mrs. Maier stepped inside, looking at her with concern. She walked closer. "I think you need to go to the hospital, Annemarie. You are sicker." She touched her forehead. "Maybe I should tell your sister. If I walk slowly, I can make it. Mrs. Krause said the subway ran the other day, so I could ride two stations. She still lives on Amburg Street, doesn't she?"

Annemarie shook her head. "Please Mrs. Maier, it's not necessary. I've caught a virus, probably when I was out the other night. That's what I get for living it up." She managed a slight smile.

"Your friend, the doctor, I've not seen him around." Mrs. Maier pulled up a chair. " He could give you something. He works with the Tommies, didn't you say? I heard Mrs. Krause say that Karl got medication from one of the soldiers. Unofficial, of course, and don't quote me, that's just what Mrs. Krause said." She opened the bag she had brought and took out a container and spoon. Here, try a few bites of this potato soup."

Annemarie gratefully took the steaming bowl and sipped a few spoonfuls. "Thank you, this is good. I am sure I will be better soon."

Mrs. Maier nodded. "I wish I could have put in meat or a bone." Mrs. Maier looked at her with sad eyes and shook her head. "I will go and visit your sister as soon as I can."

The next day Lisbeth came, carrying a large bag of food as she always did. But she did not smile, joke or offer to make coffee. Instead, she stood in the middle of the kitchen and glared.

"What the hell did you do to Doc Hartmann?"

Annemarie's face got hot. Lisbeth stepped closer and continued her tirade. "If you don't believe me, here, look at this!" She took a small box from her purse and opened it.

Annemarie stared at two gold wedding bands nestled in dark blue velvet.

"He asked me to get these for him. The man loves you, girl, do you understand? He wants to marry you. The man every nurse, every *woman* has her eye on." She stopped to take a breath. "He is important, and he'll be big in the new government." She threw up her hands. "You'll never have such an opportunity again."

"Opportunity? Lisbeth, calm down, let me explain." Holding on to the table, Annemarie pulled herself up.

"Think of your children! He loves kids, he told me so. You can bring them home tomorrow. I beg you, Annemarie, come to your senses."

With her free hand Annemarie reached to pat her arm. "Please, Lisbeth, slow down. Do you want something to drink? I have Ersatz Kaffee, but it's better than nothing and I still have a few of those English cookies."

Lisbeth threw off her hand. "Forget the damn coffee! I want to know what you could have possibly said to upset him so much."

Annemarie leaned forward, imploringly.

"What, huh, tell me, what?" Lisbeth moved even closer, her face red.

Annemarie stepped back and braced herself for Lisbeth's slap, which did not come. "I told him I can't see him again, that I am engaged, waiting for Alfred," she breathed, her body shaking.

"Are you crazy? A doctor wants to marry you, give you a future that most people will not see in their lifetime, and you turn him down because you are waiting for Alfred." Lisbeth stepped back and crossed her arms." Doc wants to rescue you from this miserable place, give your children a life, and you sick, poor, with not even a glimmer of hope, you tell him you are waiting for Alfred." Hands on her hips now, she wagged her head side to side and spread her lips in a sarcastic smirk.

The people upstairs started banging on the ceiling. Annemarie pressed her hand over her mouth. "Please, Lisbeth, don't shout." She leaned to clutch the table. "Alfred promised to--"

"I damn well *will* shout if it helps wake you up! Get over him!" Lisbeth waved her arm wildly. "Alfred is dead, has been since December of forty-two. Everyone knows what happened at Normandy. Throwing away your life and your children's future for nothing. It's beyond reason." She leaned into Annemarie and spoke softly. "You like Doc, don't you?"

"Yes, I do. But I had a dream and Alfred was holding me and he..." Annemarie stopped, tears streaming.

"Don't you get it?" Lisbeth continued, now cupping Annemarie's wet cheek. "Your Alfred has rotted somewhere in a ditch in Normandy. And you are living, and you have two small children to think of." Lisbeth gulped and her eyes shone with moisture. "Wake up, Maedchen." She took Annemarie by the shoulders and shook her gently.

"Lisbeth. Alfred and I made a promise. Can you understand that?" Her voice started to rise. "I'm not like some of those women who sleep with anybody for a dress-- like that Erika. I am not for sale."

Lisbeth's face turned dark. "Oh, we're passing moral judgment now! What entitles you to that, huh?"

Annemarie struggled to stay on her feet. "But women like Erika are common prostitutes. They -"

"Let me tell you about Erika," Lisbeth said in a cold voice. "That girl lost her parents and her home, everything, in the bombing of Dresden. Then she fled, walking days to the West. She barely survived. But lucky for her, she has good looks, a passport to a better future. So, don't knock people you know nothing about. Are you insinuating that I am a prostitute because you think I slept with the Nazis and with Nigel?" She took a handkerchief from her pocket and wiped her face.

"No, no. But the British threw bombs at the farmhouse and shot me through the legs. If it weren't for

398

them, I wouldn't be in this miserable place." Annemarie spread her hand toward Lisbeth, almost losing her balance.

"Let me tell you about the British, Missy. Nigel lost a son in the war and half of his family died in the Nazi bombing raids on London."

Annemarie stared at her.

Lisbeth stepped back "I have misjudged you, Annemarie. You are no better than others." She stepped back. "So, starve, freeze with the rest of them." She threw the food bag on the floor, and it broke at Annemarie's feet. She turned and stomped out of the kitchen. The door slammed so hard that the kitchen lamp swung back and forth, followed by another barrage of banging from the upstairs neighbors.

"How dare you!" Annemarie choked on her words. "What would you know about love? He's not dead. He will come home. And you are nothing but a cold, a common …" she sobbed uncontrollably.

The knocking from the ceiling continued. Lisbeth was gone. She could not stop shaking. It was like she had been wounded again.

Someone pounded on the door and for a moment, Annemarie thought that Lisbeth had come back. But it was the man from upstairs.

Idiot, she thought, but restrained herself from shouting at him. She sat on her chair, waiting for her heart to stop pounding. The contents of the bag lay strewn across the floor --cans, glass jars, packs of pudding, and a ham, a bag of powdered milk-- but no cognac.

Finally, she bent and slowly gathered the items, placing them back on the table. It was an awkward maneuver, reaching down without putting weight on her wounded leg. Exhausted, she finally crawled to the sofa, pulled the blanket over her head and cried herself to sleep.

CHAPTER 43

Lisbeth arrived at the club, spotted Doc Hartmann at the bar hunched over a drink and slipped onto the stool next to him.

He glanced up. "How's Nigel?"

"Oh, doing fine. I've been giving him massages and it seems to help increase the circulation in his leg. Humm, I'll have brandy."

Doc lifted his finger at the barkeeper. "Why, Lisbeth? Why? What happened? I know she likes me, I thought she loved me. I had that feeling…" He stared at Lisbeth's reflection in the mirror behind the bar. "Is it because I kept telling her that her leg has to be amputated? Was I too pushy? You know that I'm right." He downed his drink and signaled for another.

"No, Doc. You're fighting a ghost, a dead soldier. I can't get that into Annemarie's thick head. Think about it. Normandy, not many came back from there. We all know that, but not Annemarie."

The bartender came with their drinks.

Doc's fingers pushed through his hair. "You have to give it to her. She's one of the few women who can't be bought."

"Yeah, most girls I know would have said yes. You are a successful, charming doctor, plus you're good-looking." Lisbeth tried grinning but his sad eyes made her heart hurt. "I can't think of any woman in her right mind who would turn you down. Except Annemarie."

Doc grimaced and banged his fist softly on the bar. "You know, when I'm with her, I feel young. I want us to run through the meadows with her, have a picnic, play ball. I told her that I love kids, I'd give her anything she wants."

Lisbeth sipped her drink and listened.

"I know you'll laugh, but Annemarie reminds me of my grandmother. She was a poor peasant girl, only fifteen when she was sent by her parents to work as a house servant."

"Oh, well, Doc, that was a different time."

"No, listen, Lisbeth. My grandpa was a wealthy doctor, middle-aged. And he fell in love and married her against the will of his family."

Lisbeth shook her head. "A fairy tale, really."

"Grandfather taught me a life lesson. Always follow your heart. Laugh, Lisbeth, but it's true and has served me well. They were happy together many years. Some of his friends, he often said, were not so lucky."

"Old man weds young poor girl. So, he was a Don Juan. Did he teach you that too?"

"Oh, come on, Lisbeth. Go easy." Elbows leaning on the bar, he let his face sink into his hands.

Lisbeth wrapped her arm around his shoulders. "You are right. But she's ruining her life. She's got no education to speak of. Who's going to hire her when things get back to normal, huh?" Anger builds up in her throat. She drummed her fingers on the bar. "She made her bed, and now she can lie in it."

Doc did not answer, wrapped his hands around his glass and stared into his amber liquor.

"Doc, you've sat here now for over three weeks. You've been drunk almost every time I see you. That's not like you. You've got to forget her and move on." She laid her hand on his.

"Annemarie is a once-in-a-lifetime girl, and you know it," he replied glumly.

"Doc, come on. Cheer up, huh? Why don't I check with my friends? I know a couple of cute nurses. I'm thinking of Erika, the blonde. You've met her. She's nice, funny and ready for a good time. And she's built, boy is she ever!" Lisbeth formed an hourglass with her hands.

"I don't know, I really don't."

"Yes, you do. I never thought anybody would have to tell you to rebuild your ego, but you've been in the dumps too long."

He did not answer, just took another long pull at his drink.

"You'll like Erika. You'll have some fun again. How about next Saturday for the spring fling dance?" She nudged him with her elbow.

"All right. All right," he sighed. " But can you go and check on Annemarie and see how she is doing?"

"No, absolutely not. I told you I'm through with that girl."

He turned and faced her. "I will get you anything, whatever you want, if you do that. You can work with me at City General, or wherever you want to work in the city. I promise."

"What are you talking about?"

"When everything reopens under a new government, believe me, it will happen sooner than you think."

She tilted her head and saw him watch for her reaction. "You're drunk. My dear Doc, remember who I worked for? With my history, I'll never get a job in a hospital here again."

"Yes, you will. You could be my head of nursing or run the whole damn hospital if you want."

For the first time, she saw him smile again. "I'm a lot of things Doc, but I'm not a fool." She picked up her glass and took a sip.

"Oh yes." He nodded slowly. "I can make it happen, I assure you."

Lisbeth moved closer and saw some of the old spark in his eyes. "How in the world-- what are you saying?" she gasped, feeling doubt and hope at the same time.

"Remember, Lisbeth, friends in high places?" He put his arm around her.

Lisbeth smiled and said, "Thank you," very softly. "Doc Hartmann, you are-- well I admit you got me. I can't believe I'm falling for this line." She lifted her glass and downed her drink. "All right, I'll do it. And you don't have to make me promises. I'll do it because you are my friend. And I do care for Annemarie."

A big smile spread across his face. He jumped off his stool pulled her to her feet and twirled her around.

She pushed him away. "I am still angry with her though. She insulted me. You won't believe what a wild woman your sweet little Annemarie can turn into. You have put her on a pedestal, Doc. My advice - Get on with your life. I know that you hate to lose. But you can't win fighting a ghost. Nobody can."

Later at Annemarie's apartment house.

Lisbeth knocked on Annemarie's door. "It's me, open up," she shouted and knocked again, but there was no answer. She turned and rang Mrs. Maier's doorbell.

The old woman peeked through a slit between the door and her security chain. "Who is it?"

"Me, Lisbeth, Annemarie's friend. Do you know where Annemarie could be?"

Mrs. Maier fiddled with the chain. "She is home, of course. She has not been well. I can hardly get her to eat. She just stays in bed." Mrs. Maier stopped to catch her breath. "I am so glad you are here; I really don't know what to do." She wrung her hands.

"Do you have a key to her apartment?" Lisbeth held out her hand and shook it impatiently.

Mrs. Maier muttered something and turned to get the key. She handed it over, shook her head and retreated, clicking the chain behind her.

Lisbeth let herself into Annemarie's apartment. It was as cold in there as it was in the hall. Annemarie must have let the coal burn out some time ago. Lisbeth peeked into the kitchen, but there was no Annemarie on the sofa. She marched into the bedroom and flicked the switch. Miraculously, the light came on. "Hallelujah," she breathed.

Annemarie's small body lay on the bed, covered with a comforter. Lisbeth rushed over and bent to check her pulse. "Damn, Annemarie, you bullhead," Lisbeth muttered, debating what she should do. Annemarie's fever was dangerously high. She lifted the cover and saw the swollen leg. She was here as a favor to Doc, but she'd also planned to come back and have another showdown with Annemarie, tell her how wrong she had been and try one last time to change her mind. But now her nurse's instinct kicked in. The putrid smell told her all she needed to know.

"Annemarie!" she shouted. "Don't you dare die on me now."

The girl showed no sign of consciousness. Her breathing was shallow, and Lisbeth knew that the fever was raging.

"Bullhead," Lisbeth muttered again, then left the bedroom. She was glad she had asked the driver to wait. She'd have to count on her connections to get a bed on such short notice. Hospitals were filled to capacity with returning wounded and casualties from the city's bombing raids. She searched her mind for anybody who worked in one of the local hospitals. She opened the apartment door and started down the stairs to get help, but something triggered her to go back. In the kitchen she saw an envelope and a letter on the table. She picked it up, studied the old-fashioned hand and return address. It came from an Alma Schapen, Berlin, but she couldn't decipher the street address. She sat down and started to read.

Dear Annemarie:

I am sorry I could not write you sooner. It took me weeks to make it to Berlin, where I have a sister. It was hellish. I joined a trek of thousands of refugees, all fleeing before the Russians arrived, all trying to make it to the West, carrying only what they could. I will never in my life forget the horrifying scenes. Many died, even children. Riding the open cattle cars was another ordeal, but I was lucky to get on one. Those who were left behind, God, I'm sure most of them perished. You've heard what happens when the Russian Army arrives. Well, I will spare you further details.

My sister took me in. She only has a one-bedroom apartment, but we'll cope, we have to. She told me the horror stories from the firebombing that destroyed your city, but I do hope you and the children are alive and that this letter will reach you. I have sent it to a Mrs. Munster in the village of Burghof, hoping that you are still living on the farm. At least you have food. You can't believe how we suffered on the long trek. I think I will always be hungry.

Now, my dear daughter-in-law-- I hope you don't mind that I call you that-- I have sad news concerning Alfred. It is with a heavy heart that I tell you he won't be coming home. My sister handed me an official letter from the military. How it got to her I'll never know. Of course, there was no way that they could have found me. If I had received the letter, I would not have left at all. What for? I tried to stay alive for my son. I wanted to be there when you got married. Remember all the plans you two had?

He died in the first assault in the Ardennes battle. Somewhere in Belgium. I don't know more. It was just an official letter. It said, "We regret to inform you that Alfred

Schapen was killed for the fatherland..." My tears are falling as I am writing this. I am not in good health, but I hope I will live long enough to come and visit you when the trains are running again.

Annemarie, I will always keep you in my heart. I am grateful to you for loving Alfred, for giving him happiness again, if only for a brief time. I know that I will soon be united with him, and we will both eternally love you and wish you a better future with your sweet little girls. If there is a God, he will surely see to that. You deserve to be happy again.

> *In love and memory,*
> *Alma Schapen*

Lisbeth held the letter, tears in her eyes. Alfred's death must have been the last blow to Annemarie's fragile health. "Damn it," she murmured. "I think she just gave up." She wiped the tears off her face and placed the letter back on the table. No time to dwell on sadness, no time to lose.

She closed the apartment door, rushed down the stairs and told the driver to head to City General Hospital where she knew a nurse. It was a reach, but she had to get Annemarie into a hospital today.

At City General she hurried to the nurse's station, spotted her old friend Susanne and told her about Annemarie. She handed her a bag, which clanked against the desk as nurse Susanne set it down. "All right, Lisbeth. I'll put her somewhere, probably in the hallway. Who did you say is her doctor?"

"Dr. Peter Hartmann," Lisbeth lied with a straight face.

"Oh my, I'd *better* find a bed for her. Is it true that Dr. Hartmann is going to be in charge after the Tommies leave?"

Lisbeth shrugged. "So, I have heard."

"Can you put in a good word for me?" Susanne started shuffling papers on her desk as an aide walked by.

Lisbeth leaned in and whispered "You're a good nurse, Susanne. Sure, I will do that." She glanced at her watch. "I better go get Annemarie now." She sighed, thinking of the three flights of stairs at the apartment. "I will be back in a couple of hours. I'll have to bribe somebody to help me carry her down to the car" That's the only way things functioned now, and Lisbeth was a master of that game.

On Friday evening, Lisbeth stopped at the club and found Doc at the bar just like the last time. She slipped onto a stool. "She is at City General."

He jumped up. "What did you say?"

Lisbeth smiled. "Annemarie is at City General."

"Oh my God, tell me. What happened? How is she?"

Lisbeth told him how she had found Annemarie. "You probably saved her life by sending me there," she said. "With the fever and infection, she would not have lasted much longer. She never even knew I was there."

"*You* saved her life, Lisbeth. I owe you. Like I said, anything you want. The job, you just let me know." He cupped his face in his hands and sucked in his breath with a sob. He looked up at her, his eyes red. "How did you manage to get her in there? They are not accepting any more patients."

"Friends in high places." They both laughed. "And never underestimate the power of a bottle of good French Cognac."

"Aha, blackmail, I thought so. I will always stay on your good side." He waved to the barkeeper and then said, "Bring me a bottle of your best."

"A whole bottle?" She raised her eyebrows.

"You don't know what this means to me, Lisbeth. I just can't let her go. Even if I never see her again, I want her to be taken care of. She needs a good orthopedic surgeon. In fact, I'm going to see some of *my* 'friends in high places.'" He picked up the bottle that had appeared at his elbow and filled their glasses. They embraced and toasted, savoring the fine liquor.

When Lisbeth was ready to leave the club, she turned and winked.

"What?" he asked. "Just tell me what you want."

She shook her head. "You'll still be in love with her even if she never marries you?"

He shrugged and did not answer.

"One more thing, Doc. You no longer have to fight the ghost."

He grabbed her by the shoulders.

"No need to kill the messenger." Lisbeth smiled and shrugged his hands off. "She got the letter. He was killed in the Ardennes."

His mouth dropped open. "You weren't going to tell me, were you?"

"I seriously considered not." She ran to the door, waved and blew him a kiss.

CHAPTER 44
At the Wilder Clinic

Annemarie woke when a nurse touched her shoulder. She tried to lift her head and noticed the wallpaper showing sailboats, and a large painting of the ocean. She then reached beneath the covers. Her leg had been re-bandaged, and the swelling had gone down.

A woman who introduced herself as Miss Bauer came in. "I am your nurse." She had a pleasant voice and smiled softly.

Annemarie turned to her, bewildered. "Where am I?"

"At the Wilder Clinic, Mrs. Peterman." Nurse Bauer bent and placed her hand on Annemarie's forehead.

"The Wilder Clinic?" Her sister Margarete had once told her the Wilder Clinic was an exclusive private clinic, implying that it was off limits for mere mortals. It had to be Lisbeth who had pulled some strings to get her admitted. She knew her way around hospitals. But then she remembered the terrible fight. Lisbeth would not have had a sudden change of heart. Maybe Margarete had come and found her passed out. The letter! Now it all came back. Just thinking of the letter brought a wave of grief.

"Are you in pain?" The nurse adjusted Annemarie's pillow. "No? So, let's get you ready for a bath."

"A bath?" Annemarie stared at her

"I will be gentle. It it won't hurt, Mrs. Peterman. You will feel better after that. Then we will serve supper. They will stop by and ask what you would like."

409

Choose what I want to eat? Annemarie thought. This was getting more bizarre by the minute.

"We used to offer a choice of three entrees, but because of current shortages, we have only two. Due to the generosity of some of our patients, we are able to get meat and other delicacies from the Allies, oh" she looked up from her clipboard. "I see you have surgery in the morning. No food for you till tomorrow."

Annemarie's head was spinning. She was feeling weaker, and her leg hurt, the medication apparently wearing off. "Did a Mrs. Friedrich Bowman admit me to this clinic?" Friedrich might have used his connections with the shipping company.

"I don't know. After your bath you will meet with Mrs. Allmeier, our patient administrator. She will go over the surgery Dr. Strohman will perform and answer any of your questions."

Annemarie closed her eyes. *I have died and gone to heaven. But – surgery?*

Sometime later, Annemarie was still waiting for the admissions coordinator. She still wanted to find out who had brought her here. The Clinic was like a hotel, unlike any hospital she had ever been in. She wasn't sure if they had given her medicine, but she felt confused and could not concentrate.

The door swung open, banging against the wall, and Anna and Inge barged in. "Mama, Mama!" they shouted, and tried to climb into her bed.

The receptionist who had brought the girls in threw up her hands "Easy, girls, easy. Your mama is very ill." She helped Annemarie sit up, propping pillows behind her back.

"Anna! Inge! Oh my God." Annemarie didn't try to hide her tears.

"Mama, we've got a pillow, and candy," Anna shouted, chocolate around her lips.

"Oh my, you have grown. Pretty soon you will be as tall as I." Annemarie laughed, reached for a handkerchief and wiped Anna's mouth.

"And you, Inge?" She pressed her younger daughter to her chest and rocked her.

"I'm scared of the soldier. He's going to shoot us," Inge whispered.

"What soldier, child? There are no more soldiers, and nobody is allowed to shoot at us anymore."

"The soldier gave us chocolates," Anna explained.

"What soldier, Anna? Who brought you here? Did you ride on a train?"

"Aunt Lisbeth came. She gave us a pillow. She's the nicest aunt I ever had." A smile spread across Anna's face.

Annemarie's breath caught, and she could not stop the sudden recurrence of tears.

"Don't be sad, Mama." Inge cuddled up to her mother and gently wiped her cheek.

"Oh, Inge, I am crying because I am so happy that Aunt Lisbeth brought you." She picked up the chocolate-smeared handkerchief and wiped her eyes again. How could she ever thank Lisbeth, the woman she had insulted, called a prostitute, the best friend she had? Annemarie coughed, trying to suppress the sobs that rippled through her. "You know what? When we are home, we'll invite Aunt Lisbeth and bake a cake for her, and you get to decorate it."

"Yes, Mama, I want to decorate her cake." Inge clapped her hands. "Can we go now to bake it?" she asked.

"Liebling, we can't now. Mama has to come home from the hospital first."

411

"When, when, Mama, will you come home from the hospital? We've been waiting and waiting." Anna pulled her sweater over her face.

"As soon as my leg is better, Liebling. Very soon."

"Will we come home for next Christmas?" Inge looked at her with sad eyes.

Annemarie hugged her daughter and tried to smile. "Yes, Inge, we will all be home next Christmas. I promise."

After a while, the receptionist stuck her head in. "Children, we have to leave now. The car is here to take you back."

"Wait, wait, where are you going? What car? Are the children safe?"

"I am sorry, we can't keep them here. The car must take them back to the orphanage before dark, these are Nurse Lisbeth's instructions." The receptionist motioned to Anna and Inge to follow her out.

Annemarie hugged them to her. "Girls, go and tell Aunt Lisbeth that Mama is so very happy that she brought you. And don't forget to tell her about the cake we will bake for her. One more kiss." She kissed each girl and gently urged them towards the door.

Then she sank back and cried an endless stream of sadness and of joy. She wondered where Lisbeth was. Maybe she had gone to work and had asked the driver to take them back to the orphanage.

It was late afternoon when Annemarie woke again. She was reaching in the drawer of the nightstand for her wristwatch when someone knocked.

The receptionist opened the door to admit Margarete Bowman. "I will get a more comfortable chair for you, madam."

Annemarie tried to sit up. "Margarete. How did you know I was here?"

Her sister stepped over and stuffed some pillows behind Annemarie's back. "Kitty, this is the Wilder Clinic. A friend, a captain from one of the other ships, has been here. Usually, only government officials, business tycoons, famous actors -- you know, high society people -- get treatment here."

A brief, nervous laugh escaped Annemarie's lips. "How in the world did I get accepted? Surely it must be a mistake."

"Kitty, you are very ill, and when I heard that you were taken to the Wilder Clinic, I rushed over here. I talked with a Mrs.Almeier and she told me your leg has to be amputated. Poor dear." She pulled out a lacy handkerchief and dabbed her eyes. She was dressed in her best furs, fitting for a lady making an appearance at the Wilder Clinic. 'No, no" Annemarie cried out, they can't do that" then cupped her mouth with both hands.

"Don't worry, you're at the Wilder Clinic." Margarete opened her purse. "Oh no, I forgot my cigarettes again!

Annemarie fell back on to her pillow.

The receptionist came back with a chair. "Let me take your coat, Mrs. Bowman. Can I get you something to drink?"

"Coffee, please, that would be nice, with cream and a dash of sugar."

Annemarie looked up at her sister. "So, who notified you? I don't even know how I got in here."

Margarete crossed her nyloned legs and arranged her skirt just so. "I received a letter from a hospital, City General, I think, stating that you had been transferred here. I guess they are obligated to notify next of kin."

"Who brought me here?" Annemarie asked.

"I have no idea. By the way, have you seen the children?"

413

"Anna and Inge were just here. I was so happy. I've cried for an hour. I feel so relieved."

"I told you. They take good care of the children in that orphanage. Of course, you didn't believe me." Margarete took a silver cigarette case from her purse and lit up.

A young woman in a blue uniform brought in a small tray with a cup and saucer, a china coffee pot and a plate of assorted cookies.

Annemarie looked at the fancy cookies. "Where do they get these? Oh, never mind." It was useless to ask. Doc had told her things were changing, and for some, the good times were already here.

"Try one. The chocolate is exquisite." Margarete sipped her coffee.

"No, I feel queasy, probably from the medication."

"Oh, Kitty, I feel so bad for you. How are you going to get around on one leg? Your whole life on crutches. I can't imagine that. I just can't!" Margarete pulled out her handkerchief again and patted her eyes.

"A doctor friend of mine said that they are developing artificial legs that look so real, you don't notice the difference. They are doing it because so many soldiers are coming home and need artificial limbs."

"Are those free? How would you be able to pay for one?" Margarete shook her head. "You don't have any income and it could be a long time until you might be able to go to work." Margarete sighed. "My poor, poor Kitty. I'm glad Mother does not have to go through knowing this, it would kill her."

"Margarete, please stop! I feel bad enough as it is." Annemarie closed her eyes.

"I'm sorry, I can't help it, I feel so bad for you." She stood up. "Well, I'll come back and visit after the operation. Can you think of anything I should bring?"

Annemarie tried to concentrate. "Oh yes, can you stop at the apartment. There is a letter on the kitchen table from a Mrs. Alma Schapen. Can you please bring it? It means a lot to me."

Margarete sighed, "Oh, all right, I'll stop by there." Margarete reached for the bell cord to signal the receptionist to bring her coat and hat. "Oh, Kitty, I almost forgot to tell you," she said, moving toward the door. Yesterday, I signed a paper to allow a family to move into Mother's apartment. I had received an inquiry about housing for displaced families. I thought it was a good idea because they will pay half the rent."

"What, Margarete, you did what?" Annemarie choked on her words. "We have only a small kitchen and two rooms. I have two children who need a room."

"Don't get all huffy. They are a couple with one child, and that will get the front room and you keep the bedroom with the balcony."

"Three of us can't be in one bedroom." Annemarie cupped her face in her hands. "And the kitchen is small, how can two families cook there?" Annemarie's body began shaking. "You'd allow strangers to live in Mama's apartment. I can't believe it. Why our little place, Margarete? Others like Mrs. Maier live alone, they have extra space. Oh my God. What am I going to do now?"

"I was trying to be helpful, save you money. I thought it was the right thing to do," Margarete's face turned red and she did not try to hide her anger. "Annemarie, you are sick and not rational. Just sleep on it, you'll see my point once you can think straight." The young woman in uniform appeared right away with Margarete's coat and hat.

Right behind her, a nurse stuck her head in the door and saw Annemarie sobbing.

Margarete flicked her eyes towards Annemarie. "I think she is stressed about the operation and losing her leg.

Poor thing, so young and losing a leg. I just can't bear to think of it." She waved at Annemarie and left the room.

Annemarie pounded the covers with her fists. She heard the nurse talking with Margarete in the hallway.

Then the nurse returned. "Would you like some tea? Are you in pain, Mrs. Peterman? We will be serving dinner soon."

"I can't even think of food. I need to know how I got here, who brought me here?"

"I don't know. You'll have to ask Mrs. Allmeier. She'll be here before supper. And just ring the bell it you need me."

Annemarie closed her eyes, trying to absorb everything she had learned. Alfred was dead, and now she had no place to live. Her leg would be amputated, and then what? She cried again, silently, until sleep came.

When she awoke, the lamp had been turned on and it was evening. A middle-aged woman in a navy suit holding a clipboard opened the door. "I am Mrs. Allmeier, the Admittance Coordinator." She smiled. "I am here to answer any questions you may have about your case, follow-up therapy, anything you might have concerns about."

Annemarie stared at her.

"Dr. Strohman will come by soon and talk to you about tomorrow's surgery. He is the best orthopedic surgeon in the country. You will be in good hands, Mrs. Peterman." The woman sat down and straightened her clipboard on her knees.

Annemarie studied the woman's kind expression. Finally, it became reality. They were going to take her leg. She wailed and covered her face, trying to subdue her sobs. Slowly, she began to regain her composure. "Thank you, Mrs. Allmeier. I have one question. Who signed the papers to transfer me to this clinic?" She clasped her fingers together.

"Let me see," Mrs. Allmeier flipped through her papers. "Here it is. His name is Dr. Peter Hartmann."

"Doc Hartmann!" Annemarie took a deep breath. "I know him from the military hospital." Doc, not Lisbeth, had brought her here to this clinic. Why would he do this for her? She had turned him down, broken their relationship.

"Don't worry, Mrs. Peterman," Mrs. Allmeier said, looking with concern at Annemarie's tearful eyes. "We will take good care of you. We have special instructions from Dr. Hartmann and from Dr. Strohman. You have the best medical team there is." Mrs. Allmeier peered at her more closely. "You don't seem well. Let me get your nurse." She closed the door behind her.

Doc Hartmann! He was taking care of her.

CHAPTER 45
Annemarie's Apartment

Annemarie was sitting on the sofa. "My leg hurts. The one that's no longer there, ha, ha." She reached for the empty space below her right knee and swallowed hard.

Martha Dummersdorf refilled their cups. They were in Annemarie's kitchen. "It's only been two months, or is it three? They say it takes longer than that to heal." She patted Annemarie's hand. "At least we have real coffee today, thanks to your dear sister." She grinned.

Annemarie sighed. "I'm a cripple. It is finally sinking in. I'll never walk again."

"Nonsense. Look at how far you've come. It takes time."

"But it hurts, worse than before, before…" She cupped her face in her hands.

Martha slid next to her on the sofa, pulling her close, cradling her like a child. "What about that nurse friend of yours, can she get some more pain pills?"

Annemarie sat up straight and stared toward the window. "I have only seen her once since she brought me home from the clinic. I don't know why she has not come."

"Hum. Maybe she's in some type of trouble. Bernhard told me that his friend Walter, you know, the railroad man, said the British are arresting a lot of people, accusing them of being Nazis. Nobody knows where they are taking them."

"Lisbeth was not a Nazi!" Annemarie protested. She grabbed Martha's arm. "She worked at the army field hospital, but she was close to a Nazi official. Surely, they can't hold that against her."

"Well, I'm just telling you what Bernhard said".

Annemarie slumped back into the sofa. "Do you think they'd still suspect Lisbeth, now she works for the British?"

Martha handed her the crutches. "Let's not worry. Let's work on getting you back on your feet."

Two days later, Margarete stopped by. "Here's some bread, powdered milk and a ham." She spread the items on the table. "I brought some more coffee, too, all from the shipping company. Friedrich will be home next week. And if he gets a car, I want to take a trip, maybe to the Baltic Sea. I need to get away. I hope my neighbor will take the children for me."

Annemarie raised her hands, dropped them on the table and folded them. "Margarete, I am not feeling well. My leg hurts all the time and I --"

"That reminds me. I got a letter from the Wilder Clinic dated April 1946. Why do they send it to me?" She set her shiny patent leather purse on the table, pulled out a letter and pushed it across to Annemarie, who opened it. It was on Wilder Clinic stationary, signed by Dr. Erich Strohman.

Dear Mrs. Peterman:

We hope your recovery is proceeding according to schedule. I would like to see you for a follow-up examination on April 5th. After that, presuming you are healing well, we will reserve a bed for you at the Klosterbrunn Heilbad & Klinik (see address below) where you will be fitted with a prosthetic and learn how to walk with it.

Annemarie burst into tears and the letter fell on the table.

419

Margarete picked it up. "It's from Dr. Strohman. From the Wilder Clinic. Oh, my. I'll go with you. Friedrich can drive us there." She waved the letter and leaned towards Annemarie. "Why are you crying? For God's sake, a letter from Dr. Strohman."

Annemarie stared at her.

Margarete jumped up and pulled her purse off the table.

"Thank you," Annemarie mumbled, picked up her crutches and struggled to stand up.

She reached to hug her sister, but Margarete had turned and was rushing towards the door. "What am I going to wear? The mink is too warm."

Annemarie listened to her hurried steps echoing down the stairs.

The next day Martha brought over a pot of soup, and Annemarie showed her the letter. "I couldn't have done this without you. The pain in my leg, you can't imagine how bad it hurt. I owe you and Bernhard so much."

Martha leaned to hug her for the longest time. "See, soon you'll walk again. And I will go to the orphanage and tell Anna and Inge that you will come and get them."

"Let's go now so I can tell them myself!" Annemarie cried out.

"No, no, you are not strong enough for that trip." She thumped the table with her fist. "Basta! You are not going." Martha pulled up a chair and said more quietly, "By the way, did you hear from Lisbeth? And what about that doctor friend? He hasn't come around either?" Noticing Annemarie's stricken look, she said, "Sorry, I never learn to keep my mouth shut." Martha pulled a bottle from her bag.

Annemarie's mouth dropped open. "Cognac, oh my!"

"Bernhard got it from a friend. He testified for the man, vouching that he was not a Nazi." She brought two glasses from the cupboard and poured. "Prost." They toasted.

After the third glass, Martha left, and Annemarie lay back on the sofa, propping a pillow under her head. She thought of Doc. Why did he do so much for her, but not come again? Then it was clear. He'd found somebody else, perhaps Erika or another beautiful woman, not a cripple like her.

Then, a knock on the door and a familiar voice. She grabbed her crutches and hobbled to the door and pulled it open. "Lisbeth, oh, Lisbeth!" She fell into her arms. Lisbeth put an arm around her shoulder. Wordless, they gazed at each other. Lisbeth helped her back to the kitchen sofa and pulled up a chair. Then Annemarie filled her in on her follow-up visit to the Wilder Clink that she was going to the Klosterbrunn Heilbad and Rehab Klinik. "I don't know how I am going to get there. I hope Martha's husband, Bernhard, can get me train tickets. The Klinik is way down south, in Bavaria. Oh, Lisbeth, I worried about you. Martha told me that the British are arresting people and…" Annemarie bit her lip. Why had she said that? She picked up the bottle of Cognac Martha had left on the table. "Let's have a drink," she murmured, her voice cracking.

"I am all right. But I can't stay long. I'll tell you more some other time." Lisbeth took Annemarie's hand and studied her with somber eyes.

Annemarie tried to keep down a sob.

"But I will go and see Dr. Strohman," Lisbeth continued, "and ask if he can help find a way for you to get to the rehab Klinik. It is too strenuous a trip and not safe for you to go alone on the train." She sighed. "All right, I will have that drink now. She poured two small glasses to the rim. She took a deep breath and sat down across from

Annemarie. "They came and arrested Doc Hartmann." Her face showed no emotion. "I don't know where they took him." She emptied her glass in one swallow.

Annemarie wanted to scream but could not breathe, could not utter a word.

Lisbeth shook her head hard. "We know that he was not a Nazi, never, but the British have stepped up their de-Nazification campaign, and nobody is safe."

"But, Doc, he – couldn't Nigel vouch for him?" Annemarie stared at her. She noticed that Lisbeth was not wearing lipstick. Alarmed, she clutched the table. "We have to help Doc. I can testify."

Lisbeth waved her off. "Just lay low right now. Let's get you into rehab." She came close and kissed Annemarie on the cheek, turned and rushed out the door.

Annemarie felt like she had been punched in the stomach. She fumbled for her crutches, hobbled to the bedroom and opened the balcony doors. She craned her neck - there was no jeep, just two old women strolling down the sidewalk. Ahead of them, she saw Lisbeth hurrying away.

CHAPTER 46
Klosterbrunn Heilbad and Rehab Klinik

Dr. Strohman's face hovering over hers... "All went well. You'll be up and walking soon..." Feeling along her thigh , past the knee... Nothing. Oh God. Please let me die. If not for my children... Then next to her bed, swaying close and away... A warm hand in hers...

"You're back..." Lisbeth's voice.

Herself smiling... "You have come..."

Lisbeth reaching to wipe her forehead... "Doc Hartmann was here... leg looks good."

Annemarie woke with a start. She could tell by the changing light that time had passed. Her children. She couldn't die. But she turned her face to the wall anyway.

It had been a long two months since Annemarie had arrived at the rehab center. The therapist had told her, "It takes time, practice and patience to learn walking, and it might hurt the stump, but we'll be here to help adjust the prosthesis until it is right." She sighed and touched the stump, which was bandaged from the top of her thigh to below the knee. Dr. Strohman had told her she was lucky they had saved her knee. It would help her walk normally. *Lucky! Lucky, I am so lucky.* She looked away and quickly pulled up the covers. Finally she dozed, lulled by the monotony of rain pelting the window.

Later, Annemarie sat on the edge of her bed struggling to lift her knee and slide it into the artificial limb. *Why not call it what it is, a wooden leg?* It was stained tan, inflexible, the shape of a foot carved on the

423

bottom, now with one of her shoes attached. *Every day. Forever, I have to put this thing on.* She tugged on the leather sleeve that cupped her thigh and was held in place with long leather laces, stiff and resisting, to be threaded through like a shoelace. *I can't do it. I can't.* She stifled a sob, took a step, holding on to the bedpost to steady herself. It hurt.

She reached down to loosen the laces, fell back onto the bed and put her face in her hands.

Walking normally in no time, ha. Slowly, she sat up and jerked her stump out of the prosthesis. The artificial leg tumbled to the floor with a thud.

Annemarie's roommate, Monika, walked into the room on her own artificial leg. "Hey girl, let's go to dinner."

"I am not hungry."

"Nonsense. How will you get better if you don't eat?" Monika picked up her leg and handed it to her. "Here, put this on. Hurry. I'm starving."

"It hurts when I walk."

"Mine does too. They said that's usual and will go away the more you use it." Monika stood there, hands on her hips.

Annemarie sat up, slipped on the prosthesis again and started to lace it up. "I was dreaming of the surgery and when I came to, it felt like it had just happened." She sighed.

Monika walked to the door and pulled it open. "Hmm, smells like sauerkraut. Do you like sauerkraut?" She took Annemarie's hand and they hobbled to the dining hall.

Back in the room and fortified by a good meal, Annemarie said to her, "You are right. I'm going to work really hard to learn to walk. For Anna and Inge, I will dance again."

Monika pulled her close and twirled her around, and they ended up plunked on the bed, laughing.

It was May, and flowers were blooming, their aroma drifting through the open window. Annemarie sat across the desk from the head therapist.

"Mrs. Peterman, you requested to see me? How can I help you?" He smiled, twiddling his pen.

"Watch." She stood up and walked around the room with hardly a limp. "What do you think?" She twirled around and raised her prosthetic leg.

"You have made good progress." He smiled, creases forming around his eyes. "That prosthesis is one of the best fits I have seen."

"I have worked hard. I've practiced every day." Annemarie curtsied. "I think I'm ready to go home, don't you?"

"Let me see." He stepped from behind his desk. "Can you lift up your skirt for me, please?"

"Anything you ask, as long as you sign my discharge papers."

He knelt in front of her and inspected the top of the artificial leg, feeling her thigh around the leather rim.

Annemarie flinched. "Ouch! That hurts."

"Tell me where, right here?"

"Yes. I think the leather presses on my leg. Maybe I drew the laces too tight."

He stood up and stepped back behind his desk. "You have developed a pressure point. We need to make some adjustments."

Annemarie's heart sank. "So I can't go home tomorrow? I have two little girls in an orphanage. I promised to come and get them."

"Sit down, Mrs. Peterman. You are really lucky because you have healed so quickly. How long have you been here?" He opened a folder, then looked up at her. "It says here that you are to stay with us until June thirtieth."

"Why June thirtieth, and who said I have to stay?" Her face flushed. "I have the right to know, don't I?"

He tapped the page in the folder. "Your doctor, Mrs. Peterman. His instructions are specific. You are to stay until the leg fits and you encounter no problems using it. Plus, we always have a formal graduation after a group of patients have learned to walk. We hold it in the ballroom. You may have heard that room was used by the Nazi officers for their parties. You wouldn't want to miss that. You deserve it."

She weighed that thought. "Can I talk with Dr. Strohmann?"

The therapist pushed his glasses up his nose and looked back down at his papers. "It says here that your doctor is Dr. Hartmann. And he specifically noted that you are not to be released prematurely. I am sorry." He stood and glanced toward the door. "I have another meeting in five minutes."

"Dr. Hartmann?"

"Yes, Dr. Peter Hartmann. These are his instructions. And frankly, Mrs. Peterman, I dare not disobey his orders."

Annemarie sat staring at him.

"Let me help you up," the therapist offered.

"I can do it myself, thanks." She struggled to her feet and strode out of his office.

"Make sure you stop and get the technician to fix that spot," he shouted after her.

"Well, are you going home early?" Monika asked when she returned to their room.

Annemarie slouched onto her bed and folded her arms behind her head. "Nope, he wouldn't sign me out. And I found out that my doctor left instructions for me to

426

remain here until some group celebration in June." She sat up and unstrapped her leg, then lay back again.

"Yes, I heard about that. It's supposed to be a really nice party -- food, music, a good time. I think that's nice, since everyone is going back to face who knows what. The nurse said things out there have not improved-- no food, same miserable conditions." She shrugged. "Well, at least we can walk now. I'm optimistic that things will get better. And soon it will be summer. Who knows? Maybe I can plant a garden."

Annemarie stuck out her lip. "I have to find work. Remember, I have two small children. Before the war, I worked in retail at Hohman's Department Store. I enjoyed it." She stared at the ceiling. "But now, even with this new leg, I won't be able to stand on my feet eight hours a day. And the Hohman store is a ruin. Who knows if and when they will rebuild." She sighed.

"Something will come up. It always does."

"How perfect it would have been if Alfred had not been killed. We had it all planned out, like building a little house, reopening his machine shop… But he died in Normandy, for the Fatherland ha, ha."

Monika sat down on the side of Annemarie's bed. "You are young and strong, and pretty. You'll make it Annemarie, you will."

"Ja, right, I can always stand on the corner with a collection cup and hold up my wooden leg."

Monika wagged her finger. "Not funny."

"I did find out something interesting from the therapist today, though," Annemarie said. The doctor who admitted me here was not Dr. Strohmann, who did my surgery. It was Dr. Peter Hartmann. I knew him from the field hospital." She could not hide a smile.

"Aha, you 'knew him' from the field hospital? Did you sleep with him? I mean, I would have gone out with a cute doctor." Monika laughed. "Unfortunately, my doctor was at least seventy. We called him Grandpa - behind his back, of course."

"No, I did not sleep with him." Annemarie poked Monika with her elbow. "After all, I was his patient. He was just doing what he was supposed to."

"Come on, don't act so high and mighty. You know what was going on, especially towards the end of the war, and of course still. Don't act like you don't know. I bet you've had plenty of offers."

Annemarie grinned.

"See, I knew it! You've got some guy who's crazy about you."

Annemarie burst out laughing. "Well, I admit, I did. But I was waiting for my fiancé to come home. I just couldn't betray him. We met in the summer of forty-four. He was stationed at the village where we had been evacuated. God, I fell in love." She stared away, remembering. "But that's when he was shipped to the front. Damn war. I'm sorry. I'm crying again." She searched for her handkerchief.

"But -" Monika did not give up-- "then that charming doctor came along." She waited, raising her eyebrows.

"And I turned him away, told him I was engaged."

"That was it? God, Annemarie. Everybody knows about Normandy, that our boys were wiped out there." Monika shook her head and stared out the window at the budding trees. "God knows how I'll survive. Our house was bombed, and I have no place to stay."

"I'm sorry, Monika." Annemarie reached to touch her friend's hand.

"Well, I do have a sister in Munich. But she lives in a tiny apartment with two children and her husband, that is, if he has come home. He was stationed somewhere in Italy. Italy! What in God's name were we doing down in Italy? So, I'm not sure that they could take me in."

"For a short time, surely they could make room. Do you have a good relationship with your sister?" Annemarie said, thinking of Margarete and immediately regretting the question.

"Oh yes, we've always been close. She's three years older and always took care of me."

"There you go. Send her a letter. Why don't you invite her to the graduation celebration and then go home with her?"

"That's a good idea, Annemarie, thank you." Monika smiled and started to rummage through the nightstand drawer. "There are no envelopes."

"They'll give you one at the office."

"You know, if that doctor was in love with you, you should let him know how you feel. Maybe he's been waiting to hear from you." Monika wiggled her eyebrows suggestively. "He was not a jerk interested only in sleeping with you, or maybe married. Do you know where he is now?"

"You are too much, Monika." Annemarie fidgeted with her hands, thinking about Doc and the evening they'd last held each other. "I'm not sure he would wait for me. Every woman I know was after him, gorgeous women, you know. I can think of one-- Erika -- who had a figure you wouldn't believe."

"But didn't you tell me that he took care of you, that he's the one who made sure you got into this clinic? Why do you think he did that?" Monika sounded like a mother lecturing her child. "Considering how hard it is to get a bed in this place. That man still wants you, believe me. There are thousands on the waiting list. My friend Hilda Kreuzmaier in the front office told me." She stood up and started to walk around the room. "At least you could go and thank him for his kindness."

"You are right, Monika. If I see him again, I will thank him. Had I not gotten to a hospital, the infection in

429

my leg would have killed me, that's what Dr. Strohman said." Annemarie felt as if a weight had been lifted off her shoulders. She reached up to hug Monika. "I don't know though. Men don't like to be dumped. They go out and find somebody new, especially now, when hardly any men are left. But we did have a great time together." She lay back on the bed, letting her hand slide down to the stump. Then she picked up a pillow and pressed it over her face. She didn't tell Monika that Doc had been arrested by the British and she didn't know where he was." She dropped the pillow - "I fell for him; I really wanted him." Annemarie had to admit that she had fallen for him.

"Find him, thank him."

"But I just feel so guilty. And I don't want him to think that I just need a place to stay."

"Oh please, Annemarie, you think too much. What have you got to lose?" Monika stomped with her artificial leg. "I'm going to the office now for an envelope and stamps." She smiled and left the room.

An hour later, she returned.

Annemarie looked up. "Did you get your letter in the mail?"

"I just wrote that I'm alive, have been wounded and that the house has burned down."

"Did you invite her to the graduation?"

"Yes, I know she will find a way to come." Monika clapped her hands. "Thanks, Annemarie. so, what's your Doc's name? What does he look like?" She sat on the side of her bed, chin in her palms.

"His name is Peter and he's medium height, and slim. He has blond, slicked-back hair and blue eyes. Oh, he's so funny." Annemarie took a deep breath and sighed.

"So, he's a good-looking man, plus, he's a doctor. Sounds like a winner."

"And he loves to dance. We danced until my leg just about fell off!"

430

Monika laughed. "I am jealous. I could sure go for a guy like that."

"But I can barely walk now. I'm always worried that I'm going to lose my balance and fall down," Annemarie lamented.

"That's why you are here. To learn to walk. You can't expect it to happen in a couple of weeks. Remember, the therapist said that it would take time."

"I guess you are right. But I feel so hopeless sometimes. I keep thinking of all the things I won't be able to do again, like swimming."

"Swimming! Really, Annemarie." Monika raised her arms and dropped them.

"You are right." Annemarie laughed. "Do you remember when they introduced us to that man, Richard, who had been fitted only one year ago? I surely couldn't see that he had an artificial leg. Could you?"

"That's the whole point. With practice and time, we'll walk normally too. "Monika snapped her fingers. "I have an idea. I'm going to check in the office and ask Hilda if she can find us a record player. And then, girl, we will practice. We'll be ready for the celebration."

Before Annemarie could answer, Monika hopped off the bed and out the door.

After a couple of days, they got word that the clinic director had called a meeting in the ballroom. "So, let's go," Monika said.

Annemarie touched the sore spot on her thigh. "I think I'll just stay here. You can tell me what the plans are."

"Oh, no. You are coming with me, lady, if I have to drag you." She pulled Annemarie up. "Put on your leg, hurry. If you don't show up, they'll think you can't walk and they might keep you here another month."

431

Mildly alarmed, Annemarie strapped on the limb and slipped a shoe on her other foot. She grabbed her cane and followed Monika to the ballroom.

One end of the room was filled with small round tables and chairs, with a dance floor in the middle and a bar at the far end.

"Wow, these are plush." Monika settled herself into a chair. "Those Nazis sure knew how to live in comfort."

The clinic director, Dr. Hofmeister, stood in the middle of the dance floor, Hilda Kreuzmeier by his side, holding a box.

Monika waved at her. "She wants to fix me up with her brother," she giggled. "She's got three of them."

"Go for it," Annemarie whispered, trying not to laugh out loud.

The director cleared his throat, bringing the room to attention. "You know that we always conclude our program with a well-earned graduation celebration. Miss Kreuzmaier has something special she wants to tell you."

Hilda beamed and looked around. "Most of you want to dance at our celebration and we want to help you do that. I have found a record player and some records of dance music that were left behind by the former occupants, so I guess we have at least one thing to thank them for."

The patients laughed and clapped.

"I have contacted the village women, who said they would be glad to come and teach those who need it and help you learn to dance on your artificial legs. Some of them even promised to bring their husbands."

More laughter greeted her words. Annemarie was struck by the courage and cheer of these men and women who were facing grim and uncertain futures.

"I am going to pass out a paper with the details and dates of when we'll have these practices." Martha stepped to the first table and dropped off some of the sheets. Oh, and Dr. Hofmeister, is good friends with the owner of the

Hunter's Horn pub. They have started to brew their special beer again. And guess what-- he convinced his friend Alois to donate a barrel of Hunter's Gold for our party!"

The patients clapped again, and Dr. Hofmeister bowed and smiled. "I guess something good is finally coming from my love of beer." He laughed. "But I'm not sure that my wife agrees. Anyway, we will see you all in three weeks, right here. Maybe Miss Kreuzmaier can talk her other brother Hubert out of a couple of hams for our party."

Annemarie nudged her friend. "You better go for the brother with the ham, Monika. You'll have plenty to eat and a future as a farmer's wife."

"He's a butcher." Monika laughed. "The second brother is a farmer. And you won't believe it -- the third brother, the youngest one, brews the beer."

Annemarie put her arm around Monika. "Jackpot. You can't go wrong with any of them." They laughed, and Annemarie lost her balance and sank back into her chair. "Oh, Monika, I'm so glad you are my roommate. We must stay in touch when we leave here. Will you invite me to your wedding?"

"Of course. You can be the maid of honor, but first, I'll have to meet the brothers and decide which one."

Annemarie had not felt this lighthearted since she had gone to the dance with Doc Hartmann.

CHAPTER 47

Annemarie woke and let her eyes follow a ray of sunshine across the floor. "Strange, it feels like I still have both legs when I stretch." She threw back the cover, reached for her prosthesis and started putting on her leg and shoe.

Monika laced her leg. "It's getting easier, isn't it?"

Annemarie chuckled. "Well, I don't feel so much like a freak."

Monika nodded. "I don't have time to dwell on all that negative stuff. By the way, I just found out that the dance practice starts next week."

"I still don't know why they chose me to teach people to dance. I'm not sure I can do it."

"Nonsense. You dance better than anybody else. Hilda has already announced it. Besides, she already set up the record player. Everybody is talking about it."

"But that's a lot of people, and I'm still a bit rusty," Annemarie mulled. And my leg starts hurting after a while. I know I told Hilda I am a good dancer"

"Well, they can't expect you to dance with hundreds of folks, that's crazy. I can help too. Let me talk to Hilda. Women from the village are supposed to help."

"I guess, the worst I can do is break a leg." Annemarie laughed at her own joke. "I don't even know what month it is. We have a week till June first, right?"

Later that day, Monika went to the office and talked with Hilda about organizing the dance practice. When she returned, she came in the room and said to Annemarie, "I told her that you can handle maybe fifteen or twenty people at a time. So, she said she would spread the practice over a couple of days."

Annemarie nodded. "That will help. Thanks, Monika. Let's see how it goes. There may be others who can help. Remember women from the village coming?"

"Oh ja, I'll remind her. We need them."

Annemarie and Monika walked into the ballroom and looked at the ragtag bunch slumped into their chairs. Monika slapped her on the shoulder. "Let's go out there and get this bunch of old warriors going."

Annemarie stepped in front of the group. "All right, soldiers and Freuleins. Let's dance. I want those in the first two rows to take your chairs and form a circle around me, and I'll dance with each of you and show you the basic steps."

About twenty men and four women started dragging, clanking and pushing their chairs towards the dance floor. Monika rushed over to help an older woman who was struggling to pick up her chair.

"Who wants to go first?" Annemarie looked around and smiled. "Well, looks like all the war heroes are afraid of little Mama Annemarie." People laughed and clapped. "Pretend I'm your drill sergeant. You, soldier." She pointed at a man with salt-and-pepper hair, reached for his hand and pulled him up. He stumbled but let her help him out of the chair. She nodded. "Getting up from a low chair is not easy. I know. I still have trouble with that." She pulled him closer and smiled at him.

He bowed his head. "My name is Theo."

"Glad to meet you, Herr Theo. My name is Annemarie." She bowed in return.

"I know. Everybody here knows you." He smiled and put his hand on her back.

"Hm, why is that, how come they all know me?" she teased.

"Because you are so pretty and nice." He gazed down and she thought he was blushing.

"Music!" Annemarie shouted, and Monika started the record player. A lively melody echoed through the room. "Stop, too fast. Let's start with a slow waltz."

"Slow waltz coming up." Monika lifted the arm of the record player and changed the record.

"One, two, three, one, two, three," Annemarie hummed along, bobbing her head to the beat. "Follow my steps Theo. Have you danced before?"

He mumbled, "Just a little."

He stumbled over her foot. "I am sorry."

She kept on dancing. "What are you sorry for? Keep following my steps."

"But I stepped on your toes," he sighed.

Annemarie laughed out loud. "I did not feel a thing." She pointed at her right foot. "Solid oak, or maybe pine." He laughed along with her. "We make a great pair," she said, "I've got pine on the right and you on the left. You are doing well, soldier."

After a few minutes, they were dancing smoothly. Then she said, "You are in good shape. I am curious, what did you do before?"

"I was a jeweler. And I played soccer." But now…" He shrugged.

She stopped dancing and cocked her head. "What does that mean, 'but now'?"

"Well with only one leg, how can I kick a soccer ball?"

"Well, you can't. So, what can you do now?"

"I designed and repaired jewelry as well as clocks. Koerbinger's Jewelers in Hamburg. I guess I can still do that."

"Good man, you are lucky. I know Koerbinger's. On the corner of Osterstreat and Steinweg. I often lingered in front of the big window and drooled over those beautiful necklaces and rings. I was sixteen with big dreams. But that was a lifetime ago. Everything is in ruins now, no stores, no-- I am sorry, Theo. I am sure your store is still standing."

He did not answer.

After a bit, Annemarie said, "Now, Theo, you've got the basic steps and rhythm. Why don't you choose somebody to dance. Go and teach them what you have learned."

As she picked another partner and began to dance, she noticed that a couple of women were getting up to leave. She stopped and shouted, "Wait, don't leave, ladies. Monika will dance with you."

Monika released her own dance partner and reached for one of the women. "Let's go, I'll show you." She led her to the dance floor. She gestured at some of the men in the first row. "It's your lucky day, gentlemen. There are ladies waiting to dance."

After a while, as Annemarie and Monika leaned against the wall to watch the floor full of circling dancers, Monika said, "This feels good, people coming back to life."

"Yes, they are coming back to life and my hip is killing me." Annemarie looked at the clock and saw that some people had stopped dancing and were sitting back in their chairs.

"Looks like everyone is tired," Monika said, and clapped her hands. "All right, see you all next Wednesday. Did you have a good time?"

Clapping and hollering greeted her words. Monika put her arm around Annemarie as they walked back to their room. "You are amazing."

"No, you are, Monika. It was your idea. You started this dance practice." They stopped and hugged.

Back in the room, Annemarie plopped on her bed and removed her prosthesis. "My leg is tired and throbbing," she groaned, but soon, she was humming, "One, two, three, one two, three."

Monika chuckled. "By the way, that soldier, he seemed nice, don't you think?"

"Which one?" Annmarie rose on her elbows and turned to Monika.

"The soldier you danced with first."

"I danced with lots of them." Annemarie got up, took off her dress and slipped her nightgown over her head.

"Come on." Monika prodded. "The older one with the grey hair."

"Oh, him. His name is Theo. He's from my hometown. He is sort of quiet and reserved, but he is learning his steps. We'll see on Wednesday how he does." She yawned.

Monika grinned. "Maybe he is just shy because he likes you."

"Oh, please, Monika. Good night." Annemarie buried her head in her pillow.

"He is sort of elegant and distinguished-looking. I noticed he has nice hands when I handed him the instruction sheet."

Annemarie blew out her breath. "Will you stop? He is a jeweler. Lucky that he lost a leg and not a hand. He will be able to work again when things get back to normal. Someday people will want to buy jewelry again, at least a ring."

"Oh, all right." Monika blew a long sigh. "I'm exhausted."

"Me too, but it was fun, wasn't it? To see all of them dancing. It makes me feel good to look at those happy faces. I'm almost back to my old self, dancing like a pro -- ha, ha."

"See, I told you so." Monika turned to her side to look at Annemarie.

"Hm, and I can still hug my children, how lucky I am. Good night, Monika." Annemarie rolled to the wall. But as she felt her breathing, slow to sleep, she heard Monika stirring.

"You are thinking about your cute doctor, I bet." Monika's voice was teasing. "Something tells me that he will show up for the graduation."

"Go to sleep, Monika. Gute Nacht." Annemarie pulled her sheet over her face, but she was smiling.

CHAPTER 48
The Graduation

After midnight she was still tossing and turning. The graduation celebration was set for June thirtieth, and after that, what? *Bring my children home. Find work.* Maybe Friedrich could put in a good word for her at the shipping company. But she'd never worked in an office. And the big question-- When were things getting back to normal? The country was still under Allied rule, but she'd heard rumors that a new government was forming soon. And there were those other people in her mother's apartment. She sighed and stared at the ceiling. She could ask Lisbeth for help. Or... Doc Hartmann?

She leaned up and reached for a water glass on her night table, spilling some onto her gown. "Scheiss," she muttered. "Do you think we'll ever have a normal life again?" But Monika was asleep.

"Men have it easy," Annemarie grumbled the next morning. She grinned. "They don't have to worry about what to wear to the celebration. What are we going to do? All I have is an old blouse and a skirt, that's it. Maybe I shouldn't go."

"Come on, Annemarie." Monika was strapping on her leg. "We've practiced dancing. I thought you were excited about going. I have an idea. I'll be right back." She jumped up and went out the door.

Soon, she returned. "Success, Hallelujah! Hilda knows a woman in the village who used to be a seamstress."

"But I have no money, nothing to trade to pay for a dress."

"Don't worry," Monika said. "Let's see what she comes up with."

Later that day, the seamstress, an elderly, heavyset woman, appeared at the rehab center. "I am Frau Kruse. Miss Kreuzmaier sent for me." She stood in the doorway carrying a big basket. A piece of yellow measuring tape hung over the rim. "I will make a pretty dress for Freulein... You, stand up so I can measure." She pointed at Annemarie, who did as she was told. Next, Mrs. Kruse told Monika to come to be measured.

When the seamstress left, Annemarie shook her head. "Did you notice that she didn't write anything down? We need the dresses by tomorrow. How on earth is she going to get them done?" Annemarie raised her eyebrows. "And she looked like she was at least ninety. I wonder how we are going to pay her?" Annemarie raised her eyebrows.

Monika laughed. "A smoked ham! Right, a smoked ham, that's what I said. Hilda's brother Alois agreed to donate the hams. She promised him that I would go out with him. She told me that he's excited about taking out a city girl." She pulled Annemarie off the bed and twirled her around the room, one two three.

Annemarie laughed and pushed her away. "We are beginning to be good at this! Bartering a ham for a dress – or would that be a dress for a date? Have you met this Alois?" Annemarie laughed into her hand. "I've heard rumors that you have been sneaking out when you told me you were visiting with Hilda."

Monika blushed. "Yes, he came by two weeks ago. He's kind of good-looking-- dark curly hair, a little shorter than I, but he has a smiling face. A sunny disposition ran in Hilda's family. Also, I think the war bypassed their village. Some people were lucky."

Annemarie wiggled her eyebrows." I wondered where you were all those nights." She wagged her finger at Monika. "A dress for a ham! Well, we'll have some funny stories to tell our kids." Annemarie chuckled.

"The seamstress is a widow with little income, so the hams made her very happy. We will be the best-dressed ladies at the party."

"When are we going to try on the dresses? Tomorrow is graduation. I guess whatever she comes up with will have to do."

"I can't wait to find out if Alois can dance." Monika unlaced her prosthesis. "I bet your friend, the cute doctor, will show up." She grimaced while she pulled the leg off and sighed in relief.

"Hm. Maybe." Annemarie huddled under her blanket.

Early the next morning, Hilda pushed through their door, carrying a bundle wrapped in a sheet. "I have your dresses," she chirped. "Try them on. I want to see how you look!"

Annemarie pushed the blanket off and blinked into the dark room. "What time is it?"

Hilda pulled up the shades. "Get up! Hurry, ladies! I don't have much time." She turned on the light.

"How come this place always has electricity?" Annemarie asked.

Hilda stared at her. "Don't they have electricity in the city?"

"Never mind." Annemarie slipped out of her bed and put on her leg. "Monika," she shouted, bending over her sleeping friend, who bobbed up, looking confused.

"Get up. We must try on our new dresses. Hilda is in a hurry." Annemarie reached for her bra.

"Ta-dah --" Hilda dropped the sheet on the floor and held up the dresses. She handed the dark green one to Monika.

"Oh, velvet. I always liked velvet." Monika's fingers caressed the smooth pile.

Annemarie struggled into the other dress, white with small, pink roses.

"Come over here so you can look at yourself in the mirror." Hilda beamed. "Oh, you look beautiful. How on earth did the seamstress do it without even one fitting?" She adjusted Monika's bow. "You look like a queen. And you, Annemarie, well, you look like a girl at her first dance."

Monika turned in front of the mirror, pleased with her image. "Where on earth did she find the material? There's nothing available, no stores open. How did she do it?"

"Don't tell anybody that I told you. Promise?" Hilda giggled.

"We promise." Annemarie held her hand over her heart.

"Curtains!" Hilda turned to the door. "Curtains from her house!" She chuckled and went out into the hall.

Annemarie and Monika looked at each other and burst out laughing.

"Good God, we are wearing somebody's curtains," Annemarie said.

"You must have been the living room and I am the dining, or maybe a bedroom." They laughed again and pointed at each other.

Someone banged on the door. "Can you keep it down?"

Annemarie grabbed up her pillow and pressed it against her face. "Every time I look at you at the dance, I'm going to see a living room window."

That night when Annemarie and Monika arrived at the ballroom, it was already filled with people.

"I'm excited. I can't wait to dance," Annemarie whispered. "And there'll be good food, maybe our last meal, ha, ha."

Monika smacked her lips in agreement. "Oh, and Hilda told me that this graduation will really be special, you'll see."

Annemarie looked at her, puzzled, then glanced around. "Who are all these folks?" Was Doc here? The ballroom was dimly lit, and a band played. A man clad in Lederhosen blew into a tuba. Rows of chairs had been set up on one side of the ballroom for the graduates. Annemarie spotted an empty seat in the front row and another two rows back where Monika headed. On the other side of the bandstand were groupings of small tables, lit by candles, glimmering through the large hall like stars in the sky.

She waved at Monika, "See you later. You look stunning."

The clinic director, Dr. Hofmeister, stood up to address the room. He looked distinguished in his dark suit and bow tie. Hilda was standing at his elbow next to a table stacked high with folders. She wore a dark, shiny dress and Annemarie smiled, wondering which room these curtains had graced. She turned and saw Monika grinning. Hilda's brother must have smoked a lot of ham. She bit her lips and tried to concentrate.

"You have all reached a milestone in your life," Dr. Hofmeister said. "Faced many hardships, many in battles on the front, and others in the cities and towns. You all

444

have suffered. Consider yourselves the lucky ones. Today you are ready to face a new life and future. I won't tell you that it will be easy. There will be setbacks and you will struggle. But you have been given another chance. I wish you all the best of luck for the future. I am so glad to be here, giving back lives to citizens who deserve our help."

The crowd clapped and shouted.

"And now, the big moment, graduation. It will be followed by an evening of music, dancing and good food. My assistant, Hilda Kreuzmeier, will hand you a certificate. As I call out your name, please step up so I can shake your hand. We will go in alphabetical order. Let's get started."

Annemarie sat back. Peterman would be towards the end. She could not hide her excitement. She was walking again, even dancing. Somehow, she would build a new life for her children. Lisbeth had said they were survivors, and she was right. Many didn't have this second chance.

She watched as men and a few women stepped to the podium. It was moving to see the former soldiers walk and smile, waving to the crowd as they held their certificates. She swallowed a lump in her throat.

When her name was called, she walked to the center of the room. No limping, no crutches, steady and confident. Hilda hugged her and whispered, "You look lovely, Annemarie."

Dr. Hofmeister held out his hand and said something, but she was so overcome with emotion that she didn't hear. The crowd cheered and clapped. Annemarie stood clutching her certificate to her, tears streaming.

Dr. Hofmeister put his arm around her. "Are you all right?"

"I am so happy," was all she could say, and slowly walked back to her seat. She turned around to look for Monika, but her friend was not back in her chair.

Finally, the last award was presented. "Good luck to all of you." Dr. Hofmeister's deep voice resonated through the room. "Let's celebrate!" He motioned towards the band, which started to play the Radetzky march. Annemarie hummed along, moving her feet to the beat. She sat for a few moments, not sure what to do next. She had no family here, nobody was glad to see her, to celebrate with her. She fought those thoughts and craned her neck, but she didn't see Monika. She let her eyes glide across the crowded dance floor and smiled despite herself.

Then someone tapped her on the shoulder. "May I have this dance?"

"Doc!"

He took her hand and pulled her up and pressed his cheek against hers. They melted into the crowd, gliding, swaying, holding on to each other.

When the musicians took a break, Doc said, "Let's drink, Liebling."

Annemarie looked up at him. "Lisbeth told me you were detained."

He waved his hand. "The British embarked on an intensive de-Nazification campaign to flush out suspected former Nazis."

"But Doc, how could they suspect you?"

He shrugged. "Nobody was safe. They arrested thousands. I was sent to a detention center in England." He took a deep breath and pulled her closer. "I tried. I wanted to take care of you,

but. --"

"But your friends, Nigel and the others. Couldn't they help?" Annemarie fought back tears.

"Don't worry, Liebling. It's all cleared up. Nigel did what he could." He put his arm around her shoulder and guided her through the tables.

"Oh, my God," Annemarie gasped, looking up. She fell into Lisbeth's open arms.

"I knew you could do it." Lisbeth hugged her and kissed her.

Doc helped her into a chair. Lisbeth sat in the chair next to Dr. Strohman, who reached to shake Annemarie's hand. "I've come to check on my patient."

Doc stood and filled their glasses. "Champagne. Congratulations." They rose and clustered to clink their glasses.

"Thank you, a thousand times," Annemarie choked out. "I've been thinking about you," she whispered to Lisbeth. "How is Nigel?"

Lisbeth waved away the question. "Back in England."

Doc took Annemarie's hand and squeezed it. She started to pull away but didn't.

Dr. Strohman smiled and said, "Lisbeth works with me now." He raised his glass and glanced around the table. "We are so happy to have her with us at the Wilder Clinic. Prosit!" He toasted again.

Annemarie watched Lisbeth's face, noticing Dr. Strohman's arm around her shoulders.

Doc nudged Dr. Strohman. "Let's check the buffet."

"Smoked ham," Annemarie called after them. I am very hungry." As the men left, she scooted next to Lisbeth. "So sorry that Nigel left."

Lisbeth didn't reply.

"And how are you doing?" Annemarie's hand closed around Lisbeth's.

"Good. I have moved into a nice one-bedroom apartment. You'll see, it is near the Alster Lake, right downtown."

"An apartment. Near ALSTER Lake? How did you – oh, wait, I know what you're going to say."

Lisbeth chuckled and placed her arm around Annemarie. "Dr. Strohman owns several apartment buildings. And, when the British officer left for London, Erich -- I mean Dr. Strohman-- showed it to me and asked if I wanted it." Lisbeth raised her glass and drank.

Annemarie's mouth dropped open. "He said you can *just have* the apartment?"

"I moved in two days later. It is furnished. Beautiful. And a large balcony with a view of the lake." Lisbeth squeezed her hand. "As soon as it's warmer, we can lounge there and get a suntan. What? Say something." Lisbeth leaned and patted Annemarie's cheek.

"Wunderbar, Lisbeth, you deserve it. You are amazing."

Doc and Dr. Strohman returned carrying plates laden with food.

"Hmm, sauerkraut. Bratwurst. And ham." Annemarie's mouth watered. "I must remember to thank Alois for the ham, I mean the dress. He is the boyfriend of my roommate, Monika, and donated the ham. And the beer. We managed to befriend a few villagers."

"Hmm. Befriend folks from the village. Bet those boys learned a few things from the city Freulein." Dr. Strohman grinned.

"Lucky for them." Doc raised his eyebrows.

The band started to play. Annemarie waved her glass as she saw Monika and Alois floating by on the dance floor, Alois a few inches shorter than Monika. They waved and Annemarie mouthed, "Thank you."

Lisbeth and Dr. Strohman left to dance.

Doc pulled Annemarie closer. "Liebling, Erich -- Dr. Strohman -- owns a little cabin not too far from here. We can stop there and spend a couple of days. Just you and I."

"I don't know." She leaned away from him. Why did she feel doubt, she asked herself. He had done so much for her. And she wanted to be with him, she felt excited. But her children, they had waited so long. Guilt crept into her mind. Anna and Inge needed her. They had to come first. She shook her head. "I can't. No. I must go home and get Anna and Inge." She picked up her glass and took a sip of her beer. "You understand. I hope you do."

Doc pulled an envelope from his jacket pocket and placed it in her hand. "Open this."

"A letter. From whom?"

"Open it!"

She opened the envelope and pulled out a folded sheet of paper and grasped his arm. "Anna did this. She liked drawing when she was only four. Look, this one says 'Mama'. And there is a picture of Aunt Lisbeth. See?" She waved the paper in front of Lisbeth, who had returned from the dance floor. "From Anna. It says, 'Aunt Lisbeth.'"

Lisbeth laughed. "Look, how skinny she made me." She pointed at the figure with the nurses' cap and red cross on her belly.

Annemarie pointed at a small figure. "That one says, 'Inge and Lola,' A dog? Oh, and that says 'Oma Hartmann'." She pointed at a figure standing in front of a house. Annemarie turned to Doc. "Oma Hartmann?"

"Yes, Oma Hartmann. And that is her poodle, Lola." He grinned.

Annemarie reached for Doc's chin . "Talk!"

Lisbeth answered in his place. "We picked up Anna and Inge. The children are with Doc's mother. They love her already, so don't worry."

"And Miss Gertrude let them go? I can't believe that. She let my children go with strangers!" Annemarie's mouth dropped open.

"Doc is Miss Gertrude's hero now. You know him," Lisbeth grinned.

Dr. Strohman stood up and helped Lisbeth out of her chair. "Puppe, look at the time." He put his arm around

449

Lisbeth's shoulder. "We must leave. Remember, we have early morning surgery. We'll see you soon to celebrate." They walked away, waving.

Annemarie frowned after them. "Tell me, what's going on?"

"Don't worry, your children are fine. Come on, let's spend a couple of days at Eric's cabin in the mountains. I will tell you all about the children then." He reached for her hand.

She pulled away and turned her chair to face him. "No, please. I have to see Anna and Inge. I can't believe you took them to your mother's house, a woman they have never met! I don't understand why Miss Gertrude released my children to strangers." She wiped her eyes.

He handed her a handkerchief. "I can explain everything, you must believe me. I thought I was helping you since you don't know what it is like out there."

"So, you think I can't take care of my children. I am not capable. You don't know me at all." She stood abruptly and her chair tumbled to the ground.

"Calm down, Annemarie." He righted her chair.

I think I drank too much. God God, I am drunk. Annemarie thought.

"You never considered my feelings, like I don't exist." She took a deep breath. "I know, you have done a lot for me, and I will always be grateful for that."

"Please, give me a chance to explain." He reached for her.

But she stepped back, "I want to leave now and go home. If you don't want to take me, I'll find a way." She started to walk away.

He followed. "Annemarie, of course I will take you home."

"Yes, first I have to get my bag and sign some papers." She felt awkward.

"Already done. Your bag is in my car. He firmly placed his arm around her shoulder. They walked towards the exit and out into the night breeze. Doc opened the front door of a black sedan and helped her in. "Are you comfortable? It will take at least six hours to Hamburg."

"Yes, thanks." She leaned back.

He started to drive, and a young man opened the gate for them to leave the rehab center compound.

"It will be past midnight when we get there." He turned his head to glance at her.

She did not reply.

"You can stay at Mother's house. We have a guest room. And then you can surprise Anna and Inge at breakfast?"

"I have to sort things out Doc. Can you please take me instead to my mother's apartment, you know the way."

Annemarie closed her eyes. Why not accept his offer. Like Lisbeth had said, no more worries, you'll be set for life. Think of your children. What was it? Why did she hesitate. He seemed such a nice man. And all he had done for her, the clinic, the rehab center. He had saved her life. She did have feelings for him, she wanted to sleep with him, had to admit it. But was it love? Not like she had loved Alfred. That feeling, maybe it happened once in a lifetime. And what did she really know about Doc? A charming womanizer. Why would he want her, when he could have every woman, like that Erika? She could never compete with her, beauty and charm. I'm a cripple now, I'm not charming and witty.

She remembered Willie's mother telling her that she was not good enough for her son because she didn't know how to iron, and what would Doc's mother think of her, her son, a successful doctor, soon to assume a position in the new German government? And her sister Margarete told her many times that she had no taste, didn't know how to dress. She sighed and felt Doc's warm hand on hers.

451

They drove in silence. The Autobahn was deserted.

"Are you tired? The seat reclines so you can take a nap. I'll wake you when we get into Hamburg." Doc patted her hand.

"Very tired, maybe a bit tipsy," She moved in her seat to look at him. "Doc, I don't know you. Who is Peter Hartmannn?"

"I know, I know. I want to tell you about Peter Hartmannn. Get to know me. I am a doer, used to taking charge. I am sorry I offended you, hurt you. I hope you will forgive me, please."

"As I said, I have to sort things out."

They drove through the silent night arriving at her mother's apartment at three o'clock in the morning. A soft rain fell, drops sparkled on the street lantern. Doc took her bag, and they climbed up the three flights of stairs. Surprisingly the electricity worked. He waited as she searched for her keys and unlocked the door. The door opened a few inches, hitting a chain.

Doc pushed the door against the chain. "What is this? Somebody locked it from the inside?"

Annemarie leaned against the wall. "The refugees have moved in. Oh God." Carefully she closed and locked the door.

Doc shook his head. "Displaced people?"

"Yes, my sister agreed to… I'll tell you another time." She sighed and turned towards the steps.

Back in the car, he said, "I am sorry, some misunderstanding with your sister?"

"No. I am angry with her;" It was raining harder, the wind had picked up, pelting stinging into their faces. She stared at the empty street and said, "The streetlights are on."

It took another thirty minutes till they arrived at Doc's mother's house.

CHAPTER 49
Doc's Mother's House

Annemarie woke, tickled by a ray of sunshine crossing her face. She had dreamed she was picking apples with Anna in Oma Hartmann's garden. She had never met Doc's mother, but in her dream, Oma Hartmann looked like her own mother.

She sat up, not sure where she was. The rose-flowered wallpaper reminded her of the bedroom in her mother's apartment, cozy, comforting. There was just enough space in the room for a tall dresser, a night stand next to the bed, and two wooden chairs on either side of a small table in front of the window. On the table she noticed a water pitcher, a glass, a toothbrush, and a comb. A piece of paper, covered with rainbow colors letters, spelled, "Welcome, Mama." Annemarie covered her mouth with her fingers.

She slid to the edge of the bed and strapped on her leg, a daily routine now, part of her new life. "Oh God, I'm wearing a man's pajamas." She was at Doc's mother's house wearing one of Doc's pajamas. She'd been dead tired last night, and, yes, slightly drunk, all that champagne and beer. The pant legs dropped on the floor. She rolled them up.

A child's voice called, "Come here, puppy."

"Inge!" Annemarie shouted and jumped off the bed, almost tumbling to the floor. She walked into the hall and grabbed the railing to steady herself and checked her wrist watch. *Ten thirty, my God. It's ten thirty.* She gathered the

453

waistband of the pajamas to keep them from sliding down. Taking small steps, she walked down the hallway, leaned over the wooden railing and peered down into a spacious foyer. Sunlight flooded through an open door. The kitchen, she thought. The aroma of freshly ground coffee and butter melting on the stove made her realize how hungry she was. Clinging on to the rail and holding up her pajama pants she slowly walked down the steps to the middle of the foyer.

"Mama!" Inge screeched, bounding into her arms. Anna followed. "Mama, I…" she choked on her words and flew into her mother's arms.

"Children, children!" Annemarie laughed, then cried.

A short woman with dark braids around her head, wearing a red apron over a dark dress, emerged from the kitchen.

Annemarie wobbled and let go of Inge, and her pajama pants slid down to her feet.

"Oh, no." She saw Anna's shocked face. "My new leg. It's made from wood."
She guided Anna's fingers down the leg.

"It's hard," Anna stuttered.

"Yes, it's wood. I call it Woody." She burst into laughter.

The woman had joined them, laughing, then helped Annemarie pull up the pajama pants. "They are Peter's, I guess it was late when you arrived." She knotted the top of the pants, then extended her hand, smiling. "I am Helena Hartmann, Peter's mother, but everyone calls me Lenie. Welcome, Frau Annemarie. You must be hungry." She took Annemarie's hand and turned towards the kitchen. "Children, come, let's have breakfast."

All the reservations Annemarie had harbored instantly vanished. She sat on the bench in the breakfast nook between Anna and Inge, her arms around her daughters.

454

"Oma Hartmann makes the best pancakes." Anna smacked her lips.

"I'm not allowed to give some to Lola. Oma says it makes her sick." Inge leaned her head on her mother's shoulder.

"Mama, are you going to live with us?" Anna stroked her mother's cheek.

Before Annemarie could answer, Oma Lenie joined them, balancing a plate stacked high with pancakes. "We are lucky that Peter can get sugar, butter and coffee from the Allies. He is a very important person now." She beamed with pride.

"Put this jam on your pancakes. Oma Lenie made it from blueberries she picked." Anna drizzled a big spoonful of berries on Annemarie's pancakes.

A smile lit up Lenie's face and Annemarie saw a big dimple. Annemarie took a big bite. "Oh, they are delicious, so good." She turned to Lenie, "I hope you will show me how you make them."

Lenie smiled. She seemed such a happy woman, Annemarie thought. That's where Doc got his sunny disposition. But he did not look like his mother.

"More, take more," Anna piled three more pancakes on her mother's plate.

Lenie went to refill their cups. "Children, it's time to take Lola out and play in the garden. Mama and I need to talk a bit." She laughed and pulled the children off the bench. "We'll join you in a short while."

"Ja, ja, let's play with Lola." Inge hopped and skipped. "Come puppy." She picked up the little dog.

Tears rolled down Annemarie's cheeks. How sweet it was to see her children so happy. "I did not mean to cry."

Mrs. Lenie took her hand. "Peter told me so much about you." She stroked Annemarie's hand.

Annemarie wiped her face with a cloth napkin. Napkins on the kitchen table. What could Doc tell his mother about her, she wondered.

"You are a brave woman," he says, and you always make him smile." Pride shone on Doc's mother's face.

Annemarie nodded. "He's quite the funny man, so charming. All women fall in love with him. He's a real Don Juan." She looked at his mother. "Everyone likes Doc. He is a good man; he has helped me so much. He saved my life." Annemarie looked into Lenie's eyes. How lucky Doc was to have such a wonderful mother.

As though the woman had read her mind, she said, "Yes, we are lucky. My husband was so proud of him, especially when he decided to become a doctor like him. Let's go sit outside on the veranda. Such a sunny day. We don't have that often, sunny like this. We can watch the children play. They like to show off, especially little Inge, who was a bit shy when I first met her. She loves dogs. I even allow Lola to sleep in Inge's bed. I'm not sure my husband would approve."

Annemarie didn't know what to say. Finally, she said, "Thank you so much for letting me stay here last night. It was very late, and we couldn't get into my mother's apartment. It is in Eimsbuttel, and the displaced people had…" She hesitated, not sure how to explain. "And the children." Annemarie stopped. Lenie refilled their cups.

"These are hard times. We love children. Peter is our only child." Lenie smiled sweetly.

Annemarie listened. She couldn't wait to learn more about Doc. His mother leaned back and folded her arms close to her chest.

"Peter is adopted."

Annemarie's mouth dropped.

"We are unable to have children. She sighed. "Then one day, my husband told me about this young Gypsy girl who came to his clinic. She was pregnant and said nobody wanted to help her."

Annemarie pressed her hand over her mouth.

"My husband delivered the baby, a boy. The girl would not tell him who the father was. She said she had to move on and no one must find out. Later he learned that she had dropped the baby off at St. Mary Margaret convent where they take in orphans."

Annemarie listened, shocked and spellbound.

Lenie went on. "We decided to adopt the baby and named him Peter. I was so happy. We never heard from the gypsy girl again. The Nazis persecuted gypsies, and many were killed in concentration camps. My husband and Peter were inseparable. He took the boy everywhere, to the clinic and later, after he gave up his practice to teach at the university. Peter often went along to watch students dissect corpses. Peter adored his father, and I knew that he would become a doctor too."

As Lenie talked, Annemarie pondered how this was changing everything for her. How she had been thinking Doc was so far above her.

Annemarie glanced into the garden and watched Anna and Inge playing in the dirt. How could she take them away from this peaceful place to her mother's gloomy apartment, where they have to play in the ruins, share the place with a family of refugees. "Oh my God," she said out loud.

Lenie rose. "I've talked a lot. I wanted you to know our secret. No one except the nuns knows. It was dangerous to be a gypsy, and I'm sure not even my husband could have protected our son."

Annemarie saw tears welling up in Lenie's eyes. She handed her a napkin. When she finally found her voice she said, "Doc doesn't look like a gypsy. Of course, I've never met one, but you hear that they have brown skin, wild curly hair, and they steal." She glanced at Lenie.

457

"Mother told us to run away if we saw gypsies, because they kidnap little children. But there weren't any where we lived."

"Ignorance, rubbish, folklore from the Middle Ages." Lenie pounded the table with both fists.

Annemarie wished she had not said those words. "He does not look like a gypsy, with his blond hair and light skin." She felt foolish uttering those words.

"He looks like me." Lenie's face lit up. "I am from a village close to Poland."

The two of them talked for a long while.

"Oh my, it is one thirty already. I must fix dinner. Children, come help me" she shouted."

Annemarie was amazed to see her children come running.

"Mama, we are planting." Anna held up her dirt-covered hands and looked back at Inge. "Oh no." Inge wiped her hands on her skirt." Come let's wash our hands." She pulled Inge towards a metal tub under a rain spout at the corner of the house.

Annemarie chuckled. Her older daughter was still taking care of her little sister. "Oh dear, I'm still in pajamas." She had followed Lenie into the kitchen.

"Oh, I forgot to tell you. Lisbeth stopped by a few days ago and dropped off some clothes for you." She laid down a knife she had used to chop carrots. "Follow me." They walked through the foyer into a bedroom.

"Don't mind the mess, it's Peter's room, he's always in a hurry." She threw up her arms.

Annemarie stepped over a towel and picked up a shirt.

Lenie pointed at a grey bag on the bed. "That is the dress from Lisbeth. I better get back to the kitchen. I don't want the children using the knives without me." She turned and closed the door behind her.

Annemarie opened the bag and held up the dress. A navy blue skirt with a white top, blue buttons matching blue bolero. She spotted an envelope that had dropped onto the floor. She picked it up and sat on the edge of the bed and read "I hope you like it!" Signed Lisbeth. And then scribbled words, "It's from London," next to a drawing of a glass with bubbles. Annemarie chuckled. Then she took off the pajamas, easier because they were so big. She slipped the dress over her head and stood up. It fit her perfectly. "Lisbeth, oh Lisbeth." She laughed and tucked the note back into the envelope. A smile on her face, she walked to the kitchen.

Lenie put her hands on her hips. "Beautiful! Blue is a good color for you."

"Yes, you look beautiful!" said Doc.

Both women turned around to see him in the doorway. He gathered Annemarie into his arms. Anna and Inge rushed him. "Uncle Doc, did you bring us chocolate?" Anna put her arms around his waist, and Inge hung onto his leg. Annemarie freed herself from his embrace. Doc dug into the pocket of his white tunic and produced two chocolate bars.

"Peter, not before dinner," his mother objected.

"Too late." He handed a bar to each of the children.

"You spoil them." She shook her head. He stepped over and kissed her on the cheek.

Annemarie stood there, overwhelmed with emotion.

"I made your favorite, roulade. The butcher had a special meat delivery for me." She grinned. "He asked if you could stop by and look at his son, Helmut, the young one. He's got some type of cold and fever."

He nodded. "I'll stop by later."

Typical Doc, Annemarie thought. He always helps others.

"The boy has asthma," Doc explained. "I have been leaning on Lisbeth, who always finds medication that is not available."

His mother put her arm around him and kissed him on the cheek. "You two sit on the veranda while the children and I finish up. Right, Anna and Inge?"

"Yes, Mama, I know how to chop carrots and Inge helps me." Anna wore an apron too big for her, held up with rope. "I want to learn to make roulade." She jumped up and down.

Annemarie bent and kissed her. "I am proud of you." She had to suppress a sob.

Doc took her hand and walked her to the veranda. On the table, a bottle of wine. "Piesporter Michelsberg Spatlese," he announced. "My father's favorite. I tried to come home earlier to be here when you woke up. Too many patients, too many emergencies. Well, I tried. But now we have the afternoon to go out and enjoy the beautiful evening, perhaps get in trouble?" He grinned.

"Let's celebrate," Doc picked up the corkscrew and pulled the cork with a loud pop then filled their glasses.

Annemarie waved at Anna, who had turned to them, startled by the pop. "This house is an oasis untouched by the destruction all around. It doesn't feel real," she said as they held up their glasses for a toast.

"To us!" Doc wrapped his arm around her shoulder.

"A life I have not known. You circulate with a crowd living in villas, wealthy. That night at the club, those beautiful women in their fancy dresses and nylons." She moved away, "I can't be like them."

"Annemarie, all that does not mean a thing to me. You don't know me."

"Right, I know the funny man, the charmer, the man every woman falls for." She twisted the glass between her fingers. 'Lisbeth told me that you will be a big boss in the new government." She sipped her wine.

"Yes. I'm building my future. Our future. You can have the most beautiful dresses you want." A quick smile made him look like a young boy begging for candy. He reached for her hand.

"I felt so lost at that club," she continued, her voice rising. "'Where did Doc find that one? He usually brings elegant ladies, but this one, he must have rescued from a bunker,'" they said, and they laughed." Annemarie faced him, her face flushed. "I got so angry, and I …"

Doc chuckled. "I heard. You tossed your drink at Erika."

"Not funny. I then realized that I don't belong there. And now." She lifted her skirt and slapped her wooden leg. "You don't know how damaged I am, I feel ugly, broken on the inside." She choked on her words. "But I am strong, I can take care of my children, I always have."

"I know you can. I want to tell you who Peter Hartmann is. Get to know me. I am a doer, used to taking charge. I am sorry I offended you, hurt you. I hope you will forgive me. Please, Liebling."

"Your mother told me about the gypsy baby they adopted." She looked away. "Your father and you are very close, she said, that's why you became a doctor." She hesitated, not sure how to ask. "Is he, did he die at the front?"

He took a deep breath. "No. He fell ill. I tried, but I could not save him. He passed away before the fighting broke out. And I put away the past and plunged into what I do best, help save and fix the wounded soldiers."

Annemarie tried to hold back tears. She took his hand and pulled him close. They sat in silence. She heard the wind play with the leaves, and the distant voices of the children.

Finally, Doc spoke. "Lisbeth told me about Alfred. I understand how it feels so lose someone."

Annemarie choked on her words. "I am sorry." She began to sob.

He glanced at her. "One more thing I need to tell you. Anna told me about that boy at the orphanage, Robert, a gypsy orphan. I checked with Miss Gertrud. I knew she was concerned about what would become of this child. In short, I promised to adopt him."

He looked at her anxiously and smiled. "They are getting the documents ready."

She squeezed his hand. "I always wanted a boy."

"Oh, I hoped you would understand. Anna told me she likes him, sort of." Doc wiped his chin with the back of his hand. He spoke softly. "Try to see yourself like others see you. Not the little girl, not the woman with the artificial leg. You are a strong woman, beautiful, smart, funny."

She did not answer.

"Annemarie. I love you." He cradled her face in his hands, his eyes a few inches from hers.

She murmured, "Oh Doc", raised her glass and sipped her wine.

Doc knelt, took her hand and placed a ring into her palm. "Will you marry me, Annemarie Peterman?"

She stared at his face. His eyes were intense.

She held up the ring. "Beautiful," she whispered, watching it sparkle in the sunlight.

"This diamond belonged to my grandmother. My grandfather gave it to her when they were engaged."

She held up the ring. "Your grandmother's ring." She stared at it. "I can't accept it, Doc." Then gently placed it on the table.

"Annemarie. I love you. You are the first woman I have given this ring to." He slipped next to her on the bench and took her hand into both of his.

She sighed. "Doc, you are a successful doctor. You are charming, rich, and…"

He placed his hand over her mouth.

She moved his hand gently. "Peter Hartmann. What does he need?"

"A woman who loves him for himself. Would love him if he was a poor gypsy. A woman he can spoil, laugh with, have fun with a woman to play with the children." He took the ring.

"Couldn't you accept this as a token of my love? Could we just be engaged?"

Annemarie took it, and after a pause, she spoke. "But there are so many things…"

He stroked her hands. "I know you need time, Annemarie. You are grieving, for yourself and for Alfred."

"I want to go to Berlin and find Alfred's mother, have a service for him, so we can say goodbye." She covered her face with her hands, knowing he could feel her sob. "Peter Hartman. Will you wait for me?"

Doc pulled her into his arms. "Yes, Liebling, I will."

She smiled, took the ring, and slipped it on her finger.

Antje Simunac (née Keller) was born in Hamburg, Germany where she grew up during the turbulent times after World War II. She and her younger sister and mother witnessed the horrors and destruction with their own eyes and survived to tell about it.

She hopes to share this experience with readers who may well identify with how the pain and destruction affected ordinary people and how they persevered.

As a young woman she immigrated to the United States of America, where she worked in the industrial advertising business.

Antje lives in Louisville, Kentucky and is a member of the Green River Writers group, writing fiction and poetry.

www.ingramcontent.com/pod-product-compliance
Lightning Source LLC
Chambersburg PA
CBHW070928100726
47908CB00001B/142